KATHARINE SUSANNAH PRICHARD

(1883–1969) was born in Fiji, the daughter of the editor of *The Fiji Times*. Her family moved when she was three and she spent her childhood in Melbourne and Launceston. In 1904, at the age of twenty-one, Katharine went to South Gippsland to become, briefly, a governess. Her father committed suicide in 1907 and the following year she began her autobiographical novel, *The Wild Oats of Han*, though this book was not published for many years. Katharine Susannah Prichard made her first visit to London in 1908 and returned in 1912, working as a journalist. In 1915 her first novel, *The Pioneers*, won the Hodder & Stoughton All Empire Novel Competition enabling her to return to Australia to devote herself to writing 'about Australia and the realities of life for the Australian people'; her second novel, *Windlestraws*, was published in 1916. In 1919 she married Hugo Throssell and moved with him to a house on the hills of Greenmount near Perth in Western Australia; their son was born three years later. Meanwhile she continued writing novels: *Black Opal* was published in 1921, followed by *Working Bullocks* (1926), *The Wild Oats of Han* (1928), *Coonardoo* (1928) – winner, with M. Barnard Eldershaw's *A House is Built*, of the *Bulletin* prize – *Haxby's Circus* (1930), *Intimate Strangers* (1937), *Moon of Desire* (1941) and the goldfields trilogy, *The Roaring Nineties* (1946), *Golden Miles* (1948) and *Winged Seeds* (1950). Her autobiography, *Child of the Hurricane*, was published in 1964, and three years later her last novel, *Subtle Flame*, appeared. Katharine Susannah Prichard's novels have been translated into many languages including Russian, Polish and Czech; she also wrote plays and poetry and her short stories were published in four collections between 1932 and 1967.

A committed communist, pacifist and founder member of the Communist Party of Australia, she visited Russia in 1933. In her absence her husband committed suicide and, returning to Australia, she threw herself further into political work. One of the founders of the Movement Against War and Fascism, she attended the National Anti-War Congress in Melbourne in 1934 and at the outbreak of the Spanish Civil War organized the Spanish Relief Committee in Western Australia. In 1943 she became a member of the Communist Party's Central Committee. Katharine Susannah Prichard was awarded the World Council's silver medallion for services to peace in 1959. On her death at the age of eighty-six, her coffin draped with the Red Flag, she was given a Communist funeral and her ashes scattered near her home on the slopes of Greenmount.

Virago also publish *The Roaring Nineties* and *Golden Miles*.

WINGED
SEEDS

KATHARINE SUSANNAH PRICHARD

WITH A NEW INTRODUCTION
BY DRUSILLA MODJESKA

To

CELIA

Published by VIRAGO PRESS Limited 1984
41 William IV Street, London WC2N 4DB

First published by the Australasian Publishing Company by
arrangement with Jonathan Cape 1950

Virago edition offset from first edition

Copyright Katharine Susannah Prichard 1950

Introduction copyright © Drusilla Modjeska 1984

British Library Cataloguing in Publication data

Prichard, Katharine Susannah
Winged Seeds
I. Title
823 [F]   PR6031.R57

ISBN 0-86068-421-0

Printed in Great Britain by The Anchor Press at Tiptree, Essex.

INTRODUCTION

In May 1949, while she was writing *Winged Seeds*, the last volume of the goldfields trilogy, Katharine Susannah Prichard wrote to her friend Nettie Palmer:

> I'm still obsessed with Vol. III. Was ill for a while . . . and couldn't work at all. Now, am beginning again – though my solitude has been broken by friends evicted, with baby coming, so haven't the peaceful atmosphere I need most of all. Meetings have to be addressed, too. Defence of democratic rights, and so. It's really a frantic struggle always to get time for thought and creative work.[1]

The last two volumes of the trilogy were a struggle, particularly *Winged Seeds:* "(I) am more anxious about this book than the others because it must not flag, but carry interest and spiritual zest to the last gasp."[2] She wrote the very substantial trilogy, her most ambitious work, during her sixties. She was not always well, she was deeply involved with Communist politics and was often hard-up. She started work on the first volume with a Commonwealth Literary Fund fellowship in 1941. After that she was dependent on foreign translations of her work. *The Roaring Nineties* alone was translated into nine languages, mostly during the fifties. This was the first novel to make her a reasonable though sporadic living. Most of the Eastern European editions were large and the royalties reasonable. With the tiny editions that were published for Australia it was extremely hard to live by writing. But characteristically, when a Czech edition of *The Roaring Nineties* was negotiated, with a print run of 2000, she donated the entire royalties towards the reconstruction of a village destroyed in

1. Katharine Prichard to Nettie Palmer 9.5.1946. National Library of Australia (N.L.A.) MSS. 1174/1/7672.
2. Quoted in Ric Throssell, *Wild Weeds and Wind Flowers: The Life and Letters of Katharine Susannah Prichard*, Sydney, Angus & Robertson, 1975, p.149.

the war. And so again with the Slovak edition: "Yes, I know I shouldn't behave like a millionaire," she wrote to her friend and publisher Jonathan Cape, "if I don't earn even half of the basic wage as a writer, but it gives me some satisfaction to feel I may be helping people who suffered so much."[3]

Katharine Prichard's biography is both impressive and problematic. She lived for fifty years in the hills on the outskirts of Perth. In 1919 when she moved there, Perth was a small, provincial town. There she raised her son, wrote her best novels, established the local branch of the Communist Party of Australia and committed herself to political activism. Her story is crossed with paradoxes: the provincial existence of an internationally-known writer and Communist Party member; a woman who moved to her husband's town but never took his name as a writer; a communist in a conservative town. At the centre of the contradictions was her writing, itself a centre for her life and her politics:

> I write for the purpose of influencing people in the direction of ideas that I feel are important. Rodin said: "Art is the joy of the intelligence which sees the universe clearly and recreates by illuminating the consciousness . . . " I write to reach people's common sense and intelligence, to show them that if they unite they can make a different world possible.[4]

The Roaring Nineties opens the trilogy during the prospecting years of the 1890s. Through the narrative of Sally Gough and her family, it dramatises the early period of alluvial mining and the first struggles of the miners and the fledgling community. *Winged Seeds* opens in 1936 and closes the trilogy ten years later, in 1946. Sally Gough is still central to the novel, now entering the last phase of her life. The children have grown up and the focus for romance and adventure shifts to the generation of Sally'– grandchildren. At the heart of that generation is Sally's grandson, Bill, the handsome and starry-eyed socialist. It is through his character that the

3. *ibid.*, p.150.
4. Katharine Prichard in *The Critic*, December, 1967.

experiences of love, socialist politics and war are dramatised,
Nevertheless as with the first two volumes, the pleasure in
reading the novel comes from the detail of Sally Gough's life,
the unfolding through her of a narrative that always promises
tragedy. The novel ends with the burial of the old Aboriginal
woman, Kalgoorla, whose life had shadowed Sally's throughout the trilogy, a reminder of Australia's shameful history of
race relations.

Winged Seeds was not well received by the critics. *The
Roaring Nineties* had been acclaimed in 1946. The critics
equivocated about *Golden Miles*, but they damned *Winged
Seeds*. *The Roaring Nineties* was described in the *New York
Times Book Review* as "unquestionably the most important
Australian novel of recent years".[5] The *Sydney Morning Herald*,
described *Golden Miles* as "ambitious, sincere, but rather
unwieldy"[6] but it argued that with *Winged Seeds* Katharine
Prichard had "attempted too much".[7] The *Bulletin* equivocated
about *Golden Miles*, worried about its "propaganda" while
recognising it as a "challenging novel".[8] Of *Winged Seeds* it
wrote:

> The atmosphere of inertia in which this work ends, which began
> so cheerfully and so forcefully, has something of the malign
> about it. Propaganda has that effect. Dutifully parroting com-
> munist jargon . . . Katharine Prichard's characters become half
> comic and half repulsive with the disquieting unreality of the
> tortured.[9]

A review of this kind must be assessed within the context of
cold war. 1951, when it was published, was the year in which
R.G. Menzies attempted to outlaw the Communist Party.
Dorothy Hewett, a fellow radical writer, remembers Katharine
Susannah Prichard two years earlier in 1949, "frail and unafraid"

5. C. Hartley Grattan in *New York Times Book Review*, 22 June, 1947.
6. *Sydney Morning Herald*, 16.10.1948.
7. *Sydney Morning Herald*, 27.1.1951.
8. *Bulletin*, 26.10.1948.
9. *Bulletin*, 10.1.1951.

speaking from the tray of a truck in the communist election campaign, "the flying bottles and the anti-communist hysteria boiling around her".[10]

In response to the critics she insisted that she was "indifferent to what anybody may say . . . I have done what I wanted to, as well as I was able, and that's all that matters, to me".[11] Yet the fact that a major theme of her articles and talks during the fifties became a defence of socialist realism and an answer to the charge of propaganda, indicates that she felt this criticism. This is in marked contrast to the interwar years when she barely touched these themes. Her writing then was widely acclaimed and firmly established within the dominant radical nationalist tradition. Christina Stead's first novels appeared in the mid thirties, and D.H. Lawrence had visited Australia in 1922, exciting local writers including Katharine Prichard; but modernism, although its elements can be traced throughout the period, was not dominant in Australian writing between the wars. By the early 1950s there had been a significant shift. The Cold War was polarising and entrenching the Communist aligned writers into a mode that was either coming under political attack or was regarded as old-fashioned. The nationalist vision and predominantly realist conventions of the thirties were radically challenged by Patrick White's *Aunt's Story* in 1948, *The Tree of Man* in 1955 and *Voss* in 1957. It was partly because of her awareness of this changing atmosphere that she prefaced *Golden Miles* and *Winged Seeds* with verse from Furnley Maurice, a poet who had a broad political appeal.

Although Katharine Prichard had been attracted to aspects of modernist writing during the twenties and early thirties, she was unable to reconcile herself to modern trends in writing during the fifties. Or perhaps it was because of the ambivalence of her earlier attraction that she became antagon-

10. *The National Times* 25 Nov. – 1 Dec., 1983.
11. Katharine Susannah Prichard "Critics and Criticism" reprinted in Ric Throssell (ed.) *Straight Left*, Sydney, Wild and Woolley, 1982. p.169.

istic. The painful reckoning that she made after her husband died in 1933 left her more closely aligned, both politically and aesthetically, with the Communist Party during the Stalinist period. During those difficult years of the late thirties she wrote less, and with the trilogy, her writing had changed. She no longer wrote about the nexus between sexuality, the unconscious and nature, an area of writing susceptible to modernist technique. Her own writing had struck a new note in Australian fiction in the twenties: "What a revelation *Working Bullocks* and *Coonardoo* were" wrote her friend and fellow writer Vance Palmer. Even on her return from the U.S.S.R. in 1933 she was talking of describing her experience "in splashes of colour, gouts of phrases as Walt Whitman would have, or Mayakovski; paint them after the manner of the French symbolists, images seething and swarming over each other, as they lie in my head".[12] But by the trilogy she had moved unambiguously towards socialist realism. By the 1950s she had no time for modernism or avant-garde aesthetic forms which, like so many socialist writers, she linked with the decadence associated with the rise of fascism.

She criticised what she saw as a trend towards "introspective poetico-mystical illusions, frustrations and sexual aberrations". While she recognised Patrick White's flair with language, she was critical of his work: "What I find most distasteful in his writing is his pessimism and a preoccupation with what is gross and vile, mean, cruel and cowardly in human behaviour, without giving a glimpse of the heights to which ordinary decent men and women can rise in their service of humane ideals".[13] For Katharine Prichard writing was a political act which under capitalism was made in a more or less hostile context. For her the "essential function" of

12. Vance Palmer, Introduction to Katharine Susannah Prichard *N'Goola*, Melbourne Australasian Book Society, 1959 and Katharine Susannah Prichard quoted in Ric Throssell, *Wild Weeds and Wind Flowers*, p.75
13. Katharine Susannah Prichard "Modern Trends in Literature", reprinted in Ric Throssell (ed.) *Straight Left*, p.169.

writing was to interpret the struggle for existence; whereas for publishers books were a commodity to make profits and "to drug people into illusions about the possibility of happy ever after solutions to their problems . . . "[14] In an arena of ideological contestation, her purpose was "to stir and convince ·. . . readers of real values in life" and to support progressive political movements. However in doing this, she wrote, fiction should not preach or offer the writer's ideas directly as a reporter might, but indirectly through the reactions and feelings of the fictional characters as they live their lives: "The ulterior motive must never obtrude . . . It must be so part and parcel of the whole that it is swallowed in a gulp."[15] For technique she looked, by 1940, to socialist realism, which addressed exactly these issues. In this she followed Georg Lukács and the Soviet critics who underwrote socialist realism as the revolutionary mode, rather than such Marxist writiers as Bertolt Brecht and Walter Benjamin who allied Marxism with modernist strategies of writing.

While insisting that a correct theoretical approach was necessary for a correct aesthetic, Lukács argued that the relationship between socialist theory and the aesthetic of socialist realism also had to be "indirect, dialectical". In developing its technique, socialist realism was seen to have refined the conventions of the great realist writers of the nineteenth century whose mantle it claimed to inherit.[16] Similarly in Australia radical nationalist and socialist writers, including Katharine Prichard, claimed a continuity in Australian writing from Henry Lawson and the writers of the 1890s, a tradition which was more mythic than actual in a society in which Carter Brown was one of the biggest selling writers. But during the Cold War when the Communist

14. Katharine Susannah Prichard *"Literature for the Australian People"*, reprinted in *op. cit.*, p.147.
15. Katharine Susannah Prichard, quoted in Ric Throssell *Wild Weeds and Wind Flowers*, p.126.
16. Georg Lukács, "Critical Realism and Socialist Realism" in *Realism in our Time: Literature and The Class Struggle*, NY, Harper and Row, 1964.

Party was losing ground in the industrial sphere, it seemed particularly important to maintain contestation in the cultural domain. This was the context in which *Winged Seeds* appeared, and while the Cold War atmosphere must be taken into account in any assessment of the reviews, there were problems with the last volume of the trilogy. *The Roaring Nineties* is among the best of Australian socialist realist writing. *Golden Miles* had some technical problems but was a successful novel. But *Winged Seeds* falls rather flat; the problems that had been kept under control in *Golden Miles* break through. The narrative finally breaks between the continuing story of Sally Gough, which inevitably narrows as she draws towards the end of her life, and the history and politics of the goldfields which become increasingly complex with the development of capital. These are problems which should not be ascribed to a personal failing by Katharine Prichard, but to the problematic nature of socialist realism during the fifties.

The *Bulletin's* review of *Golden Miles* concluded: "Katharine Susannah Prichard as a novelist . . . has been fighting a long and losing battle with Katharine Susannah Prichard the propagandist."[17] In an obituary which was met with some protest, Dorothy Hewett made a similar point, but from a very different perspective. Forty years younger than Katharine Prichard, Dorothy Hewett grew up in Perth between the wars listening to stories of the red witch who lived in the hills. As a university student and a brand-new communist she went to visit Katharine Prichard in 1946, an occasion that made a great impact on her. Apart from encountering yoghurt for the first time, she encountered a person who seemed to her in 1946 to have integrated her life as a socialist, a writer and a woman. Not only that, but she had done it in Perth. It wasn't until much later that Dorothy Hewett realised what that strange courageous life in the hills had cost Katharine Prichard. When Dorothy Hewett wrote

17. *Bulletin*, 26.10.1948.

the obituary in 1969 she was still close to her own brush with socialist realism. Katharine Prichard, she said, had suffered a "fierce self immolation in a political dream" which had begun after 1933:

> The sensuousness, the sexual energy drained out of her writing, leaving only the husk of schematic politics to sustain her and her work. Her dogmas hardened around her like a chrysalis she was never to leave.[18]

Certainly there was a change in her writing. Only the trilogy can properly be described as socialist realist. While her much more ambiguous earlier novels foreshadowed this mode, her writing was also exploring very different modes and techniques. It may well have been that there was a "fatal contradiction" as Dorothy Hewett put it, between the "poetic sensibility of the writer" and membership in the Communist Party during the Stalinist epoch, when aesthetic as well as political demands were made of its writers. Certainly the fifties were difficult years for Communists and Katharine Prichard found many of her friends leaving the Party or expelled in the lead up to the twentieth congress and in the wake of the invasion of Hungary. There is no doubt that her politics hardened during that period when she lost friends rather than question her commitment to the Party.

Whatever one might conclude about this, there were certainly problems with the nature of socialist realism, which by the fifties, it seems to me, was out of step with the modern trends of writing. One way of measuring this gap is to remember that Doris Lessing's very different exploration of gender, writing and politics in *The Golden Notebook* appeared in 1962, only twelve years after *Winged Seeds*. Socialist realism was particularly hard to do well and did not become easier. Its reliance on the codes and conventions of an earlier period of realism wore increasingly thin as writers addressed the com-

18. Dorothy Hewett, "Excess of Love: The irreconciliable in Katharine Susannah Prichard", *Overland*, No.43. Summer 1969–70.

plex issues of the mid twentieth century. Lukács was aware of the distortions that appeared during the Stalinist era:

> Literature ceased to reflect the dynamic contradictions of social life; it became the illustration of an abstract truth . . . Even where this "truth" was in fact true and not, as so often, a lie or a half-truth, the notion of literature-as-illustration was extremely detrimental to good writing.[19]

But this was not the problem with *Winged Seeds*. Arguing the importance of historical accuracy, Katharine Prichard defended herself against dogmatic Soviet critics who criticised her characters for insufficient adherence to socialism. Although a political hardening can perhaps be detected, it is not on dogmatism or half truths that *Winged Seeds* foundered. The problem, it seems to me, is more deeply embedded in socialist realism, the guiding principle of which might be summarised as the representation of the forces of history through the lives of individuals. In the relatively simple economy of *The Roaring Nineties* this was done to good effect. Small-scale alluvial mining and the early development of the community meshed easily with the lives of its people. By 1946 when *Winged Seeds* opens, the gold mining was controlled by international capital, the war which claimed Bill had little to do with life as it was lived in Kalgoorlie; the Spanish Civil War even less. Sally, growing old, lives out her days on the verandah, concerned but by no means an actor in those events. Katharine Prichard tries to solve the problem with new characters but they are thin beside the old miners she loved so much and had lived amongst. She never really understood the "modern" generation of the forties. For the rest of the novel relies on long, cumbersome political discussions which fail to integrate with the narrative. It is not that it could not be done, but it was hard, and Katharine Prichard was not the only socialist realist to meet this problem.

There were also difficulties in socialist realism taking a

19. Georg Lukács, *op. cit.* p.119.

woman as its protagonist. The goldfields trilogy does not focus on Tom Gough, the fully committed communist, the proletarian hero, but on his mother who, like so many women, was torn between the political differences of her family and friends. It took a life-time to reconcile the struggles of home and heart and community, her primary sites of commitment, to the political struggles which took place in the workplace, the mines and the battlefield, among men and on alien territory. During the forties and fifties feminism was not a theoretical issue within the Communist Party. Katharine Prichard took "the woman question" seriously and all her novels and plays have strong female characters; but she did not consider herself a feminist and she believed, as most communist women did, that the woman question would be resolved by the nature of socialism. While she recognised the importance of women's experience, it was the workplace which was the primary and dynamic site of the political process. In a sense the climaxes of the trilogy happen off-centre: her sons die at war, go to jail and fight bitter industrial battles while she provides their continuity, and ours, and is generally confined to domestic terrains.

There is, of course, a certain advantage to a view from the periphery and in *The Roaring Nineties* and *Golden Miles* it is used to good effect. The climaxes are immediate enough when they concern her husband, and her sons are still living at home; and when they intersect with the climaxes of her own drama of love and motherhood. But the unspoken sub-text is that Sally lives through "her men". While the view from the home gives an added poignancy to the political and historical narrative, it depends on not questioning too deeply issues which have become visible with contemporary feminism. In *Winged Seeds* when Sally is alone and growing old and the political dramas are acted out through the grandchildren, the psychodynamics of independence for a woman become paramount. Yet Prichard does not allow this to dominate the novel, as she did twenty years earlier in *Bid Me to Love* and

Intimate Strangers. Winged Seeds continues the strategy of dramatising historical forces through the lives of individuals. The old pattern is maintained through the narrative of Bill's life. But while the balance between the periphery and the centre was maintained in the first two volumes, it is lost in the third. The political climaxes recede into the distance and we are left with, but never given over to, Sally growing old and reconciling herself to memory and the processes of life which are, for the most part, undramatic. In *Winged Seeds* her life does not follow a pattern of climax and resolution; it would have been dishonest to have imposed one. If the final volume ends rather lamely, it is to Katharine Prichard's credit that she remained true to her tough but undramatic vision of Sally Gough. And to her commitment to socialist realism. The year before she died she made this assessment of her writing:

> My work has been unpretentious: of the soil. Perhaps I have not made readers dream and laugh enough. The wit and gaiety I admire so much in other writers, I have lacked. But, in all the varieties of expression, my conclusion stands that the "noble candid speech in which all things worth saying may be said", is the best means of communication and fulfilling the sublime mission of art in literature. The lucid simplicity of classical masterpieces has been a guide.[20]

In 1949 Katharine Prichard was worried that she might not "hang out to finish the trilogy".[21] In fact she hung out for another twenty years writing short stories, another novel, an autobiography and at least two more plays. She continued to be surprised that her work was still appreciated. *The Child of the Hurricane*, the autobiography which was published just before her eightieth birthday, proved her most popular book after *Coonardoo*, which had caused a storm in 1929 with its depiction of an Aboriginal woman. In the twenties Katharine

20. Katharine Susannah Prichard "Some perceptions and aspirations" reprinted in Ric Throssell (ed.), *Straight Left*, p.218.
21. Katharine Prichard to Nettie Palmer, 4 Feb., 1949, N.L.A. MSS.1174/1/7594.

Prichard was breaking new ground in Australian writing; in her later years she was reworking familiar terrain. If she was old-fashioned, she could afford to be at eighty. She remained determined and clear sighted. She lived on the outskirts of a provincial town for fifty years, uneasily balancing her needs as a writer, a communist and a woman. She made mistakes perhaps, "errors of hope" an old comrade called them; she resisted compromise. Her tale remains enigmatic, conclusions elusive. Towards the end Dorothy Hewett visited her again. In an unguarded moment, perhaps, or with characteristic honesty, the older woman warned the younger: "Don't sacrifice your life to work and ideals; the most important things in life are human beings. I found that out too late."[22] There was more of Sally Gough in Katharine Prichard than she would have admitted. But that is only half the story. She remained a communist until the end, paying her last subscription for the Party three days before she died.[23] If it was a difficult relationship, it was a common experience for the left intelligentsia of the time. But it was also a source of personal and intellectual support, particularly necessary in Katharine Prichard's circumstances. Whatever the problem, her political commitment was a propelling force in her writing, a source of creative energy that underwrote her best work and was sustained throughout her long, courageous and contradictory life.

Drusilla Modjeska, Sydney, 1983

22. I am endebted to Dorothy Hewett for this quotation.
23. I would like to thank Ric Throssell for this information.

FOREWORD

It was on the Larkinville rush, I met the people whose yarns suggested the story of Sally Gough and Dinny Quin told in *The Roaring Nineties* and *Golden Miles*. But, as in the first two books, it is not intended that the composite characters in this one should be identified with any actual person, except where historical facts require mention of a well-known name.

Winged Seeds moves from the end of 1936, when the mining industry was weathering a depression, to 1946, when the prospect of a renaissance was glimmering like a mirage on the horizon.

K. S. P.

And if more blood must pour
Choose ye what things endure;
The past claims no allegiance, present years
Are crammed with falseness and the breath of fears.
Only the future lives and holds us sure
To things that never were
Being completely fair.
Then for a purpose of eternal worth
Human deliverance more vast than earth
Hath known, give gladly of your body's breath
In sacrificial birth that men call death.
Now ye, who then
Being men of men
Proclaimed your right and readiness to die,
Claim now your right to live, and all is yours
Of conquest and the honour that endures,
And all the promise future years descry.

'To Whom it May Concern'

FURNLEY MAURICE

CHAPTER I

Two slight, jaunty figures swung along in the middle of the road towards Boulder.

Mrs. Gough could scarcely believe her eyes when she saw them. It was as if two brightly coloured parakeets had alighted on the goldfields. She had been pottering about her garden, scrabbling the earth round the mauve hibiscus Bill had brought her from the bush as a seedling, cutting back the bougainvillea which sprawled, purple and magenta, over a neighbour's fence, pulling out the withered stalks of last year's sunflowers. The girls were as alike as parakeets, she thought, when they came nearer, wearing green slack suits, red sandals, and kerchiefs of red, green, blue and yellow tied over their hair. Twins, Sally guessed, and got up in the irritating fashion twins adopt in order to bewilder people.

She straightened her back, a little stiff in the joints now, and took cover behind the bougainvillea to have a better look at the girls as they passed. But their chatter and squeals of laughter stopped suddenly as they stood still.

'This is the place, I'm sure, Pam,' one of them exclaimed.

'I believe it is,' the other cried. 'There's the ramshackle old house like a broken concertina, and the creeper with masses of creamy blossom over the veranda! And, look — look, Pat —' the voice fell to a whisper, 'I believe *she's* in the garden.'

'Oh, please,' Sally found two eager faces gazing at her over the garden gate, 'are you Mrs. Gough?'

'I am,' Sally replied, wondering what on earth could bring these smart young things looking for her.

Before her imagination had time to suggest any reason, they had pushed open the rickety gate and were beside her on the garden path, both talking at once, exclaiming delightedly, and looking so pleased with themselves to have found her that Sally had to smile at their ingenuous excitement.

'Isn't she just like what you'd thought she'd be, Pam?'

'Oh, beautiful — like a Spanish peasant! If only I could paint her, just as she is in that old straw hat, eyes smiling in the shadow, faded red and yellow of her dress against that magenta blaze of bougainvillea!'

Sally was embarrassed at being caught in an old dress and working apron, and at being discussed so candidly. When she could get in a word edgeways she inquired:

'But who are you, my dears? And why do you want to see me?'

'I'm Pat and this is Pam,' the girl who seemed to take the initiative for the two explained. 'We only arrived in Kalgoorlie a few days ago.'

'And we've been dying to meet you,' the other chimed in. 'Haven't we, Pat?'

'We've heard so much about you!'

'And we do want to see Bill!'

'We've got to see Billy!'

They rattled on blithely as Sally led the way to the veranda. She began to think that the girls must be friends Bill had made while he was away in the Northern Territory, or in Sydney. Bill had returned only a week or so ago, and had got himself a job on the Boulder almost immediately. Sally was proud of her grandson: his self-reliance and the knack he had of going after what he wanted and getting it. Although, usually, he came in to see her on his way home from work, there had not been much time for intimate confidences, or to hear about casual acquaintances he had made during the years he was away from home.

But it appeared, as they went on talking, that Pat and Pam had never met Bill. They had been in England and travelling about Europe for several years. Oh, yes, they were 'dinkum Aussies', and thrilled to be at home again, although the gold-fields was not home. Not exactly. They were both born in Melbourne, but Pam loved Sydney, and thought she would be living there. She was engaged to an artist they had met abroad. Of course daddy was furious about it. He didn't like Shawn because Shawn was an artist and always hard up; he often went about with the seat almost out of his pants. But Pam didn't mind. She was an artist, too, and crazy about Shawn. She wasn't going to let daddy run her life for her. Neither was Pat. They had both made up their minds about that. They were going to live their own lives, even if they had to stick to daddy a little longer.

It was very awkward because he had control of their money. Not a penny could they get hold of at present unless he gave it to them. Actually, they could get anything they liked out of him — almost anything — while they were living with him, because he was beginning to feel old and lonely, and wanted somebody to look after him. But it wasn't good enough to waste one's life looking after a selfish old man when there was so much one wanted to do. All the money in the world wouldn't be worth it; but Pat hoped when they saw their lawyer in Melbourne, he might be able to make daddy part with a few hundreds of all the money their mother had left him. Some of it they knew they were entitled to, but how much they had not been able to discover; or the terms of their mother's will which made daddy their legal guardian until they were of age.

Sally was dazed, and beginning to resent all this inconsequential chatter, obviously a screen for something the girls were reluctant to say.

'It's no use, Pam,' Pat said, reading Mrs. Gough's troubled gaze. 'We've got to tell her.'

Sally decided that she would always know Pat from Pam. Although the girls were so alike, both ginger-haired, with greeny-grey eyes, freckled noses and the same red lips marking their thin, rather large mouths, Pat was more alert and assertive than Pam. Her eyes lighted to a quick intelligence, while Pam's remained still and mildly shining like the salt lakes after rain.

Frisco strolled on to the veranda before Sally discovered what Pat was going to tell her. Sally introduced him.

'Pat and Pam,' she said laughingly, 'I don't know who — '

'Colonel de Morfé,' the girls cried excitedly.

13

'Hello!' Frisco turned towards them with the expression of a blind man trying to remember where he had heard a voice before. 'Pat and Pam Gaggin, of course!' he exclaimed on a flash of recollection. 'There can't be another Pat and Pam who talk like young starlings.'

'Oh, Colonel de Morfé,' Pam giggled.

'You said that years ago in London,' Pat flung at him.

'Well,' Frisco walked carefully to his chair and lowered himself into, it 'what does that prove? That I haven't forgotten you?'

He was being gallant and charming, Sally realized; but a little patronizing, treating the girls as if they were still children.

'But what brings you here?' he asked. 'You haven't run away from Paddy, have you?'

'No, worse luck,' Pam murmured, and Pat glanced apprehensively at Mrs. Gough. Sally's face had lost its animation and good-humoured interest in her visitors. If they had anything to do with Paddy Cavan, they could not be friends of hers, Pat guessed.

'But we insisted on coming back to Australia with him,' she said, as if that might be considered an extenuating circumstance.

'Amy made us promise to bring a letter to Bill,' Pam added.

'We heard Amy had died.' Frisco knew that this conversation was being difficult for Sally and talked to help her. 'What happened?'

'She was motoring with a friend,' Pat said guardedly. 'There was an accident. He was killed, and Amy badly hurt. We thought she'd get over it, at first, but she died — a week later.'

'Poor Amy,' Pam murmured, 'we were very fond of her.'

'She was a good sport,' Pat spoke defensively. 'But for Amy, God knows what would have become of us. We never knew what it was to leave boarding-school, until Amy made daddy let us live with them. And when she knew Pam was dying to study drawing, she persuaded him to let her, and let me do a course in journalism. Amy was good to us: tried to do things for us as if we were her own daughters. She told us never to throw away the best things in life for what she called "the trimmings". It wasn't worth while, she'd found out after all, she said. She wanted you to know that, Mrs. Gough.'

Pat's eyes pleaded with Sally.

'Did she?' Sally said stiffly, her face unmoved. 'Amy and I had become strangers to each other for so long, I can't pretend to care.'

'But you do, missus.' Coming on to the veranda, Dinny stood beside the form on which the girls were sitting. 'We all do. Though Amy treated us badly, we can't forget she grew up here on the fields, and the pretty, artful ways she had when she was a young thing. But it was like as if she had died, when she went off with Paddy Cavan.'

'Are you Dinny Quin?' Pat asked eagerly.

'That's me,' Dinny replied.

'Amy used often to talk of you,' Pat said. 'You were her father's oldest friend, weren't you? "There's one person," she said, "will always have a good word for me, and that's Dinny." '

'Who are you?' Dinny asked.

'Pat Gaggin and this is Pam.'

'Paddy Cavan's daughters,' Sally said.

'We're not his daughters,' Pat cried, 'though we've had to call him daddy since we were children.'

'You still live with him?'

'We could have left him, and earned our own living, perhaps.' Pat understood Mrs. Gough's insinuation. 'But we had a good reason for not doing so, and after all he's never been unkind to us. Not as bossy and mean as most fathers. Usually he lets us do what we like and gives us whatever we want — particularly since Amy's death.'

'He was just helpless, at first,' Pam explained. 'You've never seen a man so distraught. He did love Amy and is lonely and miserable without her. Love's like a stroke of lightning, or an earthquake — what's called an act of God — isn't it? I didn't understand that until I knew Shawn. But I know now how

15

daddy felt about Amy. He's been quite decent to us, lately: would do anything to keep us with him.'

'Paddy Cavan's affairs are no concern of ours,' Sally said.

'That means you don't want to have anything to do with us?' Pat's voice quivered to her perception of something implacable in Sally's attitude.

'I can never forgive Paddy Cavan for what he did to me and mine,' Sally said.

'Amy told us why you mightn't want to know us.' Pat spoke apologetically.

'We're not to blame because our mother married him, and left us in his charge,' Pam wailed.

'Let's go,' Pat said, springing to her feet.

'Oh, yes, let's!' Pam jumped up and stood beside her.

'It's awful of us to have butted in on you like this, Mrs. Gough.' Sally found it difficult to withstand Pat's youthful grace, her sincerity and contrition. 'If I were in your shoes I'd feel just as you do about Paddy Cavan. But if you were in our shoes, you'd want to settle a score with him before you were through. Poor old mum, she thought the world of him, and never knew about Amy. So she left us, and her money, completely in his hands until we are twenty-one. We didn't intend to presume on your kindness . . . but we had to fulfil a promise to Amy to come and see you — and Bill. Goodbye.'

'Goodbye,' Pam echoed.

They were walking away, a little crestfallen for all their casual, jaunty swagger, when Bill ran into them near the gate.

In his working clothes, fresh from a hasty shower, with his hair ruffled and a glint in his eyes, Bill Gough still looked rather an overgrown urchin. Dropping in to see his grandmother on his way home from work, he was surprised to see two such exotic damsels on her garden path. The glint in his eye was for them. Young Bill Gough was nothing if not enterprising where good-looking girls were concerned, it was said.

'You're Bill, aren't you?' Pam gasped.

'Guilty,' Bill grinned.

'We've got a letter for you,' Pat said curtly, refusing to meet the challenge of his friendly, inquisitive gaze as gaily as she would have done a while ago.

She knew now that as soon as she produced the letter from his mother, and Bill Gough knew who she was, his expression would change, become dour and hostile, as Mrs. Gough's had done. She did not want that to happen. Not now, when she was still sore with the realization of having to share the bitter enmity these people felt for Paddy Cavan. Not while Bill was regarding her with a gay grin and bright freckled eyes: her inner springs were uncoiling to the incitement of his gaze.

Pam was surprised when Pat took the letter from the breast pocket of her tunic, gave it to Bill, and walked on without another word. Pam wondered why Pat was being so short and up-stage. It was not the way they had planned to carry off this encounter.

'But we've got to see you again!'

Pat whirled suddenly to say as Bill stood reading his letter:

'The matter is important, and strictly confidential,' she added. 'Mrs. Gough does not wish us to come here, so you must meet us somewhere else.'

'Right'. Preoccupied with his letter, Bill seemed scarcely aware of what he was saying.

'I will organize it,' Pat called with a triumphant glee which aroused him. Bill stared after her, dazed, and wondering why she had used those words. 'And please remember we are not Paddy Cavan's daughters!'

The girls turned away, with a subdued burble of laughter. They looked more like a stray pair of parakeets than ever, Sally thought, as they flipped past the plumbago hedge, swinging into the golden, dusty mist of the late afternoon sunshine.

CHAPTER II

'HEAR Sir Patrick Cavan is payin' the goldfields a visit,' Tassy Regan chuckled.

'And brought his daughters with him!' Blunt Pick added in his high-pitched, squeaky voice, as if it were the latest joke.

There was an awkward pause. Everybody knew Paddy Cavan was not a topic for conversation in Mrs. Gough's presence. Tassy and Blunt Pick looked sorry they had spoken.

To overcome their discomfort Young Bill butted in with an inquiry about the Larkinville rush.

'Well, we none of us made our fortunes on Larkinville, Bill,' Dinny said.

'Some blokes done pretty well out of it,' Dally demurred.

'Cripes,' Dinny's eyes gleamed, winnowing a smile from the wrinkles driven deeply into his face, 'when I got a wire from Mick Larkin sayin': "Feeling crook, shake a leg, bring nap," I reckoned he was on to something good!'

They were sitting on Gough's veranda in the mellow glow which follows a goldfields' sunset: Dinny, his old mates slumped along the form and a couple of boxes, Marie Robillard and Mrs. Gough in the dilapidated easy chairs with sagging bottoms, which had stood on the veranda for so many years. As the glow faded, the dusk crept up about them.

The Larkinville rush had created a sensation in 1930, but that night seven years later, Dinny started dry-blowing his reminiscences as if Young Bill, who had been away from home for a year or two, had never heard them before.

Billy Gough was still Young Bill to everybody who had known him since he was a kid, although he was a fully fledged mining engineer now. Bill had studied at the Kalgoorlie School of Mines, and been away gaining experience and doing a responsible job on a mine at Tennant's Creek in the Northern

Territory. But he had been lonely and homesick, taken a few months' holiday in Brisbane and Sydney, and recently returned to the west.

As he sprawled on the veranda steps, watching a young moon with a golden ring round it and a bright star near, swing into clear green of the evening sky, Bill looked content to be among his own people again. He had the air of a young man who has proved his ability and weathered gruelling experiences, but there was still something of the eager, irrepressible youngster beneath his assurance.

'Gee, it's good to be home!' he had been exclaiming, every now and then, during the last few days.

Bill was living with his uncle, Tom Gough, and Eily, who had taken charge of him when Missus Sally was so broken-up about his father's death. He had come round for a yarn with Dinny and his mates. And that was what he said after greeting Dinny, Marie, his grandmother and the rest of them, as he flung himself down on the steps: 'Gee, it's good to be home again.'

He sat there in the warm dusk, a funny, satisfied grin on his face: had been hungry for this familiar atmosphere, Sally thought. The yarning and tough loyalty of Dinny and his mates: the fragrance of honeysuckle and creamy blossom on the potato creeper which hung in a dark rag at the end of the veranda, mingling with the smell of red earth and the faint, acrid taint of sulphur fumes from chimneys beside the mines.

"Course, I knew Mick wouldn't be sending me a telegram like that because he was ill.' Dinny's little laugh gurgled in his throat. He spluttered and coughed over the smoke from his stubby old pipe.

'L-lucky L-l-larkin, we used to call him,' Blunt Pick stuttered.

'Knew his mates, Long Bill Matheson and Paddy Hehir,' Sam Mullett said, smoking thoughtfully. 'Paddy was sandal-wooding in dry scrubby country about a hundred miles south of Coolgardie, then. And Bill was camel man for Canning, the surveyor, when they were exploring for a northern stock route.'

Dinny went on, simmering to his recollections: 'Frisco and

19

Missus Sally and me were on the road in the old boneshaker, at dawn — with prospectin' gear, dry-blower-shaker and stores slung into the back.'

'Not before a good many other boneshakers, buggies and bikes were making tracks for Mick's camp, too,' Frisco interrupted dryly.

'Mick'd sent word to a few other old cobbers he was feelin' crook,' Dinny admitted. 'That was the worst of it, knew we'd tumble he was expectin' a rush when he declared some gold; and tipped us the wink to get in early peggin' a claim. But the cat's out of the bag when old prospectors start packin' in a hurry. So there was a bit of excitement in Kal and Coolgardie that night.'

'It was like old times,' Sally exclaimed. 'What with Dinny and Frisco mad to be off before the rush started, and the rumours going round about how rich Mick had struck it.'

'A lot of ground was pegged when we arrived,' Dinny agreed ruefully. 'Mick and his mates held the original claims and a big prospecting area. And they'd sent for Bobby Clough to locate the reef — '

'Best prospector, ever I knew, Bobby Clough,' Sam muttered.

'Fair wizard on gold!' Frisco drawled.

'Be the Great Livin' Tinker, Mick told me himself, they'd never've struck the reef but for Bobby,' Tassy burbled. 'They'd been loomin' in every direction, tryin' to trace her.'

'Thin as a rake, he was,' Dally muttered. 'Couldn't make the sign of the Cross on his face.'

Sally remembered the tall wreck of a man, withered and dry as the scrub he had been living in for over thirty years, but with its tough fibre and vitality. Few men went prospecting without a mate, but Bobby Clough had often packed his camels and set off for wild unexplored country, alone, and not been heard of for months. Once a partner had cleared out with £10,000, when they sold a good show. Perhaps that made him such an old hatter, the men said. He had struck gold, again and again, usually for a syndicate, and any money Bobby had made filtered away. Nobody knew where. Bobby did not booze or gamble. He was round about fifty when he joined Mick and his mates at Larkinville; his hair grey and his eyes bright hazel, almost gold themselves, with pupils which went to a pin's point in the sun-light and expanded at sunset.

'Mick's message didn't reach Bobby for days,' Dinny went back to his yarn like a dog to a bone. 'Bobby was away out in the mulga and couldn't be found. But he came mooching along the track, one morning, and Mick nearly hugged him! Bobby was jest about all in; had been travellin' for three days and nights after he got Mick's news. Paddy put on the billy and made tea. But Bobby could scarcely wait to eat a bite before gettin' to work. Mick pointed out where he'd picked up most of his slugs, and Bobby cocked his eye on the ridge. Down on the flat, a few trees looked as if they might be marking the course of a dead river. As Mick showed him the lay of the land, every now and then, Bobby'd stoop down and scoop up a handful of dirt: gloat over it.

' "Ye've loomed her north, a bit, Mick?" he asked.

' "Got colours in every dish," Mick told him. "But we can't pick her up on the ridge, Bob. Sunk to ninety feet by the old blackbutt, up there, and not a skereck. But I reckon the lode these floaters came down from's not far off. If we don't strike her, somebody else will."

' "We'll strike her," Bobby said.

'He went off next morning, nose and eyes to the ground, carrying his water-bag, light pick and panning off dishes. Mick went with him, at first; boiled a billy for him at midday and put out his crib. But Bob liked working on his own. Every morning, for a week, he went off at sunrise and'd come back at sundown with samples of dirt, and lumps of rock to dolly. He must've loomed for miles. When he lost a trace of gold in his dishes, he came back on his tracks and tackled the country about a mile to the north of Mick's p.a.: so hot on the scent he wouldn't eat or talk.

'But one night he muttered: "We'll strike her, soon, Mick! We'll strike her all right! She's somewhere not far off. I can feel her, now."

'It was late next afternoon, he came gallopin' through the camel bushes, his hair on end and his eyes blazin'. "Got her!" he yelled.

'Mick and Paddy and Long Bill followed him back to the outcrop Bobby'd located. No more than a half-buried snag of weathered quartz — and there was the gold showin' all through the broken stone.

' "Loomed her right up to here," Bobby cried, "and these rocks looked suspicious. Knapped 'em and there she was, first blow of the hammer."

'Paddy and Mick started in right away to dig a costeen, and everywhere they tapped the reef, she was lousy with gold. They thought they'd struck a golden hole, another 'Derry or a Carbine. Decided to apply for a mining lease in Bobby's name and the name of Frank Pimley, as Mick and his mates were holding a lot of ground. No time was lost in pegging the area, and everybody thought he'd be home and dried on the pig's back when that lease was granted.'

'You'd've thought it was another Coolgardie they'd struck, with all the excitement in the air,' Frisco murmured derisively.

'Sometimes,' Sally confessed, 'in the evening, with the claims on the flat in a haze of red dust, and tents along the ridge looking like cockle shells in the distance, I used to picture to myself the town that might grow up round the Groundlark. That was what Bobby Clough's mine was called, wasn't it? I could see it there in the sunset, the new town, with its mines, big dumps, poppet-legs and skyshafts: the streets, shops, pubs and churches —'

'We were all seein' things like that for a while, ma'am!'

Tassy's laughter rumbled in his big belly: his mouth opened and his fat jolly red face split to a wide smile.

'But after all, Larkinville was only a flash in the pan rush,' Young Bill observed lazily.

'Some pretty good alluvial come out of her.' Dinny was loath to disparage Larkinville. 'She was a poor man's field, Bill. Lots of blokes picked up slugs that went anything from a few weights to twenty and thirty ounces.'

'How did you do, Dinny?'

'Not too bad,' Dinny admitted.

'You bet he didn't,' Tassy gurgled. 'Got a nose on him like a bandicoot when there's gold about.'

'Me and my mates pegged half a mile down the track,' Dinny chortled. 'We didn't see colours for a week. And there was Frisco and me shovellin' dirt in the blazin' sun, and Missus Sally on the shaker, red with dust, so as you wouldn't know her, Bill. We were ready to pull our pegs, and lots of others like us, all over the ground. Then a couple of little beauts turned up in the ripples and I got a thirty ouncer with a nest of small slugs in the "cat".'

'Hardest ground ever I slung a pick on,' Frisco growled.

'Go on, Frisco!' The raillery and subtle melody in Sally's voice told everybody they were still lovers. 'You were a bit soft at first. But you can't say you didn't enjoy meeting all the old-timers who turned up at the rush, yarning round the camp fire and all that. Sometimes he'd play his guitar and sing like he used to on Hannans.' Her eyes went to Marie. 'Or Paddy Hehir'd get out his accordion and give us "McGinty's Goat".'

'Y're forgettin' the "Dry-blowers' Song",' Blunt Pick said slyly.

'No, I'm not!' With a flash of defiance, Sally sang:

> Here's to the dry-blower!
> When he dies to Heaven he flies
> With dust in his eyes fit to blind him
> What a rattle he'll make as he goes through the gate
> Dragging his bloody old shaker behind him.

Frisco and the old men joined in, their hoarse, quagy voices rollicking over the ditty Lorne McDougal had made, and which was so popular on the rush, though the 'bloody' was slurred over, because women were present.

'We had a good time, all right,' Dinny gurgled, 'though some blokes were shovellin' dirt and not makin' tucker for months.

Blunt Pick and me, we met old mates we hadn't sighted for years. Some of'm since we were dry-blowin' on Fly Flat. Men like Johnny Micklejohn, Chassy McClaren —'

'And Bill Jehosaphat,' Sally reminded him.

'Cripes, yes!' Dinny spluttered, his breath caught between laughter and coughing. 'You never knew who'd lob into the camp. Blokes you'd thought were dead, long ago. Seemed as if Larkinville had roused the ghosts of scores of old prospectors out of their graves. And blowed if I did't barge into Bill Jehosaphat one day on the track. Bill said he couldn't resist the temptation to pack his swag and make tracks for Larkinville when he heard all the rumours flyin' round in the Eastern States.'

'That was before the throubles began,' Tassy said.

Everybody sobered in recollection of what the troubles had been. Smoke clouded up from pipes that had almost died down.

'Rushin' Bobby Clough's lease,' Blunt Pick broke the gloomy silence. 'They'd ought to've been run off the field for doin' it.'

'There was a queer mob camped down that end of the ridge,' Dinny said slowly. 'When they started to peg right up to the reef —'

'They were within their rights,' Sam Mullett muttered.

'They were within their rights,' Dinny agreed. 'The lease hadn't been granted, and it wouldn't be, if they could prove there was alluvial gold still bein' worked on the ground. Reg'lations permitted them to peg within fifty feet of the reef. But there wasn't an old-timer would've exercised his rights against Bobby Clough — not anybody who knew the years he'd put in prospectin' and livin' on damper and parrots. We reckoned he'd earned his luck. Mick and his mates as well. They didn't make tucker for months before they struck the first slugs on the field.'

'Not like as if it was a rich man's show,' Blunt Pick growled.

'But the mob on the flat weren't dinkum prospectors,' Dinny declared. 'They were mostly the sort of riffraff follows a rush, thinkin' all you've got to do is pick up the gold and not do any hard work for it. Well, when he found those blokes measurin'' off alluvial claims within his pegs, it was too much for Bobby. He rushed round, tryin' to drive 'em off, threatenin' to shoot the first man put a pick in his ground. Mick and Frank Pimley tried to quieten him; and Paddy and Bill Matheson worded the blokes who were rushin' the lease. They asked the mob if it was a fair thing to butt in on Bobby Clough when there was miles of un-prospected country all round. They could take their pick. It was over-the-fence, Paddy pointed out, seein' all the hard work Bobby had done, and not made a bean out of it, to do Bobby out of the first bit of luck he'd had for donkey's years. But there was some tough customers in that mob. They said they weren't goin' to be soft-soaped and shoved around. Bobby Clough wasn't the only man who'd been prospectin' for years, and earned a bit of luck. A man had to stick to his rights and make the most of any ground he could peg.

' "I'll shift 'em! I'll shift 'em!" Bobby yelled, ran up to his camp, and loaded the gun he kept for shootin' kangaroos or parrots when he was short of a meal. Mick and Frank Pimley had their work cut out to stop him usin' it. He was a Cornish-man, Frank, a long-jawed, level-headed chap. Bobby'd been prospectin' for him before he got Mick's wire.

' "It's all right, Bob," Frank said, "we've got the reef. They can't touch the golden hole. All they can do is pick up a bit of alluvial, and when that's worked out, the lease'll be granted. Regulations are regulations, after all. We've got nothing to worry about. Take it easy."

'But Bobby couldn't see it that way: was fair broken up: couldn't sleep, wouldn't eat, wandered about ravin' and shoutin', tellin' everybody how he'd loomed her along the ridge to the very spot where he struck the reef, knapped a rock and there she was, "a fair jeweller's shop". Mick thought it was a touch of the sun, at first, and he'd be all right in a day or two. Frank and Mick were afraid to let Bobby out of their sight. He was wan-derin' around with his gun loaded: couldn't rest or stop talkin'. His eyes were so shifty and bright we thought he was clean off his head. Then he got an idea the mob'd be rushin' the reef,

25

stealin' the golden hole from under his nose. Frank had to take the gun off of him. Bobby collapsed and lay in his tent too weak to move for a day or two. Then Long Bill got out his truck and Mick and he took Bobby to the hospital in Coolgardie. He died there.'

'Poor old Bob!' Tassy muttered. 'After all the years he'd put in prospectin' and livin' hard out there in the bush be himself, it was too much for him to strike it rich — and be done out of his luck.'

'Not much alluvial was found on the lease, after all, was there?' Young Bill asked.

'No,' Frisco replied. 'But when the lease was granted, the Groundlark looked like being a pretty promising little mine.'

'Never forget the mornin', the same mob rushed Mick's and Paddy's and Long Bill Matheson's prospectin' area,' Blunt Pick struck up again.

'There was a lot of mutterin' about Mick and his mates not declarin' all the gold they got,' Dinny said. 'Buck Rawson reckoned he and his mob could claim forfeiture on that score. The Warden got wind of a rumpus brewin' and was comin' out on Sunday mornin'.

'But Buck and his mob didn't wait for the Warden. Jack Hehir, Paddy's young brother, heard a bit of a stir down on the lead where Mick's dry-blower was standin', and went along to see what was happenin'. He run back, shoutin': "They're jumpin' our claims, Paddy!"

'Paddy pulled on his pants, and half a dozen of us who was sharpenin' our tools at Mick's forge, went along with him. Paddy was jest about ropable, would've barged in and given any man a fistful, but we held him back. There'd've been a rough-up in no time, and only half a dozen of us with Paddy against forty or fifty men in a nasty mood on the other side. "What the hell's the matter with ye?" Tassy yells. "The Warden'll be here this mornin'. If ye've a case, ye can put it to him — and both sides'll have to abide by what he says . . . Nothin' to be gained by carryin' on like this."

'When the Warden's car came bumpin' along the track in a

cloud of dust, the jumpers were all at work on the claims they'd pegged. Paddy banged his dishes for a roll up, and first thing Warden Geary said was all pegs would have to be pulled before he'd hear what any man had to say. Buck Rawson and his mob trooped back to the claim, grousin' and cursin'. Pegs were pulled, and the Warden got a statement from Buck about why his mob reckoned they had a right to peg those claims.

'Paddy put the position for himself and his mates. The Warden retired to Mick's tent to consider his decision. Round about two o'clock, he came out and gave it. Said there was no doubt in his mind Mick and his mates hadn't been declarin' all the gold they'd got and he was going to forfeit their ground. It was like a bomb exploding amongst us. In view of the circumstances, however, Warden Geary said he had decided not to enforce the full penalty of evading the regulations, but would reduce the holding of the original prospectors to a four-man claim. He authorized Paddy and Bill Matheson to go down and peg the four-man claim in any direction they chose.

' "Y're not bein' very generous to the original prospectors, Warden Geary," ' Tassy piped up.

'Warden Geary's been praised and blamed for what occurred that morning,' Sally said. 'But Lord knows what would've happened if he hadn't come!'

'To the jumpers, he announced he was goin' to regard the rest of the area as Crown Land,' Dinny continued. 'Alluvial claims would be marked off, and these claims would have to be balloted for, so that a mad rush of prospectors for the new ground would not end in injury and disaster, or be the cause of further disputes. There were one hundred and eighty men to ballot for the fifty new claims. A surveyor was found among the diggers to tape them off. Another young chap who said he was a draughtsman volunteered to draw up a plan. The claims were numbered and numbers put on the pegs. The numbers were put in Paddy's old hat and men queued up to draw. Some of 'em, of course, didn't get a claim; some who did, didn't even have a miner's right. Buck Rawson was one of the blokes who got left.'

27

'Dinny, and some of the mugs who reckoned Mick and his mates had got a raw deal, wouldn't take part in the draw,' Frisco remembered, as if he were laughing up his sleeve at them.

'The reshuffle of claims didn't bring the jumpers much luck, anyhow,' Sally flared.

'Most of us weren't makin' tucker on our claims,' Dinny admitted. 'A lot reckoned the field was as dead as mutton soon afterwards, packed up and cleared out. Missus Sally and Frisco among 'em.' .

'And Bill Jehosaphat,' Tassy spluttered.

'He done his dash, all right,' Blunt Pick mourned.

'Bill was glad to go back to 'is sheep?' Marie queried.

'And thoroughly disgusted with shovelling dirt in the heat and dust,' Sally laughed. 'He got blisters on his hands and a sore back. Blunt Pick and he didn't see even a colour of gold. Bill was satisfied the field was worked out when he left. So were we, Frisco and I, though Dinny stayed on. He and Tassy were there when the Golden Eagle was found.'

Young Bill jerked himself up to exclaim:

'Gee, that must've been a great day!'

'It was,' Dinny agreed, 'and gave a new lease of life to Larkinville. Funny thing, we reckoned there was no gold along that end of the ridge. Nothing but hard hungry rock and cement stone. Spud Murphy, the bloke who got that claim in the ballot, put in a few weeks on her. Jim Larcombe had a look at the claim when Spud was slinging it.

' "Pullin' out?" ses Jim. "I might give her a fly."

' "Right," ses Spud. "Go for y'r life. She's too like hard work for my likin' — and nothing to show for it."

'Jim started sloggin' at the claim. She was tough all right. We reckoned he was balmy, breakin' all that rock without anything to go on. After a bit, it seems, he struck a small slug and it kept him goin'. But he'd jest about had enough and was ready to shift his pegs when his son, Young Jim, blew along — out of a job and wantin' to try his luck. His father put him on to shiftin' that cement. He hadn't been workin' more than a couple of days when he let out a yell. Jim ran over to see what he'd struck. The lad's pick had laid bare a lump of gold. Took 'em a good while to work round it.'

'Be the Great Livin' Tinker,' Tassy chortled, 'Jim said he'd've thought he was seein' double or dreamin', if the lad hadn't been there.'

'Christ A'mighty, she was a bobby-dazzler all right,' Blunt Pick put in reverently.

'When Jim yells: "Slug O!" the mob came racin' from everywhere.' Dinny was as excited as if he had just heard that yell. 'We tried weighin' the eagle, that's what she looked like — a dead bird with spread wings —'

'If you used a bit of imagination to see it,' Sally murmured.

'We tried weighin' her in the store against a bag of sugar — nobody had gold scales big enough to take her. Sufferin' cats, what a shindy there was! All of us sweatin' and cursin', and beside ourselves with excitement. She was the biggest lump of pure gold ever seen in the west. Fresh and clean but a bit rough on one side.'

'Went 1135 ounces, 15 'weights,' Sam Mullett said solemnly. 'Twenty-six and a half inches across and eleven and a half wide. Worth £5655 then; would've brought double that, today.'

'He was always unlucky, Spud Murphy,' Dally observed dreamily. 'Unluckiest man ever I knew. If it was raining pea soup, he'd only have a fork.'

When the gust of laughter had rattled away, Young Bill brought Dinny's wrath about him.

'There was a rumour going round a while ago, the Golden Eagle was smelted gold,' he said.

'Me foot!' Dinny exclaimed. 'Y' couldn't put a stunt like that over the men on Larkinville. And y' can't tell me if there'd been a trace of telluride in her, there wouldn't've been a howl about it.'

'You reckon?' Bill queried easily.

'Nothing much seems to have happened round Kal and Boulder since I was away,' he added, in order to turn the con-

29

versation and placate Dinny. 'Same old smell, same old dumps by the roadside, same old crowd yarning on Gough's veranda!'

'There were the riots, Bill,' Sally said.

'That's right.' Bill seemed to wake up. 'They blew up soon after I went north.'

'It was a bad business.' Dinny prodded the ashes in his pipe with a dead match as if his thoughts needed prodding also. 'Worse than the first anti-foreign rioting, Bill. Kind of hang-over, maybe: started in the same way with a lot of young men out of work — unemployed from all over the country swarmin' here, t'other siders as well as W.A. blokes — and foreigners in good jobs. A returned soldier who'd been on the beer, and was makin' himself offensive, was slung out of the Home from Home pub by a foreign barman. It's a foreigners' hang out. The soldier died of a fractured skull, and a crazy mob started smashing up foreign wine saloons, shops and restaurants, set fire to 'em and ran amuck, boozin' and lootin'. The west end of Hannan Street was blazin': broken glass, fish and chips, fruit, vegetables, flour, sugar, coffee, spaghetti and clothing piled up on the foot-paths, with tills that'd been burst open and furniture kicked to pieces.'

'Beer and wine pourin' down the gutters,' Dally murmured dolefully.

'It was a real night of terror: foreign women and children screaming and crying, and running after their men into the bush.' That sight still weighed heavily on Sam Mullett's mind.

'The mob commandeered the trams and went off to Boulder,' Blunt Pick butted in.

'Soon after, the sky was red with the blaze of houses burning on Ding Bat Flat,' Sally said.

'Some of the I-talians and Yugoslavs dug a trench out beyond the railway station,' Dinny went on. 'The rumour got round they were makin' bombs. The mob rolled up to chase 'em out of the trench, yellin' like mad: "Clean up the Dings! Clean up the Dings!" They got rifles and revolvers, made hand grenades out of jam tins stuffed with fracteur, and rushed the trench.

30

Y' could hear the explosions and see flashes of rifle and revolver fire. The foreigners beat it, runnin' away towards the Ivanhoe dump, throwin' bombs as they went, and the mob kept on firin' at them. Jo Katici, a Dalmatian, was killed. Tom knew him, a decent chap. Seems a miracle there were no more deaths — though six of the rioters were injured.'

''Course the coms were blamed.' Blunt Pick let fly his jibe, grinning at Bill.

'They would be.' Bill lit a cigarette.

'But they had a man here, at the time, a little bloke name of Docker,' Dinny went on. 'And he pretty soon showed that was a lie. Got out a leaflet urgin' the workers to have nothing to do with the demonstrations against foreigners who were workin' men like themselves. Pointed out the coms were against makin' ill-will between workers on racial grounds. It was playin' the bosses' game, and the unemployed had nothing to gain by turning their grouch on the foreigners. It was the mine owners and conditions of work on the mines they had to tackle if there was to be work for all. Tom and Docker were out all that night, helpin' foreign women and children to get away from their burning houses; and tryin' to make the rat-bags who'd started the riotin' listen to reason. Tom spoke at Katici's funeral. He said Jo's death had been caused by the acts of a few irresponsible fools. Every sane man on the mines was opposed to the rioters.'

'Good old Tom,' Bill's face lit up. 'You could bet what he'd do. Just as well Docker was here to give a lead, though. I know Ted, and he's all grit.'

'You're a bit of a com, y'rself, Bill, they tell me,' Frisco remarked, the idea amusing him.

'A bit of a com?' Bill whooped. 'I've been more than a bit of a com, a long time, haven't I, gran?'

'Oh, Bill —' Sally's voice held a troubled tenderness. 'I do wish Tom hadn't dragged you into his committees and things.'

Bill laughed.

'Tom didn't drag me into anything, gran. I've got enough common sense to work things out for myself.'

'That's right, son,' Dinny said. 'Always work things out for y'rself. I'm a Labour man meself, but some of us old battlers've got a bit stiff in the joints and rusty in the top piece. And the working-class movement's got to keep movin'. It's you young chaps must see to that. Here on the goldfields, there's only a handful like Tom and y'rself with the guts to tackle a tough proposition like tryin' to make people understand what communism stands for.'

'Everybody's talking about it, for or against — mostly against,' Sam Mullett said, weighing his words carefully. 'No use shuttin' y'r eyes to the fact.'

'You can't paint any real picture of what's happening in the world today, and leave us out.' Bill threw him a challenging glance. 'There may not be many coms in the mining industry, but people are beginning to realize what we're after is a decent life for everybody.'

'You think what you call "social ownership" will be a cure for all the ills the flesh is heir to, don't you, Bill?' Frisco liked to give himself an air of leisurely cynicism. 'Put an end to the whole business of exploitation, poverty and war?'

'That's about the size of it,' Bill grinned.

'I don't hold with socialism,' Tassy said heavily.

'It's against human nature,' Blunt Pick asserted, as if he had said the last word on the subject.

'You're just a lot of old stick-in-the-muds,' Bill declared heatedly. 'May have done a bit in the struggle for democratic rights in your day. But what are you doing now? Most of you are just sitting back in the traces or have become downright reactionary. And there was never a time when men and women with a spark of intelligence were more needed to organize against the dangers threatening us today.'

'I see what y're gettin' at, Bill.' Dinny tacked to support Young Bill. 'Even if some of us don't see eye to eye with you and Tom, after what's happened in Italy and Germany, we ought to do something to make sure fascism never rules the roost in Australia.'

'Too right, you should,' Bill replied with uncompromising forthrightness. 'Fascism smashes the trade unions and destroys the rights of the workers. Look at Spain! Rather than let a constitutionally elected government serve the interests of the people, it's plunged the country into civil war.'

'We're not dead yet, Bill,' Sam Mullett objected in his slow, ponderous way. 'What can we do about it?'

'Come to the meeting of the League for Peace and Democracy tomorrow night,' Bill said laughingly, 'and find out. I've got to get along now: want to call at O'Brien's and take Daph home.'

He jumped up and walked away with a casual: 'So long, everybody!' From the veranda, as he rode off on his bicycle, they could hear him whistling that gay, tuneless little air he used to whistle when he was a boy.

Dinny, Sam Mullett, Tassy and Blunt Pick exclaimed and chuckled good-humouredly about Young Bill after he had gone. They were a little sore and uneasy, on account of what he had said, and the way he had scoffed at them; but willing to concede his spirit and youthful enthusiasm. For an hour or so, they talked to soothe their ruffled consciences, recalling instances and incidents of the revolutionary zeal they had put, when they were young, into fighting for alluvial rights, union principles and labour representation in parliament.

Only Sally was vexed with Bill. She thought he had been too cocksure and arrogant with the old men.

'Stick-in-the-muds, are we?' she grumbled to Marie. 'I'd like to know how Bill would feel, now, if he'd had to battle along here in the early days. Is it any wonder some of us just want to sit back and take things easy?'

'But we cannot do it, *chèrie*,' Marie said firmly, her hands lying white and stiff, distorted by arthritis, in her lap. 'Not when there is this *fascisime* which 'as caused so much suffering in other countries, to worry about.'

'It can't affect us here.' Sally was impatient of the idea.

'The fascists will make war to achieve their ends,' Marie said with gentle obduracy.

33

'Not again!' Sally wailed. 'There couldn't be another war in our lifetime, Marie. All that horror and misery couldn't overwhelm the world again.'

Marie was spare and frail-looking in her black dress: shaken by the intensity of her emotion.

'Again and again, it will come,' she cried, 'if we — if the people everywhere — do not organize and unite to stop it. If we are stick-in-the-muds . . . if we do not think or understand . . . if we do nothing . . . can it be otherwise?'

CHAPTER III

IT was wild and stormy that night of the Boulder Town Hall meeting. After tea Tom Gough sat in his chair by the fire in the kitchen; and Bill, at the table, went over notes for the speech he was to make.

Singing to herself, Daphne blew in to press the dress she was going to wear to a dance. She threw an ironing blanket over one end of the table and switched on the electric iron.

'Sorry, Bill,' she apologized blithely, 'but I won't be a minute!' And went on singing:

> I wander-ron as in a dream,
> My goal a paradise must be . . .

'About time you woke up, isn't it, Daph?' Bill's sly grin quirked.

Daphne did not let it interfere with her singing, as she whisked out the folds of her flimsy pink dress, and ran the iron over them.

She was a pretty little thing, Daphne. As pretty as the spray of almond blossom she had stuck in a jar on the dresser and was going to wear that night. With the same zest and innocence, she was thrusting the fragile petals of her hopes and joys into the murky atmosphere of this goldfields' town. She knew well enough that rough weather might play havoc with those petals; but that did not deter her from fluttering gaily along her way. She had the same pluck and tenacity as the almond blossom. Her neat features, in profile, were firmly outlined, despite the youthful softness and immaturity of her face when it confronted you.

Tom in his chair by the fire shivered and coughed as a draught, from the door Daphne had left open, struck him. Bill got up to close the door; but Eily came in, her coat and hat on, the slightly worried expression, which rarely left it, these days, creasing her pleasant, kindly face.

'Oh, Daph,' she said reproachfully, 'I do think you might have given up your dance for one night.'

'But I hate meetings, mum!' Daphne's smile flew to Bill. 'You won't mind if I don't go, will you, Bill? Besides, there's a competition dance at the Palais tonight, and Wally thinks we can win.'

'You know dad and I don't like you going out so much with Wally O'Brien,' Eily protested.

'Don't let's go over all that again, mum!' Daphne was too happy and excited to be affected by her mother's reproach. 'Wally reckons I'm the best dancer in Kal, and I reckon he is, so I don't see why I shouldn't go to dances with him.'

'Never mind.' Tom coughed nervously. 'Daph's got her head screwed on the right way. She'll come to her senses one of these days.'

'But he's a married man,' Eily persisted.

'There's such a thing as divorce,' Daphne said lightly.

'For goodness' sake!' Eily could not suppress her consternation. 'But you'd never think of marrying a man like Wally O'Brien, Daph?'

'Depends.' Daphne tilted her head to one side, holding her dress at arm's length and eyeing it critically.

'On what, for pity's sake?'

'Whether I want to marry anyone, yet — as a matter of fact.'

With a laughing glance at Eily's troubled face, Daphne took her spray of almond blossom from the jar on the dresser and flipped out of the room.

Bill could hear her singing as she dressed in her own room, further along the passage:

> I care not for the stars that shine,
> I dare not hope to e'er be thine,
> I only know I love you,
> Love me and the world is mine.

She was always singing that sentimental ditty, Bill realized. He wondered how much of it Daphne meant, and how far her gallivanting with Wally O'Brien had gone. Daphne was eighteen, and as intent on having what she called 'a good time', as most girls of her age.

Bill was very fond of this young cousin of his. They had grown up together more as if they were brother and sister, sparring and slinging-off at each other sometimes, but conscious of a deep affection between them. When he came home Bill had been surprised to find Daphne was working as a waitress at O'Brien's hotel. He had been perturbed, too, to hear she was going to parties and dances with Wally O'Brien, younger brother of the licensee. Everybody knew Wally was the ne'er-do-well of the O'Brien family: a clever, good-looking young blackguard, at present employed as a barman in Peter's pub.

Fragments of the gossip about Wally O'Brien ran through Bill's mind as he turned over the notes for his lecture. He hoped that he could remember what he wanted to say without referring to them.

This country of ours we call a Commonwealth. Who owns it? Who owns the wealth of its infinite resources — its land and mines and industries? Do we? Do the people own the common wealth of Australia? . . .

Wally's sister, Mrs. Isaac Potter, who old friends still spoke of as Vi O'Brien, had sent Wally to the university where he was supposed to be studying law; but Wally had gone off with a third-rate theatrical company visiting Perth, toured the Eastern States and New Zealand and wired for money to return home when the company disbanded and he was stranded in Sydney. Wally arrived with a wife who had been leading lady of the company. Her dyed hair and playing of the skittish young newly-wed did not disguise the fact that she was several years older than Wally. She had been under the impression apparently that he was the beloved prodigal of a wealthy family, and it was a shock to her when Peter indicated Wally would have to start earning a crust. But good-natured and willing to give Wally a helping hand, Peter had bought a tobacconist's

37

business for him, expecting Wally to settle down and make a success of it.

. . . The biographer of a great armament manufacturer referred to 'the convenient euphemisms by which the real objects of statesmen may be cloaked and the energies of a people directed'. What did he mean by this? That statesmen cloak the real objects of their policies with flowery, humanitarian words and phrases. . . .

Living behind a small shop and doing her own housework, however, did not suit Mrs. Wally. Before long she disappeared. Wally said she had cleared out with a commercial traveller. Wally sold the business and lit out soon afterwards, leaving Peter a swag of debts to settle. Nothing was heard of him for two or three years. Then he was brought to Kalgoorlie on a gold-stealing charge, convicted and sentenced to six months' hard labour. He drifted back to the bosom of his family when that unpleasant experience was over, with the air of a martyr, having taken the rap for men in the racket for whom he had been acting as agent.

. . . We must not be deceived by the myth of a Commonwealth of Australia, or of a British Commonwealth of Nations. We must work for the reality, which will safeguard not only the welfare of our own people, but the peace and progress of the world. . . .

It had to be admitted that Wally had not betrayed the gold-fields' code and squealed. So his sister, Violet, took him in, and Wally recuperated in her comfortable home. He did more than that: he became a popular figure in Kalgoorlie society, flirted and played tennis, and entertained friends at his brother-in-law's expense until Ike Potter put his foot down and turned Wally out.

. . . Fascism in other countries, today, has trampled on the rights and organizations of the people. It is the enemy of democracy, of social justice and human dignity. It serves the interests of the war-makers, and all those who would sacrifice human progress to their greed for wealth and power. Fascist tendencies are appearing here, in Australia. . . .

Peter had come to the rescue again and given Wally a job in

the bar, to save face for the family. Wally treated it rather as a joke; but he was a good barman, Peter found, and quite popular. He could turn on a song or dirty story, and keep the beer flowing in a way that was excellent for trade. Wally, himself, enjoyed the sensation of being a profitable investment and earning high wages for the first time in his life. He was even swanking a good deal about it: talking of going into partnership with Peter, or setting up in opposition to him.

But Bill did not like Wally. He did not like Daphne to be going about with Wally O'Brien: wished he could have gone to the dance and let Wally know he had better watch his step in any philandering with Daphne.

The local committee, however, had organized this meeting of the League for Peace and Democracy in order to raise funds for Spain. Perth Molloy and Alma Leighton, who were responsible for the newly formed branch of the league, had found it difficult to arouse interest in their meetings, although Perth himself was a returned soldier, and Alma drove herself relentlessly to be a good secretary. They knew Bill had spoken at meetings in Sydney and hoped that he would prove a draw. He had been a popular footballer before he went away: played for 'Tigers', the Boulder team which sported black and yellow jerseys, and carried them so often to victory in the tough games all Boulder and Kalgoorlie assembled to watch, on Sunday afternoons, during the winter.

Of course, it was important for him to do what he could to make a success of the meeting, Bill told himself. More important to arouse people of the goldfields to realization of the dangers of fascism and the menace of the international situation, than to go to a dance and rush round trying to look after Daphne.

'Where's Dick?' Tom asked.

'He's gone out,' Eily replied reluctantly. 'I did ask him to come with us, but he said he was taking Myrtle to the pictures. Dick seems to be very sweet on that girl, Tom.'

Tom stared into the fire. Mention of his eldest son so often brought a shadow to his face.

39

'La and Nadya have been pestering me all day to know whether they can go to the town hall, tonight,' Eily said quickly. She could not bear to see Tom look so hurt because Dick was drifting away from them.

'A bit young for political meetings, aren't they?' Bill quizzed.

'I don't let them go often.' Eily smiled across at him, but her eyes went back to Tom. 'We made a mistake perhaps, taking Dick and Daphne to meetings when they were little. But La and Nadya are different. They're always asking questions: wanting to know the why and wherefore of things. Just like you used to be, Bill. Besides, they say they've simply got to go tonight, because you're speaking.'

Bill appreciated the youngsters' partisanship.

'Here's hoping there'll be a lot of others feel like that!' he said, his smile crinkling to please Eily.

Daphne tripped into the room, lissom and radiant in her flimsy finery: almond blossom pinned in a wreath on her sun-shiny hair.

'How do I look?' she queried, whirling her full skirts, and preening herself to show off the tight bodice moulding her bosom and the curve of her bare shoulders.

'A fair treat,' Bill said softly.

'Wally's coming early so that we can practise a few steps at O'Brien's before we go on to the Palais.' Daphne's laughter rippled and sang. 'We'll win the competition, you see.'

A car tooted on the road. She threw a coat over her shoulders, and ran off, carrying the pink satin dancing shoes, which were her most precious possession, in a brown paper parcel.

'Don't forget I'm taking you to the School of Mines ball,' Bill called.

'Not likely!' Wind and rain rushed through the open door as Daphne went out into them. Bill heard the car purring as it moved away. Wally had persuaded Peter to lend him his new Dodge, Bill guessed. He gathered up his notes, with an uneasy feeling he had got to do something to stop Daph going out with that blighter.

'Gran's late.' Eily glanced at the clock. 'She promised to call and drive us over to the hall.'

'I'll walk,' Bill decided.

Tucked into their coats and caps, La and Nadya burst in on him, exclaiming eagerly:

'Can we come with you, Bill?'

'No,' Eily said firmly. 'It's still raining, and I don't want you to look like a pair of drowned rats.'

'But I want to go with Bill,' La objected.

A lively, aggressive youngster of twelve, with Eily's blue eyes, La always put up a fight for his own way.

'Bill doesn't want you to go with him,' Nadya remarked crushingly.

A squabby, pale and plain little girl she was, without any of Daphne's wayward charm and ephemeral loveliness. But Nadya was definitely a person in her own right. As youngest of the family, she had learnt to keep everybody in order, particularly La, who was only two years older than herself.

'Quite right, Nad,' Bill laughed, realizing Nadya as well as Eily understood he needed to be alone for awhile. 'You see, old man,' he explained to La, 'I've got to keep my mind on my job. But we'll go for a good long walk on Sunday.

La whooped with glee, and Bill went off for his coat. As a matter of fact, he was suffering from that queer sinking feeling which assailed him whenever he had to speak in public.

He was no public speaker, Bill assured himself: had never acquired the tricks of mob oratory. All he could do was present an audience with the facts of a case and say what he thought about them. Honesty and sincerity made the best speaker, he had been told — so long as they could be heard. If he believed he had to make an effort to tell people the truth on an important matter, then he had to do so. That was the driving force behind his disinclination to assert himself: to stand on a platform, alone, facing hundreds of people, as he had done several times in Sydney.

Although he carried himself with an air of assurance, Bill

41

knew well enough it was merely to hide his shrinking from exposure of a self which had suffered some deep hurts in childhood. He was, naturally, a modest youth, Bill Gough, unwilling to claim for himself any qualities which other young men of his age did not possess. He liked to think he was an ordinary hardheaded bloke who loved life. Neither a crank nor a martyr, because he had attached himself to what he considered 'the greatest cause on earth': the right of the working people to organize for a better way of life in their own country and to unite with the peoples of other countries for world peace.

It was true, Bill would admit, he enjoyed dancing, bucking into a scrimmage on the football field, going gay with girls at a party; but, more and more, he was finding it difficult to spare time for those pleasant diversions. Study and organizational activities absorbed most of his leisure. But he was happy in the way of life he had chosen for himself: light-hearted and confident about its rightness and the ultimate attainment of its objective. That was what Sally regarded as his 'youthful idealism'. Bill thought he could afford to grin, and stack on his knowledge of economics and history in any argument; and his own conceptions of honour and courage if ever it were necessary to defend his 'youthful idealism'.

All the same, as he strode along the wide dark streets, hugging himself in his coat against the wind and rain, Bill had to scold himself for being jittery about addressing a crowd of goldfields people. Of course, he had not done any public speaking in Boulder before; and he expected that no audience would be more critical and difficult to move than one made up of folk who had known him since he was a kid.

He wished he could run off into the bush, as he had often done when he was a youngster, to get rid of some inner tribulation. It was wonderful, he reflected, how a walk about out there in the quiet assuaged any mental pain and unrest. The tough, light-leafed trees which had weathered innumerable droughts and thunderstorms gave you something of their own strength and fortitude. But it was shameful and absurd to be baulking at the post like this, Bill told himself. He must get over such weakness. It would leave him as soon as he began to talk he knew. He would lose sight of himself in his subject. The responsibility of presenting it clearly and forcibly would arouse every fighting instinct. It was only in the first moments as he faced an audience — all those eyes were focused on him and he got the impact of the massed consciousness — that he wished he were dead.

The big barn of a hall when he reached it held only a handful of people. The committee looked gloomy and depressed: agreed it was a mistake not to have taken a smaller hall as Tom Gough had advised. Alma was almost in tears, Perth Molloy apologetic and blaming the weather. Charley O'Reilly cursing, and muttering: 'Only one thing'll wake up some people, and that's a fascist bomb on their roofs.'

'They'd turn out for a fight or free beer,' Alma exclaimed bitterly.

'Never mind,' Bill tried to cheer her up. 'The people who have come along are made of the right stuff.'

He could see Sally, Frisco, Dinny, Marie, Tom, Eily and the Gough youngsters in the front row. Most of Dinny's mates were seated behind him: Tassy Regan, all spruced up in his Sunday best: Dally, a little drunk and trying to look sober: Blunt Pick, so sleek and scraggy after a shave and haircut, Bill scarcely recognized him. Sam Mullett and his wife, Eli Nancarrow and his, half a dozen neighbours and old friends, several miners and comrades, and a group of Yugoslavs, made up the rest of the audience. When two or three late-comers had shuffled into their seats, Perth Molloy thought it was time to begin. As chairman, he conscientiously introduced Bill to the audience, although almost everybody had known him all his life.

'But you're meeting not only Billy Gough,' Perth declared, aware that he must wind up his opening remarks with a suitable flourish. 'Our speaker tonight is a new and valiant young champion of peace and democracy.'

Bill hauled himself to his feet and there was a feeble clapping

43

of hands. He felt the size of an insect and as insignificant, when he faced the thirty or forty men and women scattered about the dimly lit, almost empty hall. But what he had to say was not insignificant, he assured himself, and flung out his greeting:

'Comrades and friends! . . .' He was all right then. The fire of his faith and purpose rose within him and he plunged into his subject.

'. . . Most of us here, tonight, are citizens of what is called the Commonwealth of Australia. We want to work for its welfare, and the welfare of its people.

'Why was that name chosen — the Commonwealth of Australia? It was chosen to please the people. To give them an illusion of living in a country where the national wealth is actually the property of the people. To give them an appreciation of the meaning of the word commonwealth, surely? And yet, who owns the wealth of this country — its infinite resources, its lands, mines and industries? Do we? Do the people own the common wealth of Australia? You know they do not.

'You know that powerful monopolies have seized the wealth of Australia, and use the labour of the people to maintain their own interests — and the domination of an economic system which has international ramifications. . . .'

Sally and Eily exchanged glances. They knew Bill had been nervous at first: they had been able to see him only through the mist of their own nervousness. But, presently, they could relax and smile at each other. Bill's movements were no longer jerky: his voice was ringing clearly, steadily.

'. . . But those words, the Commonwealth of Australia, should inspire us to make Australia a commonwealth in reality. They should inspire us not to be satisfied with the mere name. It should warn us, too, to be on our guard against any tendencies which would destroy the rights of our people, and their organization for ownership and control of the wealth their country produces. Fascism threatens those rights and organizations. . . .

'Just consider for a moment what the stranglehold of these

44

monopolies means to our right to organize for a commonwealth — for social ownership, which is scientific socialism. They control the work which enables us to earn a living. They control the press on which we depend for information about national and international affairs. Through these two powerful weapons, they bring pressure to bear on parliaments, on legislation, on our educational system, on the judiciary, on public opinion, and on our relations with other countries. There is only one thing they don't yet control in Australia and that is the labour power of organized workers in the trade union movement — and the intelligence of men and women who believe it's their duty to work for peace and progress.

'All over the world, men and women have been organizing in defence of their rights as workers and as intelligent beings. And against them has risen the brutal power of fascism, financed and armed by ruthless men who control the wealth of Great Britain, France, America and Australia. . . .'

Briefly, Bill described how Hitler and Mussolini had seized and maintained power. How with the support of industrial magnates, financiers and military cliques, they had launched an offensive against the democratic rights of their peoples, smashed the trade unions, tortured and murdered not only Jews, socialists and communists, but thousands of men and women suspected of progressive ideas.

'. . . No matter what fascist regimes call themselves,' Bill said, 'they will always be recognized by their deeds. The wolf wears sheep's clothing to harry the flock. National socialism was used as a cloak for the anti-working class schemes of Hitler in Germany, although these schemes have nothing to do with socialism, or the welfare of the nation as a whole. They are designed to make a German ruling class dominant not only in Germany but in world affairs. . . .'

A slight, intrepid figure, Bill looked, standing up there on the platform and defying 'Power which seems omnipotent'. That was a favourite quotation of his, Sally remembered. To her, he was like a legendary hero, determined to fight this dragon breathing fire and brimstone over Europe, and menacing even far away places like Australia.

Folk on the goldfields were too easy-going and good-natured to believe most of the stories they had heard about the ruthless cruelty and insane ambition of the fascist leaders, Bill declared. But he told how he had talked to Egon Kisch and other refugees from German concentration camps who had seen fellow prisoners beaten to death, their hands crushed, eyes gouged to bloody sockets. These men said that half of the truth about the torture and raping of Jewish and communist women by vicious guards, was not known abroad. The facts and figures Bill quoted, gave some idea of what was happening to countries under the domination of fascism.

His audience muttered and moved restlessly, as if knowledge of such brutality could not be borne.

'... This is the system of barbarous terrorism we are supporting when we fail to use all our energy against it ...' Bill's voice trembled to his anger and indignation. He went on to show the effect of fascist intrigues on the peoples of other countries.

'... Members of the Lyons Government have spoken publicly in admiration of what Hitler has done for Germany and Mussolini for Italy. They have introduced reactionary legislation to shackle the Australian workers in the exercise of their trade union rights. Papers, published in German, in Australia, boast that fascist organizations exist in every state of the Commonwealth. They are permitted to attack democratic rights the Australian working class has worked for and won after years of struggle. But when Egon Kisch came as a delegate from the World Peace Congress to a Peace Congress in Melbourne, the Federal Government refused permission for him to land. Kisch did land, was arrested and imprisoned. Gerald Griffen, a New Zealand delegate, was also refused permission to attend the Congress. You all know the tremendous indignation which was aroused and the legal battles which had to be fought in defence of the people's right to hear these men. Then we had the cropping-up of a National Socialist Party in the west, with a programme for reorganizing the trade

46

unions, on fascist lines — although that was promptly nipped in the bud . . .'

There was a rumble of laughter which heartened everybody.

'. . . Just shows what can be done when the workers swing into action!' Bill exclaimed jubilantly; and went on to explain the need for support of the Spanish workers in their struggle for a better way of life: better homes, schools and conditions of work.

'. . . The tragedy looming for humanity, in the growing power of fascism and its drive to war, is obvious . . .' He paused as if appalled by that prospect: but his voice rose to a fighting challenge as he continued: '. . . Already the Spanish conflict has revealed the secret friends of fascism in our midst. It has revealed the actual and potential enemies of democracy in a campaign to divide the people, using religious prejudices to blindfold them to the real issue — defence of a democratically elected government of the Spanish people against the forces of fascism. . . .'

Bill glanced at the paragraph he had cut from a newspaper.

'. . . Here's what a commentator said recently: "The appalling horrors inflicted on Spain by international fascism could have been prevented if Britain had fulfilled its obligations under international law to the Spanish Government and supplied the arms and material required. Instead, the National Government imposed sanctions not against the aggressor, but against the victim; it permitted, under the guise of neutrality, the uninterrupted supply of aeroplanes and munitions to Spain from Germany and Italy. Now the ghastly truth is becoming plain for all to see. The invasion and subjugation of Spain is part of the German and Italian plans for a fascist war of aggression in Europe. Was it lack of arms or lack of desire that prevented the National Government from standing by democracy in Spain?" '

Bill gazed before him, overwhelmed by his awareness of the horror and misery which lay behind the civil war in Spain. But suddenly a sense of futility assailed him. How could these few people in a back-country town of Australia make any difference to the calamity lowering, not only for Spain, but for the rest of

47

the world, if the intrigues of international gangsters queered the pitch all the time? His voice faltered and his mind became blank as he stared despairingly at the pained and patient faces turned towards him. Most of them were old and drained of vitality. Some of the old men had been shivering and shuddering under their shabby coats in the draughty hall. Bill had seen them yawn shamefacedly, now and then, and droop sleepily. There were less than a dozen young men in his audience, two or three of them working miners, the rest Yugoslavs. The Slavs, big husky men, had experienced persecution in their own land, he knew, and were willing to fight for the rights of the workers anywhere. Their burning eyes and the hungry intensity with which they had listened to him, drove the blank from Bill's mind.

They, he realized, and two or three of the miners who were friends and comrades, could be depended on to rally support for the government of Spain, and expose the activities of fascists on the Golden Mile. It was well known a fascist organizer had been busy among the Italian miners, and that he collected money among them, 'for Mussolini', as they said.

There was no need to urge the Slavs and the miners further, Bill decided. But sorry for the old people whose spirit had brought them from their firesides on this wild stormy night, and whose physical disabilities made it impossible for them to respond to his appeal for strenuous activity, he continued:

'. . . Some of you have fought the good fight for the rights of the people all your lives . . .' His voice held a whimsical challenge, and his glance flew to Dinny, Sally and Marie. '. . . I've heard it said a dry-rot has crept into the working-class movement since the great days of the struggle for alluvial rights and union organization. Maybe that's so! Maybe, we young men, today, are not as alive to the danger threatening what you fought for and won years ago, as most of you in this hall, tonight, still are. Well, we'll have to change all that. It's up to the younger generation to carry on from where you left off, and get a move on, right away.

48

'I remember a yarn Dinny told me when I was a youngster. It was about an old prospector who bought a watch from Ike Potter when he had a store on Hannans. The prospector went off to the bush with his watch and found it had stopped, so he walked fifty miles back to tell Ike just what he thought of him. Ike looked at the watch and saw what was wrong. "If you want a watch to go, you must wind it," he said. . . .'

Bill got the laughter he was seeking to make those old battlers feel pleased with themselves.

'Perhaps that's what's the matter with us young people, today . . .' Bill admitted. '. . . We all need winding-up to the problems of our own time. We've got to know what fascism means and be ready to defend ourselves from its threat "to shed rivers of blood" in order to boss the world. We've got to help to defeat fascism in Spain and any fascist tendencies which crop up in our own country. . . .'

He hurled the slogans intended to stir a working-class audience:

'Organize for the defeat of fascism and every attack on our democratic rights!

'Unite for peace and progress!

'Support the people's government in Spain!

'Unity of the workers of the world will abolish exploitation and war!

'And remember, friends and comrades, what Francis Adams, the first poet who wrote about socialism in Australia said. . . .'

Bill's voice sang as it rang through the dark, almost empty hall:

> . . . I tell you a cause like ours
> Never can know defeat.
> It is the Power of Powers.
> As surely as the sun
> Follows the great moon wave
> Will our cause be won.'

There was an outburst of applause and a clatter of handclapping when he sat down. The chinkle of coins could be heard as Alma and Eily passed round the collection boxes. Questions and discussion followed, but most people were fidgeting to go home. One of the Slavs jumped up to thank the speaker, and subsided overcome by emotion and his difficulties with the English language. Perth closed the meeting, and folk wandered away, looking reprieved, but exclaiming that it was a shame everybody in Boulder and Kalgoorlie had not been there to hear Young Bill Gough.

Mrs. Eli Nancarrow, her malicious eyes glittering, however, sidled up to Sally.

'Your grandson's got the gift of the gab, all right, Mrs. Gough,' she said. 'But I don't think he should talk about the torture and rapin' of women at a public meetin'. Fair gives you the creeps.'

'That's what Bill meant to do,' Eli said gruffly.

'Oh, well,' his wife grumbled, 'I'd rather've been at home, by the fire, with a nice book. It's no use draggin' me to political meetin's, I've told you before, Eli. If you ask me, Bill Gough's jest one of these reds, stirrin' up strife and makin' trouble everywhere.'

'Shut up,' Eli growled, hoping Mrs. Nancarrow's sharp, cracked voice had not reached Dinny and the Gough family surrounding Bill. He bundled her away.

'You don't want to take any notice of a silly old woman like that, Bill,' Dinny said soothingly.

'The worst of it is, there are so many people like her.' Bill's grin flickered. 'They don't want to hear the truth or be disturbed by it.'

CHAPTER IV

A T home by the fireside, Bill flung himself into a chair, spent and depressed.

When Sally drove them back from the hall, Eily had persuaded her to come in for a cup of tea. So they were all there, Dinny and Frisco as well as Tom, though the children had been sent to bed.

'You were wonderful, darling,' Sally said staunchly. 'I never would have thought you could speak so well.'

'Oh, gran' — Bill brushed aside her loving flattery — 'it was like talking temperance to teetotallers. Most of the people who were there didn't need convincing about the dangers of fascism, and what's happening in Spain.'

'It was a good speech all right, son,' Dinny assured him.

'Made out a case against the fascist set-up,' Frisco declared jocosely, willing to oblige Sally by buoying the lad's spirits. 'Though Hitler and Mussolini have got the wind in their sails, all right.'

He could not disguise a sneaking admiration for the performances of men endowed with no more qualities for their sensational careers than Francisco de Morfé had once possessed.

'It's a hard job to get people to a meeting in Boulder these days.' Tom was almost as glum as Bill. 'Though,' he added consolingly, 'it wasn't such a bad attendance after all.'

'Couldn't have been much worse,' Bill said.

'In the old days, we banged a panning-off dish when anybody had anything important to say, and every man in the camp would roll up,' Dinny remembered.

'What's the matter with people?' Bill burst out. 'Why aren't they interested in this question of fascism and Spain? Haven't they got any *nowse*? Can't they see that if the Spanish Government is defeated, fascism will be considerably strengthened in Europe? And war is almost inevitable?'

'Most people don't want to believe it,' Eily said bitterly. 'They'd rather jog along with their eyes shut than try to stop the bombing of Spanish workers, their wives and children, or the massacres in China.'

'I wouldn't say that.' Tom spoke mildly, reprovingly. 'There's a good few, in Australia, feel like we do — although a lot more don't understand what's happening.'

'And don't want to,' Bill interjected.

'That's a fact,' Tom agreed. 'A great many who stayed away from your meeting tonight, Bill, are like that. Daphne and Dick, for example. Others, maybe, know the facts and are just callous. Don't care what happens to anybody but themselves. But don't forget the Australian lads who have gone to fight with the International Brigade, and the six nurses. Thousands of pounds have been collected for ambulances and medical aid.'

'Not a patch on what we ought to be doing,' Bill grumbled.

'The collection tonight wasn't so bad,' Sally reminded him.

'Twenty pounds,' Eily admitted, mollified by the thought. 'Half from the Slavs, and Dinny put in a fiver.'

Bill's grin flashed to Dinny.

'Gee, it's good to have you on my side, Dinny!'

Dinny's eyes smiled. He was pleased to see that Bill's discouragement was passing.

'If there wasn't blokes like you to carry on, Bill,' he said, 'I'd die in me tracks.'

Bill stood up, stretching, and ruffling his hair.

'I'll carry on,' he cried, recapturing some of his urchinish bravado. 'Don't worry about that, Dinny. It got me down, just now, realizing what a tough job it is to reach the men on this field — and that the show tonight was rather a wash-out. Suppose I reckoned all Boulder was going to turn out to hear Young Bill Gough do his stuff.'

Two or three minutes before he had heard the front door bang, and caught a glimpse of Daphne flying along the passage, a rain-drenched, bedraggled wraith, with almond blossom stripped of its petals falling from her hair. Why had she come home from

52

her dance like that? And so much earlier than usual? Bill was worried about it, as well as about the failure of his meeting. So was Eily. She had gone off to Daphne's room immediately.

'The lad's tired and must go to bed,' Sally declared briskly.

She fussed about her old men as they put on their coats, and hustled them off. Then she kissed Tom and Bill, and stood looking at them, a glisten of tears in her eyes.

'You two make me feel there's something of Dick in the bond between you,' she said quickly, and disappeared into the windy darkness.

'Poor old gran,' Bill murmured, 'she still grieves for dad, and I scarcely remember him.'

'Sometimes I forget you're not my own son, Bill.' Tom's voice had the grave, deep tone it took when he was moved. Bill did not miss the sadness in it, though, when he added: 'I wish young Dick were more like you.'

'I wonder, sometimes' — Bill hesitated and then continued — 'if that's what's the matter with Dick. If, perhaps, he feels you've given me a good deal of what should have been his. And he's struck out on his own — cut himself off from us — in self-defence.'

'Maybe,' Tom said. 'But I've never given Dick less than I gave you, Bill. It had to be the way it was. He ought to know that.'

'He'll understand, one of these days,' Bill said reassuringly. 'He'll feel, like I do, that we're brothers, really, Dick and I — like you and my father were, Tom.'

'Cripes, lad,' Tom grasped Bill's hand. 'It's a comforting thought, that.'

Eily came into the room, her face ruckled in bewilderment and distress.

'I don't know what's the matter with Daphne,' she said. 'She won't tell me. She's lying on her bed, with her face to the wall, sobbing her heart out. All she'll say is: "Go away, mum! Leave me alone! Leave me alone."'

'Had a row with O'Brien, I suppose,' Tom said.

'Something's gone wrong,' Eily fretted. 'Usually, he brings

her home from a dance. But she must have walked tonight. Her dress and shoes are soaking wet and all muddy.'

'If it means a break with Wally, so much the better,' Bill said. 'She'll get over it.'

But he was as concerned as Eily about the cause of Daphne's homecoming in disorder and tears. When Tom and Eily had gone to bed, and he was lying on his own stretcher on the veranda near her room, Bill could hear Daphne's muffled crying. It was more than he could bear.

He opened a door from the veranda, went quietly into her room and sat on the edge of the bed.

'What's up, sweet?' he asked gently. 'Tell Bill. It's no use keeping things bottled up inside of you.'

'Oh, Billy,' Daphne turned swollen and streaming eyes to him, 'Wally's dumped me.'

That was good news to Bill, but he contrived to hide it.

'Damn his eyes,' he said, with suitable indignation. 'I'd like to kick his behind.'

A faint smile struggled through Daphne's tears.

'So would I,' she said plaintively.

'Let's!' Bill cried. 'You give him one, good and hard, and then I'll have a go at him.'

But Daphne could not rise to the banter in his sympathy.

'It was awful, Bill,' she said tragically. 'We'd had the first dance, and then two girls came in. You never saw such flash janes: twins, with ginger hair, dressed exactly alike — in black satin with big sprawly flowers and birds and pomegranates all over it . . . Wally was mad about them the minute he saw them. He got somebody to introduce him, and danced with them all night, doing the craziest stunts. Once I heard one of the girls say: "Who's the pretty little thing in pink?"

' "Which?" Wally said.

' "The one with blossom in her hair."

' "Oh that," Wally said. "That's Daph Gough."

' "Daphne Gough?" They seemed quite excited and wanted Wally to introduce me.

' "I'd like to paint her," one of them said. But I didn't want to speak to them. I just couldn't, Bill . . . And Wally didn't come near me until it was time for the competition waltz. Then he couldn't talk of anything but Pat and Pam.

' "They're Paddy Cavan's daughters," he said. I was so wild, I just wouldn't answer him.

' "Jealous?" he said.

' "You can't treat me like this, Wally," I said. "I won't stand it."

' "Who's asking you to?" he said, cool and distant like. "Don't be a little fool, Daph. You shouldn't take things so seriously. God knows I never meant you to." But he did — oh, he did, Bill. At first — and every time he said he loved me, I'd laugh at him. And then he'd look miserable, and say it was a case of "give a dog a bad name". Wouldn't I try to believe he'd never been so gone on a girl before. And then he'd kiss me — and everything was so lovely between us. I just didn't think he could ever treat me like this.'

'It's rotten,' Bill put his arms round her. 'But you mustn't let it get you down, Daph.'

'I know,' Daphne sobbed. 'I didn't let anyone see, there, at the Palais, what I was feeling. I danced and flirted with Steve Miller and any boy who came along. But when Wally said that, I just walked off and left him standing in the middle of the dance floor. I didn't care about the competition — or anything. I think I must have run all the way home, Bill. Forgot about my shoes, and to get my coat. My dress is ruined.'

'Never mind,' Bill said soothingly. 'I'll buy you a new one.'

'Oh dear,' Daphne sighed. 'I didn't know being in love could be so awful.'

'It's not all it's cracked up to be,' Bill said cheerfully. 'But you've got plenty of spunk, Daph. You're not going to let people start saying: "Poor Daphne", and being sorry for you, are you?'

'Too right, I'm not!'

'That's the style,' Bill said gently. 'You must get a bit of

55

shut-eye, now, and stop crying — if you want to put a good face on it, at work.'

'I suppose so,' Daphne sighed. 'What a comfort you are, Bill. I could tell you anything, and you wouldn't fuss and be all cut up like mother or dad. You'd just take it, sporting, and help me all you could, wouldn't you?'

'You can bet your sweet life on that, darl,' Bill replied, more disturbed by this query than anything Daphne had said.

Daphne closed her eyes and turned away as if she were sleepy now. It was not the moment to put further pressure on her confidence, Bill thought. She was too exhausted to talk any more tonight.

Stretched on his own bed again, Bill's blood seethed at the thought of Daphne's hurt and humiliation. Daph, the lovely, laughing, little scatter-brain who had been the spoilt darling of her own family for so long, it was hard for her to take the sort of knock-out Wally O'Brien had given her. Bill cursed him indignantly.

But it wasn't so much a broken heart Daphne was suffering from, as outraged vanity, he suspected. And if there was more to it than that — What was it Daphne had said? 'I could tell you anything . . .' Bill sweated in consternation. Surely Daph did not mean there was more to tell: something she was reluctant to talk to Eily and Tom about? Bill rejected the thought. It was too incredible and harassing — although he knew Wally O'Brien: had heard him boast that girls on the fields were easy. A man had only to flatter them up: give them a few glasses of wine, and they were his without a struggle.

'Damn him!' Bill groaned. He could not sleep for a while: nerves were tugging and jangling all over his body. He fretted about Daphne. His brain ticked off scraps of what he had said at the meeting that night. The white blobs of faces in the dark swam before him. He could feel again the horror and misery he had talked about; he felt as if he were drowning in an abyss of despair because people would not listen or understand when he was trying to warn them about the tragedy overhanging them. Mrs. Nancarrow's wicked eyes glittered at him; he could hear her cackling voice telling everybody that it was Bill Gough, not Hitler or Mussolini, who was responsible for the crimes of fascism.

'God,' Bill moaned in his dreaming unrest, 'what is a man to do?'

'He was reviled and persecuted of men' . . . the voice seemed to come from a distance. And then Tom was talking to him, reminding him that no man or woman who had ever tried to better the lot of the working people escaped abuse and calumny in their own time.

'Cripes,' Bill told himself, 'I'd forgotten that.'

The poem he had quoted at the meeting rang through his brain:

> I tell you a cause like ours
> Never can know defeat. . . .

He went to sleep on it, and slept soundly, peacefully.

CHAPTER V

EVERYBODY was talking about Paddy Cavan's daughters.
It made no difference that the girls announced firmly on
all and sundry occasions: 'We are Pat and Pam Gaggin,
Sir Patrick Cavan's step-daughters, not his daughters.' Sir
Patrick, nevertheless, took an unctuous pleasure in playing the
indulgent parent to two wayward young women, and in intro-
ducing them as: 'My daughters, Pat and Pam.' So as Paddy
Cavan's daughters they continued to be known.

They were attractive girls; they naturally created a sensation.
When they walked through the streets, they wore either gaudy
slacks and pullovers, or brightly patterned dirndls; and at night
sweeping satin gowns from which their pale faces rose on a thin
stalk of neck, with lustrous hair, square cut across the forehead,
falling in a straight sheath to their shoulders. Their eyebrows flew
upwards like fine dark wings, and long gingery lashes shadowed
greeny-grey eyes always shimmering to an intense vitality.

The gossips were busy in no time recounting to each other
the 'goings-on' of Paddy Cavan's daughters. There was nothing
unusual about girls drinking and smoking with men in the lounge
of a pub, these days, they agreed; and it was well known that
smart young things were entertained at beer and petting parties
by eligible young men on the goldfields. At first, Pat and Pam
got the reputation of breaking all the records for going gay with
young men of the town. But before long another rumour was
on its rounds: that Paddy Cavan's daughters were too fast and
blasé for Kalgoorlie's younger set, and had taken to bedevilling
the older men. Married men and middle-aged rips fluttered
round them wherever they went: took them to the races, showed
them over the mines, sat yarning with them in the lounge at the
Palace Hotel: delighted, it appeared, to bask in the presence of
such glamorous youth and indulge the twins' taste for violent
arguments.

Restless and excitable, the two certainly were: nobody knew quite what to make of them. They smoked readily but drank as cautiously as two old maids. Although they danced with sensuous pleasure — often together, to the disgust of waiting partners — from all accounts they were a disappointment at close quarters to would-be lovers.

Bill got an inkling of this when he overheard two young sparks of the town discussing Pat and Pam with Wally O'Brien. He had gone into the bar at O'Brien's with Abe Carlson, a wealthy bookmaker.

Abe was a good sort, generous and sympathetic to any move-ment likely to defend his race from anti-Semitism. Bill had run into him outside O'Brien's and was explaining the situation in Spain when Abe said:

'Come and have a drink,' and led the way into O'Brien's.

They stood breasting the bar where Peter O'Brien, shirt sleeves rolled up, was serving. Further along, Toby Dowson and Kim Lindsay were leaning over Wally's end of the bar. Bill stood with his back to them; but their talk rattled on his ear drums.

'Too damned uppish and inseparable!' he heard Toby Dowson say.

And Kim Lindsay: 'Those bitches will lead a man up the garden, discussing "the psychology of sex" until the cows come home. But there's nothing doing when there's a chance for a bit of love-making. "Don't like being mauled" and "Mugging is barred".' A light, indifferent voice was mimicked disgustedly.

Bill guessed that Paddy Cavan's daughters might be the subject of this conversation. He was curious, although it did not concern him in any way, he told himself. To be sure, one of those girls he had met on his grandmother's garden path had struck a nerve with an exhilarating effect which still lingered. But as soon as he discovered her association with Paddy Cavan, he had put the thought of her away from him: almost forgotten that she and her sister had said they must see him again about something 'important and confidential'.

There was nothing important and confidential they could have to tell him, Bill decided. Or, if there were, in connection with his mother's affairs, it could wait. She had told him in her letter that in her will she had left him the cottage at Cottesloe where they used to stay when he was a child: assured him it was bought with her own money and had nothing to do with Sir Patrick, so he need have no qualms about accepting it. Bill was not sure whether he should: but his grandmother and Dinny both said there was nothing to be gained by making a present of the cottage to Paddy Cavan. So when Lady Cavan's lawyers wrote to him, he had signed the documents which made him a landlord, as Frisco pointed out. Bill, himself, could not grieve for his mother. She had been almost a stranger to him, and he felt slightly embarrassed because she had remembered him with some affection before she died.

He had been too busy, after work, collecting money for Spanish relief, organizing study circles, attending union and party meetings, to bother about seeing those girls again, Bill assured himself. Besides he had heard the gossip about them, knew they were in demand at all the dances and keg parties of the smart set, and could not imagine that he and the Misses Gaggin would have anything of interest to say to each other.

'You don't understand the type.' Wally's patronizing drawl impinged on the facts and figures Bill was giving Abe Carlson about Spain. 'You've got to talk art and literacher, if you want to get anywhere with Pat and Pam. And politics!'

'Hell,' Toby Dowson groaned, 'it's beyond me.'

'They like to think they're intelligent young women: got no inhibitions,' Wally explained blandly. 'But it's a bluff really. They're not as eaten up with intellectual enthusiasms as they make out. All women are the same in the dark.'

An appreciative guffaw drowned the rest of his remark. The lads added bawdy comments and exclamations.

'You can always trust girls with highfalutin ideas to go the pace — any pace you want — if you handle 'em the right way.' Wally served another round of drinks, assuming the slightly bored air of a man of the world. 'They're more bed-worthy, in the long run, than the gold-diggers who fall for you easy.'

Bill's impulse was to whirl round and bash his face. But he could not give himself that satisfaction, he realized. There was Daphne to be considered. Wally must not be given the gratification of thinking he was sore on her account. And he must concentrate on Abe and getting a decent contribution out of him.

'That's the size of it, Abe,' Bill burst out. 'If we want to stop the growth of fascism, we've got to give the Spanish people a hand. God Almighty, in common decency, a man can't refuse a few quid when women and children are being bombed, refugees massacred without mercy.'

'No need to get so hot about it, Bill,' Abe replied equably. 'You'll get your few quid from me.'

He had noticed Bill's reaction to the talk of the half-drunken youths beside him, and guessed there was something in it that made him go suddenly haywire and want to let fly at Wally O'Brien. Abe had no desire to be involved in a brawl with young men who were all good clients. To pacify Bill and get him out of the pub was his immediate concern. He understood what had annoyed Bill as he finished his beer, and heard Toby Dowson snigger:

'They're just a pair of "modern young things", Paddy says, "no vice in 'em".'

'Don't you believe it,' Kim Lindsay grumbled. 'Pat left the marks of her finger nails on me at Middleton's party.'

'As vicious as a pair of wild cats if you try any rough stuff,' Wally drawled. 'That's not the technique to make a girl shed her panties.'

'Come on,' Abe said gruffly.

Out in the street, he took a wad of notes from his pocket and gave Bill a fiver.

'Maybe I'll double it next month,' he said, and jerked his head towards the hotel. 'Gets your goat, hearing young blighters like that talk about women in a bar. But you don't want to do your block about it, Bill.'

61

'I know.' Bill shook off his fury. He was grateful to Abe for removing him from the bar, and for the fiver. 'It's all I can do, though, to keep my hands off Wally O'Brien, sometimes.'

When Abe had sauntered away, Bill picked up his bicycle and rode off, perplexed by the frenzy which had seized him, an almost ungovernable desire to grapple with O'Brien and wipe the vicious complacency from his face. It was not entirely on Daphne's account he had become so incensed, he suspected, although he felt hot under the collar when he thought of Wally O'Brien's treatment of her. Daphne seemed to have got over it quite well. She was going out with Steve Miller, a young miner, who had been her boy friend before Wally appeared on the scene. She did not sing so much, and was looking rather peaky, but all the same had put a good face on her break with O'Brien. She wouldn't even talk about it any more. Every time Bill had tried to draw any further confidence from her, she had retreated behind a hard shell forming over her mind on the subject.

'That's over, Bill,' she said irritably. 'It was my own fault if I let Wally make a fool of me. I ought to have had more sense. But I'm finished with him now.'

Bill was relieved to hear her say that, but uneasy about Daphne's defiant reticence. She was secretly fretting a good deal, he thought, despite a forced gaiety and reckless flying about with Steve or some other lad. It was apparent she could not forgive Pat and Pam for commandeering Wally. Daphne retailed all the spiteful gossip about them with naive gusto; and slung-off because Wally was always hanging about, dancing attendance on them, and often getting snubbed for his pains.

It was the way everybody was tearing those girls to pieces that riled him, Bill assured himself; and after all, it was 'over-the-fence' for Wally and his cobbers to talk about any women in a bar as they had done.

He was not personally concerned about Paddy Cavan's daughters, Bill told himself. He wasn't going to lose any sleep over what they did, or didn't do; but it amused him that Pat and Pam had amazed and horrified old-fashioned sinners and scandal-mongers. More by the careless audacity with which they went about doing as they pleased, than anything else, it appeared. They had a green sedan in which they dashed about the country; but latterly Paddy had bought them a pair of horses and the girls had taken to going off together on long rides in the moonlight. One night, they had camped in the bush when they lost their way. Paddy was sending out a search party to look for them, when they rode in next morning as if nothing had happened.

What set the whole town agog, though, was their attempt to visit the 'swy': the famous two-up ring on a sand hill near the old Rising Sun Inn. The game was illegal: no woman had ever been permitted to invade the sacred precincts. Pat and Pam hit on the bright idea of dressing up in men's clothes and getting Wally O'Brien and Kim Lindsay to take them there. The ring was run by a well-known old-timer who boasted that his game was well-conducted and orderly; two-up the fairest gamble in the world. For years, the police had not interfered with him, although every afternoon in the week there was a crowd of men and boys betting deliriously on the fall of a penny, behind a brushwood screen, on that hilltop a mile or so out of Boulder.

Look-out men stood at strategic points to warn players of the approach of the dees, or any suspicious strangers. But the only seats round the ring consisted of upturned sanitary pans; and Wally guessed he was in for trouble when two men offered their seats to the sprightly lads accompanying him. The boss, however, would not allow disregard of his authority to pass unchallenged. He asked Wally to introduce him to the young ladies, and politely requested them to leave. In the heat of the game, the language of some of the men became rather lurid, he explained. Pat and Pam tried all their wiles, begging him to let them remain. But with lordly courtesy, the old man in his rusty coat and weathered felt hat, a diamond flashing on his little finger, escorted them beyond the brushwood screen, opened the door of a shining Rolls Royce drawn up there, and directed his chauffeur to drive the Misses Gaggin back to Kalgoorlie.

'I may be any sort of blackguard, mesdames,' he said sweeping off his hat, and bowing with urbane dignity, 'but there's one thing I won't stand for. And that is bad language in the presence of ladies.'

Dinny had got the story from Pat and Pam themselves. That was another thing which amazed and amused Bill: Dinny's friendly alliance with Paddy Cavan's daughters. Dinny discounted any malicious gossip and would not hear a word against them. The girls were a bit high-spirited and unconventional, he said; they had to be to hold their own against Paddy.

'And they do that, believe me,' Dinny chuckled. 'If Paddy knew some of the things they do with his money, he'd have a fit.'

As Dinny had handed Bill ten pounds for Spanish relief funds, and intimated that the donor wished to be anonymous, Bill had a shrewd idea from whom he had received the money.

Dinny, it seemed, had come across the girls on one of his prowls round Maritana, shown them the site of the first claims and yarned to them about old times. He had met them more than once. Sometimes by appointment, Bill discovered, as did his grandmother. She had been most indignant about it. But Dinny declared Pat and Pam were as nice, sensible girls as he had met for many a long day; and after all, they couldn't help it if their mother had married Paddy Cavan.

Pam had painted a portrait of Dinny. A queer daub of a thing, it was! No more like Dinny than the man in the moon, Sally Gough said. She could have done better herself. But Dinny was very proud of it, and said Missus Sally did not understand modern art.

The artist had not intended to make a likeness of him, Dinny explained. All she wanted to do was paint an old prospector in a glare of sunshine with red earth of the goldfields all round him; give an impression of the demon which possessed him in his search for gold.

'Pam says,' he said, a quizzical glint in his eyes to be talking like this, 'pure art springs from what an artist feels about something, not from just what anybody can see.'

Frisco's roar of laughter did not put him out of countenance; neither did all the chiacking he got from Tassy and Blunt Pick about his girl friends. It was comical to see Dinny, all dressed-up and excited, going off to meet Pat and Pam. Sometimes he took them for a walk round the mines, and sometimes went to yarn and have tea with them in a room they had rented for a studio.

They lent him books containing coloured reproductions of pictures by some of the modern painters, and Dinny tried painstakingly to give Missus Sally useful instruction about them. She gasped incredulously, gazing at pictures by Kadinsky, Legèr, Braque and Picasso.

'They're just crazy, as far as I can see,' she exclaimed, refusing to be impressed.

Bill was intrigued that Dinny seemed to have come to a vague understanding of what modern artists were seeking: new conceptions of form and light, dramatic reactions to familiar objects, interpretation of the fantasia of memory and subconscious emotions. It was all very confusing to Bill, and remote from the everyday struggle for existence, although he could appreciate some revolutionary theories of visual expression which made for simplicity and strength in pictures and sculpture.

He had heard them discussed among young artists in Sydney, and learnt to value what they admired in the work of Gaugin, Picasso and van Gogh. As a matter of fact, he recognized that Pam's portrait of Dinny bore some resemblance to van Gogh's 'Old Peasant'. But Bill had heard too much about the irresponsibility of artists and intellectuals, where the working-class movement was concerned, to allow himself to attach much importance to them. It was true, he acknowledged to himself, he had been taking a sneaking interest in Dinny's talk about art and the girls, although he repudiated the idea that he would have liked to be on such friendly terms with Paddy Cavan's daughters. Not likely! He and they could have nothing in common.

Two or three times, as he came from work, Bill had seen Pat and Pam sauntering along the Boulder road. The first time, as he whizzed past on his bicycle, he wondered whether they might have intended to waylay him in order to give him that information which was supposed to be important and confidential. The second time, he had no doubt of it, because they looked towards him; but he jerked his head and passed them on the road. He was conscious of behaving churlishly: ashamed of having showered them with dust, and of that jerk of the head with an unsmiling glance.

Bill wished he had worn a hat and could have raised it with easy nonchalance. But he wore a hat only to a funeral or wedding, and when he was going on a trip to the coast. When he was working underground, he dragged a dirty white cap over his rough dark hair to keep off the dust and grease. This cap, he decided, would do to play the little gentleman, next time he met those damned girls.

It was several days after he had heard young Dowson and Kim Lindsay talking to Wally over the bar at O'Brien's, that he came across Pat and Pam again. He had worn his cap two or three times, and discarded it in favour of an old felt which could be used for a polite gesture, if need be.

The girls were standing gazing at the high, grey, pinkish and mulberry coloured dumps of the South Kalgurli mine as he came level with them. He contrived to raise his hand to his hat and was passing when Pat called:

'Heigh, Bill!'

Bill stopped automatically. He could not pretend not to have heard. A little sheepishly, he wheeled his bicycle back to where the girls were standing, beside the road.

'What do you mean, passing us like that?' Pat demanded furiously. 'I told you I had to speak to you about something important and confidential, and three times Pam and I have walked out to the mines to meet you, and you've dashed past.'

'Is the matter so important?' Bill felt he had to be on his guard with these sirens.

'It is to us.'

The freckles in Bill's eyes danced. It was ludicrous, somehow, for Pat to try to look angry and imperious in green slacks, a red jacket and beret: but he wasn't going to be beguiled by this damsel, Bill told himself.

'Well, let's have it,' he said dryly.

Pam had seated herself on a boulder by the roadside as if she were tired. She gazed at Bill, a hurt expression in her mild eyes.

'You shouldn't be so rude to us,' she said.

'I'm sorry,' Bill felt mean about saying it like that: as if he were not in the least sorry for having been rude to them. He wondered what was the matter with him. It was not natural for him to be so stiff and offhand with girls. Even with social butterflies like these he had gone surfing and dancing on summer holidays at the coast, and enjoyed himself hilariously. But that seemed a long time ago, before he began to take a serious interest in life and work, and he could not forgive these two for being associated with Paddy Cavan.

'We've got a letter of introduction to you from Jack Stevens,' Pat said. 'Jack's fighting with the International Brigade in Spain, now, and so is Shawn Desmond. Pam's engaged to Shawn.'

'What?' Bill could scarcely believe his ears. Jack Stevens had been a good friend of his, and one of the first communist organizers in the west. But Jack was an Englishman. When he received a small legacy from his grandmother, Jack returned to England, and Bill had not heard from him for a year or two.

'Here's Jack's letter,' Pat said. And with an inflexion of gleeful malice: 'You'd better read it.'

Bill opened the envelope she handed him, and glanced through Jack's letter.

'I'll be damned,' he exclaimed, looking up at Pat with a shy grin. His hand went out. Pat took its firm grip and then Pam.

'Glad to meet any friend of Jack's,' Bill said.

'That's better,' Pam sighed.

'Does Paddy Cavan know — about your friendship with Jack?' Distrust crept back into Bill's mind and eyes.

'Of course not,' Pat said impatiently. 'We've got to be careful.

67

When we're twenty-óne we'll have control of our own money and can do as we please. If daddy had the faintest suspicion we've learnt to think for ourselves, he'd cut off our allowance.'

'I see.' Bill was still dubious.

'We can't be of much use at present,' Pat went on. 'But we want to do all we can to help Spain.'

'Crikey!' Bill began to laugh. 'It's the best joke I've heard for a long time. Who'd've thought it? Paddy Cavan's daughters — '

'We're no more his daughters than you're his son, Bill,' Pam reminded him. 'He married our mother, and then yours.'

'Eh?' Bill looked startled. 'Gee, that's right,' he admitted after a moment's thought. 'But I don't call him daddy.'

'You didn't have to,' Pam replied.

'You weren't a pair of kids he took over with all of their mother's belongings,' Pat said gloomily.

Bill was laughing again, laughing in a jolly, irrepressible way that set the girls laughing, too.

'If only I could tell gran,' Bill exclaimed.

'We did tell Dinny,' Pam confessed.

As they walked along the road towards Kalgoorlie, Pat and Pam talked eagerly to win Bill's confidence.

'It was Shawn who opened our eyes to everything,' Pam said. 'We used to go to cafés and studios with students from the Slade School, and met Shawn at a party. He wanted to paint me. His friend, Ian Foster, painted Pat — and you'd never have known we were twins.'

'Shawn and Ian would argue about everything under the sun,' Pat went on. 'Pam and I felt such nitwits.'

'We were "aesthetically and politically immature", Shawn said,' Pam giggled softly.

'All sorts of interesting people used to come to Shawn's and Ian's studio,' Pat explained, 'writers and artists, most of them reds. They gave us books to read about art and scientific socialism.'

'And took us to exhibitions, meetings, demonstrations, concerts and music halls,' Pam chimed in. 'We'd sit on the studio floor, eating yards of spaghetti, drinking red wine, and arguing until we were all quite sure we could settle the affairs of the universe, if only we got a chance.'

'But it wasn't always like that,' Pat said quickly, sensing Bill's disapproval of such a bohemian approach to matters of grave importance. 'We did see life in the slums of London, and learn what the extremes of wealth and poverty do to people. We were convinced that a system which causes so much misery and injustice has to be changed, and that we ought to help to change it.'

'Shawn said, at first, we were "slim gilt souls",' Pam interrupted. 'He's so vigorous and passionate about everything. His painting and work for the movement, most of all. I never thought I could mean anything to him. He didn't like my drawing, and I loved his beard and laughing eyes. Shawn's got the laughingest eyes you ever saw, hasn't he, Pat?'

Pat smiled at her sister's query.

'He has,' she agreed. 'And Shawn went to jail for six weeks because a cop laid his hands on Pam. It was that day the Mosley black shirts marched into the East End, and the people barricaded the streets. We were in the crowd. The police started bustling everybody along: the crowd surged back again, and suddenly the police were batoning all round them. I saw one of them catch hold of Pam.'

'I only called him a big, ugly brute because he hit a man standing near me,' Pam murmured.

'Shawn went mad and barged into the cop,' Pat went on. 'I managed to drag Pam away, and Ian got us out of the crowd. We ran for miles down back streets and alleys. When we were far enough away, we went into a picture show and stayed there until it was dark.'

'But Shawn got badly knocked about,' Pam wailed. 'He couldn't paint for weeks.'

'It was no joke,' Pat said soberly. 'We didn't want to leave Shawn, but Ian said it was no use hanging round. That cop would have grabbed the lot of us, and Shawn told him to get us away if there was a rumpus.'

'Paddy never knew?'

'No,' Pat said slowly. 'Amy guessed, I think, that we'd been with Shawn when he was arrested. It was all in the papers next day — about the battle of the East End, Shawn assaulting a policeman, and two young women who had obstructed the police in the execution of their duty. Amy tried to make us promise to give up our "rackety, bohemian friends" — but she didn't tell daddy.'

'Let him think we were just smart young things and having a good time at parties and dances,' Pam chimed in. 'He'd fly into a rage, now and then, and grouse about the amount of money we were spending. But if he'd known where a lot of it went, goodness knows what would have happened.'

'After all, it was our own money,' Pat said defiantly. 'And daddy had no right to interfere with our political opinions. There'll be a show-down when we claim what our mother left us. Meanwhile if he thinks we're irresponsible hussies, so much the better. We can still do what we like with any cash we've got.'

'While Shawn's fighting in Spain, how can I think of anything else?' Pam asked. 'We must send things to him, and to the International Brigade.'

'When the revolution broke out, so many of our friends thought they ought to go and help the People's Government,' Pat said. 'Jack Stevens, Ralph Fox, John Cornford, Ian and Shawn, and Aileen Palmer. Pam and I wanted to go too; but we weren't of age, and nobody would have us without our parents' consent. It was no use trying to get Amy and Paddy to agree to our going.'

'I wanted to go myself,' Bill confessed. 'Tried to get away when I came down from the north. But Tom was ill, and after the first batch of men had left, I thought it was my job to come home and take over his work.'

'Queer, isn't it,' Pat queried, 'that we should be so het-up about Spain?'

'It's not Spain so much as the struggle against fascism going on there,' Bill said.

'And a better way of life the people want to make for themselves,' Pam murmured.

'Who'd believe it,' Pat laughed, 'the three of us against Sir Patrick Cavan, and all he stands for?'

'Perhaps because of him,' Pam said.

Bill laughed and exclaimed with them at the dirty trick fate had played Paddy Cavan.

'But after all it's up to the younger generation to move on,' he said. 'We're not exceptions. In tune with the big ideas of our time. That's all.'

'What's struck Young Bill Gough?' miners going home on their bikes, or in the rattling trams, asked each other when they saw Bill walking along beside the girls and on such good terms with them. 'About the last bloke you'd expect to be hob-nobbing with Paddy Cavan's daughters.'

CHAPTER VI

Mɪɴᴇʀѕ on the road were not the only ones surprised to see
Bill Gough on such friendly terms with Pat and Pam.
Dick dropped in on his grandmother with the news.
By the time Bill called, an hour later, Dick had left and passed
it on to Tom and Eily. He was waiting to chiack Bill as soon as
he got home; and when Daphne came in let her know how Bill
had glad-eyed Paddy Cavan's daughters, and made quite a hit
with them, on his way from work that afternoon.

Daphne glanced from Dick to Bill, unwilling to believe what
Dick had said.

'Cripes, can't a bloke speak to a couple of good-looking girls
without everybody getting on to him?' Bill asked good-
humouredly.

Daphne looked hurt, as if Bill had gone over to the
enemy. She joined Dick in his slinging-off during their evening
meal.

Bill would not defend himself. He took Dick's and Daphne's
baiting as lightly as he had taken Sally's caustic comments, with
a self-conscious, rather sheepish grin.

'They're to be the star turn at the School of Mines ball.' Dick
polished off his jam roll and pushed back his chair. 'You ought
to go along, Bill, and show the lads of the village they can't have
it all their own way with such swanky sheilas.'

'Bill's taking *me* to the ball,' Daphne said. And with a twinge
of remorse for having joined Dick in trying to discomfort Bill:
'My new dress is a dream, Bill! There wasn't anything in the
shops that was just what I wanted so Marie said she'd make it.
She can't do much sewing now, but mum and gran helped her,
and it's the duckiest thing you ever saw. Pink taffeta with silver
thread on the flounces.'

'Been winning the lottery, Daph?' Dick queried.

'It's a present from Bill,' Daphne told him.

72

'We've got to be a credit to the family when we mix in high society, haven't we, Daph?'

Bill tossed off Daphne's glance of contrition and gratitude. He was anxious, as well, to spare Dick any qualms for not having given her the dress himself.

'Daphne's always that,' Dick said, with a flash of the affection for this lovely young sister which he rarely showed. 'No one a patch on Daph at Kal dances.'

'Oh, Dick!'

Daphne knew Dick had witnessed her humiliation at the Palais dance, and that this was his way of bucking up her spirits. Dick was taking Myrtle Langridge to dances and tennis parties, these days, and although Daphne did not like the plain and inane girl Dick had attached himself to any more than the rest of the family, she had tried to please Dick by being 'very sweet', as she said herself, to Myrtle whenever they met.

Myrtle was the only daughter of a mine manager with an unsavoury reputation for using old mines to screen extensive transactions of the illegal traffic in gold, but he had recently been appointed to the board of the Golden Star and Long View, by which Dick was employed. Mr. Langridge, it was understood, disapproved strongly of Myrtle's going about with Dick Gough, although she was not a popular or attractive girl and had been rather left out in the cold at social gatherings of the younger set, until Dick constituted himself her escort and devoted admirer.

As he dressed to take Daphne to the School of Mines ball, two or three nights later, Bill grimaced at his reflection in the mirror on his chest of drawers. It was small and dusty like the room which he had screened off for himself on the end of the veranda.

His fingers were stiff and clumsy as he knotted his bow tie. Sally would not approve of the result, he was sure, remembering her instructions years ago when he was disporting himself in Kalgoorlie society. The dinner-jacket she had given him then felt tight on his shoulders: the sleeves were too short. Bill wished

73

he could have worn his best navy suit, which fitted him better; but Daphne would be disappointed if he did not dress up for her on this occasion, and his grandmother had aired and pressed the black trousers and dinner-jacket, so that he could make a distinguished appearance. They still smelt of moth ball, Bill fancied.

A smile twitched the muscles of his grave, squarish face as he thought of how fussy she had been about their cut and fit when she first presented them to him, and how she had retrieved them from the drawer into which he had thrown them when he went north. 'Gran thought no one else could keep moths and silver-fish from devouring them,' Eily said. His grandmother, she said, was responsible, too, for the new shirt, collar and tie he had found laid out on his bed with the dress suit, when he came home from work.

Bill had showered, shaved, slicked his rough dark hair with brilliantine, and struggled into that 'party clobber', as he called it, with a queer feeling of being as excited as a kid, and deriding his excitement about this night out. It was a long time since he had gone to a School of Mines ball, which was regarded as one of the social events of the year in Kalgoorlie. As a student, he had never missed the great night, or any of the diversions of the young people with whom he came in contact. He had danced and played tennis with the sons and daughters of mine managers and the *élite* of the town, as avid as any of them for the enjoyment of every pleasure they could devise. To the disappointment of Tom and Eily, and Sally's dismay.

She had been astounded to read in the daily paper that Mr. Wilbur Fitz-Maurice Gough was to be best man at a fashionable wedding.

'If you want to call yourself a Fitz-Maurice Gough and shine in Kalgoorlie society,' she said tartly, 'you must behave like one.'

He had nothing to do with having the Fitz-Maurice tacked on to his name, Bill protested. The mother of the girl who induced him to be best man at her wedding, had given his name to the press like that. But Sally had taken him in hand. Talked about seemly behaviour for a young man of good family: how he must bow and stand to attention, show a deferential courtesy to parents of the bride and bridegroom at the wedding: learn to fold his tie neatly and precisely: carry one glove with negligent grace: never fiddle with things, or fuss nervously if anything went wrong: hold himself with a modest but dignified self-confidence.

Bill laughed to himself as he thought of it, and of this suit which she had ordered because the wedding was to be in the evening.

'I'm not going to have you look a hobbledehoy in that crowd,' she said defensively.

He had never reached the standard of tails, Bill thanked God. His excursion into fashionable society did not last long enough. An argument with old Berryman about a strike on the mines ended it. And Bill had been very fond of Lucille Berryman at the time, and thought his heart was broken when Lucille would have no more to do with him because he refused to desert Tom and the miners over that strike. It was then he threw his black trousers and dinner-jacket into a drawer and forgot about them. Soon after he had gone up north. Since then, and those months in Sydney, he had taken more interest in industrial and political affairs: become so engrossed with them that he had had little time, or inclination, for social functions of any sort.

But tonight, he found he was looking forward to 'going gay', dancing and feeling young and care-free again. At first, he had promised to take Daphne to the ball as a sort of duty, and to let Wally O'Brien know he could not play fast and loose with her. Then, when Wally was out of the picture, he wanted to make the ball some sort of compensation and defence for Daphne. Now, he was conscious most of all that Pat and Pam would be there! How would they meet him with the eyes of Kalgoorlie society watching their every movement? Perhaps Paddy Cavan would accompany them, curse him! Some of his cobbers and mine managers would certainly be present, and retail any gossip likely to interest Paddy. Dare he ask Pat to dance with him, Bill asked himself. That obstreperous nerve still stirred when he thought of her. Bill could imagine himself swinging in dreamy, sensuous delight with that slender figure in his arms, Pat's bright head near his own. What rot, Bill told himself sternly. He wasn't going to allow himself to be carried away by any thrill over this girl. She was too glamorous for his liking; and he was mistrustful of her interest in any of the matters which were of vital importance to him. But still — his urchinish grin flickered as he glanced at himself in the mirror — Paddy or no Paddy, they might risk that dance, if Pat were willing.

'Ugly mug,' he told himself, 'I don't like your chance.'

Daphne looked as lovely, in her new dress, as she had done that night a few weeks ago which had ended so disastrously. The dress stood about her in stiff folds of pink silk; her silver slippers showed beneath it, and a rose sat sedately in her hair. But her break with O'Brien had affected her insouciance more than he had imagined, Bill thought. She would never admit how much it had hurt her; and was putting on a pretty show of being as gay and light-hearted as ever.

Eily and Tom were delighted to see them going out together; they admired and flattered Bill as well as Daphne until the taxi Bill had ordered arrived.

'Doing things in style, tonight, Bill,' Tom commented happily.

'You bet!' Bill winked at him. 'It's not often I take the prettiest girl in Kal to a ball.'

The ball made a gala spectacle in the shabby, dust-raddled Town Hall. Women and girls crowded round the shining floor, bare arms and shoulders blocked by the black backs of the men hovering about them. Bright lights splotched and blurred the maroon, green, pink, mauve, white and blue of the women's dresses as they moved. Brisk, brassy music of the band broke the colours into fragments, bizarre patterns which slid this way and that, revolved, fused and fixed themselves again beside the drab wall when a dance ended.

Bill smiled to see it all like a picture in that book of modern paintings Pam had lent Dinny.

There were always more men than women at a function among

workers on the goldfields; but tonight prosperous citizens had come to patronize an event of social importance. Women were in a majority: heads, young and old, fixed in permanent waves, faces made up to look beautiful, gowns of the latest fashion moulding slim or obese figures.

It was curious to observe how parties and cliques kept to their own particular eddy, except when they were dancing. Then they shuffled and pranced on the polished floor, packed together and sharing an explosive geniality.

Bill found himself infected by the gaiety and exuberance which filled the old hall. He danced with Daphne and several of her friends, yielding to the conscientious efforts of the town band to produce a merry racket, and enjoying rhythmic movement with a partner whose bright eyes and fragrance set his senses whirring in a careless pleasure he had denied himself for a long time.

Now and then old friends greeted him. He saw Lucille, married now and a buxom matron, dancing with her fat stockbroker husband, although she did not recognize him. Daphne flitted past, flirting gaily with various admirers. She was the centre of a lively group between dances, Steve Miller standing guard. When Steve was not dancing with Daphne, his eyes followed her, lingering on her radiant face. It was from Steve's slightly apprehensive movement Bill discovered that Wally O'Brien had arrived. And with him Pat and Pam.

They were late: made a dramatic entry, wearing Spanish costumes, just before the exhibition dance they were due to give. In full-flounced skirts of golden satin, black shawls heavily fringed and embroidered with huge red flowers wound round their busts and hips, mantillas of black lace hiding their hair and surmounted by high carved combs, they looked like exotic flowers in a suburban garden.

'Paddy Cavan's daughters!' Bill heard the whisper run round the hall, and his resentment surged, although Paddy had not accompanied Pat and Pam, and that was something to be thankful for.

77

Their dance, in the middle of the ballroom floor, an audacious whirl of voluminous skirts, with a seductive strutting and swaying of lithe bodies, stamping of red-heeled shoes, snapping of fingers, shocked as many as it delighted by its wild grace.

Men surrounded the Misses Gaggin when they found seats in a far corner of the hall. They held court there, and danced with Toby Dowson and Kim Lindsay after the band tuned up again.

Wally O'Brien remained, lounging against the wall, somewhat disgruntled, until they returned. When Pat and Pam danced again, it was not with him.

Bill was surprised to see Wally make his way round the hall to where Daphne was standing, laughing and chattering with her following of students and young miners.

'The next's ours, Daph!' Wally announced, as if his right to her dances could not be disputed.

Daphne's casual glance veered to him.

'Oh, hullo, Wally,' she exclaimed lightly. 'Sorry!' she added, and went on talking to the lad beside her.

'Well, which?' Wally demanded with amusement and displeasure.

'I'm booked up,' Daphne replied sweetly, and went off with Steve.

It gave her a lot of satisfaction to do that, Bill knew. Her laughter lilted back to where Wally was swallowing his discomfiture. He shrugged and went back to his post near Pat and Pam. They, too, seemed to be ignoring him. Bill watched Wally settle in an empty chair and play the bored and cynical man of the world as he surveyed the couples, jigging and jogging, pacing with grim solemnity or swaying rapturously, clutched to each other, as they swung round the ballroom floor.

Bill could not bring himself to join the throng round Pat and Pam. It would mean exchanging agreeable remarks with O'Brien, Dowson and Lindsay, and that he had no intention of doing.

The exhilaration of this plunge back into the careless days of his youth was gone, Bill realized. The whole show had fallen flat for him. He no longer desired to dance with Pat. It was difficult to believe she and Pam were the same girls who had walked along the Boulder road with him, only a few days ago. His distrust of them stirred. But it was not only a vague disappointment which made him feel uneasy and depressed. He had begun to think he should not be here.

During his first excursions into Kalgoorlie society, he remembered, he had been as eager as any other young man to drain such a night of its delirious excitement. He had gone out to a friend's car for a spot between dances, smoodged with a girl in some dark corner, and gone home in the early hours of the morning, lit up and longing for his next adventure in the fascinating world of music, bright lights and lovely girls which happened like a miracle on the goldfields, only at the big balls. But, now, as he watched the swirl of the dancers, at the back of his mind lay a consciousness of the economic and political problems with which he had become involved. He could not rid himself of a sense of the injustice and chicanery which was at the bottom of them. All this gaiety seemed spurious, a festive screen for the deprivations working people were enduring on the goldfields and everywhere else. He should not be here, Bill told himself. He had no right to forget even for an instant the bitterness of the class struggle: the suffering of the Spanish people: the menace of fascism and war looming on the not very distant horizon.

What did these well-to-do men and women care about all that? The men with powerful mining interests, mine managers, bank officials, wealthy shopkeepers, publicans and their wives and daughters. Nothing disturbed them except any interference with their prospects of an easy, comfortable existence. Of course there were lads from the School of Mines who were working miners, and their girl friends, among the less affluent patrons of the ball, but most of them also were indifferent.

It was true, Bill thought, that even the business men were glad to relax in an atmosphere of glamour and jollity. On a night like this they could escape into an illusion of security, and fantastic hopes that 'all was for the best in the best of all possible worlds'. For many young people, tonight was the realization of a dream and a compensation for the dullness and dreariness of their everyday lives. That's how it was with Daphne. She loved dancing, to wear pretty clothes and exercise her airs and graces. You couldn't blame her when you knew her days were spent in the back premises of a dingy pub, washing dishes and rushing backwards and forwards waiting on half-drunken men. Bill hated her doing it and so did Dick. After all, Daph was 'a Fitz-Maurice Gough', he said — to Eily's and Tom's amazement. Daphne had giggled and stuck to her job. Wilful and flighty she might be, but she had a streak of her grandmother's pride and independence, Bill knew.

It was Dick who had badgered Sally into telling him about his grandfather's family. As far as Tom and Eily were concerned, it might not have existed; but Dick derived a lot of satisfaction from knowing he was not just a miner's son. Ever since that remark of his, it had been a joke between Daphne and Bill to say: 'Don't forget you're a Fitz-Maurice Gough!'

Dick did not forget it. He had become Mr. Richard Fitz-Maurice Gough of late. To impress Myrtle's father, Bill suspected. During the evening, he had caught a glimpse of Dick dodging about among the best families, being obsequious and gallant to well-groomed, middle-aged women and their paunchy, sozzled husbands, or steering Myrtle, stodgy and unsmiling, in blue satin, through the dancers. The floor was packed with them: some of the men becoming riotous as a result of frequent potations in the parked cars lining the street outside the Town Hall. All the evening, couples had been drifting out to the cars and returning to the ballroom after a spot and a little love-making in the cool darkness. The men's faces had become red and swollen. They sweated as they danced, exuding an odour of stale beer. It was a hot night for early summer. Bill himself began to feel he would not object to a long beer, and a breath of fresh air.

He wished that he could get away: felt he had outgrown his capacity for enjoyment of this sort of thing. But he was reluctant to destroy Daphne's pleasure. She would be dancing, laughing and chattering blithely into the small hours. But Steve Miller would not leave until she did. He could ask Steve to take Daphne home, Bill decided. Good old Steve, he had always had tickets on Daph, and would think his luck was in to have this honour thrust upon him.

'Right, Bill,' Steve said, beaming when Bill explained that he wanted to clear out. 'I'll look after Daph. See she gets home safely.'

Bill was making his way to the door when Pat and Pam waved to him. Bill caught the jerk of Wally O'Brien's surprise and the quick glance he cast at Pat and then towards himself. When Pat crossed the floor to speak to him, Bill saw Wally lean forward, a vaguely ironical smile on his bland, handsome face.

'We didn't dream you'd be here tonight,' Pat said.

'I brought Daph, my young cousin,' Bill said.

Pat followed his eyes to where Daphne was dancing.

'Isn't she lovely?' she exclaimed. 'We saw her at the first dance we went to in Kal, and Pam was crazy to paint her. She had blossoms in her hair: was so blossomy herself. Tonight she looks different. Not so young and —'

'Unsophisticated.'

'Mmm.' Pat smiled that he had understood what she hesitated to say. 'We'd like to know her, Pam and I. Will you introduce us, Bill?'

'Better not!' Bill's grin flashed. 'You see Daph's a bit sore with you for having captured her boy friend that night.'

'For goodness' sake!' Pat's eyes widened. 'Who?'

'O'Brien.'

'But we can't get rid of him,' Pat protested. 'Of course, after we met him that night, he made himself useful doing all sorts of things for us, fixing up the studio, and taking us about. But he's an awful bore, really: one of those conceited idiots who thinks he is a genius *manqué*, and is a pain in the neck really. Surely, your cousin couldn't be bothered with him!'

'She's giving him the bird tonight, all right.'

81

Pat's laughter was a little uncertain.

'Was that what you were doing to us, Bill? You were just going.'

'I couldn't see myself being agreeable to some of the men hanging round you,' Bill admitted rather lamely.

'I thought that,' Pat said. 'And we do need a little moral support tonight, Bill.'

'What's wrong?'

Pat put her hand on his arm.

'Let's dance,' she said. 'I feel as if I'd know you better — and can tell you afterwards.'

'I'm not up to your standard,' Bill demurred.

'Oh, Bill,' Pat pleaded with a desperate earnestness, 'don't be so stand-offish! We used to think you'd be a sort of brother to us, and we must have somebody like that we can talk to sometimes.'

They began to dance, and Bill was aware of dejection and appeal in Pat's movement towards him. She did not speak. Drooping and serious she hung in his arms, and Bill held her with the gravity and tenderness of a dream they were sharing. A subtle communication flowed between them from the light pressure of her finger-tips on his arm, and the firm hold he had taken of her waist, its yielding towards him, and the swaying rhythm of their limbs together. There was nothing of the delirious pleasure of dancing with Pat that Bill had anticipated. Instead, he felt they had found an understanding and confidence which would indemnify them from any further hurts they might receive from each other.

'Thanks, Bill,' Pat said, throwing back her head when the music ceased and arousing herself to be vivid and charming again. 'I know now what you're really like.'

Her voice faltered: she turned away to hide her distress.

'Pam and I didn't want to come tonight. But we had promised to dance. We've had bad news. Jack has been killed, and Shawn is seriously wounded.'

Bill put his arm through hers to steady her. He saw the tears in her eyes. They made their way out of the ballroom and into the street.

'It's damnable,' he muttered.

'My poor Pam,' Pat said, on a sobbing breath, 'she's beside herself with anxiety. Wants to go to England and then to Spain to find Shawn. Paddy will never agree, of course. And Shawn may not be there when we arrive. What are we to do?'

Bill was at a loss what to say.

'Go and get Pam, Bill,' Pat begged. 'I shouldn't have left her. There's no one we can talk to but you. Our car's along here. I'll sit in it until you come.'

Pam jumped up as soon as she saw Bill re-enter the ballroom. She came to him, her face quivering.

'Where's Pat?' she cried. 'I can't stand it here, any longer. Oh, Bill, did Pat tell you? I feel as if I'm going crazy.'

Bill took her arm, and men in the crowded door-way stood back for them to pass. Out in the street, Pam sobbed quietly beside him. Pat drove towards them and stopped to pick them up.

'Oh, darling, it was too much for you!' she exclaimed. 'I was afraid it would be. You sit in the back with Bill and tell him all we know.'

Bill helped Pam into the car. She leaned against him as they sat there, crying brokenly.

He forgot they were almost strangers, trying to comfort her. And presently, she began to tell him about the cable they had received from Ian Foster. It said nothing but: 'JACK KILLED IN ACTION STOP SHAWN SEVERELY WOUNDED.' They had cabled Ian asking for further particulars. Where was Shawn? When had it happened? Would they be permitted to go to Shawn if he were still in Spain? They had sent money to Ian for cables 'because he was always hard-up', and told him to send some to Shawn in case he might need it.

'You've done everything you could,' Bill said soothingly. 'Don't lose heart, Pam.'

'It's so awful, waiting and not knowing,' Pam wailed. 'And yet better than thinking he's dead. Oh, Shawn, Shawn! Why did I let you go? Why didn't I go with you? If only we could go to him now, Bill!'

'Maybe it would be better to wait for further news,' Bill said.

'That's what I think,' Pat flung at him gratefully.

'You'd be such a long time travelling,' Bill pointed out. 'And, most likely, the worst would be over, before you could reach England.'

'I suppose so,' Pam agreed reluctantly.

'Perhaps Shawn will come to you when he's better,' Bill ventured. 'At least he'll be out of the fighting, and a long sea voyage may be just the thing for him when he's on the road to recovery.'

'Oh, Bill,' Pam sighed, 'if only he could come here.'

'He will, you'll see,' Pat declared.

She had been driving slowly up and down quiet streets until they drew up at the hotel.

'Don't go in yet,' Pam pleaded. 'Could you stay and talk to us for a little longer, Bill?'

'Of course,' Bill said.

So Pat drove out along the Coolgardie road, and turned off into a side track. There among the trees, in the peace and quietness of the moonlit night, they talked about Shawn and Jack Stevens, and the heroic struggle they had gone to take part in with such selfless gallantry.

Clouds drifted over the moon, obscuring the silver light which had filtered through the scraggy grey trees all about them. There was a sudden chill in the air. Bill glanced at the watch on his wrist. It was two o'clock.

'We'll take you home,' Pat said. 'It's helped us a lot, talking to you, Bill. Thanks for coming.'

Pam shuddered as they drove through the gloom of the trees, headlights of the car just picking out the track from dense scrub on either side.

'Shawn used to say, it will be a dark day for the world if we're beaten in Spain,' she murmured. 'And I feel that day is getting nearer and nearer, Bill. It's like a doom hanging over us.'

CHAPTER VII

'WHEN you take a girl to a ball, don't you usually see
her home afterwards, Bill?' Daphne queried petu-
lantly as she finished her meal next evening.

She was late and Eily had kept it hot for her. Dick had gone
out: the children were doing their lessons. Tom had had a
haemorrhage that day and Eily would not let him move from
his bed on the veranda. She was worried about him, and went
out to sit with him as soon as she gave Daphne her dinner. Bill
had been helping with the washing-up, and stayed to talk to
Daphne. She had slipped off her shoes, looked 'washed out' as
Eily said, after dancing until the small hours and working all day.

'Stow it, Daph,' he replied good-humouredly. 'I got fed up
with the show, and knew you wouldn't mind Steve bringing
you home.'

'Did you?' Daphne's temper had a frayed edge. 'Well you
let me in for a nice scene. Wally wanted to "make it up" and
bring me home. Steve and he nearly had a fight. I said I wasn't
going with either of them. You would take me home. Wally
said you'd gone off with Paddy Cavan's daughters, and I could
have brained him. But he was as mad about it as I was, so I just
laughed and said: "Too bad, Bill cutting you out like that!"
And came home with Steve.'

'Sorry, Daph,' Bill said gently. 'But Pat and Pam were
awfully upset by some news they had just got. I had to try and
help them.'

'Oh, yeah?'

Bill hated these Americanisms which were seeping from the
films into the everyday talk of people on the fields, Daphne
knew. 'Oh, well,' she added, with peevish exasperation, 'if you
want to make a fool of yourself with those janes, it's your own
affair, Bill. But don't expect me to be pleased when you leave
me in the lurch — and I've got to explain to Steve for the

85

umpteenth time that I don't want to marry him, and that . . . that. . . .'

She was on the verge of tears.

'I thought you were sweet on Steve,' Bill excused himself blunderingly.

'Sweet on him?' Daphne exclaimed. 'I like Steve well enough. He's a good sort. But can't you see I've been playing round with Steve, just to get even with Wally?'

'Cripes, darl, I didn't think it was as bad as that.' Bill stared at her.

'It's worse — much worse — if you only knew!' Daphne put on her shoes and whisked out of the kitchen.

Bill went after her; but she had shut herself in her room. He knocked, and Daphne called:

'Go away. I'm tired. Don't want to talk, Bill.'

Bill opened the door, walked into her room and sat on the bed where Daphne had thrown herself. She turned away from him.

'It's no use,' she said irritably. 'I don't want to talk to you, Bill. I'm peeved, I suppose, because you went off with those girls. It was such a thrill going to the ball with you. And then when I had to wrestle with Wally and Steve, I felt you'd let me down.'

'I know it looks bad, sweet,' Bill said humbly. 'I should have told you I wanted to clear out. I wouldn't let you down, you know that. I was just going when Pat — '

'It's all right.' Daphne squeezed his hand. 'I'll be all right when I've had a sleep, Bill. But I hated those two to snaffle you — as well as Wally.'

'Are you sure that's all that's bothering you?'

'Of course!' So mild and innocent, Daphne's eyes were, Bill's fears scurried away from them.

'I really am dog-tired,' Daphne murmured impatiently. 'Good night, Bill, dear.' She kissed him and Bill left her.

But Daphne was as tired and nervy next day as she had been that night. All the same, when she came home from work, despite Eily's objections, she rushed off to have a shower and

86

change, before snatching a hasty meal and going to the pictures with a lad she had met at the ball.

'I don't know what to do about Daph,' Eily fretted. 'She's wearing herself to frazzles carrying on like this. Working all day, and out nearly every night. I'm glad she's taking a few days off and going down to Perth for the week-end.'

'Is she?' Bill was surprised. Daphne had said nothing to him about this jaunt.

'One of the girls who used to be a waitress at O'Brien's is going to be married, and Daph's been asked to the wedding,' Eily explained, ironing the white linen cuffs and collar Daphne wore with her black dress to wait on the tables at O'Brien's.

'It'll do her good to get away from the fields for a while. I wish she'd take a real rest, go down to Warrinup and stay with Den and Charlie for a month or so, or try to get a job at the coast.'

'Where's she going to stay in Perth?' Bill asked.

'Oh, at Shirley's,' Eily said. 'That's the girl who's going to be married.'

'I must have a word with her about it.' Bill lit a cigarette and smoked thoughtfully. 'Some friends of mine could look her up and take her to a show, perhaps.'

'Thanks, Bill,' Eily said gratefully. 'She needn't worry about going back to O'Brien's at all, if they make a fuss about this week-end. Tom and I'd be only too pleased for her to take a holiday, or have a rest at home.'

But Daphne wasn't grateful for Bill's suggestion that those friends of his should go to see her and take her out, during her visit to Perth.

'I'll only be there two or three days,' she said offhandedly. 'And I dare say Shirl and I'll be dashing round together.'

'When is she being married?' Bill asked.

'On Monday, and I'll catch the train back next day.'

'Where does she live?'

'Mind your own business, Bill Gough,' Daphne snapped. 'And leave me alone!'

'Well, don't bite my head off,' Bill replied equably. He was perturbed all the same, because, apparently, Daphne did not want him to know anything about this trip of hers. At the moment, though, he was more worried about Tom than Daphne. And so was Eily.

'He's never been so weak, Bill,' she said anxiously. 'Every time he coughs there's this wretched haemorrhage.'

'Do you think we ought to let Daph go away?' Bill asked.

Eily looked scared. 'But she'll only be gone for the week-end,' she said quickly. 'I can't think that Tom . . . that he will be so much worse, before she gets back. And it would be a pity to spoil her holiday, Bill.'

'I suppose so,' Bill agreed.

He wondered afterwards why he had not been more concerned about that visit of Daphne's to Perth. To begin with, it never occurred to him she had been lying to Eily, or that there was anything unusual about her going to the wedding of a girl who had been a waitress at O'Brien's. Daphne was too ingenuous to hide a thought in her head from anybody, Bill imagined.

She had never been away from home alone before, and went off in a fever of excitement, her new evening dress carefully packed in tissue paper. But she took only one suitcase with her: did not want to be bothered with a lot of luggage, just for two or three days, she said. Tom seemed better that afternoon, and Eily had gone to the railway station with Daphne.

'You'd have thought Daph was going away for months when she kissed me goodbye,' Eily told Bill. 'She was worried about her father, I suppose. They've always been very close to each other, Bill.'

'She'll be all right,' Bill said, to cheer Eily, although his own mind was uneasy about Daphne going away like this when Tom was so ill.

He called in at O'Brien's and found Wally behind the bar, as usual. That disposed of any lurking suspicion that Wally might be making a trip to the coast, also for the week-end.

A telegram came from Daphne next day to say she had

arrived safely; and Bill wondered whether there was any cause for his misgivings after all.

On Saturday, Tom took a turn for the worse. Eily sat beside his bed all night. The following morning, the doctor warned her that Tom could live only a day or two longer.

All the week Eily had been torn with anxiety, watching over Tom, day and night. She had known for a long time that some day the end would come like this; but now it was near, she broke down and wept despairingly. Bill's heart ached for her. He put his arms round her.

'Oh, Bill,' Eily cried, 'how can I bear it? My darling Tom! It's been hard to see his suffering, for years — knowing everything we did for him was hopeless. But now the pain and ghastly weakness are too cruel! Would it have been better if I'd let him go to the Sanatorium? He wanted to go, just to save us trouble. As if anything I could do for him were a trouble. At least it's a comfort to know he's here with us. We can take care of him and make things as easy as possible. He's been asking for Daphne. I do wish she were home.'

'There, there,' Bill murmured with incoherent tenderness. 'I'll send her a wire.'

'I mustn't cry like this,' Eily pulled herself together. 'It would distress Tom so if he saw me crying.'

Bill made her go and lie down.

'I'll sit up with Tom, tonight,' he said. 'You must have a sleep, Eily.'

'Good lad,' Tom whispered when Bill settled into the chair near his bed. He guessed that Bill was insisting on Eily taking some rest.

Too weak to talk much, every effort broken by the raucous breathing that racked his wasted body, Tom's eyes on Bill said so much of what was in his mind that Bill grasped his hand to reply:

'It's all right, Tom. I'll look after Eily and the kids — and our work. You've put up a great fight, comrade. Something for me to live up to. You know I'll do my damnedest, don't you?'

In Tom's brilliant and glazed eyes the spirit which had directed his existence was flickering out.

'Better,' he whispered. 'You'll do better than I could, son.'

'Take it easy,' Bill pleaded. 'I know what you want to say, Tom. You don't have to tell me. And you've just got to keep quiet and rest, till Daph comes home.'

Tom's grip relaxed and his eyes closed, as if obeying Bill's injunction. 'Daph . . . yes, I must wait to see her. . . .'

'Daph! My poor little Daphne,' he muttered presently, the words scarcely audible. 'She's . . . in trouble . . . big trouble . . . Daph! Daph!' he called, and his voice fell away moaning.

Bill wondered if he were still conscious. Tom's mind had been wandering during the day, but he seemed to have fallen asleep as he spoke, and to be uttering that hoarse cry in a nightmare.

'Don't worry, I'll look after Daph,' Bill murmured, afraid to arouse him, and yet alarmed by Tom's subconscious warning that something disastrous had happened to Daphne.

But Tom had a fairly peaceful night. Sitting beside him, and watching his ravaged face by the subdued light of the night lamp, listening to his laboured breathing, Bill cursed the mining industry which had made such a wreck of a man like Tom Gough. There never was a purer, more noble soul, Bill told himself. There never would be a man he could love with such gratitude and veneration.

Eily came to relieve Bill in the early hours of the morning; and Bill went off to get a few hours' sleep before he went to work.

He wanted to send a telegram to Daphne, telling her to be sure to catch the next day's express, although she was expected to return that day, anyhow. But, in the flurry of seeing Daphne off and her anxiety about Tom, Eily had forgotten to get the address of the girl Daphne was staying with. Bill dared not let her see how disturbed he was about that.

In every fibre Bill was aware of an inexpressible misery and anguish because Tom was dying. Tom, who had been more than a father to him. Tom, the big, quiet man, who had given him all he knew of strength and courage. A young warrigal with a sore mouth, he had been, when he knew that his mother had deserted him and that his father was dead. But wisely and firmly Tom had taken him in hand, removing the pain and bewilderment of those childish years; arousing his interest and awe by telling him stories of the earth and the stars, the peoples of other lands, the wonders of scientific discovery, the struggle of mankind through the ages against oppression and injustice. As soon as he began to understand something of the nature of the universe and his place in it, his secret grievances had fallen away, Bill realized.

By giving him a critical mind, a respect for scientific knowledge and teaching him to search for the facts of any situation, Tom had helped him to find firm ground on which to build his life. Tom's love and understanding had been always there to be depended on.

Bill slept uneasily, unable to lose consciousness of Tom's suffering and his own grief. His thoughts tangled with a fuming and fretting anxiety about Daphne. When he wakened the memory of a horrible dream clung to him. He had seen Daphne sinking in dark swamp and Tom struggling hopelessly to reach her.

'Christ,' Bill groaned, 'what has happened?'

Dick insisted on remaining up with his mother, the next night, and Sally sat with Tom all day.

CHAPTER VIII

P A T met Bill on the road as he was coming from work. 'Hop in,' she said, opening the door of the car. 'I've got to talk to you.'

Bill seated himself beside her, and she drove on.

As Pat talked, the picture of what had happened that morning hung before Bill as if he were looking at a rather amateurish film, distorted, blurred and incredible.

Pat and Pam had gone to the railway station to pick up a package of canvases and paints Pam was expecting from Perth. They saw Daphne come past the ticket collector with other passengers who arrived by the train, but Daphne hung back when the rest of the passengers had taken taxis or hurried away. She looked dazed, and so wan and queer, that Pat exclaimed to Pam:

'It's Daphne Gough. She must be ill.'

Daphne was standing with her suitcase beside her, and suddenly clutched at a post as if she were going to faint. Pat ran to her and was beside her before she collapsed.

'The porters got us some brandy,' Pat said, 'and when Daphne revived, we put her in the car and drove her to the studio. She was all in, didn't seem to care where she was going, or who we were. We thought she'd been to a party and mixed her drinks, perhaps. Was suffering from a hang-over, and might not want to go home until she felt better.'

'It was awfully good of you, Pat,' Bill murmured.

'Nonsense!' Pat smiled at him. 'We'd have done the same for any girl, but we were glad to do anything we could for Daphne because she belongs to you, Bill. Pam made her lie down on the divan. She was too exhausted to say a word. The tears dripped down her cheeks. We just fussed over her and petted her until she went to sleep.

'When she woke up, I took her a cup of tea. She was very upset and wanted to go at once.

92

' "There, there, honey," I said, "Pam and I know how it is. Rest a bit longer. You don't have to bother about us."

'The poor kid, Bill, she said: "I didn't think you were like this." But she seemed to realize Pam and I would stand by her if she was in a spot of bother.'

'Is she?' Bill asked.

Pat nodded.

'Hell,' Bill groaned. 'I was afraid something was wrong.'

'After a while, she told us about it,' Pat went on. 'Not because she wanted to, really, but because she was so shaken and had to tell somebody. I think, too, she felt after all we could be trusted — and might know what she could do.'

'What is it?' Bill asked, unable to restrain his anxiety. 'Is it just that she's pregnant, and scared?'

'She's been to an abortionist, and had a horrible experience,' Pat said flatly.

'God!' Bill was flabbergasted.

'When we'd talked things over, Daphne decided I'd better come for you,' Pat said. 'Because you've got to help her, Bill. Pam and I'd do anything we could; but you know how Daph's father and mother, and her grandmother, will feel about her having anything to do with Paddy Cavan's daughters. In some ways, things are not as bad as they might have been. Daphne didn't let the brute she went to touch her. She ran away . . . she'll have to tell you about that herself. She's in no danger, at present. But what are we going to do? How are we going to get her out of this mess?'

'Makes me feel murderous to think who got her into it,' Bill muttered.

'That doesn't help,' Pat said dryly. 'There are not many men who haven't got a girl into the same sort of mess, some time or other.'

'I suppose not,' Bill agreed. 'But at least a bloke with any decency sees a girl through.'

'She may not want him to,' Pat replied. 'As often as not a girl thinks it's her affair, not his. A lot of girls take this abortion business quite easily, Bill. Of course, sometimes it ends in a dirty tragedy; but there are doctors and nurses who do the job skilfully, I know. Costs a lot — but at least you get hygienic surroundings.'

Bill's quizzical glance relieved the tension between them. Pat laughed.

'I'll tell you a funny story. Pam wouldn't mind I'm sure— under the circumstances. We were awful lambs when we first started going about by ourselves. Brought up in a convent, you see, and we didn't know anything. Not a thing about V.D. or precautions. And Pam had an affair with a married man. It was before she met Shawn. He was a writer, very charming and all that; but furious when he knew she was two months gone. Called her a little fool and God knows what: gave her filthy stuff to swallow that made her so sick I nearly died of anxiety. Then we heard about a doctor, and made an appointment with him. But, oh, we were scared, when we were going to keep it, Bill! My poor little Pam was shaking like a leaf, so sick and terrified, and I was beside myself. We took a swig of brandy before we went off in the car, and another from a flask I kept in the side pocket in case of accidents. We were both a bit squiffy when we arrived at a dreary looking house they called a convalescent home, in an outlying suburb of London. Pam started crying, and what with being so upset about her, and a bit drunk, I felt I just couldn't let her undergo that beastly operation.

'Then the doctor came in, and said in a breezy way: "Well, which of you is the patient?"

' "I am," I said, and jumped up.

' "Oh no, no, Pat!" Pam cried, trying to stop me.

'But I had quite persuaded myself I could have the operation instead of Pam. It wasn't until the doctor had me well and truly laid out, he discovered that I wasn't the patient. And was he wild! But very kind, too. Assured me Pam would be all right, made her stay two or three days in hospital, and told us, afterwards, to forget all about "an unfortunate incident" in our lives.'

Bill's and Pat's eyes met and they laughed with frank and easy camaraderie.

'I've known girls who paid a visit to some quack in the morning, and had to go on with their work all day,' Bill said.

'Most people don't realize the tragedy and misery that go on in a girl's mind when she has to face up to this problem,' Pat said quietly. 'Either she's got to have a baby and be regarded as an outcast all her life, or risk an abortion and be able to remain an ornament of respectable society. We've got to be sensible about Daphne, Bill. Let her choose what she wants to do, and make it as easy for her as possible, either way.'

'I suppose so,' Bill agreed. 'I can't begin to thank you and Pam, but—'

'Shut up.' Pat pulled up at the big ramshackle bungalow where Pam had rented a room as a studio. 'Don't you understand, my lad, that girls stick together in these crises. It's no use being sentimental. Besides, who could help doing what they can for Daphne? Such a woebegone little waif she looks, at the moment. Be very gentle with her, Bill.'

In the big untidy room, filled with Pam's pictures and painting gear, Daphne ran to Bill, and clung to him, speechlessly.

'Gee, I'm glad to see you, sweet,' he said. 'I've been worried: had a feeling you'd got something on your mind.'

'Pat's told you?' Daphne asked.

'A bit,' Bill said, sitting on the lounge and pulling her down beside him. 'She said you'd do the rest yourself.'

'They've been so good to me, Bill.' Daphne's voice quivered. 'I don't know what would have happened if they hadn't looked after me last night. I couldn't bear to think of going home, letting mum and dad know what was the matter.'

'Nobody's kinder when you're up against things.' Bill's loyalty would not allow any reflection on Tom or Eily.

'That's the worst of it,' Daphne wailed. 'If they weren't so good and kind, it wouldn't be so awful to hurt them. And it would just about kill dad and mum to know what I've been through.'

'Why didn't you tell me you were in a jam, darl?' Bill asked. 'Didn't you tell anybody?'

'I couldn't bear to,' Daphne said wildly. 'I couldn't bear anybody to know. I was so angry, thought I could manage things myself. The girls at work, I've heard them talking about having "a shot"; and it being nothing to make a fuss about. One of them went round, screwed up with pain all day, and came to work just the same next morning. And I knew Shirley had been to a man in Perth who fixed her up, last year. So I wrote to her and got his address: said it was for a friend of mine.'

'Did you stay with her?' Bill asked.

'No. She's not even being married, Bill.' Daphne drooped under the shame of her confession. 'I made up that yarn to get away. But after all, I hadn't the pluck to go through with it.'

'You had a darned sight too much pluck, trying to on your own,' Bill said.

'It was too awful and horrible, the whole business. I just got mad with fright and ran away.' Daphne was shivering and crying as she talked. 'That man — he looked like a murderer, Bill. He had bony hands that clawed at me. And the house was so dark. It was near the river ... I didn't go there until it was night, and there was a dog. One of those big dogs like a mastiff only it was black with green eyes and a mouth that hung open and was blood-red inside. . . .

'A woman came and talked to me. She said I'd have to stay the night, and pay her right away. I gave her the money and she put me in a back room and told me to undress. The man came in then and went away to get something. I could hear a woman in another room moaning and moaning. I just lost my nerve, Bill. Got all panicky or something. The river was shining like black glass so near the house, and I was terrified of them all, the man and the woman — they had such cruel eyes — but most of all of the dog. I dressed as fast as I could. The window was locked, but I managed to open it and jumped out. Then I ran, but it was a long path to the gate and the dog came after me. I never thought I'd get away from him. He chased me through some scrub. It was so dark I couldn't see where I was going and every minute I thought the dog would pounce on me. But there was an old banksia tree, and I scrambled up into it. Then I heard the man calling and the dog went back to him.'

Bill sweated with rage, as he thought of Daphne's escape from the house near the river, and her flight through the dark scrub. She was trembling and still terror-stricken as she huddled beside him.

'Never mind, darl.' Bill's arm tightened round her. 'You did the right thing to get away.'

'But I dropped my suitcase when I was running through the scrub,' Daphne sobbed. 'My handbag was in it, and my ticket and money. So I had to stay there, in the scrub, until it was light enough to look for my case. Fortunately, I found it, and went back to the road where there was a bus. Then I went to the waiting-room at the railway station and sat there until the train left.'

'Forget everything now, but that you're home again and there's nothing to be afraid of,' Bill said. 'Your father's pretty low, Daph. I think he's just waiting to see you.'

'Oh, Bill.'

'You must pull yourself together and pretend it was a good holiday, darl. We'll decide what to do, about other things, later.'

Pat and Pam came in with a bottle of beer and some sandwiches.

'A little drink wouldn't do us any harm, I feel sure,' Pat said.

'Cripes, no,' Bill grinned gratefully. 'Daphne's going to tidy up and come home with me.'

Daphne went to a mirror over the mantelpiece.

'Is that me?' she exclaimed at her reflection; but she took foundation cream, lipstick and powder from her suitcase, combed her hair, and presently her pale face looked as fresh and pretty as usual.

'You were more paintable this morning.' Pam eyed Daphne critically.

'Of all the callous little beasts!' Pat exclaimed.

'I'm not,' Pam protested. 'Daph knows that, don't you Daph? But I can't help wanting to paint the reality of things. This morning Daph was all the girls who've been in her position. Such a wilted blossom. Now she's hiding everything. You don't get the tragic innocence and damage done by rough usage to her youth and loveliness. But I like the courage and pain in her eyes. Will you let me paint you sometime, Daph?'

'Oh dear,' Daphne shrank shyly and nervously from this summing-up of her plight, 'if you really want to! I can never thank you enough for all you've done for me, Pam — you and Pat.'

Pat kissed her.

'Don't say any more, honey. Come and see us whenever you can. And don't get down-hearted! We'll find a way out, you and Bill and Pam and I — even if you don't do as I suggested and tell your grandmother.'

'Oh, I couldn't do that.' Daphne's face puckered to her distress.

'I could,' Bill said, as if a responsibility that had been weighing on him too heavily could be lightened. 'Gran's been up against so many tough propositions, herself. She'll know how to handle this one, I reckon.'

T HE purgatory of Tom's slow dying overshadowed everything else for his family that week. He was conscious that
she was there when Daphne went into the room and knelt
beside his bed.

Tom lifted his hand and caressed her bright head. His
eyes lit with their tender smile.

'You're . . . all right, Daph? You're — ' he whispered unable
to express the thought which troubled him.

'As right as rain,' Daphne said, trying to chatter in her usual
blithe inconsequential fashion. 'I had a lovely time in Perth,
darling. Shirley made the prettiest bride — but . . . but I'd
never've gone if I'd known you were so ill.'

Tom patted her head. '. . . bad dream . . . thought you were
in trouble.' The words were almost inaudible. 'It was dark and
you were so frightened . . . Nothing can hurt you, Daph — if
you don't let it. You can only . . . hurt yourself. Remember.'

He closed his eyes and seemed to fall asleep, though Bill saw
the effort to talk had exhausted him. As Tom lapsed into the coma
of weakness caused by any exertion, Bill lifted Daphne and drew
her way from the bedside.

'It's almost as if he knew,' she cried brokenly.

'He couldn't,' Bill consoled her. 'It's just that he's always
believed you're good stuff, Daph, and wants you to be
brave.'

Eily went about preoccupied with nursing Tom: she could
scarcely bear to leave him for a few minutes. The children
glanced at her, and away again, as if it scared them to see how
stiff and strange her face had become. This dying of their father,
his raucous breathing and low, unconscious groaning, terrified
them. Daphne gave up all idea of going back to O'Brien's. She
was eager to help her mother by doing the cooking and housework, looking after La and Nadya. Sally came to sit with Tom

during the day, and Dinny hovered about anxious to do any chores, or trot off on messages for Eily.

'It will be a mercy when it's over,' Sally said, dry-eyed. 'My poor Tom, he didn't deserve to suffer like this.'

'He was a miner,' Bill reminded her. 'It's what almost every man who's worked underground as long as Tom did, has to go through.'

'If he'd gone to the San, it would have been easier for mother,' Dick said.

'You don't know what you're talking about,' Sally rapped out. 'Do you think your father wouldn't have done anything in the world to save Eily pain and trouble? But the doctor said no treatment would make much difference. And the only comfort your father and mother have had, for years, is that they could be together at the end. They've never fallen out of love with each other — and you can't say that for many people, Dick.'

'Dad knew we'd never feel he was a burden,' Daphne said. 'He knew we'd want him to be with us.'

Only a few days before, a miner in the last stages of tuberculosis had taken a plug of dynamite, gone out into the bush and blown off his head. It was to escape the torture of these last hours, everybody understood; and to save his wife and children the burden and expense of his illness. Other men had hanged themselves, or cut an artery to expedite the sentence of death hanging over them.

It was hard on the women whose men took this desperate course. They felt 'father' had put a shame on them, although they knew well enough that he had been worrying chiefly about them. The cost of special foods and medicines was rarely covered by relief funds, and his long illness inevitably wore down the health and patience of a wife and children.

Tom would never have wounded his family by taking the short cut, Sally thought. That was something Eily could not have got over. As it was, she would have the consolation of having done everything possible for Tom, and then when her sorrow abated, she would rally to a sense of her duty to

100

the children, and the work she and Tom had undertaken together.

Only Eily and Bill were with Tom in his last struggle for breath. Bill held him until the struggle subsided, and in relief Tom lay back.

'My darling, oh, my darling, if only I could go with you,' Eily cried.

An expression, rested and peaceful, stole over Tom's wasted features. His conflict with life was over, Bill knew, and death had claimed all that was left of Tom Gough.

Bill stood back as Dick took his place beside Eily, putting his arms round her, more moved by her grief than the dead face of his father. He stared at it sullenly, abashed by the power and serenity with which death had invested it. Bill went for Daphne and sent her to her mother. La and Nadya were asleep. They should not be wakened, he thought. He went out into the yard and sat down on a box near the vegetable garden Tom had made, feeling outside the family circle, strangely alone in his grief and sense of irretrievable loss.

Everything seemed to know Tom was dead. The almond tree stood stark and black against a sky silvering in the dawn. A flight of curlews passed overhead with an eerie wailing. There was something desolate and deserted about the way the fence posts sagged between their wire railings. A row of cabbages, Tom had planted, squatted against the dark earth as if turned to stone. A door banged and, in the distance, Bill heard the rumble and drone of batteries at work on the ridge. Tom had stopped; but that grinding rush of ore, feeding the batteries, the crushing tramp of the giant treads would never stop, Bill told himself. The mines had broken two generations of men. How many more would they destroy before life became of more value than profits?

Tendrils of Bill's affection as a child had clung round Eily and his grandmother. His love for Tom was something different. Tom had been not only the wise and patient guardian of his youth, but the steadfast comrade of later years, incorruptible and selfless in his devotion to the cause of the working people. Bill thought no one would ever arouse in him an emotion so profound as Tom had done.

When he was a youngster, he remembered, Sam Mullet had said:

'There are not two men like Tom Gough born in a century.'

And now he was dead. Tom was dead. Bill was appalled by what that was going to mean to him. There would always be a spiritual loneliness: a blank in his life no one else could fill. Only on the plane of mutual service to the great ideals of humanity could their bond be maintained. Bill swore to himself to keep faith with Tom in that respect.

A few hours later when they were all in the kitchen for breakfast, Dick, assuming the duties of the eldest son, said he would make arrangements for the funeral on his way to the office.

The first gust of her passionate weeping having spent itself, Eily realized there were still practical things to do for Tom.

'It must be a red funeral, Dick,' she said. 'I promised your father that.'

'But there'll have to be a parson,' Dick demurred.

'No.' Eily spoke firmly. 'Bill knows what Tom would have wished, and will ask a comrade to speak. You can talk over the other arrangements together. But everything must be done as simply as possible.'

It was galling for Dick to submit to this evidence of separation from his father's confidence. He loathed the idea of making even death, as he said, 'an occasion for propaganda'.

'Your father's whole life was propaganda,' Eily told him. 'If his death could serve the interests of the workers, that's what he would want.'

'I'll see the undertaker and leave the rest to Bill,' Dick said with as good grace as he could muster.

Den came up for the funeral and Sally was shocked to see the change the last few years had made in her youngest son. He had been thrown from a young horse and broken his leg, was still limping and screwing up his face with the pain as he walked. Den had lost weight, too, and looked as thin as a rake, in his loose and shabby suit, and there was grey in his hair.

'I'd have given anything to get here sooner, mum,' he said. 'But the blasted cows have to be milked, and I couldn't leave Charlie until I got someone to help her.'

'How is she?' Sally asked, knowing Den's wife was expecting another baby soon.

'She's fine!' Den's face crinkled in a smile. 'We're hoping for a boy this time. Four girls aren't much use to a dairy-farmer with a gammy leg. But tell me about Tom. God, it's hard to think of him gone! We haven't seen much of each other for years. Only when you come down for the summer holidays. But it was good to know he was here: good to have the old chap to talk things over with now and again.'

Sally said sadly: 'We'll all miss him, Den. But I can't grieve now his pain is over. Tom suffered too much. I reproach myself for having let him work in the mines when he was so young. And for not realizing it was to help me he insisted on doing it. It's remembering that I'll never get over.'

Den tried to comfort her. He could not believe his mother had anything to reproach herself with, although he knew that Dick had been dearer to her than any of her sons.

Sally had never before attended a funeral; but there was a strange compulsion on her to stand among the men and women who had loved and honoured Tom. Den and she huddled close to each other as they sat in a mourning coach on that slow and painful journey to the cemetery. They two, the last of the family circle she had made, and Tom before them, with a red flag draped over his coffin. They could not see it, because the first coach in which Eily, Dick, Daphne and the children were driving, lumbered along ahead. The coaches must have come from Morris's old establishment, Sally thought: they were so dilapidated: creaked and rattled drearily on their rusty axles.

Bill was walking with members of the Communist Party: Dinny with his mates, and Frisco in the long trail of miners and workers from every union on the fields, moving along the dusty road towards the Boulder cemetery.

Bill had arranged for Perth Molloy to pay a last tribute to Tom at the graveside. Perth was no orator. He said simply what everybody was feeling about Tom Gough: that Tom had been a good mate and a good comrade, a man whose honesty and nobility of character had been respected, and whom many had loved even when they did not agree with his political opinions.

'Goodbye, Tom,' Perth concluded. 'You've earned your rest if ever a man did. And given us an example of how to live. The courage and goodness of a man don't die with him. We, your comrades, friends and workmates, will remember them. We will remember you, Tom Gough. And we will try to be worthy of all you did — for us — and for the future of humanity.'

Someone started to sing 'The Red Flag'. Men and women joined in, until hundreds of voices uprose, singing over the grave, and carrying far over the sun-blasted plains, into the mists of the distance where the barricade of the mines with all their chimney stacks and poppet-legs fretted pale blue the sky.

Every worker on the goldfields knew the words of that song, had sung them at social functions and funerals for years. Across the heads of the crowd, Bill caught a glimpse of Pat and Pam. Bill wished it had been 'The Internationale', or the funeral hymn for a good comrade, that was being sung for Tom. But only he and two or three others knew those songs. Singing of 'The Red Flag' had been a spontaneous outburst.

Bill saw several well-known citizens in the crowd as it moved away from Tom's grave; and there was a group of aborigines standing at a little distance, their superstitious fear of death preventing them from coming any nearer. He noticed that Sally stooped to speak to an old gin sitting on the ground, and guessed it was Kalgoorla.

'It's only after a man's dead, people can afford to acknowledge his worth,' Eily said sadly when they were back at home after the funeral.

'They're scared — we're all scared, to a certain extent — of trying to change a system which seems "Power omnipotent",' Bill reminded her.

'I suppose so.' Eily looked forlorn and hopeless.

'But it isn't, we know,' Bill's faith asserted itself to cheer her. 'Systems change. They're just a stage in social evolution. And history's with us because we're blazing the track ahead.'

'Oh, Bill,' Eily sighed. 'I wish you could make Dick realize that. He's drifted so far away from us.'

Bill said loyally: 'They've been putting the screws on him at the office, and Dick feels he's got to steer a safe course.'

Bill knew, what Dick had not yet told his mother, that there was a vacancy for chief clerk in one of the Golden Star and Long View subsidiary companies and that he, Dick, had been offered the position, if he would sign a document stating he was not a communist or member of any political organization opposed to the interests of his employers. Dick had signed the document, and was prepared to go to any lengths, Bill was afraid, to dissociate himself with the views held by his father, and secure that job.

Defending himself to Bill, a few nights later, Dick said that his father's funeral, and the talk about it, had embarrassed him a good deal with his bosses.

'I'm fed up with the workers and the working-class movement, Bill,' he said angrily. 'Ever since I was a kid I've seen dad sacrifice everything for them. And what did he get out of it? The workers of the goldfields wouldn't even listen to him when he talked about communism and socialism.

'Oh, yes, they beefed out "The Red Flag" at his funeral and most of them agreed with what Perth Molloy said. Dad was a good bloke. Nobody could deny it. But I'm not going to waste my life for a mob who'd rather swill beer and bust up their pay at the two-up, than try to better themselves and live as well as they could. I've got no confidence in the workers, I tell you straight, Bill. I don't believe they ought to have the power to run the state. I don't believe they care a bloody damn for what you call their democratic rights — not the crowd working on the mines these days. I've heard them shout dad down when he talked about a fair deal for the Soviet Union. Do they want to hear the truth about Spain? Not on your life! They take the line of least resistance, siding with the priests and the bosses, when it's a question of putting up a fight for anything that doesn't touch their pockets. The blasted coms they say, are white-anting the labour movement, stirring up trouble: "Give them the boot in the union and in the A.L.P!" Think I'm going to smash my prospects and lay down my life for the swine, like dad did his? Not if I know it! I hate the workers, Bill. I hate the stupid, cowardly crawlers. "Feed 'em and make 'em work for you," that's what old Langridge says. And I reckon he's about right. You can't do anything else with men who only live to booze.'

'Or booze in order to live,' Bill interjected.

'Things will never be any different,' Dick flung at him, his passion running down. 'Not in our lifetime at any rate. I'm going to get what I want out of mine.'

'You talk like a damned fascist,' Bill said.

'Everybody's a fascist who doesn't agree with you,' Dick replied.

Bill argued with him half the night. The workers were what the system had made them, he maintained. They were the victims of circumstance, creatures of their environment; exhausted by heavy and monotonous toil, they sought relief in the stimulus of alcohol, the excitement of gambling. Doped, duped and demoralized by the press, radio and cinema, run to exploit their credulity, how was it possible for the workers to think and act clearly in their own interests?

'We've all absorbed some of the poison of the system,' Bill said. 'Would like to make a success of our own lives, grab some luxury and security, and let the rest of the world go hang. I don't blame the workers for blundering in their ignorance, letting themselves be pushed around by religious bigots and political spielers, so that they can't see straight, or act in their own interests. I reckon most working men and women've got an instinctive understanding of what's wrong; but they know the cost of going against the tide. They know what unemployment and poverty mean too well, to risk having to face them until they've got to. A lot of them don't know they are being doped about Spain and the Soviet Union. Or why. But you do, Dick. You know the facts — the facts of any case your father stood for. I blame you for signing that document, and the men like you who'd rather play the bosses' game than put up a fight for your own rights, as well as the rights of the workers.'

'I want a decent home. I want a wife and kids who will be well-dressed and well-educated,' Dick said stubbornly. 'I want to earn enough money to pay my way, and to have some influence in the community.'

'Cripes, so do I,' Bill laughed. 'But I'm not going to sell myself, body and soul, to get them.'

Their argument made no difference to Dick's decision about accepting that job, and breaking with all the ideas his father had held, in order to ensure a successful career for himself. Bill hoped Eily would not hear of it, and that Dick would do nothing to add to her distress for a few months, at least.

She was looking like the ghost of her old self: going about her usual work in the house, and at meetings, with conscientious thoroughness, trying to appear sensible and reconciled to Tom's death, although her blue eyes told everybody how bereft and lonely she felt without Tom.

A paragraph in *The Miner* struck her like a blow. It announced Dick's appointment, and that he had signed a contract requiring him to sever any connection with activities or political organizations opposed to the interests of his employers. Moreover, a statement by Mr. Richard Fitz-Maurice Gough was appended which declared he had never taken part in the activities of such organizations, and that he wished to dissociate himself entirely from the opinions and organizations sponsored and supported by his father, the late Mr. Tom Gough.

Dick would not discuss the matter with his mother.

'It's no use,' he said. 'I'm going my own way. If I can't have any peace at home, I'll go and live at a pub.'

'Oh, Dick,' Eily cried reproachfully, 'your father and I never interfered with what you wanted to do. But I can't understand — '

'I don't expect you to,' Dick interrupted as if it were a matter of indifference to him anyhow. 'Or to approve of my marrying Myrtle Langridge in the Roman Catholic Cathedral, next month.'

Eily's face ruckled painfully. It was not what he had said but the way he had said it that hurt her, Dick knew. He had spoken with deliberate cruelty to make his mother realize he was severing old ties. He added with a pang of compunction:

'I'm sorry, mum. But I've got to get out of the rut this family has sunk into. Mr. Langridge offered me that job because of Myrtle, really. And he won't consent to our marriage except on his own terms.'

'You're a man, my son,' Eily said quietly. 'You must make your own decisions.'

'Dad disagreed with his father,' Dick reminded her.

'But to go forward, not back,' Eily said. 'And for very different reasons than yours.'

'Oh, well,' Dick shrugged, 'we'll leave it at that. I'm going to make up for the failure of other Goughs to get anywhere in this town.'

It was from his younger brother and sister Dick got more galling criticism than from any other member of the family.

'Are you a rat, Dick?' La asked bluntly when Dick came into he sitting-room where they were doing their lessons.

'What do you mean — a rat?' Dick asked.

'The boys at school say you are,' La told him. 'They say you've ratted on the labour movement.'

'He has, too,' Nadya chimed in. 'I heard Dinny say to Bill, dad would turn in his grave if he'd heard what they said in *The Miner* about him. Do dead men turn in their graves, Dick?'

'No,' Dick said curtly. 'And if they did, what difference would it make?'

'I don't know,' Nadya admitted. 'But I suppose Dinny meant you've done something dad wouldn't like. If you have you ought to be ashamed of yourself, Dick.'

'Mind you own business,' Dick cried furiously. 'You're a precocious brat, Nadya.'

He walked out of the room.

'Gee, he is cross, isn't he?' Nadya remarked placidly, chewing the end of her pencil.

'You're our brother and it is our business,' La yelled after him. 'Darned if I'm going to get into any more fights on his account,' he grumbled, returning to an essay he was supposed to be writing on the whale. 'How do you spell Antarctic, Nad?'

Nadya spelt the word slowly.

'Well, I've said the whale is a large fish,' La remarked. 'And that it's most prodigious in the Antarctic regions. What can I say next, Nad?'

Nadya, counting scrupulously on her fingers, scowled at him until she had finished her sum.

'Oh, La, I've told you before all about whales,' she said, with her odd old-fashioned air of superiority. 'There are so many different kinds and the whale is not altogether a fish. It's an aquatic mammal. It suckles its young, and they don't stay in Antarctic regions, they come to the warmer waters along our coast to breed. Haven't you read *Moby Dick* and *The Cruise of The Cachelot*? You ought to know lots about whales.'

'Well, you can't do your twice times tables,' La jeered.

'I can so,' Nadya protested. 'But not the big numbers.'

'You know, Nad,' La looked up from his laborious writing again, 'I don't believe Dick is a rat.'

'No?' Nadya sounded dubious but willing to give Dick the benefit of the doubt.

'I remember dad said once, "A man who rats on his principles is the meanest thing alive." Dick's not that. What's "principles", Nad?'

'Oh, things you believe in; know are right,' Nadya replied vaguely.

'Well, Dick wouldn't go against things he knows are right,' La decided. 'Let's go and tell him we don't think he would.'

They went along the passage to Dick's room where he was reading at a small table with a green shade over his eyes.

'I don't believe you're a rat, Dick,' La blurted out. 'Neither does Nadya.'

'You couldn't be,' Nadya said firmly. 'Because dad said, "A man who rats on his principles is the meanest thing alive."'

'Clear out, both of you,' Dick shouted angrily. 'I don't care what you think.'

'My, he was riled, wasn't he?' La remarked when they had settled down to their lessons again.

'That's because he's got a guilty conscience,' Nadya said solemnly. 'I always feel as cross as two sticks when I've got a guilty conscience, don't you, La?'

Tom's death and Eily's concern about Dick were so much on Bill's mind that he had delayed having the straight talk with Daphne which he knew must be tackled.

It was late on a Sunday afternoon they went for a walk, and sat down on the brow of Maritana. The hill that lolled behind the town was nearly bald now, ruddy-brown, its weathered flanks scarred by more shafts and pot holes than there had been a few years ago. New workings were being driven into its cavernous interior. The gold bonus, and profitable treatment of low grade ores, had revived interest in old mines from which the visible gold had been torn recklessly and low grade ores left as worthless in the early days. On Hannan's Reward, too, there were signs of renewed activity. Red earth and rubble piled beside the mine, struck great wedges against the sky, that immaculate blue sky of the goldfields, like porcelain, frail and lustrous near the horizon. Bill never forgot it was round about here, at the foot of Maritana, that the first alluvial gold had been specked, and that the town, lying outspread for miles in the sunshine below, had sprung from the invisible resources of this weathered hill.

There were still vestiges of low-growing native herbage on

the slope where Daphne and he were sitting. Bill had picked a mauve flower with leaves of silky grey plush and was marvelling at the hardihood with which it grew in such sterile ground, when Daphne said:

'Poor mum, she's had so much to put up with lately. I'd give anything not to add to her troubles, Bill.'

She had made up her mind it was too late to consider anything but having the baby, Daphne explained listlessly. She was resigned to the idea, but wished she could go away so that no one on the fields could discover what had happened.

'We'll fix it, sweet,' Bill told her, racking his brains as to how he could. 'But I'll have to be sure that you go to a decent place.'

'I don't know any.'

'Neither do I,' Bill admitted.

'I've been thinking,' Daphne went on, after a moment. 'P'raps Pat was right. Gran would know what's the best thing to do.'

'Let me tell her,' Bill begged. 'I'll go along right away.'

Daphne had gone home, and he had walked off down the road to see his grandmother. It would be a relief to discuss with her what they could do for Daphne, he thought; and she would help him to decide whether Eily should be told, just yet, or not.

'Well, it knocks the stuffing out of you, doesn't it?' Sally exclaimed, when Bill had taken her into the kitchen, shut the door and told her why Daphne made that visit to Perth, and what she was up against. 'Daphne? The poor child! Thank God Tom didn't know. But Eily — it doesn't seem fair not to tell her. Yet, maybe you're right, Bill. She couldn't cope with anything more just now. Ask Daphne to come and see me in the morning and we'll talk things over.'

'Oh, gran,' Bill hugged her, 'I knew you'd handle this better than anybody. I've been so worried. We could send Daph away, somewhere, to have the baby, couldn't we? And manage to keep the whole thing to ourselves?'

'We'll find a way to look after Daph, and beat the gossips,'

Sally said, frowning thoughtfully. 'Though mind you, Bill, I'm no prude. I've never believed a woman should bear a child if she doesn't want to. We've learnt to control other natural forces. Why not this one? But there's so much prejudice — and danger — attached to these illegal operations, I wouldn't — couldn't let Daphne take any risks like that, now.'

'You're on your own, Sal-o-my,' Bill grinned, rejoicing in the way his grandmother had taken the news of Daphne's trouble, although he knew how hurt and disturbed she was by it. 'That's what dad used to call you, didn't he?'

'Do you remember him, Bill?' Memory of the dear voice which had called her by that name, shadowed Sally's face.

'Only a tall man who used to romp with me, and sing out: "Sal-o-my! Sal-o-my! Where are you, Sal-o-my?" when he came home from work,' Bill said. 'You were great mates, weren't you?'

'We were.'

'And we are?' Bill queried, with that winning smile, so like his father's.

'My beloved sonny-bun,' Sally pulled his head down to her and kissed him. 'You're a great comfort to me.'

'MARIE'S going down to the coast for a few weeks,' Sally said when she went to see Eily. 'She wants someone to go with her. I can't get away just now.'

'I couldn't, either.' Eily was ironing in the hot kitchen. Her sweet face showed the stress and unhappiness of the past few weeks.

'You shouldn't drive yourself so hard, my dear,' Sally said.

'It's better for me to keep busy.' Eily pushed a wisp of hair from her damp forehead. The nervous tension she was under was evident in every word and movement. 'I'd like to oblige Marie, of course. But there are the children to think of — and Dick. I don't want him to go and live at a hotel before he's married, as he's threatening to, if things don't run smoothly at home.'

'I'd like to give Dick a piece of my mind,' Sally exclaimed, her indignation getting the better of her resolution not to worry Eily by saying what she thought about Dick.

'It's no use talking to him.' Eily put another freshly laundered shirt on the clothes-horse beside her. 'I feel we've got to let him go his own way.'

'That's all very well,' Sally agreed. 'But Dick can't expect to keep our affection and respect. I could forgive him for signing the contract, but not for the statement.'

'I find it difficult to forgive him for either,' Eily said. 'But Dick doesn't care about anything except making a good position for himself, just now.'

'If that's the way he feels, we must leave him to his own devices, I suppose,' Sally retorted. 'But I never thought any grandson of mine would be such a spineless creature.'

'Neither did I,' Eily said wearily.

Sally returned to the purpose of her visit:

'If you really can't go with Marie, why not let Daphne?

The child's been looking a bit run-down lately, and Marie'd love to have her.'

'Oh, gran, it would be just the thing for Daph – if only she'd go.' Eily looked so pleased at the suggestion, so guileless and grateful in her loving simplicity that Sally felt conscience-stricken about deceiving her. An implicit confidence had existed between them, and under ordinary circumstances, she knew no one would be wiser and more helpful to Daphne than her mother. But as things were, Sally was sure it would be better to spare both Eily and Daphne any further emotional strain. Later, Sally promised herself, she could tell Eily, and Eily would understand why she had acted as she thought best.

'I'll have a word with Daph as soon as she comes home,' Eily continued. 'She's having her portrait painted, and has gone to that Miss Gaggin's studio this afternoon. Daph won't let us call those girls Paddy Cavan's daughters any more. Funny, isn't it? She seems to have struck up quite a friendship with them.'

'So does Bill,' Sally said dryly. She had revised her opinion of Pat and Pam since her talk with Daphne.

'I wonder if Bill's really smitten,' Eily mused.

'He laughed when I asked him,' Sally told her. 'Said he was too busy to fall in love.'

'He's busy, all right,' Eily agreed. 'Bill rarely has a night to himself. That wouldn't stop him from being in love, of course. He may not have any time to give to a girl, but there can be the spark in his mind. Tom and I were lucky because we could work together. All the same, I hope Bill hasn't got a crush on one of these girls.'

'Bill's no fool,' Sally said staunchly. 'But you never can tell what girls like those will do to a man.' She paused and added reluctantly: 'I suppose I must climb down and let him bring them to see me. He half-suggested it the other day. Dinny's been at me, too.'

'You're wonderful, gran!' Eily's admiration and affection for Sally fused in a tired smile. 'The children always turn to you when they're in any difficulty. I heard La and Nadya talking when they wanted to go to the new Olympic Pool that hot night last week. They knew I couldn't go, and that I wouldn't like them to go by themselves. "I know," Nadya said, "we'll ask gran!" "She'll take us, you bet," La said. "Gran loves the pool as much as we do." '

'Of course I do,' Sally laughed. 'You've no idea what a thrill I get out of that pool — remembering how precious water was in the old days when we couldn't afford a drop to wash with, sometimes. And now, the youngsters can disport themselves in a great blue-tiled bath that looks as if a bit of the sea had been dropped down here on the goldfields! At night when it's strung round with coloured lights you feel as if you were dreaming.'

'Why has Dick been so different from the others?' Eily reverted to her perturbation about Dick. She was ironing one of his shirts. There were several on the clothes-horse beside her.

'It's hard to say,' Sally replied. 'I thought I was going to care more for Dick than either Bill or La, because of his name. But I never did, somehow. There was always a streak of meanness in him. Even as a little boy he'd grab things for himself in a sly, greedy way. As if he were afraid of being deprived of them. Apples or cakes I'd put out for the children. He never liked sharing, even his toys. I remember, one Christmas time, I gave Bill and Dick each an engine. Dick took possession of both. When I went out, Bill was sitting, looking on mournfully, while Dick played with both engines. I saw what had happened, and told him he must give one back to Bill. But do you think he would? Started to yell and scream, and ran away clutching the engines. "It's all right, gran," Bill said. "He's only a kid. Doesn't understand." But, of course, I went after Dick, took one of the engines from him and tried to explain that I'd given it to Bill and the other to him.'

'I know,' Eily said, on the verge of tears. 'It's always been like that. Perhaps, at first, he was jealous of Bill. It's been my fault not knowing how to manage him better.'

'Nonsense,' Sally declared emphatically. 'There's a throwback to some ugly strain in most families. Dick's young and ambitious and behaving like a conceited puppy. But he'll come to his senses when he gets a few hard knocks from life.'

'I hope you're right,' Eily said, grateful that his grandmother could make any excuses for Dick.

Sally was far from believing what she had said to console Eily. She felt that Dick was like a changeling in the brood of her grandchildren. She had no patience with the lack of guts and personal dignity he had shown in that attempt to dissociate himself from his father and all he represented.

But her mind was too full of Daphne, and the carrying out of the plans she and Marie had made, to be bothered about Dick and his shoddy behaviour just then. Marie had agreed to take Daphne to Amy's cottage at Cottesloe, which belonged to Bill now. Marie would arrange for Daphne to see a doctor, and find a suitable hospital into which she could go. Daphne was to wear a wedding ring and be known as Mrs. Gough for the time being.

Sally was pleased that she had advised Bill not to refuse his mother's gift of the cottage. After all, she pointed out, the houses at Mullingar which Amy had sold to buy the cottage at Cottesloe were her own property. Tim McSweeney gave them to Laura and Amy, so Paddy Cavan had nothing to do with them. If Bill owned the Cottesloe cottage, the family could go there for summer holidays, so Bill had been persuaded to sign the documents which made him a man of property, despite some misgivings. And then, when this difficulty arose about finding a place where Daphne could escape from prying eyes until her baby was born, the cottage at Cottesloe occurred to Sally as a godsend. Although it was out of repair, and not close to the beach, Marie and Daphne would be quite comfortable there, she assured Bill, and not so conspicuous as in a boarding-house.

A few days before they left for the coast, Mrs. Ike Potter had come to see Sally.

'I found a letter from Daphne, the other day, in a coat Wally left at my place, Missus Sally,' she said in her blunt fashion.

'It was written some months ago, and I understand Daphne's not seeing anything of Wally now. He's a blackguard, of course; and I could strangle him for bringing any pain or trouble into your family. If there's anything I can do —'

'There isn't, Violet,' Sally said brusquely. 'Except to hold your tongue — and see he holds his.'

'I'll do that,' Violet promised. 'But forgive me, my dear. I know you're not well off, and — '

'We can look after Daphne,' Sally said with quiet dignity. 'But if ever your brother crosses my path, I'll take a horse whip to him. And you know I'll do what I say.'

'Steve Miller has already broken his jaw and given him a black eye,' Violet remarked, her complacency unruffled, 'Wally's talking of leaving the west — for good.'

'The sooner, the better,' Sally said. 'But does that mean there's been a fight about Daphne?' She could not conceal her dismay. 'The whole town will be talking next!'

'I don't think so,' Violet replied imperturbably. 'Steve managed it rather well, I understand. Wally said something in the bar Steve didn't like, and Steve let him have it. But Peter tells me Wally has been helping himself from the till a good deal lately, and he's told Wally to clear out, or he'll take action.'

When Bill called on his way home that afternoon, Sally asked him what had happened in the bar at O'Brien's between Wally and Steve.

'Steve's awfully fond of Daphne, you know, gran,' Bill said. 'He came to see me after he'd cracked Wally: was a bit upset that he'd done his block. Seems some of Wally's cobbers were twitting him about having lost his pretty little dancing partner, and he made a dirty remark. Steve let fly as quick as lightning. "That's to stop your mouth, O'Brien," he said. "And there's more where it came from if you talk that way about any decent girl in this town." I was nearly bashing Wally's face in, myself, not so long ago, for the same sort of thing — though not on Daphne's account. Wally's no fighter, and Peter took charge. "He'll remember, Steve," Peter said.'

'I hope so,' Sally snapped.

'Maybe the men who were there will think Steve's keen on Daph,' Bill said slowly. 'But that's no secret. Steve and Daph were sweethearts before she started going out with Wally. And do you know what Steve said to me the other night, gran?'

'How could I?'

'Don't be so cross, darl,' Bill chided. 'I'm telling you, aren't I? Steve said: "I wish Daph would marry me, Bill. I would stop any talk about her and Wally — and I don't mind what there's been between them. I know Daph's got no time for him now, and I could wait until she's ready to — to make it a real marriage." '

'Well — ' Sally exclaimed, and paused to think about what Bill had said. 'I always liked Steve, but I never thought he had that in him.'

'Daph won't marry him,' Bill went on. 'She says she couldn't take advantage of Steve's generosity.'

'I'm glad she feels that way about it,' Sally replied. 'Shows the child has the right spirit, in spite of everything, Bill. We've always thought she was such a little scatter-brain. But she's got grit to stand up to this business as well as she has done.'

'You're telling me!' The urchin in Bill rose to his grandmother's defence of Daphne. The complicity between them delighted him. 'Daph will come through, all right, won't she?' he asked more soberly. 'A rotten bit of luck like this isn't going to ruin her life?'

'We won't let it,' Sally said firmly. 'It's no joke for a girl to be an unmarried mother. She's regarded as a miserable sinner, or worse still, damaged goods, by most people. But I'm not going to have Daph victimized like that. The baby can be adopted, or — '

'I'm backing Steve to win in the long run,' Bill laughed. 'Daph's very fond of him, really; and I can't see her being "a miserable sinner" as far as he's concerned.'

Sally laughed with him, the light dancing in her brown eyes and their subdued witchery glowing.

'The gossips say I'm a "miserable sinner" myself, Bill,' she said, as if they were both youngsters and understood each other very well. 'But what does that matter? I don't mind, and I hope you never will.'

Bill remembered that his grandmother's love affair with Colonel de Morfé was still a scandal busy-bodies in the town discussed a good deal. He did not like Frisco any better than Tom had done, but he loved to see Sally looking so handsome and full of the joy of life as she did at the moment.

'Oh, you!' he said gently. 'You could get away with murder, darl, and nobody blame you!'

AFTER Marie and Daphne had gone away to the coast Sally found herself moody and restless.

Since Frisco had opened a small business office in town, they no longer went to the gardens to listen to the birds and indulge in a little billing and cooing themselves like a pair of youthful sweethearts. At first Sally was pleased that Frisco could do something which would enable him to endure his blindness. But latterly, she had begun to fear he was becoming too deeply engrossed again by the racket of share-mongering.

She was worried about Den as well. He had looked so middle-aged and care-worn: worked too hard and was harassed financially, she knew. Her two elder sisters had claimed a share in Warrinup when Fanny and Phyllis died. Den raised a mortgage to pay them; but a fall in the price of butter fat, and poor prices for his stock, made it difficult for him to meet liabilities to the bank.

'Living on the land's not all it's cracked up to be,' he had said, half-jokingly to Dinny. 'Maybe I'll chuck it and try prospecting, some day.'

That Den could contemplate leaving Warrinup where she had thought he would be safe from the hazards of existence on the goldfields, filled Sally with consternation, although she could not believe he would ever be willing to do so.

During the depression, it was estimated that 400,000 men were unemployed, or working on short relief terms, throughout the Commonwealth, and that 25,000 farmers had become bankrupt. Another 30,000 continued to work their land under crippling mortgages.

Although the mining industry in the west had been brought almost to a standstill at the onset of the depression, granting of the gold bonus brought renewed activity to many mines which had been idle. Within four years of granting of the bonus the number of workers on the mines rose from 4000 to 13,000. But workless farmers and unskilled youths from all over the country were flocking to the goldfields and still found themselves a drug on the industrial market. They had been living in appalling conditions, ill-clad and half-starved, sleeping in the Open Cut on Maritana, or in the shelter of any old lean-to of bagging and brushwood on Misery Flat. When they appealed for food and clothing an ironic correspondent in *The Miner* suggested that they should collect chaff bags to cover themselves, and apply to butchers at the abattoirs for the offal usually given to the owners of whippets. The unemployed were advised also that they could gather up the stalks of celery and cabbage which the green-grocers usually threw away; and stale bread and scraps from the restaurants, to make themselves a nourishing soup.

It was disturbing to think of Den ever being forced to leave Warrinup and join this horde of hopeless and desperate men seeking any sort of work on the goldfields. Dairy farmers in the south-west were in a better position than wheat growers who had been broken by droughts and mortgages in the dry areas, Den said. But still, hundreds of small farms in the south-west had been abandoned, because it was impossible for men to make a living and pay the interest on loans and mortgages under the terms of which they had been induced to develop virgin land.

There were thousands of young unemployed men, working in relief camps in the southern forests and earning no more than sustenance: married men with their wives and children, too, living in tents and shacks of bark and corrugated iron, near construction jobs inaugurated by the government to provide part-time work for destitute families. It was said that the worst of the depression was over; but still on the goldfields, and every-where else in the west, there was a great deal of unemployment and anxiety about work and wages. If a man lost his footing in the struggle for existence, it was difficult for him to find any means of earning a living.

When she heard the mine whistles in the morning, and saw the ramshackle trams rattle by with their freight of gaunt, shabby men, Sally thought of Tom, and Bill who was often working underground. The eerie shriek and wail of the ambulance siren sent her rushing to the gate. She would exchange exclamations with neighbours over their fences, and go back to her housework, or potter about the garden, wishing she could slip across the road and talk to Marie.

For so many years, she and Marie had run into each other's houses for a chat whenever they felt inclined. They had discussed every small happening in their lives as if they were matters of great importance. Of course, she missed Marie, Sally confessed to herself, although it was a comfort to know Marie was looking after Daphne.

The minutes Bill spent with her when he blew in as he came from work were a bright spot to which Sally looked forward. He could banish her doldrums with his gay greeting and peck on her cheek, though the dear lad often sprawled on a chair, looking tired and despondent himself, Sally perceived. She decided that she must do something about it.

'Well,' she said briskly, 'when are you going to bring your girl friends to see me?'

'Gee, gran,' Bill's voice leapt in surprise and delight, 'I'd love to some evening.'

It was so easy to please him, Sally told herself. She loved to see his eyes light up and smile at their understanding, the secret joke they seemed always to be sharing. Bill was still feeling Tom's death very deeply, she knew, and worrying about Eily, Daphne and Dick, besides all the work he had to do in connection with his committees and organizations. He took other people's troubles too much to heart, Sally told him: carried the woes of the world on his shoulders, as Tom had done. But her sympathy had never been with Tom, somehow, as it was with Bill.

She suspected that an evening with 'those girls' would tempt Bill to a little relaxation, and she was prepared to give him anything a young man of his age should enjoy. Even if he were in love with a girl who flirted as casually as she breathed.

Dinny would be as pleased as Bill to know she had relented about having anything to do with Paddy Cavan's daughters, Sally surmised. She realized now that Pat and Pam were not Paddy's daughters, and that they intended to break with him next year, when they would be of age.

Sally wore her best dress, a brown taffeta with pipings of rose round a smart bolero, the evening Pat and Pam came to see her. She forgot to look like a grandmother, Bill said, even though he was there to remind her of her obligations.

'She'll always be a charmer, Missus Sally,' Dinny chuckled. 'Although she pretends, now, she doesn't care how she looks.'

'Don't you believe it,' Bill laughed.

'How does she look, Dinny?' Frisco asked grudgingly.

'Jest the same as when you last saw her,' Dinny replied. 'Not a day older. Her hair's a bit greyer, perhaps. She's got it in a big plait round her head, and that red stuff on her lips.'

'But her eyes, Dinny?' Frisco queried. 'Have they got the light and smile in them they used to have?'

''Struth,' Dinny exclaimed, 'they're like they always were when Missus Sally was up to mischief. It's a sort of party we're havin' tonight, Frisco. And Missus Sally means to put it all over Pat and Pam, unless I'm greatly mistaken.'

She did 'put it all over' Pat and Pam by her reception of them, Bill was gratified to see. No one could have met them with more pleasure, and begged with such grace to be forgiven for discourtesy when the girls first called. Pat and Pam fell for his grandmother, as most people did when she chose to exert herself on their behalf. Whether she were playing the charmer and lady of quality, or a harassed boarding-house keeper, her natural quality shone through every part. She was his own Sal-o-my with a vitality and distinction all her own.

Pat and Pam had been a little in awe of her: rather afraid of her disapprobation, so they had dressed in plain white frocks of some soft, filmy material to give Missus Sally the impression they were quite ordinary girls who would appreciate her kindness, and not the fast young things about whom, no doubt, she had heard.

Bill's eyes lingered on Pat, critical and bemused. If she caught his gaze, her eyes held it happily. Pam was quieter than usual. She played with a kitten, the only survivor of a litter Sally's old tabby had presented her with, a few days before. Pam was more interested in the kitten, apparently, than anything else.

It was a hot night. As they sat on the veranda, light from a lamp near the door burnished gingery-gold the girls' hair, so that they looked like Lorelei maidens in their white frocks. They had come out of the dark pool of the night and were stranded on her veranda, Sally thought. She was not surprised that Bill appeared a little daft as he stared at them, although he was keeping his head, she noted: wary and on the defensive. He joked light-heartedly as he talked to Pat, deriding her interest in the mines and local happenings. Only the glad eyes Pat and he bestowed on each other, and the lilting current of their voices apprised Sally of the age-old irresistible attraction between them.

The girls had been out in the bush with one of the forest rangers the day before, and were full of excitement about their adventures.

Barb Reidy was one of the best bushmen on the fields, Dinny said. Born and bred in the country, he knew it for hundreds of miles like the palm of his hand. Barb had been a good deal responsible for breaking up the sandalwood racket, which was ruining crown lands, and under-selling on the Chinese market. He had shown plenty of pluck, too, dealing with timber thieves who would have despoiled the green belt around Kalgoorlie. It was being preserved to prevent erosion. Often when Kalgoorlie and Boulder were shrouded in dust, out in the forest there was not a stir. Cutters could obtain a licence to fall and truck dead wood, or green wood from specified areas further back; but big prices were offered for mulga sticks, salmon gum and gimlet, so that the timber thieves were always busy trying to outwit the ranger, and run their loads along dark tracks at night, particularly at the week-end when they thought he would not be on the job.

But Barb worked overtime and all night, when it suited him,

to see whether green timber was being cut indiscriminately on an unlicensed block. He would leave his truck two or three miles from a camp where he suspected men were working illegally, walk through the bush in carpet slippers in order to take them unawares, and had risked his life by doing so on several occasions.

'There's some rough customers amongst the "scrooges",' Dinny said. 'A bunch of Slavs, Barb says, are the worst offenders. They were mostly mountaineers in their own country and are always at loggerheads with their own people. A big, dirty old ruffian went mad when Barb walked into his camp one night and seized the wood he and his mates had been cutting: put the government brand on it, that is. He yelled to his mates to beat Barb up, but Barb was armed and ready to shoot if he had to. But he's got a way with him. Barb made the old man listen to reason: confiscated his wood all right, but let him off a prosecution.'

'Another time a dago threw a knife. Barb just ducked in time to miss it,' Frisco chortled.

'Did he tell you about the time he caught some blokes burning charcoal?' Bill asked.

'No,' Pat's smile played to his.

'Barb pulled his hat down, and walked into their camp at night. It was a long way out, and a risky thing he was doing, he knew, because that bunch might be treating gold.

' "What are you chaps doing?" he said.

' "What's that got to do with you?" one of them asked truculently.

' "I'm the forest ranger," Barb said. "You've got to have a licence to burn charcoal."

' "Hell, if that's all you want!" "You should have seen the faces light up," Barb says. The whole outfit whooped with glee and bought licences, and he went on his way. It was none of his business what they were doing, so long as they weren't burning charcoal illegally.'

'We chased a timber thief, yesterday,' Pat explained eagerly.

'Passed a truck on the road loaded with green timber. Mr. Reidy decided to follow new tracks into an unlicensed area. He drove for miles, winding through the bush, just following a track of wheels, and sure enough came on the remains of a camp, and the stumps of young salmon gums.'

'It was fun.' Pam chimed in. 'Then we lit a fire, boiled the billy for lunch on the old Jubilee rush. There were paper daisies growing among the dumps and torn red earth all round: the mallee yellow with blossom.'

'Afterwards, we went to see Jim Cox,' Pat went on. 'He told us about the time two hundred camels used to camp on the flat, going out to Gindalbie when three thousand men were working there, though it's deserted now. His humpy and his mate's are the only ones left on the track. The bush seemed to flow like a grey sea all round them. Those old men, Mr. Reidy says, have been there for donkey's years, and are the only two within cooee of each other for nearly a hundred miles in every direction.'

'I know Jim,' Dinny told them. 'Went out with Barb to see him, couple of months ago. He still likes to potter about the rush. Says the old prospectors never sank where the sixty-ounce slug was found, but further along. "She's where you find her," Jim says, and reckons there's a lot of good gold round about. Did ye notice how he'd built a kind of barricade round his place of all the crooked sticks and bits of timber he could lay his hands on, and made a gate with a couple of native relics hangin' over it? He's such a hatter, he didn't like the natives coming round. There was a lot of them about at one time, and Jim found those carved wooden pieces stowed away in a cave on the hill, thirty-odd years ago. They were painted red and white then. One of the old men begged Jim to give them back to him; but Jim reckoned they gave him a sort of power with the natives and wouldn't part with 'em. He wouldn't have even his mate, Alec Cockburn, livin' with him. Cockburn used to be a great ladies' man in his day, but he camps down there on the track so as to be near Jim. He's over seventy, but bought a motor bicycle a while ago. Thought he'd like to ride into Kanowna, now and then, to see the girls. But the only time he tried, he ran into a tree and broke his leg.

' "He couldn't ride, poor old Cock," Jim says. "He couldn't ride a fence if he tried. He'd get on one side and fall off the other." '

The girls laughed, and Pam said softly:

'He's the happiest man I've ever met, Mr. Cox. He says he wouldn't change his life out there for anything you could offer him.'

'That's right,' Dinny agreed. 'He's got the old age pension: can live on it with nothing to worry about. Speck a bit of gold when he feels inclined, and the boys take him a wild turkey or bottle of beer, if they're shootin' or prospectin' out that way. Jim likes the peace and quiet, feelin' he's his own boss to the last. He said, last time I saw him: "I'll die here where I've lived, Dinny. Seen forty-seven of me old mates go down the track: carried some of 'em, and dug a grave for 'em. Me mate'll dig mine. That's all I want, to stay here and have the sky and the stars over me when I pull me pegs." '

'Pam made a sketch of him,' Pat said. 'We would have liked to stay all the afternoon yarning to him: but Mr. Reidy had to look at some young timber fifty or sixty miles away. And we nearly got bushed, just at twilight. He said such a thing had never happened to him before. We went backwards and forwards along a track where the young mulga had grown very thick since he was last there. It looked so grey and ghostly; there was scarcely any light. Pam and I were quite excited at the thought of being lost in the bush. But, of course, Mr. Reidy found the turn off at last!'

'Coming into Kalgoorlie again,' Pam exclaimed, 'there was a clay pan, near Lake Gwyn — red earth, burnished and glowing in the sunset, samphire spreading out from it, ruddy brown, and smelling of violets. The great bosom of a timbered hill loomed up purple and dark. The sky faded after a while to tangerine and orange, a lemony-yellow and green. The evening star glittered through — '

She paused, as if it were impossible to describe that transcendental beauty. 'It was marvellous,' she sighed. 'If only I could have painted it.'

The girls soon had Dinny yarning about the early days. Frisco brought out his guitar and sang for them, more jolly and debonair than he had been for a long time. The mere presence of such desirable wenches exhilarated him, Sally imagined. There was a fragrance about them: the sound of their laughter had a youthful joyousness. It was just as well he could not see Pat and Pam, with their shining hair, and slim, lithe figures.

In all the years she and Frisco had been together, he had never given her any cause for jealousy; but Sally wondered with a twinge of regret whether the romantic ardour of their passion was waning. They had become almost as used to each other as any thoroughly respectable married couple. The idea was disturbing — and absurd. She brushed it away hastily, and listened, amazed, to Pat holding forth about the disastrous possibilities of what was happening in Spain. Was she talking for Bill's benefit, or did she really understand what 'the menace of fascism and war' meant, Sally asked herself.

Paddy had financial interests in Spain, Pat explained. He had taken Amy and the girls with him once when he was visiting the country. They had met people who were working for a Republican government before it was established. Not that Paddy knew anything about that. He would have been furious had he suspected who some of their friends were. She rattled on about Shawn and an artists' colony near Barcelona: argued heatedly with Bill about the strength and significance of the anarchist movement in Spain. When Pam joined in, Bill got the worst of it, and Sally smiled, thinking how astounded Paddy would be if he could have heard the violent opinions expressed by his 'daughters'.

So strangely the threads of individual lives entwined, Sally reflected. Who would have thought a man, made on the goldfields like Paddy Cavan, would be concerned about Spain? That Bill and his step-daughters would be brought together by it, fighting against him? Could it be true that what happened in Spain might affect her, Sally Gough: that another world war was brewing there, as Bill said? Sally shuddered away from the thought.

The young people seemed to enjoy their argument. It wasn't her idea of love-making, Sally confessed to herself; but if Bill had found a girl who could talk about the things which interested him, and they got some satisfaction out of political arguments, so much the better. She was pleased Pat and Pam had made a success of their evening, and that they were pleased with her.

Afterwards, the girls often came in the evening to see Sally, whether Bill was to be there or not. Pat would sit on the veranda steps and listen to Dinny and his mates yarning, while Pam, in the background, made rough sketches of the old men and Missus Sally. She had coaxed Sally to hang a lantern on the wall behind them so that she could get all the light she needed, and nobody noticed her as she sat there, working intently. Sally did not like her drawings. But she liked Pam; she liked Pam better than Pat as a matter of fact. Pam would help her to get supper, and chatter ingenuously about Shawn: how he had been wounded, but was getting better, and coming to Australia: how they intended to be married as soon as he arrived and were going to look for a studio where they could live and work together. Pat usually could not tear herself from the old men, their yarns and arguments, to have a quiet talk with Sally, although occasionally she insisted on taking a turn to help getting supper. Sally would have preferred that she did not. She was conscious of some constraint between herself and Pat, as though their feeling for Bill made them slightly apprehensive of each other.

Pat's eager questions and the sound of her laughter reached Pam and Sally one evening when they had set out the tea-cups, cut the cake and were waiting for the kettle to boil.

'Pat sounds happy, doesn't she?' Pam remarked thoughtfully. 'It's made such a difference to us, Mrs. Gough, knowing we could come here, and be good friends with you.'

'And Bill?' Sally's brows lifted and her eyes smiled.

'And Bill,' Pam said gravely. 'Pat's in love with him, I think — and I don't know what we're going to do about it. Bill doesn't care for her so much. He thinks Pat's "a slim gilt soul", as we say, and too irresponsible to believe in, altogether.'

'Do you?' Sally asked.

'No,' Pam said slowly. 'But Pat needs love more than I do. I've got my work.'

'Oh, well,' Sally lifted the steaming kettle from the hob, and poured water into her big, flower-spattered tea-pot, 'so long as they don't hurt each other, there's nothing to worry about, is there?'

When they went back to the veranda, they found Pat had persuaded Dinny to take her out to a blacks' camp in the bush near Bulong. Pat had been making inquiries about the aboriginal tribes who wandered about the goldfields in the early days and was disgusted to discover that nobody knew much about them.

'Kalgoorla could tell you,' Sally said.

'That's what I thought, missus,' Dinny explained. 'And the mob Kalgoorla's getting round with, just now, are sittin' down in a corner of the Rill Station property. Ralf was tellin' me the other day. He's wood-cuttin' for Mr. Brown.'

'That's Maritana's son — ' Sally remembered and caught her breath. Her eyes went to Frisco. Did he remember who was supposed to be Ralf's father?

'He's a fine type,' Dinny continued, having forgotten Ralf's parentage himself. 'One of the best workers he's got, Bob Brown says, although Ralf's not a full-blood.'

The twitching of a muscle in Frisco's jaw betrayed his interest. He had not forgotten the name Maritana had given his son, Sally realized. There was so much in Frisco's past she had had to ignore in order to be happy with him. But every now and then, something like this occurred to revive a memory which filled her with sick, angry shame.

CHAPTER XII

THE days slipped imperceptibly into the blaze and glare of summer. Soon the white roofs of the wide-spread gold-fields' towns were shimmering in the heat. Every breath of wind stirred fuming dust from the dry red earth. The light had a dazzling incandescence. Here and there a tree stood black against it, and dingy mists veiled the distant scrub.

Daphne wrote from the coast that she and Marie were having a glorious time, sea bathing and loafing on the beach. She felt so fit she thought she ought to take a job in one of the cafés, she told Eily, but Marie had persuaded her not to. Marie had suggested teaching her to be a dressmaker. What did Eily think of the idea? It might be less strenuous than earning a living as a waitress, and the pay would be better if she could work with Marie, and ultimately have a business like Marie's.

Eily had written to say she hoped Daphne would learn all she could from Marie. Dressmaking would save her the back-breaking rush and strain of waitressing, particularly if she could do it in her own time and be her own mistress. Bill posted Eily's letters. When he was going off in the morning, he asked if Eily had any letters to be posted, and changed the Miss to Mrs. D. Gough on the envelopes addressed to Daphne.

Dick was married in the Roman Catholic cathedral towards the end of November; but not before the high altar, which caused the bride's mother to weep all through the ceremony. A homely body who had had only her religion to support her in the trials of her life with Edward J. Langridge, she considered her new son-in-law had brought disgrace on her by refusing 'to turn'. Dick was prepared to do anything, short of that, to marry Myrtle. By way of compromise he had agreed to Mr. Langridge's demand that any children he and Myrtle might have, should be brought up in their mother's faith. And Myrtle had threatened to marry Dick in a registry office if her parents made any further objections to her wedding. The only legal part of any ceremony the church could perform was provided for at the Registrar's Office, she pointed out to them, and, with or without the church's blessing, she intended to marry Dick Gough.

So, making the best of a bad bargain, Mr. and Mrs. Edward J. Langridge had sent out invitations to the wedding of their daughter Myrtle Grace to Richard Fitz-Maurice Gough; and to a reception at the Palace Hotel afterwards.

When Dick brought Myrtle to see her, Eily had done her best to win the girl by an easy friendliness. But Myrtle's set smile and the hardness in her pale blue eyes did not relax. She was as trim and self-contained as the neat little bun of fair hair which sat on the nape of her neck. There was nothing warm or generous about her; but Eily supposed she must love Dick to put up such a fight to marry him.

'Myrtle's as predatory as a female spider, if you ask me,' Sally had said. 'And she's several years older than Dick, so it's not surprising she's made up her mind to hang on to him.'

Bill sensed that it would be a relief to Dick if he did not attend the wedding. Frisco accompanied Eily and Sally. Dinny was not invited, and at first Sally had been so indignant she declared she would not go.

'Oh, gran,' Eily wailed, 'I did hope you'd come to stand by me.'

'If that's the way you feel, I will go — for your sake, my dear,' Sally replied. 'But everybody knows Dinny's one of the family, and Dick should have seen he was invited.'

'Of course he should,' Eily sighed.

But Sally was just as pleased afterwards that Dinny had not been there.

'It was more like a wake than a wedding,' she said. 'The Langridges treated the whole affair as a calamity. At the church and during the reception Mrs. Langridge was dabbing her eyes and heaving huge sighs all the time, and Pa Langridge going round bemoaning the loss of his "one ewe lamb", and the head-strong ways of "young gurrls". You couldn't have stood it,

Dinny. I was furious, and poor Eily looked almost as depressed and miserable as Mrs. Langridge.'

For months Eily seemed unable to shake off the depression which had taken hold of her. She forced herself to do her work as usual, Sally knew, but could not overcome her grief for Tom and unhappiness about Dick.

She was smiling, however, and more like her sonsy, good-humoured self, the afternoon she came to see Sally, a few days before the schools broke up for the Christmas holidays. Eily had taken Nadya the night before to the annual concert of children who went to the convent school.

'Nadya begged me to go,' Eily explained. 'She was very excited because Lucia Rossini was going to play the piano by herself, and the nun who teaches Lucia says she's as promising a pupil as Eileen Joyce was at her age.'

Sally knew all about the Rossinis who lived next door to Eily. The father was a dusted miner, and Nadya had adopted the whole family. There were so many Rossinis that you lost count of them. Sally remembered three small boys as well as the baby, and knew that Rosa, Lucia and Maria were Nadya's 'best friends'. Rosa, the eldest, had left school to help her mother with the younger children, although she was only twelve. She took her responsibilities more seriously than Mrs. Rossini, Eily said, and was a care-worn little drudge, but Nadya adored her.

Everybody had heard about Eileen Joyce who was now a famous pianist, living in London. Eily knew her when she had been a freckled little girl, running about Boulder. Now they could turn on their wireless, and hear her playing at grand concerts in England. This was Lucia's first public performance and a great night for the Rossinis.

'It was a good concert,' Eily said. 'The children sang beautifully in their hymns and choruses. And Lucia! There's no doubt the child is gifted, gran. She was so self-possessed and absorbed in her music, sitting there on the piano stool, playing her pieces from memory. Quite difficult things by Mozart and Bach! You'd never have thought it was the same child who plays kick-the-tin with Nadya and other youngsters in the back-yard, yelling as loudly as any of them. There was a good deal of chattering and fidgeting among the children in the front rows, until Lucia began to play. Nuns in their black dresses were standing in the aisles and saying "Ssh! Ssh!" now and then. But there wasn't a whisper or shuffle while Lucia was playing. The kids sat with their eyes glued on her, and clapped like mad when she made her little bow and walked sedately off the platform.

'But oh, gran, it was during the last item, the "Ave Maria", the dreadful thing happened.' Eily's laughter fluttered. 'The children marched on to the platform for it, and knelt down with their backs to the audience. The old nun conducting the singing stood facing them, so she couldn't see the row of little girls furthest from her. One child's black dress got caught up, and there she knelt, with her bare bottom exposed to the audience — the most innocent, lovely little bottom.

'The nuns in the hall were so shocked they didn't know what to do. They couldn't interrupt the singing, or distract the attention of the child on her knees, and closed their eyes prayerfully, hoping the audience would do likewise, I suppose. Only a few of the younger children gasped and tittered. It was Maria Rossini whose dress had got caught and Nadya nearly died of shame. But I heard Rosa say with great dignity: "She *has* got a pair of drawers, but they're in the wash this week." '

It was a long time since Sally had heard Eily laugh as she did then. The humour and irony of the incident kept a smile shimmering in her eyes even when she said:

'It was such an indictment of poverty on the goldfields, that little bare bottom!'

Frisco had made several lucky speculations over recent years. Shares in the Sunset mine, near Lawlers, which he had thought worthless but hung on to, rose after the granting of the gold bonus.

When the financial depression sweeping the world struck the goldfields, the mining industry was brought almost to a standstill. Several mines closed down. The Ivanhoe and Golden Horseshoe were supposed to be worked out: the Perseverance in not much better shape. Other mines kept a few tributors working spasmodically. Big proprietary companies on the Golden Mile blamed rising costs and the decline of ore resources for their decrease in production. Older, less prosperous mining camps were dead: Coolgardie deserted and derelict. Prospecting, it was said, had become a lost art.

Thousands of shareholders had been ruined by over-capitalization of the mines, Dinny contended. Unscrupulous mine managers and company sharks overloaded their plants with machinery for the treatment of ore which did not exist. Their huge stamp batteries had to be fed, and a cut-throat competition to get tonnage at the lowest cost to impress directors killed many a good mine and robbed shareholders of a decent margin of profit.

Most business men agreed that the curse of the industry was rabid company promoting and over-capitalization. Mines had fallen into disrepute and water was rising in abandoned workings where rich shoots of gold were known to exist, because chicanery and mismanagement had destroyed their prospects of becoming satisfactory producers. Substantial grants had been made to the Wiluna Gold Mining Company and several other companies in order to enable them to carry on. But mining magnates maintained that the grant of a bonus by the Commonwealth Government for the increased production of gold was essential to revival of the industry.

Mr. Claude de Bernales campaigned vigorously for the gold bonus. Of recent years, he had put Sir Patrick Cavan in the shade as a company promoter and the presiding genius of various spectacular mining enterprises. Sir Patrick, it was well known, preferred to remain in the background of most of his activities in the mining world. Since he had been living in London, and acquired financial interests abroad, his reputation for being the power behind every move to consolidate the position of mine owners on the Golden Mile had faded. During the slump, however, it was rumoured that Paddy Cavan was backing de Bernales and associated with him in the campaign for the gold bonus.

Australia needed gold more than any country affected by the crisis, the mining magnates argued. Her gold reserves, depleted by the war, were disappearing from the treasury, yet mines were standing idle and gold was lying hidden in the vast auriferous areas of the west. The price of gold had never been higher. There could be no over-production of gold; the variation in basic value turned only in the direction of a higher price. No other commodity enjoyed such a unique position or such prospects for the future. So the government was urged to assist mine owners and the big proprietary companies to shoulder the burdens of gold production. Any suggestion that nationalization of the industry would be a more permanent solution of the problem, however, brought forth threats to fight, tooth and nail, any legislation aimed at depriving the mining companies of properties which they could no longer work effectively without government assistance.

The granting of the gold bonus was regarded as a feather in the cap of Mr. Claude de Bernales. To be sure, when it was granted in 1931, the bonus fell short of what had been expected: £1 an ounce on all new gold produced in Australia. The bonus applied only to quantities produced in excess of the average of the past three years. That meant only chicken feed for the proprietary companies and big producers on the Golden Mile unless they increased their output tremendously; but it did promote a vigorous working of many old mines and mining fields which had been abandoned.

The mining of low grade ores became a profitable proposition and a galaxy of new companies sprang into existence to exploit any likely show. Unlimited capital, it seemed, was being made available to launch and equip these enterprises.

De Bernales had returned to London, and soon afterwards announced the flotation of Anglo-Australian Gold Development Limited. This was followed by the flotation of several other mining companies.

Newspapers referred to Mr. de Bernales as 'the inspiration behind the mining revival of the west', and credited him with having brought millions of capital into the industry.

In the rising fever of speculation, and the spurious prosperity created by it, Frisco had bought and sold shares. Just to give him some interest in life, he told Sally; and to feel he could still put through a business deal, if only to amuse himself.

Time hung heavily for him, she knew. It was irksome for any man to be cut off from the work to which he was accustomed; and for Frisco, whose mental and physical energy was as vigorous as ever, to sit inactive and brooding in darkness was a disaster to which he could not reconcile himself. He had made a gallant attempt to take it lightly, but often sank into gloomy and irritable moods she could not exorcize. It was harder for Frisco than most men to sit like a 'great useless hulk', as he said, and drag out a monotonous existence. He had talked of putting an end to it.

What was the use of living like this he demanded. Of course, he loved Sally. To be with her was the only thing that made life possible. But how could a man be a burden for ever to the woman he loved? It was amazing how Sally had put up with him — but soon she would hate him. His exactions, black moods and rows with Dinny had become intolerable. No, no! Sally protested. But they had argued and quarrelled until it seemed as if the halcyon days of their love affair were over.

In desperation, it was Sally herself who had encouraged Frisco to buy shares in a show Tassy Regan advised them was going to be a good thing. Dinny and she both bought 'Gold Specks', which rose steadily. Frisco sold at a good figure, although Tassy declared it was too soon. Dinny and he and Sally were caught when the shares fell rapidly, and Frisco had the crow over them.

But that gamble renewed his zest for the game. All the year he continued to buy and sell script in the new mines opening up everywhere. His good spirits and pleasure at having found something to do, dissipated Sally's anxiety about those black moods. She read the Stock Exchange reports to him every day. Before long she was writing so many letters and spending so much time book-keeping and running about for him, that she said jokingly:

'You'll have to get an office and a typist, if this goes on!'

'That's an idea,' Frisco declared jubilantly.

Next day, after a walk into town, he announced he had taken a room in a block of offices, not far from the Palace Hotel. It was in a straight line from home. There would be no need to cross the main road, and Frisco had worked out how he could walk into his office every morning and set himself up in business, in a small way, as a stock and share broker. Sally could not begrudge him the prospect of overcoming the handicap of his blindness, and finding some outlet for the energies which tormented him when he sat brooding over his helplessness.

She went with Frisco to see the room, bought the table, chairs, shelves and typewriter to furnish it, and interviewed girls who answered Frisco's advertisement for a typist.

The room was in a shabby block of buildings where the back premises were let in flats. But when Frisco was installed with his typist, he regained something of his old boisterous vitality and assurance. Sally had qualms about his being drawn again into the frantic whirl of share-dealing, but Frisco laughed at the idea.

'Trust me, me dear,' he reassured her. 'I won't go too deep into anything. This will just keep me amused — and busy. At least, give me an excuse for pretending to be. And that's something.'

Who could deny him any relief from the darkness which encompassed him, Sally asked herself. She understood the sense of frustration Frisco had been wrestling with, and those black moods which overwhelmed him. When Dinny said something about 'a dog returning to his vomit', she was very angry. Frisco and Dinny had never ceased to snarl at each other, occasionally, although they contrived to get on fairly well. Dinny was chiefly to blame, Sally considered. He would look after Frisco as if they were really good mates, clean his shoes, cut his toe nails, and worry about him if he were out by himself and late coming home. But the latent animosity between them smouldered: would sometimes burst into furious altercations, or reduce them to surly silence.

Frisco was in great fettle when he had established himself in that office. Old acquaintances blew in to wish him good luck. Some of them put odds and ends of information in his way which Frisco was able to turn to profitable account. In answer to the circulars he sent out, men and women who had small savings to invest sought his advice.

While the Hampton Plains and Bullfinch booms were soaring, Frisco's office was packed with clients willing to risk their all in the frantic scramble for shares. He recommended caution, and sounder, if less glittering, prospects for would-be speculators. When those booms collapsed he reaped the gratitude of a number of folk who had not lost their savings.

If Sally called in to see him in the afternoon, after she had been shopping in Kalgoorlie, his room was always full of smoke. Miss Drew, the typist, clacked away on her machine at a small table, and Frisco was often busy with a client. Sally knew he liked her to see him like this.

Very soon he was on good terms with everybody in the building: being hauled out for drinks with the men and given a cup of morning and afternoon tea by a woman who lived in a flat behind Frisco's office. She was a coy, round-faced little woman with a cast in one eye and an ample bosom: a newcomer in the town and said to be the girl friend of old Lindsay, manager of

139

the Yellow Feather. Sally was there one afternoon when Mrs. Rooney brought Frisco his cup of tea. Miss Drew clearly did not approve of these attentions to her boss. She frowned and kept her eyes on her work when Mrs. Rooney ambled in with an amiable gurgle and: 'Here's your tea, Colonel de Morfé, and a scone I've just made.'

Miss Drew had her own paraphernalia for making tea in a cupboard beside her, and obviously resented this infringement of her right to provide Frisco's cups of tea.

Sally liked Nora Drew, a plain, awkward girl with buck teeth, but so competent and unassuming that she ran the office without Frisco's suspecting how much he owed its success to her handling of his business. She had brought order out of the chaos of his correspondence and the accounts with which Sally had wrestled in vain: introduced a system of book-keeping, filing and cataloguing which enabled Frisco to check his interests and commitments at a moment's notice. Nora had every detail of his banking and Stock Exchange transactions at her finger tips, dealt firmly with unsatisfactory clients, and kept Frisco up to the minute with his appointments.

'She's a jewel,' he would say exuberantly, and took advantage in every way of Nora's services. Often, he kept her working at the office half the night, in order to get out circulars and statements which he insisted must be dispatched immediately, without the slightest compunction for the demands he was making on her health and devotion.

'You're working too hard, Nora,' Sally said, noticing how pale and fagged the girl looked after a while. 'You mustn't let Colonel de Morfé take advantage of your good nature.'

Frisco was out, that day, and Sally had decided to wait for him.

'Oh, I don't mind what I do for Colonel de Morfé.' Nora raised brown eyes so humble and devout that Sally was troubled by them. 'He's very good to me, really. And, so wonderful — blind and trying to run an office like this! I've got to do everything I can to help him, Mrs. Gough.'

CHAPTER XIV

THOROUGHLY pleased and excited to be going underground on the Great Boulder, ~~Pat and Pam~~ donned oilskins
and hard hats, clutched their lamps, entered the miners' cage
and were dropped to the one thousand eight hundred feet level,
from the whitewashed plat of which visitors usually saw something of the workings of the mine.

They walked miles through winding dark tunnels, drives
and stopes, the girls said. Pam made some rough sketches of
boggers shovelling ore, truckers pushing off the heavily loaded
skips, machine miners working under the flare of their headlamps in a cavernous end. But the heat and fumes there were
too much for Pat. She had to confess she felt sick and faint. The
underground manager, who was showing the Misses Gaggin
round, by special request of Sir Patrick Cavan, had to hurry them
back to the plat where there was a down-draught of fresher air.
He looked glad to bundle them into the cage again, and to get
rid of them when they landed safely on the surface.

Pat was disgusted with herself for being so squeamish. Paddy
made a great joke of it. 'Not so tough as ye thought ye were,
me dear?' he queried jocosely. Nothing would ever induce her
to go underground again, Pat declared. She had seen enough of
work in a mine to last her a lifetime. It had terrified and appalled
her: the sense of being enclosed in that vast subterranean warren,
the heavy darkness, dank musty atmosphere of the place. She
could not get them out of her mind, or the faces of the men
working in the mine. Doré could have drawn them, she said.
Pam would never be able to.

'You didn't give me much chance,' Pam demurred.

'Sorry, darling,' Pat glanced at her, impenitent but smiling.
'Pam's immune to any emotion when she wants to draw,' she
told Bill. 'But if I get wrought up, a point comes when I just
can't stand things. That's all.'

141

'It wasn't altogether the fumes in that hot end upset you then?' Bill's quizzical grin flickered.

'No,' Pat admitted. 'I was sick with horror all the time. How can men spend their lives working in that awful darkness and suffocating atmosphere?'

Bill shrugged. 'They've got to earn a living, I suppose. Every man I know wants to get out of the mines as soon as he's made enough money to keep himself and his family in ordinary comfort. But to some of us, like myself, born and bred on the fields, there's a fascination about the industry. Mining engineering performs miracles, and every phase in the process of gold extraction is a triumph of human skill and ingenuity. While gold's a necessary commodity, I reckon all we can do is try to get a better deal for the man whose labour power is most necessary to production. Above ground and below.'

Paddy had arranged for the girls to see the workings of a mine on the surface, the next day; and accompanied them to the treatment plant.

He trotted with them through an old shed on the Great Boulder, gloating over its hidden wealth. Like a ghost of the past, the shed stood dismantled and unused, but still heavily laden with gold dust which had permeated its tall wooden framework, uprights, scantlings, platforms, rows of crumbling brick ovens, cyanide vats stained with verdigris and the primitive machinery used for treating rich oxidized ores. They were being preserved for future treatment. The ruddy brown earth underfoot was still rich with gold, Paddy boasted. The course of an underground creek had been exposed by excavations under the shed, and half a million pounds worth of gold had been won from its pinkish and white rubble fairly easily. Behind the shed a huge dump of tailings reared itself against the clear blue sky. Left there in the open, gold was being released from particles of iron ore as the iron rusted.

Three shafts towered over the underground workings of the mine. The engineer's and manager's offices were ranged round the treatment plant.

Paddy's gout was plaguing him, so he decided to sit in the manager's office while Pat and Pam were being escorted over the treatment plant. The old engineer, Mr. Ebenezer Wilde, to whom Paddy introduced them, somewhat grumpily accepted the honour thrust upon him. He had lived for the mine and recently retired, although he still pottered about doing odd jobs. Sir Patrick should get one of the smart youngsters now in charge to explain the new processes of gold extraction to his daughters, Mr. Wilde objected. Of course, he approved of the company's adoption of labour- and cost-saving devices in the treatment of low-grade ore.

'But you've got to admit a lot of good gold was won by the old methods, Paddy,' he remarked defensively.

'And lost,' Paddy growled.

They would have argued indefinitely had not Pat strolled off to investigate for herself. Pam and Mr. Wilde followed her. Presently they were all squatting round a diagram the old man drew on the ground.

'This is the way we used to get the gold from the broken rock you saw in the mine,' he said, quite affable now and flattered by the girls' eager interest. 'The grizzly, here, sized out fine ore. It was carried on to the cracker which reduced it in size: dumped in the battery bin for storage and fed to the stamp mill for further crushing. On the strakes the free gold was taken out — about forty-two per cent of the final output. The tube mills reduced the rest to pulp. Classifiers graded the pulp. Thickeners took out surplus water. Agitators mixed cyanide solution into the pulp. A vacuum filter separated the gold pregnant solution from the pulp, leaving residues which were pumped away. A recorder measured the gold solution and it was turned into the zinc boxes. Zinc has an affinity for gold: picks it up from the sludge. Then the zinc went to the smelters and the bullion was roasted out. It had to be retorted before it became fine gold and went to the bank.'

'Is that all?' Pat gasped.

'Crikey, no,' Mr. Wilde laughed. 'That's only one method,

still used a good deal, although we've got all sorts of electrical gear and new machinery to simplify production these days. Oil flotation gave us a headache for a while, but it's a profitable proposition now.'

They went into the engine room, housed in a new building of corrugated iron. A black mammoth there was hauling ore from the depths of the mine, its double engines controlled by one man, on the saddle of a stool, up aloft, before a huge dial. The dial indicated the movement of skips from various levels to the surface.

Pat and Pam watched skips rise from the shaft, automatically unload and send ore crashing into the bins. They saw it carried by a conveyor belt to the cracker and crushers. Dazed and bewildered, despite Mr. Wilde's shouted explanations, they followed the pulverized ore as it passed through the agitators, rotary filters and precipitating gear. They could not hear themselves speak in the terrific din and clatter of huge, crouched machines driving angled elbows with indefatigable energy, wheels flashing silverly, pistons thudding up and down, ceaselessly, insatiably: grotesque monsters slobbering over their auriferous gruel. The grey pulp being slapped to a dingy froth, as oil dripped over it in the flotation cells, looked a veritable witch's brew.

' "Double, double, toil and trouble," ' Pat murmured, gazing at it. ' "Fire, burn; and cauldron, bubble." '

'The bubbles collect infinitesimal particles of refractory minerals,' Mr. Wilde explained. 'But the pulp, pregnant with gold, is swept away to the filter presses which squeeze out all the moisture so that dry, lumpy fragments emerge, and are carried on to the roasters.'

In the roasting ovens, at first, mauve flames could be seen rising from the molten ore. A smell of sulphur hung in the air until the sulphide was exhausted. The precious metal glowed rosy-red, but still did not look like gold.

'Not yet, it doesn't.' Mr. Wilde beamed as Pat said so. He had the air of being a magician in charge of operations. 'Free gold from the strakes is amalgamated with mercury and goes direct to the gold room. But these cakes here, in the roasting ovens, are repulped in cyanide solution and agitated for seventy-two hours, then filtered; and this solution goes to the precipitator in which the principal agent is zinc. Other products from the filter return to the grinding section, and go through the whole process again. Zinc slimes are passed on to the gold room to be retorted.'

In the gold room, the 'holy of holies', which visitors were rarely permitted to enter, the girls saw the amalgam roasted and pure gold run off into moulds. The room was like a prison cell with its barred door and wet floor. There was nothing beautiful or awe-inspiring about it. Yet here in its locked safe and on shelves along its high dark walls, the reserve wealth of the mine was stored: thousands of pounds worth of gold in heavy grey dumplings, cones of amalgam and bullion.

Out in the sunlight and open air again, Pat took off her hat, and let the light breeze fan her face. She felt shattered by her visit to the treatment plant, she said. Not sick and faint as she had been underground, but overwhelmed by a sense of the terrific and diabolical energy which had gone into its machinery and processes.

'Yes, I know,' she exclaimed with an intensity which amazed the old engineer who had never thought beyond technical problems of the mining industry, 'years of scientific research and experimentation have gone into the perfecting of those machines and processes. They're the creations of man's brain and labour — not the brain and labour of one man but of thousands. It's true, isn't it? And to think all that energy and ingenuity is devoted to chasing the tiniest specks of gold! That the miracle of this place is subservient to the skill of a few workers operating the controls, and to the will of men behind the scenes whose wealth and power it serves!'

'Why can't as much tenacity and genius be used to clean up the mess of the world?' Pam inquired.

Mr. Wilde's shrewd eyes glimmered. 'You'd better ask Sir Patrick,' he said.

They had just glanced at the tool-repairing workshop, on their way through the plant. Pam wanted to go back there and make a drawing of the men as they swung to and from the roaring furnaces. Machines thundered, shaping and pounding the red-hot steel, and showers of sparks flew; but Pam was oblivious of all that, as she stood in a corner of the workshop getting the outlines of gaunt figures in the swoop and fling of rapid movement, or slouched over the blinding furnaces.

Pat was surprised to see Bill among the workers in the tool shop. In his blue jeans, grimy and oil-stained, he stood talking to the foreman. They walked over to the entrance.

'Bill!' Pat exclaimed delightedly. 'But this isn't where you work, is it?'

'Slipped over to see if they could do a repair for me here,' he replied with a shy grin. 'Thought I might catch a glimpse of distinguished visitors, too.'

'Hullo, Bill,' Mr. Wilde trotted up. 'There's been another break-down on the Little Boulder, they tell me.'

'The company's economizing: been patching up gear for the hell of a time,' Bill said, a wry twist to his mouth. 'If things don't look up on the Little 'Un, I'll be looking for a job.'

'We'd take you on here, tomorrow, lad, if I had my way,' Mr. Wilde assured him. 'But I'm a back number, these days.' He looked across to the tall chimney stack, stately shafts and white buildings of the Lake View and Star, shimmering in the afternoon sunshine. 'How about trying the Yanks? They've spent half a million on reconstruction, lately: electrification, new machinery, oil-burning furnaces.'

'Nothing doing,' Bill grinned. 'I'll stick to an Aussie show.'

'There's a sandgroper for you!' Mr. Wilde beamed, appreciating Bill's back-handed compliment. 'Can't say I blame you, Bill. I'm a sandgroper meself. The "View and Star" may have got the most up-to-date plant and be the biggest gold producer on the field; but the Yanks've introduced speed-up and stand-over methods that aren't popular with Australian workers.'

'That's about the size of it, Mr. Wilde,' Bill agreed.

'What's a sandgroper?' Pat queried.

'A man who thinks the Golden Mile is the centre of the universe.'

'A lad born and bred in the dust of this field.'

While they were chiacking each other, laughing and arguing over the meaning of 'sandgroper', Sir Patrick Cavan's black and shining Rolls swung into sight. It drew up a few yards away. Paddy heaved himself out of the car and waddled towards them.

Seeing him, Bill said: 'So long, Pat!' and disappeared into the workshop.

'Who was it ye were talking to?' Paddy demanded, squinting at Pat.

'Oh — that — that young workman?'

Pat could not make up her mind whether to tell Paddy, or evade his rage for the moment. But Mr. Wilde broke in:

'Why, that was Billy Gough. One of the smartest young engineers on the G.M. Where did he get to? Like you to meet him, Sir Patrick.'

As Sir Patrick regarded his step-daughter with glowering suspicion, Eb. Wilde remembered why there was likely to be no love lost between Sir Patrick and Young Bill Gough. He had glimpsed a subtle attraction and familiarity between the young people, also, and cursed himself for having embarrassed the lovely girl beside him.

'Have I not told ye,' Paddy demanded, breathing hard, his heavy red jowls quivering in an effort to restrain his wrath, 'y're to have nothing to do with that young man, or his family?'

Pam came running from the workshop. 'Oh, there you are, daddy?' she cried blithely. 'Sorry to keep you waiting. But there were some effects round those furnaces I just had to have a shot at.'

Mollified by her greeting, Paddy growled: 'That's all right, kitten. If ye're quite ready, we'll be getting along.'

Pam had seen her talking to Bill, Pat surmised, and Bill on his way through the workshop had told Pam of Sir Patrick's arrival. Pat was furious with Paddy for speaking to her in that hectoring way. Like a mettlesome filly under the flick of a whip, old Wilde observed, she had flung up her head, and with bright eyes confronted Sir Patrick, clearly intending to tell him she would do as she pleased. But Pam intervened and gently shepherded Sir Patrick to his car.

Pat turned to Mr. Wilde, her anger subsiding. He was perturbed by Paddy's outburst, she realized: a little disconcerted also by the way Paddy had ignored him.

'It's been a marvellous afternoon,' she said, smiling to charm the old man and relieve his discomfiture. 'My sister and I are very grateful to you, Mr. Wilde, for giving us so much of your time. And for showing us something of the mysteries of gold extraction.'

'It's been a pleasure.' Eb. Wilde jerked himself to an old-fashioned bow, a twinkle in his grey eyes. 'A pity, though, I made trouble for you with Sir Patrick.'

'Don't let that worry you.' There was a defiant raillery in Pat's glance. 'It won't make any difference to my friendship with the Goughs.'

She swung away to join Pam and Sir Patrick; but her lithe, graceful figure turned before she got into the car. Her smiling glance and the wave of her hand were intended for Young Bill in the workshop as much as himself, Mr. Wilde imagined.

CHAPTER XV

SALLY drove Dinny's old car when Pat and Pam went
with them to the blacks' camp on Rill Station.
   It was a Sunday morning and Bill had to attend a union
meeting, so could not go. Frisco made an important business
engagement his excuse for not joining the party, although Sally
imagined he was concerned not to embarrass her, because Ralf
would be there, in the blacks' camp. Kalgoorla's presence, too,
always disconcerted him.

Sir Patrick had twinges of gout and was in the worst of
humours when they left, the girls said. He expected them to
dance attendance on him, and couldn't see why Pam wanted to
go to Rill Station to sketch 'a lot of filthy abos'. The girls did
not tell him with whom they were going to Rill Station.

'You've got to have your nerve with you when you're driving
with gran,' Bill warned them. 'She says herself she feels as if
she were handling a bucking colt, and has got to break him in
or die in the attempt.'

Pat and Pam understood that when they sat in the back seat
of Dinny's bone-shaker. Never had they experienced anything
like the way Missus Sally drove Jiggledy Jane, bashing and
bullying her along the rough road, dashing recklessly over stumps
and corrugations until the old car nearly fell to pieces. The
engine groaned, stuttered and coughed on an up-hill climb,
water boiled in the radiator, and the brakes shrieked as Jane
scrambled down the far side.

Every now and then Dinny would yell back to them: 'All
right?' or: 'Still there?' And the girls managed to gasp: 'G-good!
G-good as g-gold!'

'We were so scared we could hardly speak,' Pat confessed to
Bill afterwards. 'How Missus Sally got over fifty miles like that,
and back, I don't know!'

They had to leave the car on a track winding through the

scrub and make their way to the spot near a dry creek bed where Dinny said the natives were camped. Standing still, he scanned the surrounding thicket of mulga and thorn bush, from which tall, slender trunks of blackbutt and the white-barked trunks of salmon gums, stained a dull pink, reared themselves against the blue sky.

'There they are,' Dinny cried, having detected the shape of a wurley and a few black figures through the scrub. Protected by their natural colouring and faded, dirty clothing, among fire-blackened tree trunks and the grey-green of the mulga, the natives were at first scarcely visible.

'Hi there!' Dinny called, and Sally and the girls fell back until he had talked to the man who came towards him.

The natives would be aware of their approach, Sally knew: curious and alarmed, ready to fly off and disappear through the unending wilderness of the trees if the strangers with her and Dinny had anything to do with the police, or inquired about little half-caste girls in the camp.

It was Ralf who spoke to Dinny, and Sally was glad Frisco had decided he had an important engagement and would not come on this excursion with them. Ralf showed little of his white blood; he was more of an aboriginal than a quarter-caste, although he wore better clothing than the rest of the men, except Dungardie who was a stockman, another station hand, and Charley, a police tracker. Their khaki trousers, washed and rubbed to a yellowy buff, clean shirts, wide-awake felt hats and spurred boots, made the stockmen look quite dandies among the rest of the natives who gathered quickly and sat down on the red earth, at a little distance from where Dinny was talking to Ralf.

Ralf called in a native dialect for someone to tell Kalgoorla that Dinny Quin and Missus Sally wanted to talk to her. Two or three women scuttled away from behind the bushes.

There were a dozen or more wurleys of leafy boughs scattered round an open space of gravelled earth, taking advantage of the sheltering scrub. They looked like mounds of dry leaves with here and there a few bags thrown across: the blackened ashes of camp fires lay before them. Dogs, women and children crawled out of the wurleys. There was shrill, excited laughter among the women, callings and an eager chattering.

Kalgoorla walked past the wurleys, no longer as stiff and straight in her dirty rags as she used to be. The man's hat on her greying hair looked as if it had not been removed for years. It rarely was, Sally knew. Kalgoorla scowled at the girls in their green slacks beside Sally. Kalgoorla did not appreciate this invasion of her solitude, Sally guessed. She distrusted white people and any stranger suggested some danger to her. Dinny broke down her taciturnity with a sly joke which set everybody gurgling and spluttering delightedly.

'By Cri', Kalgoorla,' he said. 'You got'm big belly! Make'm gee-gee (baby)?'

'Gee-gee, rubbish!' Kalgoorla replied, a smile chasing the gloom from her heavy dark face.

She slumped down on the ground beside him, and her eyes turned to Sally with pain in their shadowy depths.

'Got'm guts ache,' she murmured apologetically.

'Tell Ralf to come and see me, next time he's in Boulder, and I'll give him some pain killer,' Sally said.

'Eh-erm,' Kalgoorla glanced at her own folk, squatted on the ground and standing about her. 'That one,' she nodded towards a man in dirty blue trousers, an old coat wrapped round him although it was a hot day, and a pot hat perched high on long curls caked in mud which fell to his shoulders. 'That one, nadaerie (medicine man). Jump on belly: make'm well feller.'

'Him spinifex man,' Ralf explained, 'come walk-about long way, from Ooldea.'

'Wild native, probably from the McDonald Ranges,' Dinny told Pat. 'Don't like the look of him meself — broken some tribal law, maybe, or hiding from the police.'

The spinifex man screeched angrily at Ralf, bright brown eyes snapping beneath his mud curls. He strutted about with an air of authority, excited and hostile to the visitors.

An older native, tall and powerfully built, naked but for a loin cloth round his thighs, strings of red wool binding crisp brown hair back from his high forehead, stood up and looked at the spinifex man. He did not speak; but the spinifex man slunk away among the women, muttering at that silent rebuke.

'Bardoc, my father,' Ralf murmured with pride in the dignity of that dark figure.

Pam had already taken out her sketch book: her pencil was flashing over the white paper. Some of the women crept behind her and exclaimed at her quick drawing of Bardoc. He sank to a squatting position on the ground again as soon as he saw what she was doing.

'You feller, all about, not belonging same family Kalgoorla?' Dinny asked.

'Wiah,' Kalgoorla muttered.

'Wongi, all scattered and mixed up,' Ralf explained. 'This man comes from Norseman,' he indicated a wizened old man, wearing a grimy crocheted cap of many colours and what had once been a school blazer of blue flannel over threadbare tweed trousers. 'That one from the Laverton ranges.'

The Laverton man, a big strapping fellow with a broad splay nose, his skin much darker than the others, beamed in recognition of this introduction.

'He's the only one who's nearly black,' Pat whispered. 'All the others are bronze —'

'Long time ago, Kalgoorla,' Dinny persisted, 'what name Wongi people walk about Coolgardie, Kalgoorlie? Before white man come . . . before goldfields.'

Kalgoorla shook her head as if she did not wish to remember that time, or talk about it.

'Go on,' Dinny wheedled. 'You remember your father, what name his people, Kalgoorla?'

He took out his tobacco pouch: Kalgoorla's eyes fastened on it hungrily. She pulled a pipe from under her dirty coat. Dinny let her fill it from his pouch. The older men crowded round, eager for their share of the tobacco. Dinny gave his pouch to Bardoc, and he handed it round until it was empty. Pat hauled a gold cigarette case from her trousers pocket, and spilled the cigarettes out to give one to Ralf, Dungardie and the others. There were not enough to go round, but seeing this was a popular move, she called to Pam, and Pam, too, produced a gold cigarette case and handed cigarettes to the women swarming round her.

Ralf scolded Kalgoorla, and squatting down on his haunches picked up a twig and scratched a circle in the sand. He drew lines across it, pointing to the areas of various tribes: Yalindarra, Yulbarra, Kakarra, Wiloora — north, south, east, west. Then he cut the circle to give the quarters: Kieelie, north-east; Murrinee, south-east; Yilbarra, further east; Waooloo, north-west; Yaberoo, south-west. Kalgoorla argued and quarrelled with him. But all Dinny could make of their argument was that Yalindarra wongi were people of the north, Kakarra wongi, people of the south, and so on.

'Kalgoorla say wongi properly word belonging to Edjudina people,' Ralf explained. 'Now all native people mixed up and scattered round about call themselves wongi or wongudda — mean the same thing: different dialects.'

'But that's not telling us names of the tribes, Ralf,' Dinny objected. 'I remember a man from down Norseman way used to say he was a Mulba man.'

'Kabul,' Kalgoorla muttered, and went on talking to Ralf n their own language.

'She says she's a Kabul woman, and her tribal country was all about Coolgardie and Kalgoorlie,' Ralf interpreted. 'Dooidie, her man, went north with one of the early prospectors and she went with him. Long time, they sit down with Yalindarra wongi. There was a big fight. Dooidie finish'm. Kalgoorla come back to her own people.'

The spinifex man had come round again buzzing like an infuriated wasp. Clearly he was very disturbed by this intrusion of the white people and their curiosity about tribal words and tribal secrets. He had scared the women away from Pam, and tried to intimidate the others about letting her draw them.

'Whiskers Johnny says it is a bad thing to let the white woman catch their shadow,' Ralf laughed.

'It's a native superstition that if somebody takes a photograph or draws them — catches their shadow, and takes it away, they'll die,' Sally told Pat. 'The younger ones like Ralf don't worry; but the old folk are still quagy about it.'

'This my woman, Lucy,' Ralf said, looking down at the young gin who had sidled up beside him. Her loose wavy hair, sun-bleached and fairish, might have been badly dyed. It had a golden gleam in the sunshine. But she was a full-blooded aborigine, Dinny said. He had seen others with hair like that who were not half-castes. Lucy giggled, hiding behind Ralf, a dress of faded pale blue cotton stuff wrapping her slender figure, and a small boy hanging on to her hand. The boy was quite naked but for a fragment of shirt which came to his navel.

'My son,' Ralf said fondly and proudly.

A thin little girl, very dirty and bedraggled, hovered near.

'That one Berenice,' he said, 'she very sick feller. All over sores.'

The woebegone little figure with big hungry eyes made Sally's heart ache. She realized the child was suffering from venereal disease and that something should be done for her. The natives would resist any attempt to remove her from the camp, she knew. Berenice was the promised wife of one of the men.

An old woman with a sour, wrinkled face and sore eyes hurried up and hustled Berenice away.

'That nadaerie tell her it is the white man's sickness,' Ralf said. 'And old Gininga's scared the police will come some day and take the kid away.'

Sally distributed boiled lollies, apples and oranges to the children. She gave packets of biscuits and two tins of jam to Kalgoorla, who she knew would share everything with the other women.

Pam had made friends with several of them.

'This is "Laughing Mary",' she told Pat, laughing at the clean, plump and pop-eyed young gin in a red dress beside her. 'She works for Mrs. Brown at the station, and this is Kanageera. They call her Broken Nose — poor thing!'

Kanageera's nose had been broken so that only the end of it was left on her broad shy face above a wide distorted mouth. It had evidently been smashed by a heavy blow in her youth. Her brown eyes were sad, as if conscious of her ugliness, and her blue dress dirty and torn.

'They're both Cobber's wives,' Ralf explained. Cobber was the other stockman. 'And they fight plenty. Cobber likes Broken Nose best.'

Mary burst into a merry gurgling, and the shy, ugly young gin's mouth grimaced in a smile, as if this were a joke between them.

A tall, round-faced, jolly-looking, middle-aged woman came from behind one of the wurleys. A crumpled print frock sprigged with flowers hung over her skinny black legs. She was tying a blue apron over her high protuberant stomach.

'Shame on you, Mary,' she cried, 'you'm petticoat hanging down!'

Laughing Mary hoisted her red skirt unconcernedly and hitched up a dirty rag, hanging from under it.

'Why it's you, Nalka,' Sally cried. 'You used to come to see me, long ago, on Hannans with Maritana, didn't you?'

'Eh-ermm,' Nalka murmured, her face clouding. It was a mistake to have mentioned Maritana, Sally realized. The faces about her became sombre and unsmiling, furtive glances were exchanged and feet stirred uneasily in the dust. The aborigines never speak of their dead, and the mere name of Maritana reminded them of the tragedy which had befallen her: and that the mystery of her death had never been cleared up. Sally could have kicked herself for mentioning Maritana.

'But you bin mission girl,' she went on cheerfully talking to Nalka. 'Work up at station, Mrs. Brown tell me: mighty fine cook, wash'm clothes like nobody's business.'

Nalka grinned, gurgled and the shadow lifted from every face.

'Bin lazy bones, now,' she remarked complacently. 'Sit down in camp, go walk-about. Good place here, plenty tucker, plenty flowers. My kid Saidie in mission: big girl, write me letter.'

From a little bag hanging at her belt, Nalka produced a scrap of dirty paper. She could neither read nor write herself but was very proud of her daughter's accomplishment.

'Tell'm,' she said, jerking her head towards Pat and Pam, 'what my girl Saidie bin write in letter.'

Sally read the letter, which was in a round, well-formed hand-writing.

'Dear mother,' it said, 'I hope you are very well as it leaves me at present. I am very happy here. We are singing praises to the Lord all day. I hope you sing praises and love the Lord. And I hope you do not drink beer and go to the pictures. It is very wicked. I am very happy because Jesus is my personal Saviour. Your loving daughter, Saidie.'

Everybody looked impressed, and Nalka beamed happily, taking the letter from Sally and folding it back into her dilly bag. But Mary's laughter bubbled and flew merrily.

'Nalka not drink the talking gabbie, all right,' she spluttered. 'Weeah? (No.) She not get'm drunk and fight Gininga. Weeah. Lie in shade all day, goon-goon, whuff-gurr — whuff-gurr.' She mimicked the heavy breath and snort of a drunken sleeper.

Nalka turned on her shouting furiously, but the other women joined Mary, laughing and spluttering over the fun of taking Nalka down a peg because she had been giving herself airs before the visitors.

Kalgoorla raised her voice, calling to them. Nalka shut up and the laughter spluttered away.

'Would they sing to us, I wonder?' Pat asked eagerly.

But everybody seemed suddenly to be overcome with shyness. The women giggled and huddled together. The men looked at the ground, all reluctant to oblige.

'By Cri',' Dinny exclaimed, 'you fellow all scared to sing a song for the young lady?'

Ralf had sat down beside his gin and their child. Clicking a pair of kylies, he started to sing quietly to himself. Sally guessed that he might be the yenma, or poet of the tribe and a leader in the tulgoo, which was the local word for corroboree. Pat went over to listen to him.

'Tell me what it is about,' she said.

'About wilga — that tree,' Ralf said, indicating a slight, graceful tree standing nearby. 'Sing:

> Yungandarra, (sun-up)
> Wilga throwing light
> Wongi wake up
> Gindoo (sun) walk in sky
> Wilga throwing scent
> Wongi go hunting

('Chase'm job'), he added with a grin.

> Gindoo stand still
> Wilga —

He could not find the word — hung his head.

> leaves hanging down,
> Giving nothing shade —
> Wongi weary bugger.
> Sun sit down.
> Wilga throwing shadow
> Wongi sleep.'

An old man with clipped beard and small eyes matted with pus had seated himself under a tree. His coat and trousers were red-brown of the earth. Several of the men went over and squatted near him. They seemed to be part of the landscape even at so short a distance, their faded, dust-raddled clothes melting into the foliage of broombush, blackbutt saplings and salt bush about them.

Presently he was clicking two pieces of stick and singing:

> Bee-dil, bee-dil, minongrila,
>   Boombo-yogonning.
> Keern-del, keern-del minongrila
>   Boombo-yogonning.
> Marra-bree, breebo-ganning,
> Jahrra-bree, breebo-ganning.

The lines were repeated: some of the men joined in the singing, following the rhythm and quarter tones of the fragmentary melody in perfect unison. It ended with a dramatic flourish which set them all smiling.

'The man on a hill is cutting down a tree,' Ralf explained. 'He looks towards the south and sees a storm coming. "Keerndel, keern-del", the sound of his axe, and "jahrra" the sound of wind and rain slashing the trees, making everything tremble.'

Pam made a quick sketch of Ralf's wurley, beside which a line had been strung. A couple of shirts, a pair of pink scanties and a child's little pants were flying on it. Lucy had been a mission girl, Ralf said, and carted water from the station to do her washing.

'Every day, wash'm, make'm clean feller,' he boasted. 'Tell me bring'm scented soap and talc powder from the Boulder when I been in with wood for the boss. Lucy can sing mission songs. Sing'm "Follow Jesus", Lucy.'

Softly, with the wail and inimitable native rhythm and cadences, Lucy sang:

> Wan-algoo, wan-algoo, gnar-u
>   Jesus wan-algoo
> Nung-uh good-oo, bala good-oo
>   gnar-u balauna wan-algoo,
> Wan-algoo, wan-algoo, gnar-u
>   Jesus wasn-algoo
> Nung-uh good-oo, bala good-oo
>   gnar-u wan-algoo.

Follow the track, follow the track,
 Me, Jesus, follow the track,
This way, that way, me, that's the one,
 Follow the track.
Follow the track, follow the track,
 Me, Jesus, follow the track.
This way, that way, me, follow the track.

Three women coming into the camp caused a stir. Everybody, men, women and dogs swirled towards them. They had been out hunting, and a scrawny, elderly gin with a tuft of ragged grey hair under her chin was yanking a wild turkey over her shoulder. She threw it to the ground, still alive, its legs tied together.

The bird was no bigger than a pheasant, with beautifully patterned feathers, faun, brown and black. It had a long neck and snake-like head, with grey-lidded yellow eyes which searched the scrub desperately for a way of escape. The bearded woman had broken its leg with her throwing stick and was very pleased with herself.

'We bin give her to Charley,' Ralf explained. 'Him lonely and want a woman.'

Charley, the smart young police tracker, taking a holiday with his people, seemed quite satisfied with his bride.

'Good woman,' he said approvingly.

'This one Nelly,' Ralf introduced the other gin with a clamped-down mouth and bleary eyes, her cotton dress grey and grimy.

'Kukah-u-ah!' he exclaimed jubilantly as she spilled a load of hard wild pears, tinged with bronze, from a bag she had been carrying.

'Kalgurluh,' Kalgoorla stretched out her hand and picked up one of the pears.

'That's the origin of the name Kalgoorlie,' Dinny said. 'It grows on a wiry sort of creeper — used to be plenty of it along the Boulder ridge. Comes up quickly after a thunderstorm, has yellow flowers and then this fruit forms. It's very sweet when it's ripe. The natives put it in the ashes of their fire and cook it until it's soft. They tramp miles for it. That's why they used to come round the Boulder. It was the place of the kalgur-luh — your place, eh, Kalgoorla?'

'Eh-ermm,' the old gin muttered. The fruit had a sacred significance for her, Dinny told Pat, Kalgoorla believed the spirit of the dream ancestors, who created it, had entered into her mother before she was born at the place of the kalgurluhs. It was there she belonged; there her own spirit when she died would seek reunion with the kinsmen of her tribe, allied by this totem.

Kalgoorla would not talk about that, Dinny knew, before so many white people; or before the natives of other tribes who had drifted together in this camp of refugees and renegades from tribal customs. The young people laughed at and disregarded the old ways, she said, although they were afraid of this nadaerie from the north-east. Even Kalgoorla was a little afraid of his glittering eyes and mad rages. But the young people, she told Dinny, would rather follow the track of the white people now than the track of their own people.

The old man who had sung the wood-cutter's song was sing-ing away to himself as he stoked one of the camp fires:

> Pigian, pigian, bululun bululun
> Carboodmaan bunun, carboodmaan bunun,
>
> (Charcoal, charcoal, bell-bird singing, bell-bird singing. Turkey gobbler on the ground.)

'He says the fire's ready, and his heart's singing like a bell-bird, because there's a turkey for tucker,' Ralf commented.

The whole camp accompanied Dinny and Missus Sally back to the car: men, women, children and dogs, a raggle-taggle gipsyish crew, laughing and chattering, exclaiming with awe and consternation as Sally climbed into her seat. Dinny and the girls seated themselves, and Jiggledy Jane began to snort and growl, getting into action. They shrieked their fear and delight when Sally reversed and, plunging and bucking, Jane turned on to the track.

The natives could be heard jabbering excitedly as the car trundled away down the track, rocking and bumping over the roots of trees and ruts left by heavy rains. Their voices in the distance were like the crying of birds, high to low, with a long drawn out note, laughing and wailing.

'We're so near we must drop in and see Mrs. Brown,' Sally said, when she struck the main road.

'Bob Brown'd never forgive us if he heard we'd been calling on the wongi and hadn't paid him and his missus a visit,' Dinny chuckled.

'Maybe we could run into Bulong, show the girls what happens to a mining town,' Sally suggested, 'and drop in at the Browns on the way back.'

'Oh, let's!' Pat and Pam exclaimed, eager to make the most of this adventure.

So Sally had stepped on the gas and Jiggledy Jane ambled along towards the green belt of big salmon gums, wadgil and morrel, surrounding the site of a once prosperous mining town. Nothing was left of it now except one corrugated iron shack, a line of old pepper trees where the main street had been, and the Queen Margaret mine on the ridge, with dumps and pot-holes stretching over the gravelled flats all round.

They stopped for lunch on the ridge. Dinny made a fire and boiled the billy. Pat and Pam dispatched their thumb pieces of brown bread and bacon and cuts of chookie with hearty appetite. They exclaimed rapturously over Sally's lemon cheese tarts: said, of course, they had never tasted such a delicious meal, and that the tea, which Dinny swung round in his fire-blackened billy to settle the leaves and show them the bushman's trick, was 'super'. Sally smiled at their appreciation of her picnic, pleased that they were enjoying this day out with her and with Dinny.

When the meal was finished, she repacked the tucker box, and they chuntered down to the deserted town site.

'Hard to believe this used to be a town of three thousand people with smart shops and seven pubs,' Dinny said mournfully. 'But when the "Maggie" finished, the town jest faded away.'

They had stopped for a moment near the only shack left standing, and a tall, spry old man stalked out from it.

'If it's not Peter Cohen himself,' Dinny exclaimed. 'Mister Cohen and his brother were the big men in Bulong in its palmy days,' he explained, introducing Mr. Cohen to the ladies. 'They owned stores and pubs and sunk a lot of money in the mine.'

'It doesn't make sinse,' Mr. Cohen remarked with the brogue of an Irishman, 'to see the place now and remember what it used to be. But I reckon Bulong'll come agin, Dinny. They're talkin' now of doin' exploratory work on the "Maggie". A prospector got twelve ounces in an old shaft, beyant, three feet from the surface, last week.'

'Any of the old crowd about?' Dinny asked.

'There's the Mayor, camped a bit along the road,' Mr. Cohen said.

'Cripes, we must have a word with him,' Dinny declared. Mr. Cohen suggested that the ladies might like a cup of tea, and said he would boil the billy for them. But Dinny assured him they had just had lunch and must be getting along, as they were calling at Rill Station on their way home.

'Mr. Brown — that's Bob's father, used to be the Mayor of Bulong,' Dinny said, as they drove off along a scarcely visible track overcast by black ironstone gravel. 'He's a grand old chap, used to be a school master, and then took up land out this way: started the station to run cattle, built the homestead and reared a big family. There's no town left to be mayor of, but Mr. Brown's still the Mayor to old-timers.'

They had sat yarning with the Mayor, in the hut of corrugated iron where he lived, among scattered, slender trees on rising ground strewn with the black ironstone gravel.

The hut was tidy and clean, but cluttered with books and papers. Shelves made of fruit cases were filled with books; piles of papers lay stacked on top of them. In a mug on the table there was a bunch of paper daisies. The Mayor showed Pat and Pam the little bottles in which he kept crumbs of gold he had specked or dollied from specimens picked up in the bush. He too, believed Bulong would come again when the 'Maggie' was properly developed.

On the opposite side of the track, a prospector's hut crouched against the earth, with a tub of red lilies flaring magnificently under a brushwood screen.

Dinny went over to have a word with their owner, and came back chuckling.

'Y'd think they was the holy ghost, them lilies,' he said. 'That bloke can't talk of anything else. How he got 'em and reared 'em — kept 'em alive through all the dry seasons. Got nothing belonging to him except those red lilies — they're a sort of miracle to him. He doesn't want anything else.'

'I don't wonder,' Pam murmured. There were only these two huts for miles and miles of dreary country under black ironstone gravel, and the red lilies made a flare of miraculous beauty for anybody to gaze at.

'Well, we must be gettin' along,' Dinny said after a while. 'How about comin' in to the station with us, Mr. Mayor?'

The old man hesitated. 'But I can't leave my dog,' he demurred.

'We'll take him along — if Pat and Pam don't mind.'

'He'll sit on the floor and I can hold him,' the Mayor said eagerly.

'Of course we can make room,' the girls exclaimed.

They squeezed together in the back seat and the old man and his dog clambered into the car.

The station buildings were like an isolated village in the surrounding wilderness of trees. The cleared paddocks formed an island of tawny summer-dried grass, and the whitewashed corrugated iron buildings rose from the red earth as if they had grown there. They looked old and dilapidated when Jiggledy Jane chuntered up to them. The wooden verandas of bush timber were sagging and sun-rotted in places. Two windmills scratched the sky beside dams half-filled with muddy water;

but the green of a vegetable garden flourished beside them and the rounded bouquets of a few fruit trees, oranges, lemons and figs.

'It's not like the big stations up north, or in the south-west,' Dinny explained. 'Raising sheep and cattle in this country has been a tough proposition, what with the droughts, shortage of feed and water almost any summer. How Bob Brown manages to do it beats me. He works harder than any man I know, and his missus has worked with him, as bright and chirpy as a bird, though it's a hard and lonely life she lives out here. She's reared six children and doesn't see a white woman for months, sometimes.'

When Jiggledy Jane pulled up in the station yard, Mr. and Mrs. Brown came out to meet their guests.

'This is a pleasant surprise,' Mrs. Brown said cordially, by way of greeting.

'Go on,' Dinny grinned, 'we reckoned the wongi'd let you know we were on our way.'

'They did,' Bob Brown's lean, kindly face lit with an answering grin. 'We've had half the camp up to tell us Dinny Quin and Missus Sally make'm walk-about in that old bus of his, "buck like two-year-old". "Got'm mighty fine kambie (pretty young girl) in back seat. One make'm pictures",' he pretended to make quick sketches, 'all time, all time, other feller askin' plenty questions. Paddy Cavan's daughters, Charley say –'

'We're not,' Pat and Pam piped up automatically, 'Paddy Cavan's daughters.'

'Pat and Pam Gaggin,' Dinny introduced the girls. 'Trust the wongi to know all the news of the countryside.'

'Come in! Come along in, all of you,' Mrs. Brown said eagerly. 'You'll stay the night, won't you?'

The sun was already low in the western sky. Sally glanced at it anxiously. She did not like the idea of taking Jiggledy Jane over the rough tracks back to town after dark. Her eyesight was not as good as it used to be, and Jane's lights always feeble and liable to fail altogether.

'We ought really to be on our way in a few minutes,' she said dubiously.

'Oh, couldn't we stay?' Pat and Pam chorused.

Sally understood that this visit to a way-back station was an experience for them and was reluctant to disappoint them.

'We've got a telephone. You could send a message to your folks,' Mrs. Brown pleaded. 'You can't just run away in a few minutes.'

'Oh, well,' Sally conceded, 'p'raps we could stay if it's not putting you to too much trouble.'

'Trouble?' Mrs. Brown laughed in her brisk, cheery fashion. 'It's such a pleasure to see you, Mrs. Gough, and have a yarn about something besides cattle and gold. That's all the men can talk about. Come along and I'll show you your rooms, and then we'll have tea.'

The station, like most out-back stations, was built in a rough square with the kitchen, dining-room and sitting-room on one side, and the living-quarters on the other; store rooms and offices across the end. There were so many big, simply furnished bedrooms along the wooden veranda of the sleeping quarters that the whole party could be stowed away comfortably: Pat and Pam in one room, Mrs. Sally in another, and Dinny in the room reserved for stray male visitors.

Pat and Pam washed quickly, combed their hair and touched up their faces with lipstick and powder. Then they stood on the veranda gazing about them, over the cleared paddock before the homestead, and out to the distant scrub surrounding it on all sides like the sea.

So isolated and remote from the busy life of the goldfields towns, this collection of white weather-beaten buildings: this home in the wilderness! The solitude of the place pressed in on them. How lonely and quiet it was! The spaciousness and tranquillity filled them with awe. Sunset painted the sky a glittering crimson, which faded on drifting strata of clouds to the faintest pink. Golden mist drenched the earth and was lost in the haze hanging among those distant trees. The smoke of fires at the blacks' camp put a fragrance of sandalwood in the air, though probably it was only mulga that was burning. Native voices could be heard far away like the cry of birds, with a drift of singing, eerie and wailing.

The girls held to each other, exclaiming incoherently. It was inexplicably moving to them, this breath of the country; this glimpse of its immensity and primitive mystery.

'Oh, there you are,' Mrs. Brown exclaimed, coming to find them. 'Come and have something to eat, now. I'm sure you must be dying for a cup of tea.'

To be dying for a cup of tea, Pat and Pam recognized as a custom of the country.

'Oh, we are,' they agreed.

A table was spread at one end of the long kitchen, and everybody sat there to eat the salads and cold meat Mrs. Brown set before them. She poured tea from a huge enamel tea-pot, and Missus Sally scurried about cutting bread and handing round the cups of tea. Plates of cake and pots of butter and jam stood on the table to be passed along when anybody requested.

It was a leisurely, jolly meal, with Mr. Brown and Dinny swopping news of the countryside, Missus Sally and Mrs. Brown exchanging their own items of gossip, children clamouring to get a word in edgeways, and another piece of cake while their parents' attention was occupied, the old man adding some reminiscences, and Pat trying to talk to the handsome young stockman who had taken his place at the table.

The women washed up afterwards, and the men sat round the table, smoking and yarning. Pat could not tear herself away from the yarns; but Pam helped Mrs. Brown, and Sally went off to ring a neighbour about asking Dally to give Frisco and the boarders their breakfast.

'Sure,' said Dinny, 'the "Maggie" 'll come agen. There was always rich patches in her. When Chris and me had a show on the flat, we reckoned there was a lot of good gold never come out of her.'

'That's fact,' the Mayor remembered. 'And when they struck

166

a rich patch, the miners reckoned they were share-holders: filled their billies. An old bloke, going home with a lot of gold in his billy one evening, struck the manager, who stopped to have a yarn with him.

' "Have a swig er tea," says the old bloke, thinking the manager was looking a bit suspiciously at the billy.

' "No. No, thanks," says the manager, not fancying having to swallow the black brew the miners made for themselves. And the old bloke sauntered away.'

'That was in the good days,' Dinny chuckled. 'It's not so easy for a working miner to get away with a bit of gold now.'

'How's the cattle, Jack?' Mr. Brown asked his stockman. He had been mustering, and was to be on the road with a mob for the sale yards in Kalgoorlie at dawn next morning.

'Quiet as mice,' Jack Ross, the stockman, replied, 'though there's a big white-faced bullock gone a bit lame.'

'You don't have to worry much about mustering and droving in flat, open country like this,' the Mayor observed. 'Not like the rough, timbered country up north, eh, Jack?'

'Cripes, no,' the stockman stretched his long legs with a smile. 'I don't want any more stampedes like the one we struck coming down the Canning Stock route, not so long ago.'

'Tell us about it,' Pat begged.

The stockman swung his lazy smile on her. Women had been rare birds in his wandering existence, and it amused him to think he could cut quite a dash in Boulder and Kalgoorlie when he swaggered around in his loose shirt, wide-brimmed Ashburton felt and close-fitting riding pants, with spurs jingling. The movies and yarns about wild westerners had done that for him; and his dark eyes, brilliant with the sunshine in which they were accustomed to watching for stragglers in a mob of moving cattle, or cutting out prime beasts from the scrubbers, intimated willingness to cut Pat from any mob of young females, although he maintained the casual disinterested air of a warrigal, mistrustful of strangers.

'Oh, there wasn't much to it,' he said easily. 'We were bringing four hundred stores down from Billibuna Station. Cross-eyed Charley and Ruby, his woman, as good as any man on a cattle camp, a couple of native boys and old Jack Barr as cook. The beasts were as wild as flies, and first night out it was so dark — you couldn't've heard a dog bark. Away they went. We chased 'em for a couple of hours in thick, scrubby country and brought 'em back: most of 'em. Next night it was the same: a native spear sent them off. The natives are a bad lot along the stock route. Speared a couple of drovers, two or three years ago, stampeded the cattle and got all the beef they wanted for months, so they reckon it's a good game, scarin' cattle. We staked two horses that night, and one of the boys was killed.'

'If bullocks start breakin' like that they make a habit of it,' Mr. Brown said.

'Third night,' Jack Ross went on, 'Cock-eyed Charley and Ruby were goin' on night watch, changing horses with me and Bindi — and the blasted brutes broke again. Ruby pelted after 'em, and somehow we got them back, Charley and Ruby and me. But Charley was all in — fell off his horse and there was no getting a kick out of him till he'd had a bit of shut-eye. We took it in turns to have a bit of sleep during the day. But next night, the blasted brutes could've broke to kingdom come, I was dead to the world as soon as I hit the ground before my go on night watch. When I came to, there was Ruby and old Jack, going round the cattle, singing quietly, and not a move out of those blasted scrubbers . . . We got about half the mob to Wiluna. Worst bit of droving ever I done.'

'It's tough country along that stock route, all right,' Dinny consoled him. 'A couple of drovers I know lost their whole mob — breakin' back like that to where they come from, not so long ago. And I remember when two stockmen were speared by natives, on their first trip down.'

So the evening passed with yarns about cattle and gold and the natives, revealing the stuff of which the everyday life of these people was made.

Pat and Pam felt as if they were taking part in a play, sitting there in the station kitchen with its floor of rough-hewn timber, walls of corrugated iron, whitewashed and stained with red dust, glow of the fire dying down in a big stove at one end. A carbide lamp spluttered on the table and threw white light on the worn leather of the men's faces. Mrs. Brown's work-worn hands and white dress, a stock whip and rifle hanging on the wall, the dresser loaded with china, the Mayor's dog wandering restlessly between the fireplace and the open door, which framed a panel of blue night sky and the station yard washed by moonlight.

It was so different from any way of life Pat and Pam had ever known, the stark simplicity, the struggle for existence so grim and unremitting, requiring every nerve and muscle to overcome the toil each day demanded through the long summers when the sun sapped the vitality of every living thing; dearth and dryness reduced the land to an inferno of blasted hopes. Yet with humour, kindliness, indomitable spirit, these people battled along, their pride and independence surviving every hardship and disaster.

On the veranda, before going to bed, the girls gazed about them, at the white roofs of the station buildings, the trees stretching to infinity in the moonlight, the sky overall of a soft blue-grey like the salt bush and mulga, unreal and enchanting. So still and silent everything was: the stars misty in the heat.

'It's as if we were living in a dream,' Pat said.

'Or at the bottom of the sea,' Pam murmured. 'I feel lost without Shawn.'

'And I seem to have found myself,' Pat mused. 'I'm happier than I've ever been.'

She shivered in a spasm of unruly nerves.

'Somebody walking over my grave,' she cried and laughed quickly. 'It's unlucky to say you're happy, I suppose. Let's get some shut-eye, as Bill says. Golly, wouldn't Paddy be mad if he knew we've been gallivanting with Dinny and Missus Sally!'

PADDY was sitting propped up in an armchair in his private room at the hotel, one leg stretched out on a footstool, when Pat and Pam rushed in to see him next morning. He scowled at them and they knew they were in for a bad time when he burst out:

'What the hell do ye mean — gaddin' round the countryside with Dinny Quin and Mrs. Gough, stoppin' out all night, and havin' me worried to death about what's happened to ye? To say nothing of clearin' out when me gout was so bad I didn't know what to do with meself, and not a soul in the blasted place to do a hand's turn for me, bein' Sunday and the maids off duty. If Wally O'Brien hadn't come in, and later, Detective-Sergeant Smattery, I'd've been on me own all the afternoon and evenin'.

'God damn it!' Paddy roared, 'I've been pretty easy-goin' with you girls. I've let you go y'r own ways and given ye everything ye've wanted! And all ye can do is take advantage of me good nature: leave me in the lurch when I need a bit of lookin' after — and start all the tongues in the countryside waggin' about y'r disgraceful goin's on! I won't have it, I tell ye!'

Paddy pounded the table beside him with a heavy fist. The pale, bloodshot eyes above the ruddy heave of his fat cheeks flashed wrathfully.

'We told you we were going to Rill Station!' Pam said. 'So we took it for granted you'd know where we were.'

'I won't have it,' he shouted again. 'Ye've got to stop behavin' like a pair of spoilt brats. And I won't have ye gettin' round with the Goughs — people who haven't got a good word to say fer me, and always rakin' up the past! Young Bill's the worst red ragger in the town, Smattery's been tellin' me, and ye've been seen in his company a good deal. "Y'd ought to put your foot down, Sir Patrick," Smattery says. "The young ladies'll get into hot water if they go round with Bill Gough. They're a bad lot, these communists on the goldfields: will be stirrin' up trouble before we know where we are — blackmailin' you, as likely as not, if they think they can get anything on your daughters"!'

'It's a lie,' Pat exploded.

'Bill Gough is Amy's son,' Pam reminded Paddy.

'I know. I know,' Paddy's rage was exhausting itself. 'That doesn't mean Amy would have anything to do with his rotten communistic ideas, or want ye to be settin' y'rselves agenst me.'

'Amy asked us to see Bill and give him some messages from her,' Pat said.

'She did, did she?' Paddy's rage spluttered out, and he gazed at her miserably. 'That doesn't mean,' he added, pulling himself, together, his anger reasserting itself, 'that ye've got to be visitin' Mrs. Gough — goin' round with her and that blackguard, Dinny Quin, in their broken-down motor car.'

'Now, listen,' Pam said quietly, 'you've got yourself all worked up about nothing. It's not good for your gout. Sit back and I'll tell you what we've been doing.'

She shook up the cushions on his chair, made his bandaged foot more comfortable on the footstool, and sat down on a chair beside him.

Pat stood at the window, looking out, indisposed to placate Paddy in any way, although she realized Pam was handling the situation more wisely than she. Their lawyer had advised them not to break with Paddy until they were of age, and some complications in their mother's will could be straightened out.

'You know I like to paint all sorts of queer places and people,' Pam said gently. 'And Pat likes to write about them. Well, we've been going about meeting all sorts of people here — among others Dinny and Mrs. Gough. They're old identities, and —'

'Aren't I one, meself?' Paddy's eyebrows lifted, and the grin of the urchin who had deserted from his ship and made his way with the first team to Coolgardie, flickered.

'But we've heard all you've got to say about the early days, and I've drawn you lots of times,' Pam objected. 'We like to make friends with new people, and it stands to reason the people we like won't always be the people you like. They never have been.'

'Now, now, me dear, if y're meanin' that disreputable young artist feller —'

'He's my fiancé,' Pam jumped up. 'You've got no right to talk like that about him!'

'Sit down,' Paddy said testily. 'I hoped ye'd be forgettin' him. It was for y'r own good, I didn't like the idea of y'r marryin' him.'

'Well,' Pam went on, 'Pat and I are old enough now to know what's good for us: to choose our own friends, and to marry the men we want to. You mustn't interfere.'

'God damme,' Paddy blustered, 'I'm y'r legal guardian. I've a right to —'

'We'll soon be of age,' Pat flung at him from the window.

'So you will.' The thought wrought a change in Paddy's demeanour. Pam felt she could see his brain working over the changes and complications that fact would bring into his affairs. 'But I hope it won't make any difference to — to our gettin' on well together. You girls are all I've got in the world to care about. Maybe I'm a crusty old curmudgeon, a bit hot-headed and interferin' at times. But I've tried to be a good father to ye —'

'Since when?' Pat interrupted. 'You left us at school for years: didn't care whether we lived or died.'

'Don't be hard on me, Pat.' Paddy's voice trembled. 'Ye know a business man can't call his soul his own, and in those days when I was makin' me way in the world, and had so many irons in the fire I didn't know which way to turn, what was I to do with a pair of kids? I did the best I could for ye, puttin' ye in a good school and gettin' the reverend mother to send me reports regular.'

'You could have come to see us occasionally.'

'That's all past.' Pam was a little vexed with Pat for bringing up their school days just now.

'Afterwards, Amy was good to ye, wasn't she?' Paddy said eagerly. 'We got along pretty well together, all of us, didn't we?'

'Yes,' Pam agreed, 'we were fond of Amy.'

'We want you to understand now,' Pat said impatiently, 'we intend to live our own lives and — '

'What does that mean?' Paddy demanded suspiciously. 'I've given ye plenty of rope, haven't I? Let ye carry on as ye pleased so long as it doesn't interfere with me interests. If ye want to flout me, go ahead. But y'll not get a penny of my money to squander. I'll cut off y'r allowance, I'll — '

Pam's warning glances curbed the angry retort Pat was ready to hurl at him.

'How can you expect us to have any respect for you when you talk like that?' she asked reproachfully.

Paddy mopped his fat red face, sweating profusely in the sultry heat.

'See here,' he said brusquely. 'I don't expect very much — I don't expect ye to to feel about me as I do about you. It's true y're young and ye've got y'r lives before ye. But I've got nobody else in the world to care for, neither kith nor kin. And I'm fond of ye both. When people call ye Paddy Cavan's daughters, I feel as if ye were, and as proud as a turkey cock! If y'll stick to me — if y'll be like daughters ought to be to their old father — y'll have every penny I've got. God knows, I'm not askin' for much — jest a little affection, jest a little consideration. I know I've been a bit over-bearin' in the past — and I'm sorry I spoke the way I did jest now, but I was that lonely and miserable, yesterday, and Wally O'Brien made me boil when he said —'

'You shouldn't have discussed us with Mr. O'Brien,' Pam said.

'God,' Paddy spluttered, 'I thought he was one of y'r boy friends. He came up to see me about a job or something, and stayed talkin'. Mentioned havin' seen ye drivin' out of town with Dinny and Mrs. Gough and that it was a pity you were gettin' so thick with them.'

'What's it got to do with him?' Pat cried angrily.

'It's got this to do with him — and you,' Paddy growled. 'Everybody in this town knows they're no friends of mine.'

'Why?' Pat asked.

As if a wasp had stung him, Paddy shouted:

'How the hell do I know? — except that I've got on in the world, and the Goughs've all been such blasted failures.'

'Wally O'Brien's an immoral young man,' Pam said primly. 'We don't like him, and won't go out with him any more.'

'My God,' Paddy growled, 'how was I to know?'

'He just wanted to upset you and make mischief,' Pam pointed out. 'But Dinny and Mrs. Gough have never said anything to us about you — except that they didn't want to know us at first because we were "Paddy Cavan's daughters".'

Paddy swore, grimacing with pain as a sudden movement jerked his leg.

'Oh, well, they've got reason enough to hate me,' he said sombrely. 'Only I don't want them turning you two against me.'

'You're the only person who could do that,' Pam told him.

'Well, what did ye do? Where did ye go?' Paddy demanded irritably, squirming and wriggling with the pain in his great toe, trying to overcome the unpleasant impression of his first outburst and restore something like amiable relations between himself and his step-daughters.

'Oh, we had a marvellous time,' Pam said chirpily. 'We went to a blacks' camp out near Bulong, and stayed the night at Rill Station. Wait a minute, and I'll show you some of the sketches I made.'

She ran to get her sketch-book.

Paddy contrived something between a grunt and a doleful chuckle.

'Queer idea of a good time some people've got. Spendin' the day in a blacks' camp!'

'Dinny knew some of the natives,' Pat remarked with pacific intentions. 'It was very interesting, talking to them and to some of the old people at Bulong.'

'Hmmmh,' Paddy growled, 'I remember when they struck the first gold there: used to be called I.O.U. Couple of chaps put down a shaft on the ridge, reckoned they'd struck a duffer, and cleared out. Year or two later an old swagman came along and used some of the rock lyin' about to make a wind-break for his camp fire. As he sat eatin' his tucker, the gold glittered out of the rock at him where his fire had been. He did pretty well out of that show — and the Queen Margaret was a good little mine in her day.'

Pam returned with her sketch-book. She pulled her chair up beside Paddy, feeling a little sorry for him, and thinking she could divert and interest him with her drawings.

She turned over the pages, chattering amiably.

'They're very rough sketches, of course, just dashes and out-lines . . . That's Dinny the first day we met him when we were exploring Hannan's Reward claim . . . and those are some miners' cottages out near the Boulder.'

'Y've got Dinny, and no mistake,' Paddy admitted grudgingly. 'And that's Missus Sally, I suppose!' He held back a page as Pam was turning it. 'She used to be better lookin' when I first knew her. A sonsy young woman: had a way with her. The men would've done anything for her. But she stuck to Morrey Gough, as far as I know, though Frisco did make up to her, even in those days. Pity she ever had anything to do with him. He's no good — never will be.'

'There,' Pam said hurriedly, 'that's a group of natives at the camp. Whiskers Johnny, a spinifex man, and Bardoc. Doesn't he look a noble savage? And he seems to be a person of authority in the tribe.'

'God, is he still alive?' Paddy muttered.

'And that's Kalgoorla,' Pam babbled, 'one of the oldest natives in the district, Mrs. Gough says.'

'Thought she was dead, long ago,' Paddy stared at the bold outlines of Pam's drawings as if he were seeing the ghost of these people he had once known. Kalgoorla might have been any old gin in Pam's drawing; but Paddy's fat cheeks became flaccid as he stared at it. A queer, haunted expression stole into his eyes and he breathed heavily. Pam turned the page, fearing some unpleasant memory had disturbed him.

'And that's Ralf,' she said cheerfully, 'with his wife and child. He's an awfully handsome specimen, a stockman on the station.

175

Mrs. Brown says he's a quarter-caste really, though he thinks Bardoc was his father. His mother was Maritana, the native woman who was murdered — '

Paddy dashed the book out of her hands.

'What are ye gettin' at?' he shouted harshly. 'What's y'r game, rakin' all that up and tryin' to make trouble for me. I see it all now! It's Missus Sally put ye up to this, and Dinny Quin. But by God, they've got nothing on me. They can't prove anything. Think ye can trap me, do ye? Think ye can trap Paddy Cavan. By God, I'll show yer! I'll show the whole mob of stinkin' hypocritical swine they can't trap me.'

Pam was gazing at him, terrified by the insane fury that consumed him.

'You're mad,' Pat said sharply. 'We don't know what you're talking about.'

Paddy stared at her, suddenly aware of how far his raving had committed him.

'Yes, I'm mad,' he mumbled. 'It's this pain and all the worries I've got on me mind at present. I've had nothing but worry and trouble since I came back to this damned town. And on top of it all, here's a letter from some shark of a lawyer in Melbourne askin' for a statement of trust funds, invested on behalf of y'r mother, and falling due to the Misses Patricia Mary and Pamela Anne Gaggin. Who the hell does he think he is, puttin' a gun at me head like that? I'll give him all the statements he wants, and a flea in his ear into the bargain. Blasted interferin' nincompoop. And what've ye got to do with it? That's what I'd like to know. Damned ungrateful hussies, tryin' to stab me in the back. Get out of me sight! Get out of me sight the pair of ye!'

'When you're in a more reasonable frame of mind, we'll discuss the position with you,' Pat said coolly, as she and Pam went out of the room.

'Well, ye better pack y'r bags,' Paddy shouted after them. 'We'll be leavin' for Melbourne on the train, the day after tomorrow.'

CHAPTER XVII

In their own room the girls gazed at each other, aghast.

'He thinks he can order us about as he pleases,' Pat burst out. 'We've got to show him he can't!'

Pam, still shocked by the wrath and brutality of Paddy's face when she had mentioned the murder of Maritana, was thinking more of that, than that they were to go away. As if it had been photographed on the sensitive tissue of her brain, Paddy's face, tortured and malevolent, held her in a trance.

'I wish we need never see or speak to him again.' She spoke breathlessly as if by speaking she had broken the tension she was under, and could comprehend that Pat was chiefly concerned about leaving Kalgoorlie. 'But there's Mr. Braithwait's letter. We'd have to go to Melbourne soon.'

'That's all very well,' Pat flung back at her. 'But we needn't go — like this.'

'How much money have you got?'

Pam's mind turned to the practical issue. She was reluctant to oppose Pat; but there was no other way to convince her, at the moment, that they must act cautiously if they were not to put themselves at a disadvantage with Sir Patrick Cavan.

Pat picked up the scarlet satchel which she had thrown on the bed, and turned out its contents.

'Not much more than two pounds,' she exclaimed disgustedly.

'And I've got five pounds, two shillings and seven pence,' Pam reported, having investigated the purse in her satchel. 'My bank account's down to about a fiver. And so is yours, I suppose. If we hadn't sent that money for Shawn's passage to Australia — '

'We had to, of course,' Pat interrupted.

'Well, that settles it, doesn't it?' Pam queried.

'Our allowance will be due next week,' Pat objected.

'But we won't get it if we don't go with Paddy,' Pam pointed out. 'We'll have no money for travelling, later, or paying our board here. And we've got to see Mr. Braithwait, as soon as possible.'

For Pam to take charge of a situation and come to a decision for both of them was quite unusual, but she realized Pat's mind was too full of how going away would affect her relationship with Bill Gough to think about anything else.

'It's insufferable!' Pat snatched a packet of cigarettes from the dressing-table, took out a cigarette herself, and handed the packet to Pam. They lit up and Pat exploded again: 'Why should we put up with his bullying?'

'It won't be for much longer,' Pam reminded her. 'As soon as we get to Melbourne, Mr. Braithwait will be able to arrange a loan for us, and we needn't stay with Paddy after that.'

'But I don't want to leave Kalgoorlie just yet,' Pat cried stormily. 'I don't want to go away until Bill — until Bill and I —'

'I know.' Pam's eyes held the balm of their understanding and feeling for each other. 'But there's nothing else we can do, as far as I can see. Paddy's got the wind up about Braithwait's letter. Suspects, evidently, we're not going to live with him when we have our own money. I've got an idea it's going to be awkward for him to account for the trust funds he's supposed to have invested for us — and he's going to fight handing over more than he can help.'

'You bet he will,' Pat said grumpily.

'Well, we mustn't let him have things all his own way,' Pam insisted. 'The sooner the whole business is settled, the better. After what Paddy said this morning — his crazy rage — there was something horrible behind it, Pat, I feel I can't breathe the same air with him. Before that, he was trying to cajole us into staying with him.'

'I suppose you're right,' Pat conceded. 'But damn him. Damn and blast him, all the same!'

'You're awfully fond of Bill, aren't you, darling?'

'I've never been so het-up about anybody,' Pat admitted angrily. 'And the worst of it is, sometimes I think Bill doesn't care two hoots for me. At first, he didn't want to like us. But lately there's been a look in his eyes, as if he couldn't help being caught in — what there is between us.'

'Of course he is,' Pam said.

'Oh, I don't know.' Pat was thoroughly despondent. 'If we go away, and he hasn't said anything, he'll just get absorbed in his work and forget I ever existed.'

'I don't believe it.' Pam moved across the room to sit beside her and their arms entwined. 'But after all, Bill's about the only man we've met here you could fall for. Perhaps when we go away —'

'Pamela Anne,' Pat pulled away indignantly, 'are you suggesting I've just got a crush on Bill? It doesn't mean much more?'

'You've often been in love before, darling!'

'Not like this!' Pat protested. 'Other men have made love to me. I've never had to do all the wooing myself. And I'm just aching for Bill to say he loves me; but he won't. He's never even kissed me.'

'That's an insult,' Pam murmured, tenderly, derisively.

'It is,' Pat laughed. 'A kiss these days doesn't mean anything, of course. I'm glad Bill doesn't kiss me like that. But I'll be dancing mad if he wants to shake hands when we say goodbye!' Her blithe spirit reasserted itself. 'What are we going to do? Start packing, I suppose.'

'We may as well,' Pam agreed.

'In the morning, we can go to see Dinny and Mrs. Gough,' Pat said, hauling a trunk from under the bed. 'They could give Bill a message to come to the studio in the evening. We'll have the afternoon to fix things up there.'

They made short work of hanging coats and frocks in long travelling-wardrobes, stowing shoes and lingerie into elegant blue leather trunks, sorting books and papers, and pinning hats into their hat boxes. Sir Patrick was dining in his room that night, the waiter informed them when they went down to dinner.

The girls did not see Paddy until breakfast next morning, when he hobbled downstairs and greeted them as if nothing had happened to disturb his jocose urbanity. His gout was better, much better, he assured them.

Pat's and Pam's 'good morning', however, was cool and distant. It brought forth an apology for his ill-humour the day before.

'I'm sorry, me dears, that I was so short wit ye yesterday,' Paddy said ingratiatingly. 'But this cursed gout plays the divil with a man's temper.'

As neither Pat nor Pam replied, he went on:

'I hope I'll not be upsettin' y'r arrangements too much, leavin' Kalgoorlie at such short notice. But I got a wire on Sunday morning about urgent business that's cropped up in Melbourne, and sent word I'd be over on the next train. It's out of the question y'r stayin' in this pub without a chaperone; and I don't like the idea of ye travelling alone.'

The wisp of a smile betrayed Pat's amusement at Paddy's pose of solicitude for her and Pam.

'We're quite ready to go,' she said.

'As a matter of fact, we'll be pleased to get to Melbourne sooner than we expected,' Pam added.

Paddy darted a suspicious glance at her quiet, faintly smiling face, but contented himself by saying: 'Ye'll have a good time there. Be able to entertain and cut quite a dash in Melbourne society.' The twinkle in his eyes was intended to convey good-natured forgiveness for any indiscretions they may have committed here. 'This dead-and-alive hole is no place for the beautiful Miss Gaggins. It'd drive anybody to drink — or gettin' into all sorts of mischief to pass the time.'

During the morning the girls paid Sally a flying visit. They told her and Dinny about Paddy's wrath over the Sunday excursion and his sudden decision to go to Melbourne. Pat did not attempt to disguise her anger at being bustled off like this, or the reason for her reluctance to leave Kalgoorlie.

'I'm sure, whatever he says, Paddy made up his mind to go to

Melbourne at once, because he doesn't want us to be friends with you — and Bill,' she said heatedly.

'Couldn't you refuse to go until you're ready,' Sally asked.

'We haven't got enough money,' Pat wailed.

'Paddy'd stop our allowance,' Pam explained. 'And, in any case, we'd have to go to Melbourne in a month or two.'

'I'll tell Bill you want him to go to the studio tonight,' Sally promised. 'But I hope your going away won't make him too unhappy.'

'You don't believe I love Bill,' Pat cried. 'Nobody does — not even Pam. But I'd rather stay here just to be near him, and see him now and again, than go away and risk losing him altogether.'

'You won't do that, if you really care,' Sally assured her, smiling.

'That's what I tell myself,' Pat said ruefully. 'And I can't let Pam go through all the unpleasantness there's likely to be with Paddy over mother's will, alone, can I?'

'Of course not,' Sally agreed.

They had spent the afternoon in the studio, packing books and pictures. They bought a couple of big cases from one of the stores, and Dinny had come along to nail them down and fasten metal bands round the rough deal boards to hold them securely together. Pam gave him a portrait of herself, and a pastel drawing of Pat for Bill. Dinny was to come, next day, after they had gone, and take away the old chairs and the divan he thought Missus Sally might be able to use.

There were only a few odds and ends to stow in a suitcase when they went back to the studio after dinner that evening. The spirit-lamp, coffee-pot, cups and saucers had been left out for their last supper with Bill, and several books to give him.

The room looked dreary and depressing, with the big packing-cases standing ready for the carrier, the walls bare of Pam's vivid and provocative masterpieces, the furniture deprived of its gay covers and cushions, the Spanish wine jar, every brass bowl and piece of colourful pottery gone from the empty bookshelves. It had been a pleasant place the girls had made for themselves to be at home in during their months on the goldfields. But now, with scraps of rubbish littering the jarrah floor, which had been polished until it shone, and dust everywhere, her studio was no longer the setting for a tender love scene, Pam reflected.

'It looks like a deserted bird's nest,' she lamented. 'A bower bird's nest, with all the broken bits and pieces about.'

Pat was too tired and dispirited now to care where she saw Bill.

Seizing a broom, she swept round the room with vicious, futile energy, while Pam started to paint her name and their destination on the packing-cases. Pat brushed up the rubbish and took the bin into the yard. Returning, she threw herself into a chair, and glanced at her wrist-watch.

'Bill's late,' she exclaimed fretfully. 'You don't think Missus Sally would forget to give him our message, do you, Pam?'

'Oh, I know,' she replied to the lift of Pam's brows and her quizzical glance, 'it's mean of me to suggest it. But after all, she doesn't want Bill to be drawn into anything with me. She hopes there won't be any fond farewells. She still thinks we're just smart young things: only concerned about getting a thrill out of everything.'

'She likes us, though she didn't intend to,' Pam said in a dove-like murmur to soothe Pat. 'I'm sure she'll tell Bill we're expecting him. Don't start imagining things Patsy.'

Pat's eyes closed and she stretched wearily.

'I wonder why we like Bill so much,' Pam ventured, sitting back to survey the bold black strokes of the MISS PAMELA GAGGIN, MELBOURNE, she had painted on the rough yellow boards of a packing-case. She was tempted to attach a symbolic design: add a few birds on the wing, suggestive of the contents and of the wrath to come if any of them were damaged. She set to work gleefully, taking tubes of colour from the paint-box beside her.

'He's not good-looking: not a sex-appeal artist,' Pat exclaimed. 'It's a sort of quality about him, I suppose. Like pure silk, easy on the eye, and lovely to touch — psychologically I mean. I like his mind, his intransigence and honesty; the glint in his eyes — that grin of his, and the way he gets under your skin with a charm that doesn't even know it's there. And he's decent and durable, Bill! You could stack on him.'

'Yes,' Pam agreed, vaguely, intrigued by her illumination of the packing-case. 'But he'd be more satisfactory as a friend, than a lover — or husband, don't you think?'

'I do not,' Pat retorted. 'Bill would be infinitely more satisfactory as a lover, or husband, than Shawn, who's got you all mixed up with his art, and politics.'

'Funny, isn't it?' Pam murmured placidly, busy with a caricature of herself as an infuriated female, in her comic strip. 'That doesn't worry me. I'm so sure of myself and Shawn.'

'Oh, hell!' Pat sprang up and moved restlessly to the window. 'There's ten striking.' She could hear the chimes of the Town Hall clock in the distance. 'What can be keeping Bill?

'I do think he might have tried to come earlier,' she went on. 'P'raps he doesn't want to come! Perhaps he's afraid of giving himself away. Perhaps he'd rather let us go without a word — and cut us out of his life, for ever.'

Pam's little laugh gurgled. 'You sound like the tragedy queen in the last act of a melodrama. Pull yourself together for goodness' sake, my lamb, and do something to your hair. You look a wreck.'

'It's the way I feel!' Pat cried. 'You don't mind being yanked off like this, Pam. But I've been so happy lately. And now — everything's shattered. Oh, damn, damn, damn!'

She flung away from the window.

'I don't care how I look. I don't care about anything! Why doesn't he come? What in the name of blazes is keeping him?'

'Oh dear,' Pam was working on the second case, with a design which amused her, 'I wish we didn't fall in love so drastically.'

'It's awful, isn't it, being in such a dither?' Pat combed back her hair with swift, fierce gestures. 'Not a bit romantic or joy-making.'

'I could brain Bill for not admitting he's madly in love with you,' Pam murmured.

'He's not,' Pat said gloomily. 'That's the worst of it. I wish he were.'

There was a familiar drubbing on the door. Pat sank limply into a chair. Pam went to the door and let Bill in.

'Sorry I'm so late,' he said breezily. 'Had a meeting and couldn't get away sooner.'

He seated himself on the edge of a packing-case, and glanced round him with a wry smile, abashed, a little nervous and defensive.

'Cripes, this is a blow! Gran tells me you had quite a breeze with Sir Patrick about going out with her and Dinny.'

'And being so friendly with that young blackguard, Bill Gough!' Pam exclaimed, giving Pat time to collect her wits.

'Did he bring me into the argument?' It seemed news to Bill that he had anything to do with their departure.

'He did,' Pat said dryly. 'Dective-Sergeant Smattery informed him we were going about with one of the worst red raggers in the town.'

'I'm sorry, Pat.' Bill's brow ruckled. 'I'd hate to think I've made things awkward for you.'

'Don't worry about that,' Pat said impatiently, curled into her chair and regarding him with tragic eyes. 'The only thing we're worried about is being bundled off in a hurry — and saying goodbye to you, Bill.'

'It's tough luck,' Bill spoke as if he were trying to evade the personal implication. 'Is there anything I can do for you?' he added cheerily. 'Any packing or clearing up?'

'You could try to look a little more concerned about saying goodbye — even if you don't feel it,' Pat said bitterly.

She wished she knew how much Missus Sally had told him of what she had said that morning. But instinctively she realized Missus Sally would not betray her confidence. Bill's demeanour was guileless of any self-consciousness or compassion.

184

'I feel it, Pat,' he said quietly. 'You know that. But I've got to crack hardy.'

Pat stared at him with rebellious eyes.

'I don't want to go, Bill,' she said. 'I don't want to go away from you.'

Bill did not pretend to misunderstand; but apparently he was determined to maintain a non-committal attitude.

'We've been good pals, Pat,' he said unsteadily, and attempting to be facetious. 'I'll be grateful to Paddy Cavan for one thing, at least. That's bringing you here.'

His grin glimmered, infuriating Pat. Was that all she had meant to him, she asked herself. A good pal? He wouldn't even say a good comrade, which would have meant more to him and to her. He knew — he must have felt, she assured herself — the subtle magnetic current between them, the response of her whole being to his nearness, the joyous tumult which possessed her when he came into a room and his eyes sought hers. It was only tonight he had shut himself off from her, and looked so stubborn and grim.

To gain time and break down his reserve, she said defiantly.

'He's a wicked old man — and after the way he spoke to us yesterday, I feel sure he's got something on his mind, worse than anything else we know about him.'

'Who was Maritana?' Pam asked.

'That's an old story,' Bill said. 'She was a native girl gran knew when she first came to the goldfields. Later, she married a white man, at least she was living with him and they had a swag of kids. He was supposed to be in charge of a treatment plant out in the bush. Maritana used to collect gold for him. There was a case in which granddad and Uncle Tom were charged with being in possession of gold suspected of being stolen. Gran swears Paddy Cavan framed them. And Maritana, it seems, threatened to give evidence which would be awkward for Paddy, who everybody knew was associated with the Big Four in the gold ring. But Maritana disappeared: her body was found months afterwards in an abandoned shaft. Her husband cleared out at about the same time — and it's always been suspected that he killed Maritana — although Paddy had something to do with the row there was between them before Maritana's death. Dinny says the men who know something about it reckon Paddy told Fred Cairns to send Maritana bush and see that she kept her mouth shut. There was only one way he could do it, evidently.'

Pam shuddered.

'I knew there was something horrible about Paddy's memory of that name. He just went mad when I showed him a sketch of Ralf, the stockman on Rill Station, who they say is Maritana's son.'

'And that's the sort of man we've called daddy,' Pat exclaimed. 'He's afraid people here have been telling us about him, Bill. But as a matter of fact they haven't. We didn't know why Dinny and Mrs. Gough hate him so much — except on account of Amy. But we're beginning to understand.'

'There's much more to Sir Patrick Cavan's record on the goldfields than that,' Bill said. 'I'll be glad when you don't have to live with him.'

'So will we,' Pat assured him.

'You've no idea what lonely, uncared-for brats we were at that school in England,' Pam said. 'When we went to live with Paddy and Amy, we were so pleased to belong to anybody, and somehow we've always been trying to accommodate ourselves to the sort of people we were with. Amy's society crowd, and Shawn's friends. And now, here, meeting you and Mrs. Gough and Daphne and her mother, we feel as if, for the first time, we could be ourselves and have the sort of friends we need. Kind and sincere people we can love, and who'd love us, perhaps, if they knew us better.'

'I'm sure they would,' Bill said. It was easier to express his affection for Pam than for Pat.

There was no danger in the glances they exchanged. The flow in the sympathy between them was tacit and peaceful. But Pat's eyes played the very devil with him, alluring and taunting him to swim in their grey-green depths until he almost drowned in them, hearing the siren song she sang to him there. He had dragged himself from its enchantment only by the skin of his teeth, Bill told himself; but he could not deny that the shape of her head, the sweep of her eyelashes, every line and curve that was Pat, were inexpressibly lovely and dear to him.

'Man's love is from his life a thing apart,' Bill believed. That went for woman too. He did not intend to allow any sexual-cum-sentimental weakness to interfere with his work. Pat knew that. They had discussed and laughed at the romantic illusion they called 'loove': willing to admit delirious emotions conjured up by the biological urge, and that there might be imperious psychological affinities involved; but to be trapped into admitting themselves the victims of a confidence trick which had been played on generations of young people, was another matter.

It was not the urge and affinity part of what was called love they rejected, but the illusions, bargains and fantastic conception that two people could mean more to each other than anything else in the world, for ever and ever, amen. Why did young people laugh at sloppy sentiment on the films and in the theatre? Why did they deride romances in which the young couple lived happily ever after? They were children of their generation, and had learnt that love which was supposed to transmute life to a paradisaical existence was a myth. A pleasant interlude this delightful sensation of tenderness and desire might give. But to let it interfere with any serious purposes they might have, sheer stupidity! Yet, here they were, both caught in a hunger for each other, the recognition of a joyous entente, and a devastating misery, because they were going to be separated.

Pam left them together. As the door closed behind her, she could hear Bill saying:

'I'm not going to say goodbye to you, Pat.'

'Do you want me to come back? Do you really, Bill?' Pat asked eagerly.

Their voices followed Pam as she sat on the doorstep which led down into a dry and neglected garden.

'Of course I do,' Bill said heartily.

'Listen, Bill,' Pat sounded distraught and angry, 'it's no use putting on an act with me. If you've got a martyr complex, I haven't. As soon as you came in I knew you'd made up your mind to let me go away without saying a word to show you care for me, or that you know I care for you.'

'Not quite that.' Bill's voice had its beguiling charm. 'I can't believe you do, and that this between us matters very much to you.'

'Oh, it does! It does, Bill,' Pat protested. 'I feel all torn and bleeding at the thought of leaving you — and nothing being settled between us. It's hurting you, too, I know. Don't be so hard on us. Give me a chance to be all you want, Bill.'

There was silence in the room behind her for a moment. Pam lighted a cigarette and gazed out into the starlit darkness. She hoped Bill had dropped the queer restraint with which he had armed himself, and that Pat was seducing him to a more loverly attitude. She had no doubt Pat would put her arms round him and try a little physical nearness to win him from any decision to exclude her from his mind and work.

Bill's voice, strangled and husky, reached her.

'It's no use . . . I couldn't live your life, and you couldn't live mine, Pat. Better to realize that, now, than let bitterness and disappointment break us by and by.'

'You don't trust me! You don't believe in me,' Pat wailed.

'No,' Bill agreed.

'Damn you! Damn and blast you!' Pat cried. 'I hate you. I hate myself for having been such a fool about you. You think I've just got a pash for you that won't last. P'raps you're right. P'raps that's how it is. You win, Bill. Better go now. Sorry to have embarrassed you: made it hard for you to turn me down. Goodbye.'

'Pat!' Bill's voice was broken and pleading. 'Don't say that . . . Don't say I —'

'Go — for goodness' sake,' Pat cried hysterically, and on the verge of tears.

Pam heard the door open and shut. She rose from the step as Bill stumbled towards her, his face wrung by a pain he could not hide. It told her all she wanted to know.

'Go back at once and tell her you love her, or I'll never forgive you, Bill,' she said with an intensity Bill obeyed automatically.

When he went back into the room, Pat was crumpled up in the chair where he had left her, sobbing tempestuously. Filled with compunction and tenderness Bill squatted beside her and put his hand on her hair.

'Pat, darling,' he said huskily, 'I do love you. I can't leave you like this.'

Pat's sobbing abated. Presently she sat up, blowing her nose and looking at him with tear-drenched eyes.

'Devil, aren't you?' she queried, trying to smile. 'That was all I wanted you to say. Never thought I could be such a dill as to cry about any man. We don't cry, do we, Pam, unless we're really up against things?'

Pam had come in and was making coffee on the spirit-lamp.

'We cried when Shawn went away,' she said in her literal fashion. 'And when we heard he was wounded.'

'I was so concerned about myself — being able to hold out against you,' Bill confessed, trying to atone to Pat for having hurt her. 'Didn't realize I was being —'

'Clumsy and cruel,' Pam interpolated.

'A woman scorned, that's how I felt,' Pat declared jerkily, determined to make a joke of her tears. 'I should have demonstrated that hell hath no fury, etc., shouldn't I, Pam, instead of just weeping?'

'Cripes, I ought to be pole-axed.' Bill looked contrite and wretched. 'We got at cross purposes somehow: each pulling our own way, and not trying to understand the other's point of view. I meant all I said, Pat, but I didn't say all I meant. I do love you and want you to be with me. But it can't be, because — '

'Don't say it again,' Pat implored. 'All I want is to know you love me, Bill. The rest's up to me.'

She put her arms round him and their lips met in a kiss which closed the subject very satisfactorily, Pam thought. The magic between them had its innings at any rate. Moving quietly in the background, Pam was sure of that. She heard murmurs of: 'Darling!' 'My sweet!' 'Oh, Pat!' and 'Bill!' as if the language of love were reduced to these muted exclamations and murmured endearments.

'As soon as things are fixed up, and we can do what we like,' Pat said, after a while, 'I'll come back, Bill — that is, if you want me to.'

Bill smiled into the depths of her eyes.

'Will you?' he murmured. 'I wonder.'

'There you are.' Pat tore herself away from him. 'You don't really believe I love you. But I'll come back, whether you want me to or not.'

'Listen, darling,' Bill said. 'Love's a big word. I've been afraid to admit it's the only one that fits what I feel for you. But we know love's not all it's supposed to be. At the moment, we feel the joy and sweetness of having found we belong to each other. We've had a little bit of something that neither of us will ever forget. But — '

'That's idealistic tommy rot,' Pat said furiously. 'I don't want to be just a bit of glory in your life. I want to live and work with you, Bill. I want to be with you always, sharing everything that happens to us. You can't divorce me before we're married.'

'The worst of it is,' Bill grinned, 'I ought to be firm now, and say you're romanticizing.'

'You believe I'm just "a slim gilt soul", as they used to say in London,' Pat wailed. 'But I'll show you, Bill. I'll show you I can be just as staunch as Pam — and she's never thought of another man since she knew Shawn. At least he gave her a chance. But you'd like to just turn me down and say: "Not today, thank you. Some day, perhaps, if I'm not otherwise engaged." '

'Or you're not.'

'Time!' Pam called, as if she were umpiring a fight and came towards them with two cups of coffee.

'Here's your coffee, and stop quarrelling both of you!'

Bill stood up and took a cup of coffee from her for Pat, the other he held shakily for himself.

Pam stretched up to kiss him. 'You're the sort of brother I've dreamed of, Bill, dear,' she whispered. 'Don't disappoint me, will you?'

CHAPTER XVIII

'NORA needs a holiday,' Sally said brusquely.

Having finished his dinner Frisco had lighted a cheroot and was leaning back in his chair, fagged and thoughtful.

'A holiday?' Frisco exclaimed in consternation. 'What on earth would I do without her?'

'You could get another girl, temporarily,' Sally replied, conscious of twinges she did not like because anybody else could be so indispensable to him. At the same time, she realized Nora was necessary to the effective running of Frisco's office: doing something for him that she, herself, could never do, and largely responsible for the success of his business. She was grateful to the girl, she assured herself; and really concerned about her health.

Nora had been working for Frisco without a break, since the opening of his office, soon after granting of the gold bonus. She was looking worn out and so nervy, now, Sally was afraid she would not be able to carry on unless something was done to relieve the strain she was working under. 'Nora could arrange to train another girl,' she suggested. 'I feel she'll crack up, if you don't make things easier for her.'

'I'll have a word with her about it,' Frisco promised, disturbed by the idea.

But Nora would not hear of taking a holiday. She was upset at the thought of handing her work over to anybody else. Frisco compromised with an office boy to do some of the running about for her.

'I'm all right, Mrs. Gough,' Nora said earnestly next time Sally saw her. 'Really I am. I couldn't leave Colonel de Morfé just now. As a matter of fact no one else could handle things for him. There's too much important business to deal with. I've got to remind him about so many matters in connection with it — and see he doesn't get into difficulties. By and by, when things are slack, I can take a holiday.'

'You're very good to him, Nora,' Sally said gently. 'I don't know what on earth he would do without you.' The girl knew more about Frisco's commitments and financial position than she did, she realized. 'Let me know if I can help you in any way.'

'Thank you, Mrs. Gough, I will,' Nora said meekly. But her mind tightened and closed, Sally saw, at the idea that a reliable secretary could in any way betray her employer's confidence.

Nevertheless, Nora was worried and anxious on Frisco's account, Sally divined. She had let slip that word 'difficulties'. What did it mean? Was he getting out of his depths in the dangerous whirlpool of the share market?

Frisco brushed aside her fears.

'I'm not in the running for any big deal,' he said. 'Besides, once bitten twice shy.'

'You've been bitten more than once,' Sally reminded him.

'Don't rub it in,' Frisco replied.

The first period of spurious prosperity which had been brought about by the gold bonus and a fever of speculation was waning, Sally knew.

There had been quite a stir about the American Gold Bill in 1934. It fixed the gold content of the dollar and was hailed as a measure to nationalize gold. An order of the Secretary of the United States' Treasury required gold coins to be turned into the Federal Reserve by a certain date and authorized the banks to confiscate any presented later by individuals. It was understood that confiscated money would revert to the government as part payment of the penalty for violation of the gold regulations. This penalty was to be double the value of the gold held. There had been almost unanimous support for the bill, the most conservative elements of Congress backing it, so that threats of an inflation revolt had been withdrawn.

Dinny and his friends chewed over the significance of this move. Frisco thought he knew the answer, but was too busy with his own affairs to argue with Dinny about it, just then.

Goldfields people were concerned that the flotation of 'wild cats' which had been a feature of the recent prosperity, and the tying-up of large areas in the interests of overseas capital, would deprive the community of much of the benefit they had anticipated from the bonus.

Mr. Norbert Keenan, in the Legislative Assembly, had drawn attention to the recent epidemic of 'wild cats.' He said that he could not recall anything in the history of the mining industry more calculated to breed mistrust than many flotations of the past two years. Not only had the public been offered so-called mines on which little or no exploratory work had been done, but mere options over wide areas in their virgin state had been put on the market.

Business men in Kalgoorlie and Boulder agreed with him that exploitation should be regulated and kept within bounds. They considered that the Minister for Mines should refuse to register the transfer of any mining property until certain conditions were complied with. One of these conditions, they believed, should require a statement of the names of all parties who had an interest in a property, and that the price at which the property had been acquired, and was being passed on, should be furnished to the proper authorities.

When the price of gold began to soar, it was considered, there was no justification for the granting of huge reservations. The price of gold was sufficient to induce reputable companies to take leases on ordinary terms, without permitting the holding-up of thousands of acres when there was phenomenal prospecting activity. The holders of some reservations may have brought a fair amount of capital into the country, but there was no doubt better results would have been obtained if ground had been left open to prospectors and companies satisfied to take up two or three claims in twenty-four-acre leases.

'Auriferous areas of the state will never be developed,' Mr. Keenan protested, 'by companies permitted to hold-up huge areas indefinitely while actual work is confined to a few acres.'

Nobody knew the rackets being worked off on unsuspecting shareholders better than Frisco, Sally was certain. He had told her about some of them. How the reports of two mining experts had been introduced into the prospectus of one company, giving details of a surface ore body four feet wide extending for two hundred feet through a lease, and yielding an average of from four to six pennyweights. But there was no mention of the fact that a shaft already existed on lode to a depth of fifty feet with drives a hundred feet north and south, and samples taken from them disclosed only two 'weight ore. After making two or three calls the mine was abandoned; but some smart manipulators had been able to rake off several thousands before the company ceased operations.

On another mine, a report of large tonnage and high values indicated the possibility of profitable production for fifty years. Shares jumped from threepence to one and ninepence. After three months' operations the phenomenal deposit had not been located. Shares stood at 'sellers one penny' and shareholders were left lamenting.

'How can you be mixed up in such a rotten business,' Sally asked indignantly.

'Knowing the ropes and beating the smart alecs gives me a lot of satisfaction,' Frisco admitted. 'If only I can queer Paddy Cavan's pitch for him, now and again, I'll die happy. Since I've been back in the game, I've heard some pretty crook deals Paddy's put over lately.'

'Don't let him have another crack at you, for goodness' sake,' Sally pleaded.

'No chance of that,' Frisco replied. 'I'm too small fry for him to bother about these days.'

All the same, Sally was apprehensive of the grip his old interests were taking on Frisco. He went back to the office almost every night, and was restless and ill at ease when it was closed over the week-end.

When Sir Patrick Cavan arrived in Kalgoorlie, Frisco wondered what had brought him. The need to convey a soothing report to the English directors of some of the companies with which he was associated, Frisco suspected; or to boost some recently acquired leases.

By increased production, the established companies would benefit by the bonus within two years, it was estimated, and meantime the premium on gold arising out of the exchange rate should provide a sufficient profit to justify reorganizing their plants. To be sure, they had made promises of individual expansion during the bonus campaign, and the industry depended on the fulfilment of these promises. But the big proprietary companies had not put as vigorous an effort into improving the gold yield and raising the bonus to a level which would make it of as much value as was expected.

Sally no longer dropped into Frisco's office as often as she had once done. He and Nora seemed to be so busy always, and reluctant to waste any time talking to her. On several occasions she had run into Mrs. Rooney, either taking a cup of tea to Colonel de Morfé, or returning with the empty cup. Sally could not get over an aversion she felt whenever she saw this fat, jolly, middle-aged woman, whose flat adjoined Frisco's office, although Mrs. Rooney was always very affable to her.

Nora, too, did not like Mrs. Rooney, Sally gathered. She would sometimes meet Mrs. Rooney at the door, take the tea from her and say Colonel de Morfé was busy: he could not be disturbed. Frisco laughed at Mrs. Rooney's attentions and treated them as a joke. She was 'a silly little woman, but kind-hearted', he said. Lately, though, he had taken to calling her Beulah.

It was quite useful to be on friendly terms with Mrs. Rooney, Frisco explained. She could often pass on tips Old Lindsay had given her about inner manipulations of the share market.

Frisco had his own sources of information, naturally; but it was just as well to keep track of what a shrewd speculator like Gordon P. Lindsay was up to. Beulah had a little money to invest, herself, and liked to dabble in shares. She attached more importance to Frisco's opinion than Mr. Lindsay's, apparently — which added to the humour of the situation as Frisco saw it.

CHAPTER XIX

WHEN Sally went down to the coast at the end of the summer, she explained that Marie and she had been promising each other this holiday together for years. Now, Marie was saying, she and Daphne would be coming home soon, and if Sally didn't join them, those days at the sea Marie and she had dreamed of might never happen.

'Do go, gran,' Eily pleaded. 'I can take the children over to your place: look after the boarders and Dinny and Frisco.'

'I wish you could go instead, my dear,' Sally said, still uneasy about not telling Eily her real reason for going to Cottesloe that month.

But it was out of the question for her to get away, Eily protested. La was studying for a scholarship this year and had to be helped with his lessons: Nadya was reading too much and must be chased out of doors to play more. Eily was very busy with the unemployed organization as well, addressing cottage meetings: trying to keep the League for Peace and Democracy together, and helping girls in the Waitresses's Union to improve their conditions.

Sally knew how important all this work was to Eily; but she knew too how eager Eily would have been to go to Daphne had she known Daphne's baby was expected within a few weeks.

Those days Sally spent at Cottesloe stretched into a month. When she came home, she said Daphne had got a job in one of the seaside cafés and wanted to keep it for a while. But the fact of the matter was, she told Bill, Daphne refused to be parted from her son. At first she could not endure the sight of him; she had been disappointed the baby was not a girl, and wept and wailed for fear the child would be like his father. But, gradually, her pity and tenderness had been aroused, and now she was the most devoted of young mothers. She would not hear of the baby being adopted, or even for Sally or Marie to take him home and look after him. So Marie had found a decent old woman to live with Daphne and mind the baby while she was at work.

'The only thing troubling Daphne now,' Sally smiled happily, 'is that her mother doesn't know. "I feel we're not being fair to her, gran," she said. "No one's more loving and understanding than mum. It was better not to tell her when she was so broken up about dad. But we shouldn't keep it from her now." Of course, I agree with Daph,' Sally concluded. 'Eily ought to know.'

'Eily's still got a lot of worries to contend with,' Bill demurred. 'Dick's one of them.'

'Dick?'

'He never comes to see her. He's broken completely with all of us. He and his wife are living with her father in a bungalow at Lamington. Eily went to see Dick the other day, and I've never seen her so angry as when she came home. She says . . . well, it's difficult to explain . . . but some men who weren't known as communists were sacked from the Golden Star a week or so ago. Eily must have suspected Dick had something to do with it. She accused him, evidently, and he denied it, but looked so shifty and self-conscious, she knew he was guilty. He admitted afterwards that he had told Langridge who were "possible trouble-makers" on the mine. And defended himself by saying he'd do the same thing again. He's got to "safeguard the interests of the company".'

Sally exclaimed incredulously.

'Eily was very broken up about it,' Bill went on. 'She insisted on telling the committee and criticizing herself for carelessness, because Dick had seen the comrades when they came to meetings at home. She's so conscientious and unsparing of herself. I tell her not to worry; but she feels responsible for those men losing their jobs; and that they'll get the black alley on every mine on the fields.'

'It's too bad,' Sally was fuming. 'My poor Eily!'

'The bosses are scared of men likely to try to improve conditions on the mines,' Bill said. 'There's nothing in the work of the Communist Party of Australia on the goldfields, or anywhere else in this country, that's illegal, or need be hidden, except the names of members who might be tramped like this. Eily feels she's got to work harder than ever to make people understand that.'

'It breaks my heart to see her,' Sally said. 'She walks miles, I'm sure, distributing papers and leaflets round the town, like she used to with Tom. But she looks so sad and frantic, as if she must keep on doing what they used to do together. I wish she'd go down and stay for a while with Daphne —'

'That's it,' Bill whooped. 'Daph could tell Eily about the baby. It would be good for both of them. We'll fix it, gran; push Eily off as soon as possible.'

Eily was on her way before the end of the month. Daphne had written, hinting she was in some trouble and needed Eily's advice and help. Sally said she would love to have La and Nadya and Bill with her for a while, and Bill promised to look after her work and committees. So Eily had packed a small suitcase, and gone off in a couple of days, concerned only about what was distressing Daphne.

Sally heaved a sigh of relief, and felt she could rid herself of any compunction about have deceived Eily when she read the letter which came from Daphne a few days later.

'Mum was wonderful,' Daphne wrote. 'I met her at the station, and we had a good talk and a cry before we went to the cottage. Tommy did the rest. She's as much in love with him now as I am. It means a lot to her that I called him after dad. He's getting so fat and jolly, gran, gurgles and spits all over me. And mum says she's glad I don't want to be separated from him.'

When Eily came home, she looked so much better that Bill and Sally congratulated themselves on the success of their strategy. Eily had regained her normal sweet smile, and capacity for finding hope and happiness wherever they gleamed.

'I wanted Daph to come back with me and let me mind baby while she's at work,' Eily said. 'But she thinks it's better not for a while. By and by she'll come home. We're not going to allow anybody to think we're ashamed of this baby.'

'I should think not,' Sally retorted, up in arms at the idea. 'But it's going to be hard for Daphne to take all the grins and gossip.'

'Daph's a very different girl than she was before this happened,' Eily said. 'More serious and responsible. I've got you and Marie and Bill to thank for that, gran. You helped her to stand up to everything and pull through like she has done.'

'Daphne's got grit,' Sally said warmly. 'Tom would have been proud of her.'

'He would, wouldn't he?' Eily's eyes brightened. 'I used to be very impatient with Daph sometimes. But Tom always said: "She'll be all right, Daph. She's got good stuff in her."'

During the winter, Daphne came home, bringing the baby, because he had been ailing and she was anxious about him.

La and Nadya were wildly excited when they heard that they had become an uncle and aunt. They asked all the questions Eily expected. She told them quite simply the baby's father did not want him, and that Daphne had changed her mind about liking the baby's father, so he had gone away. No, Daphne had not been married to him, and some people thought it was a disgrace for a girl to have a baby without being married.

'But,' Eily said, 'I believe, and so does gran, that motherhood is sacred, however it happens. No matter what anybody says we'll and look after Daph's baby, won't we?'

La was old enough to understand her explanation better than Nadya.

'Too right, we will,' he said.

And Nadya exclaimed happily:

'You know, I've been asking you for ages to get a baby, mum. And you haven't done anything about it. But now we can have Daph's, so you needn't bother.'

Of course tongues wagged when Daphne came home with a baby in her arms. The gossips had a good innings. But Wally O'Brien had left Kalgoorlie, and whatever scandalmongering there was, did not affect the usual kindly attitude of goldfields folk to a girl who had been 'left in the lurch by some blackguard', as they put it.

Daphne was as proud of her baby as any other young mother going about with a plump, rosy infant in his pram. And there were hundreds of young mothers taking their babies for walks in push carts and perambulators along the earthen footpaths and asphalt pavements round about Boulder city. Daphne's baby had as pretty fixings in his pram as any other baby, a downy blue blanket, embroidered pillow case and coverlet. He was as daintily clad, and as fresh and sweet as the most pampered of the youngest set.

Friends and neighbours nodded and smiled to Daphne as she passed with her pram. If now and then she caught a sour or disapproving glance, it did not disturb her. There were so many cheery and good-natured greetings as she walked along. Men and women would stop and say: 'Hullo Daph!' 'Glad to see you home again!' 'How's the little feller?' 'My, he's coming on fine, isn't he?' 'Tell your mother I'll be coming round to see her soon.'

'How kind they are,' Daphne exclaimed to her mother. 'I've never taken much notice of most of these people; and they go out of their way to say something nice to me.'

'Goldfields folk are like that,' Eily said. 'They've been through so much themselves, the working people, they like to show their friendliness when they think you may need it.'

'It's a good deal on your account people are being so kind to me,' Daphne demurred. 'Everybody comes and pours out their troubles to you, mum. You've helped so many.'

'Nothing of the sort,' Eily protested. 'You're just one of them, and they'd stand by you through thick and thin.'

'I had no idea there was so much suffering and trouble all round us.' Daphne's young face became overcast and thoughtful. 'Just fancy Mrs. Young with cancer of the stomach and a crook heart, as she says herself, nursing a husband dying of T.B! And old Mrs. Colquhoun, over eighty, crippled with rheumatism, and nearly blind, bringing up Mabel's four children. And now — she was telling me yesterday — Jack's wife has left him, and he's brought his little boy for her to look after. "It's a shame, Mrs. Colquhoun," I said. "You shouldn't have to work so hard at your age." "What does it matter, dearie?" she said. "I haven't got much longer to live, and a little extra work won't make any difference." '

Eily's brow furrowed. 'I must go over and see what I can do for her.'

'And there's Mrs. Tudor — ' Daphne was trying to express a new perception of the way people were living round about her, Eily realized — 'with her only son a nervous wreck from the war, laughing crazily day and night! She's afraid to let him out of her sight. Hardly ever leaves the house, looks like a ghost and almost insane herself after looking after Paul all these years. And Mrs. Stubbs who went up to Coolgardie for her mother's funeral, last week, and came home to find her husband had been injured in an accident on the mines and lost both his legs.'

Eily was afraid the troubles of her neighbours were having too depressing an effect on Daphne.

'Don't forget Mrs. McNab,' she said lightly. 'She came in this morning to complain of the way Mrs. Colquhoun's goats are always breaking into her garden. And that Frankie — he's her youngest son and the only one at home with her now — is "carryin' on" with a fat, lazy trollop who's got four children! The husband is likely to come home from Wiluna any time, start a brawl and land Frankie with this woman and the four children! Mrs. McNab is sure she'll have the lot to cope with.'

'Oh, dear!' Daphne laughed; but her eyes still held the shadow of her thoughfulness. 'How on earth you can smile, and keep going, mum, I don't know.'

'There's nothing else to do,' Eily said cheerily. 'If I didn't laugh sometimes, and feel there's something to work and hope for, other people's troubles would get me down. Your father used to say he never ceased to marvel at the heroism of ordinary people. So although there's so much suffering and sorrow round about us, and very little we can do to help, I try to look beyond it all, and organize for a better way of life.'

'Oh, mum,' Daphne's eyes lighted with the love which had grown between them, 'if only I could be more like you.'

WHITE-COLUMNED eucalyptus, kurrajongs with great bouquets of satiny green leaves, pepper trees trailing pink berries in long drifts, enclosed the gardens that were an oasis in Kalgoorlie. They were full of birds, little warblers, honey-eaters and doves whose cooing, chirruping, long fluting notes and cadenzas vibrated through the sunshine of any afternoon in early summer.

Sally loved the gardens, and would go whenever she could to sit there for an hour or so listening to the birds, and delighting in the plots of wallflowers and pansies, marigolds and roses which made bright posies on lawns over which wide-armed sprays swished ceaselessly. Particularly if she were worried, or depressed. There was always some old-timer with whom she could chat if she felt inclined. Children playing about on the grass, whose games she could watch and smile over: the old swimming pool near by where thousands of goldfields youngsters had learnt to swim, her own lads among them. The Turk's cap of the band-stand, shawled with bougainvillea in virulent magenta bloom, reminded her of the time when she and Frisco used to come to the gardens like a pair of young lovers. They had often laughed about the Turk's cap, and the new coat of silver paint it got occasionally.

That was one of the things distressing her, Sally realized. Frisco never had time to come to the gardens with her now. More and more he had become absorbed in his office and business, and, since she had returned from the coast, Sally was afraid all was not going well with them. Frisco had been drinking more than usual. She was as concerned about that as his financial position. He had never been a man who drank for the sake of drinking. His drinking, she suspected, was to cover some mental unrest. Dinny thought that too.

'If Frisco's come a cropper, share-dealin', you'd ought to

'know about it, missus,' he said. 'It's got my goat the way he's comin' home boozed, and worryin' the soul-case out of you.'

She had got to tackle Frisco about it, Sally decided, after she had been sitting in the gardens a while, thinking what she should do. The sooner she knew the actual state of his affairs the better. There might still be time to extricate him from any mess he might have got into.

She shook out her skirts and walked quickly towards the gate. It clapped behind her, and the wide bare streets in the glare of hot sunshine struck her eyes, as if she had been dreaming in the shadowy peace and beauty of the gardens.

Frisco was out when she reached his office. Nora said she did not know where he had gone, or when he would return. She seemed a little flustered, Sally thought; did not want her to wait. But Sally had made up her mind that what she had to say to Frisco must be said immediately. It must be said while she felt the need was urgent. She thought, too, she might get some idea from Nora whether Frisco's financial position was as critical as she feared.

'I wouldn't wait, if I were you, Mrs. Gough,' Nora said, obviously anxious to get rid of her visitor.

For that reason, Sally's behind settled firmly into her chair. Nora was sniffling: her eyelids red-rimmed. She shuffled her papers as if to intimate to Mrs. Gough that she was very busy and irritated by her presence. But Sally had no intention of moving until she found out what was the matter with Nora. Nora had been like this before if Frisco was out when she called unexpectedly, uneasy and nervous about her being in the office.

'I wouldn't wait, Mrs. Gough,' Nora repeated fretfully. 'Colonel de Morfé may be a long time. I've just remembered he had an important engagement and —'

'What on earth's the matter with you, Nora?' Sally asked. 'You've been crying.'

'It's nothing,' the girl replied nervously. 'I must be getting a cold or something. But I wouldn't wait, Mrs. Gough, I really wouldn't.'

'You said that last time I came,' Sally reminded her. 'What is the matter, Nora? I know things haven't been going too well in the office lately. Business has fallen off and you're worried. I am too. If I knew what the position really is, perhaps I could help.'

'You couldn't,' Nora almost sobbed.

For a moment, she looked as if she were going to break down and confide in Sally the cause of her unhappiness about Colonel de Morfé and his affairs. But she pulled herself together: her back stiffened and her mouth set in taut lines.

'I'm sorry,' she said steadily, 'but I really can't discuss Colonel de Morfé's business with you or anybody, Mrs. Gough. Excuse me, please. I have some work to do. If you'll come back in an hour, Colonel de Morfé might be in.'

'What nonsense, Nora,' Sally replied. 'You're not busy. And you haven't got any work to do. I noticed it when I came in. I've noticed, once or twice, when I've called lately, that you're listless and depressed — and pretending to be busy. Is that what's worrying you? It's worrying me too. The office doesn't seem to be going as well as it did. Goodness knows I don't want Colonel de Morfé to get into difficulties, if I can use any influence I've got with him to prevent it. Don't you realize that, you silly girl? Or is it too late for us to do anything?'

'I do realize you want to help him, Mrs. Gough,' Nora cried distractedly. 'I do realize it! But you don't understand, it's as much for your sake as his I'm concerned. Please go now, and I'll get Colonel de Morfé to make an appointment with you. Then you can ask him all the questions you like, and — and advise him to close the office, perhaps.'

'I'll sit here till he comes in, if I have to wait all night,' Sally said quietly.

She was really alarmed. If Nora thought the office ought to be closed things must be in a bad way.

'I wish you wouldn't,' Nora said miserably. She put paper and carbon in her typewriter and set the keys clacking at a frantic pace.

Sitting on her chair near the window, Sally was angry and resentful of Nora's attitude. Paint had blistered on the wooden frames, flies buzzed drearily on the dim, bleary pane. Hot sunshine beat against it, drenching a back-yard cluttered with overflowing garbage tins and rusty machinery; a dirty white cat prowled among them. Sally would have liked to open the window, but that would have been an unwarrantable interference with the law and order of Nora's domain: send her papers flying if a breath of wind stirred. And the last thing she wanted to do, Sally assured herself, was to give Nora the impression she was interfering in any way with her rights in this office. She admired the girl, had a genuine affection for her: was grateful for the devotion she lavished on Frisco, and for the capable way she looked after his business interests.

Sally thought Nora was aware of the friendly, sympathetic feeling she had for her, and regretted the antagonism which had cropped up between them this afternoon. Was it because Nora was in love with Frisco and jealous of her, Sally wondered. Perhaps that had something to do with it. She was jealous, anyhow, of her rights in this office, and her knowledge of Frisco's business. Sally could concede her those rights and appreciate her loyalty. But latterly, she had been bringing Frisco home late at night, the worse for too many drinks. He was supposed to have been attending some business meeting, of course; but, after all, it was going a little too far for a young girl to be running about after a drunken man at all hours.

Yet she could not be jealous of Nora, Sally told herself. There was something too idealistic and selfless about the services Nora rendered Frisco. Sally did not believe Nora's attachment to him could affect the relationship between herself and Frisco. That had become as taken for granted and well-established as if they were married. Nora, like everybody else, accepted it as a matter of course. Sally had hoped Nora did not feel any personal hostility to her, and rather that they had achieved a curious sympathy for each other because of their devotion to Colonel de Morfé. But why had Nora been so agitated and almost rude to her this afternoon? Why was Nora so anxious for her to go away and not wait for Frisco to return?

The typewriter made a busy clatter; but now and then, when Nora's flying fingers paused, Sally thought she could hear voices in the flat next door. Once, she caught a rumble of laughter. The typewriter rattled over it. Again, there was smothered laughter: a man and a woman were laughing together. The typewriter crashed against it. But that laugh rose above all the noise Nora could make. It was a short, gusty laugh Sally knew well. Frisco's laugh, although muted and restrained. Was he somewhere in the building? Sally could feel Nora's glance straying to her. Nora banged frantically on her typewriter, trying to drown out every other sound. But it was Frisco's voice Sally heard in an exclamation that twanged on her heart. A woman's cry and repressed giggle filtered through the intensity of her listening.

The inner walls of the building were thin, paper-covered hessian on a framework of light timber where it had been partitioned into offices and apartments. Despite the rattle of the typewriter, Sally was sure the voices she had heard were coming from Mrs. Rooney's flat, which adjoined Frisco's office.

She rose and walked to the door.

'Mrs. Gough!' Nora jumped up, entreaty in the gasp of her exclamation.

She knew Sally had heard those voices next door, and was frightened by the look on her face.

'Why on earth didn't you tell me Colonel de Morfé is having tea with Mrs. Rooney?' Sally demanded angrily.

She whirled out of the office and into the passage, Nora following her.

'Don't go in,' the girl begged. 'Wait until he gets back, Mrs. Gough.'

'Mind your own business, Nora,' Sally said sharply. 'This is mine.'

She rapped on Mrs. Rooney's door, and Nora scurried back into the office like a rabbit flying for its burrow. There was no answer to Sally's knock, and silence on the other side of the door. Sally banged again on the frail panels, angrily, imperiously. Still not a sound came from the room beyond. Her brain seethed, suspicion and jealousy rising to a fury which destroyed reason.

'Open the door, or I'll break it down,' she cried.

There was a murmur of voices, the creaking of a wire mattress and hurried movement in the room, as incriminating as the silence had been. In her demented state Sally could not wait for the door to open, she hurled herself against it. The lock parted from the rotten woodwork. As she stepped into the room, she saw a fat naked woman disappearing behind a bead curtain, and Frisco, on a broad low couch against the wall, pulling on his trousers.

Sally stood staring at him. She could not speak. Her rage had left her. The frenzy of her jealousy was over with this proof of his abuse of her confidence. She felt only cold and aghast, as if there were nothing to say or do which would affect the knowledge she had acquired.

'Well, my dear,' Frisco said jauntily, 'you wanted a scene and you've got it.'

Mrs. Rooney had wrapped herself in a kimono, and sidled into the room, smirking coyly and with brash satisfaction.

'There's nothing to make a fuss about, I'm sure,' she giggled. 'A gentleman likes a bit of fun sometimes, and you can't expect to be the only pebble on the beach.'

'Shut up,' Frisco growled. 'If you take this seriously you'll be making a great mistake, Sally. It shouldn't have happened, I'll admit. But you know the sort of fool I've been all my life where women are concerned. You can't turn me down, now, because — because —'

'Can't I?' Sally queried. 'But that's why I can. Because, in spite of everything, I believed in you.'

She began to laugh: to laugh in a crazy anguish of broken faith and passionate resentment. 'Now, I don't any more. You're just absurd and contemptible.'

He looked it as he hung before her, crumpled and unstrung.

The sardonic grin with which he tried to cover his discomfiture, and the rough grey hair on his bare chest, made Sally realize the aged and impenitent Don Juan he was.

'I love you, Sally,' Frisco said harshly. 'You know I do. This woman doesn't mean a damn thing to me.'

'Well, I like that!' Mrs. Rooney bridled indignantly. 'Not an hour ago I was your "little honey pot" and "the best cuddle on the G.M.".'

Sally moved towards the door, saying: 'I'm sorry to have disturbed you. But I had to know.'

She wanted now to get away as quickly as possible. But Mrs. Rooney had no intention of letting her escape so easily.

'And so you should be,' she cried, with triumphant indignation, 'bursting into my flat like that, and trying to make trouble for me and Colonel de Morfé. You and your high-mightyness! You haven't got any more right to him than me! He's got all he wanted from you, and if he wants something younger and warmer, you can't blame him.'

'No,' Sally agreed.

'I love him, and I don't believe you do, or you wouldn't let this make any difference,' Mrs. Rooney persisted, her swivel eye squinting maliciously and the soiled kimono falling away from her huge floppy bosom.

'There's nothing to argue about,' Sally said flatly.

'Sally! Sally!' Frisco called and stumbled towards her. Half-clothed and dishevelled, he tried to follow her into the passage. Mrs. Rooney pulled him back.

'You can't go out like that,' she expostulated. 'Nice reputation I'll get. Everybody in the building knows by now why Mrs. Gough broke down my door, I'll bet. And what's going to happen to me if Mr. Lindsay hears about it?'

Sally fled along the passage. As she passed the door of Frisco's office, she caught a glimpse of Nora, crouched over the table with her head on her arms. But Sally could not think of that. She could think of nothing but Mrs. Rooney's flat, with a pink flamingo winking obscenely from a crude painting on the wall, a naked woman scuttling through the bead curtain, and Frisco on the rumpled divan among plush cushions plastered with gaudy flowers.

She was free of the insane torture which had driven her to break down Mrs. Rooney's door. There was no pain in knowing Frisco had destroyed her faith in him for that stupid, slovenly woman who was another man's mistress. She felt only dazed, beaten — and more guilty for having deceived herself about Frisco than outraged by what he had done. After all, as he said himself, she knew the sort of man he was. She had taken him, knowing it, and built up a conception of him to justify herself. And now, she could no longer endure it — or him.

CHAPTER XXI

'Y o u must forgive him, Mrs. Gough,' Nora said when she came to see Sally next morning. 'You've no idea how broken up he is. When he came back to the office, Colonel de Morfé collapsed in a chair. Wouldn't move, and I sat with him until nearly morning. Then dad came round to see what had happened to me, and we took him home.'

'That was good of you, Nora,' Sally said. 'But it's not a question of forgiveness.' Her smile quivered. 'It's like when Humpty Dumpty fell off the wall: All the king's horses and all the king's men couldn't put Humpty together again.'

'Oh, dear,' Nora sighed, 'what is to become of him? It wasn't his fault really, you know, Mrs. Gough. That woman pestered the life out of him. She was in and out of the office all day. Like a fly, buzzing round and oozing sex all over the place. First, it was morning tea, then morning and afternoon tea, or a glass of beer in the flat. I was downright rude to her: kept the office door shut and wouldn't let her in — if I could help it. But it was no use. She'd call out: "It's me, Frisco! Can't I come in? Miss Drew won't let me!" And last night, half a dozen times, she came knocking at the door and saying: "It's only me, Frisco — Beulah. Your little Beulah. Come and have supper with me. Don't turn me down, Frisco. I'm that lonely and miserable." He said: "Go to hell" once, and she went away, snivelling. But she's so persistent, and so — so cunning for all her soft silliness. I think she knows she's fat and ugly, and he wouldn't have anything to do with her if he could see. So she got hold of him the only way she could: the way any woman can get hold of a man if she wants to — by making out she's hot stuff and mad about him.'

'Nora!' Sally was amazed to hear Nora talking like that. She looked such a staid, frumpy little person with her round glasses and mouse-coloured hair pulled straight back from a broad, putty-coloured face.

'Oh, girls in my position haven't any illusions about men and the women who run after them,' Nora said bitterly. 'The good ones are too good, and the others just bitches.'

'It's not as simple as that,' Sally said. 'The goodness and the bitchiness are mixed up in most women, I think. And I don't know why a bitch should be blamed for being what she is. But all that's got nothing to do with Colonel de Morfé and me. I thought we were old enough to rely on each other, I suppose. But I was mistaken, you see. I can't feel I care for him any longer, or want him to be with me.'

Sally was surprised she should be talking like this to Nora; but the girl's distress was so naive and sincere she had to respect it and try to explain to her.

'Oh, dear,' Nora exclaimed dejectedly. 'I knew you'd feel like that! And that's why I did my best to prevent you from finding out. But Colonel de Morfé isn't really a bad man, Mrs. Gough. He doesn't make a pass at every woman he comes in contact with, like some men I've met. He's never said a word out of place to me. And God knows I'd be quite pleased if he had.'

'You've been wonderful to him, Nora,' Sally said gently.

'Have I?' Nora queried, her voice dry and hard. 'I just couldn't help myself doing anything to make things easier for him. If he weren't blind and so helpless, and charming — and bluffing so hard, all the time —'

'It's no use, Nora, as far as I am concerned,' Sally interrupted, realizing the girl was still pleading with her. 'For years, I've told myself that about him, but now it has no effect on me. Frisco can always look after himself, or get someone to look after him.'

'That's the worst of it,' Nora said passionately. 'She will. She tries to make out Mr. Lindsay's still keeping her. But he isn't. He hasn't been near her for months. Everybody knows she's got hold of Colonel de Morfé and won't let go unless —'

Sally had not reckoned on the gossips being better informed than she was about Frisco's affair with Mrs. Rooney.

'Oh, well, if Mrs. Rooney will give him bed and board, like

I did, there's nothing to worry about, is there?' she said lightly.

'You know there is,' Nora began to cry. 'She'll ruin him. And Colonel de Morfé's finances are in a bad way already—'

'Are they?' Sally sounded indifferent.

'You're hard, aren't you?' Nora sobbed.

Sally supposed it was true. 'It's as if we had become strangers,' she said reluctantly. 'I can't even feel sorry for him.'

Nora went away with handkerchiefs, two clean shirts, and two or three pairs of socks, in a small suitcase.

'I'll send the rest of Colonel de Morfé's clothes to the office tomorrow,' Sally said, promising herself she would wash and iron several soiled things before doing so, and that Frisco's suits would be meticulously pressed as usual.

Frisco came to see her in the evening. After a violent and painful interview, he too went away having made no impression on Sally's resolution. As she watched him groping blindly, and stumbling along the track to the gate which he used to tread with such buoyant familiarity, for the fraction of a second Sally was tempted to run after him and bring him back. But Nora was there, waiting beyond the plumbago hedge. Sally saw her take Frisco's arm to guide him: Frisco leaned heavily on her slight, girlish figure.

'Are you sure y're not cutting off y'r nose to spite y'r face, missus?' Dinny asked, no longer able to pretend he did not know what was happening.

'I don't know. I wish I did, Dinny,' Sally cried wildly. 'Now he's gone, it hurts more than I thought it would. But it had to be done. Frisco's offended my sense of decency too deeply for me ever to feel the same about him. If it had been Nora, I wouldn't have minded so much. But to destroy all there was between us for that sloppy, cross-eyed female—I can't get over it.'

'Oh, well,' Dinny murmured. 'There's some things beat cock-fightin'. And this is one of 'em. But I reckon what Nora says is right. Mrs. Rooney isn't the sort gives a man the ghost of a chance if she's after him.'

BILL's eyes lit up, and a shy, self-conscious grin chased the weariness and abstraction from his face as he grabbed the square pale blue envelope, which sometimes stood waiting for him on the kitchen mantelpiece when he came home from work. He shoved it in his pocket and went off whistling that queer, tuneless bird song of his.

He never spoke of Pat or Pam; and Eily forebore to ask questions, although she and Daphne were dying to know whether Pat and Bill had 'come to an understanding'; or were merely disentangling the threads of a passing attraction.

'I suppose Bill feels he can't talk about Pat because their love won't come to anything,' Daphne mused. 'He thinks she would come between him and the things he wants to do.'

'That's it, I'm afraid,' Eily said. 'Bill couldn't be happy unless he were "on active service" for the workers, as your father used to say. And how could Pat share the sort of life he leads?'

'But I'm glad Bill's got this spot of joy about Pat, just now,' she added thoughtfully. 'He's working so hard: got so much on his mind, what with the strike at Youanmi, party work, getting more relief work for the unemployed, and worsening of the international situation.'

'You're the limit, mum, you and Bill.' Daphne's glance took in her mother's fretted concern about each of the matters she had mentioned. 'Why should you be so worried about what's happening in Europe? Why should you and Bill feel morally responsible for arousing people to "the dangers of the international situation", as he says? You've got enough on your hands, surely, helping the unemployed? And the men at Youanmi?'

'I don't know,' Eily admitted. 'Except that we're made that way. It seems absurd to think we can have any effect on the drive to fascism and war going on overseas, I suppose. What can we do to prevent them sweeping down on us? Not much. But we've got to do what we can. Perhaps because we understand better than most people what's involved. The struggle for human rights — and we must help people to understand and unite against injustice and oppressive conditions, here, and everywhere.'

'Oh, dear,' Daphne exclaimed impatiently, 'it's beyond me!'

'Getting the little things done, here and now, is moving in the right direction,' Eily said gently. 'And you're helping Bill to collect funds for the men on strike at Youanmi aren't you?'

The strike at Youanmi had aroused indignation among miners all over the goldfields. It arose when a miner was killed and another injured working in ground that was considered dangerous by men on the mine. Bill had borrowed Dinny's car and gone over to Youanmi: got the story from the miners' representative himself.

'They've been asking for trouble on this mine, Bill,' he said. 'Young Bob, that's the bloke who was injured in number two stope, was wording the shift boss for a hard hat on the morning of the accident. "Y're bloody lucky to have a job," he ses. "Never mind about a hard hat." Ted Morrison, another bloke working in number five, says the underground boss came along the other day and said to him, "You fellers've got to be careful to dodge the stones falling here." "Hell," Ted ses, "I'm no acrobat. How about gettin' some decent styes put up?" "None of your cheek!" ses old Bandy, "we don't sack men on this mine. We put 'em in number two stope." It was murder, plain murder, that's what it was, Bill, putting Mick Wall and Bob Read in that stope.'

'They'd been out of work a long time: were ready to take any job, the boys tell me,' Bill said.

'That's about the strength of it, Bill,' Dick Flynn, the miners' representative, replied. 'Mick and Bob had been pretty active in the Glory Hole strike. No victimization and all that, when the men went back to work. Just any excuse to tramp militant unionists after a bit. And the black alley on every mine from

215

Norseman to Wiluna. They'd been foot-slogging and chasing a job for six months when they were taken on here.'

'They knew it was bad ground they were working in?'

'Too right, they knew,' the rep. said. 'Just three days before, we sent a wire to the Government Inspector and the Workers' Inspector to come down and inspect the ground in number two and number five stopes.'

'What did you say in the wire?'

' "Serious danger loss of life on this mine. Request immediate inspection." And a fat lot of good the inspection did us. The inspectors recommended that owing to the unsafe nature of the ground, the stopes be worked at a height of not more than ten feet. Those men were working at twenty-five in number two when the accident happened.'

'The inspectors recommended,' Bill remarked. 'They could have made it an order.'

'Death-trap, that stope, if ever there was one. There's great fissures in the overhanging wall where she's fallen in. Boulders hanging over the styes. Well, the long and the short of it was, after our mate was killed we held a stop-work meeting. Men on shift came out, and at a mass meeting in the Workers' Hall that night it was decided no shift would go below until the recommendations of the Government Inspector and the Workers' Inspector, that number two stope be mullocked-up to ten feet and adequately timbered, were put into effect.'

'And the mine manager wrote to inform you "the company was not prepared to incur the heavy expenditure which would be required, if the demands of your union were acceded to", I understand,' Bill said. 'I've seen the letter, and a further one which stated that "the company would not discuss the matter further until the men returned to work". Paddy Taafe showed them to me.'

Mr. Patrick Taafe was the president of the Mining Division of the A.W.U., an old miner and popular with the men on every field. A complication had arisen in connection with the strike, which began during the last days of April, because a penalty clause had been introduced into the new mining award coming into operation on May 1st. The award would introduce a forty-hour week on the mines; but the penalty clause provided for the deduction of one day's pay, from holiday pay, for every day a man took part in an unauthorized stoppage of work. The men were anxious for the strike to be settled before the new award came into operation. The company was prepared to let it drag on until after May 1st.

Paddy Taafe had got a car and driven over from Boulder as soon as he heard of the trouble at Youanmi. He was an old man, 'dusted', and could scarcely speak for coughing now; but, that morning, with delegates from the strike committee, he had gone below to inspect the number two stope. And what did he say when he saw the place where the accident occurred? 'Get me out quick, boys! Get me out before the whole damn place comes down.'

Bill was in Youanmi for the meeting in the Workers' Hall that night.

'Paddy made a great speech,' he said. 'He told the men of Youanmi he was proud to be with them: proud to see their spirit: proud to know miners have got the guts to put up a fight for their rights, penalty clause or no penalty clause: "Forty years' experience I've got behind me — forty years of industrial organization and work on the mines — and I've got this to tell you. No men ever had a clearer case for action than the men have got on this mine. I went below, meself, this morning, and you can take this from me, boys. Number two stope is the worst and most badly worked stope I've ever seen — and I've seen a good many. When it's matter of life and death, Arbitration Court Awards and Trade Union Constitutions count for nothing." The poor old boy was coughing and struggling for breath as he talked; but he kept on: "I've got to congratulate you on the stand you've made. I've got to congratulate your committee on the way it's handling the struggle. It's going to be a bad business for the mining company when the facts about conditions on this mine get round. You men'll have the backing

217

of the unions and all the miners on the eastern goldfields. I'm going to promise you the support of the Mining Division of the A.W.U. — so long as I'm president of the union. Solidarity's a great thing, boys. Stick to it. The fight's on. And don't forget the fight's always on when it's a question of being forced to safeguard our lives and working conditions." '

Miners cheered Paddy Taafe until they were hoarse that night at Youanmi. And the old man had been as good as his word: fought the cause of the strikers in the union and in the Chamber of Mines, until repairs on the mine were made and the men went back to work.

But the struggle took on a new significance when men found money deducted from their holiday pay for days prior to May 1st when they had been on strike. There was an upsurge of indignation, which threatened to stop work on every field, in support of the Youanmi men's resistance to this attempt to deprive them of holiday pay. Paddy Taafe told the Chamber of Mines if they wanted a fight they could have it. The Chamber of Mines announced that the penalty clause was not intended to be retrospective. Youanmi men won this recognition, not only for themselves, but for miners on every goldfield of the west.

Bill was so pleased about the outcome of the strike that he whistled and sang as he went to work, for days.

The penalty clause nevertheless was a thorn in the flesh of most working miners. They complained that they had been stampeded into accepting it with the forty-hour week, and that mine managers were taking advantage of the penalty clause to introduce new methods of speed-up into the industry. Miners' representatives who reported disregard of safety and sanitary regulations had been sacked on several mines, without any action being taken by the men they represented on the mine and in the union, to defend them from victimization. There was no doubt the penalty clause was having its effect; and that many men were unwilling to forfeit holiday pay in order to redress an injustice done to a fellow worker or to defend the rights of the mining fraternity.

Steve Miller and several other men who, as miners' representatives, were responsible for protecting the interests of the miners, urged a more vigorous policy to prevent further deterioration of conditions on the mines. Their moves had been frustrated by a union official who was suspected of being more concerned to collaborate with the mine owners than to serve the interests of the workers.

'Bureaucratic methods are destroying rank and file control of the union,' Bill said.

'It's worse than that, Bill,' Steve protested gloomily. 'The bosses are putting the boots in, and the miners are taking it lying down.'

Then men on the big Lancefield mine downed tools in defence of a mate who had been sacked on the trumped-up charge of an underground manager known as 'The Tramper'. Every man on the mine was a member of the union and Alf Jones a staunch and popular unionist.

The strike aroused tremendous enthusiasm because it vindicated the spirit of miners who would not be intimidated by the penalty clause from fighting for their rights. It lasted nine weeks and Bill was in the thick of it, addressing meetings at outlying camps during the week-end, collecting funds, and counteracting the influence of the union official who was advocating the acceptance of terms for the settlement of the strike which would have defeated its purpose. The Lancefield men took management of the strike into their own hands; and their committee conducted negotiations which brought the struggle to a successful conclusion.

Soon afterwards, a meeting of miners called for the union official's resignation, on the grounds that he had become too far removed from contact with the miners to work in their interests, and had come close to sabotaging their efforts in the Lancefield strike.

'This strike's shown they can't leg-iron miners with the penalty clause,' Dinny chortled. 'And that if a man's paid by the workers to serve their interests, and doesn't, well, he knows what to expect.'

'The Workers' Inspector is getting a bit of hurry-up on the Lancefield, too,' Bill told him with a good deal of satisfaction. 'Seems the boys drew his attention to several breaches of the regulations before he went below, a while ago. But he didn't notify the management of the need to do anything about them. The union executive instructed him to carry out his duties more energetically. He got busy and had those matters adjusted. But after his last visit, it appears, his notice on the office door stated that he found everything in order. Next day, the Government Inspector came along, and after he'd been below, stuck up his notice. It pointed out important matters which the management had to rectify in connection with sanitation, safety rails to be provided at several places on the ten level, guards on plates to be kept in position, and cartridges to be provided and used in firing. So old Greg's in for a spot of bother again!'

During the strikes and conflict in union affairs, Bill found himself plagued by his thoughts of Pat. He felt as if she were a siren sitting on a big rock, far away, combing her golden hair with a golden comb and singing a wonderfully melodious little song to lure him from the class struggle and his duty to the workers. He tried to thrust her out of his mind; but she returned, laughing, indignant and reproachful. Sometimes he could feel her hair blowing across his face, as it had done when they were driving together, and an exquisite vibration flew through all his senses. The fragrance of wild cassia was like a whiff of her presence. Furiously, he brushed away these fantasies of a love-sick dreamer, and turned to the tasks chewing at his brain for immediate attention.

One of these was obtaining work and fuller measures of relief for the unemployed. Over a thousand workless men still drifted about the goldfields, sleeping in the Open Cut on Maritana, and in the rotten shacks of tin and bagging on Misery Flat.

Dinny and his mates were discussing the subject when Bill dropped in for a yarn with them one evening.

'Y' can't walk down the street without being bitten half a dozen times for a feed,' Dally grumbled.

'The johns'll vag a single bloke and run him out of town if he's caught askin' for tucker.' Blunt Pick's voice cracked to his indignation. 'But what's he to do if he can't get work, and got no money to buy a bit of bread and meat. Starve? Blowed if I would!'

'Seen a one-armed man, swingin' a shovel by a hook on the stump of his right arm, coupler days ago,' Tassy muttered. 'Shovels full of ballast he was slingin' into a truck, and sloggin' like mad to make believe he could do it as well as his mates.'

'Only yesterday a chap was telling me he'd been twenty-eight weeks trying to get a job,' Sam Mullet said. 'He's got a wife and four kids. Decent sort: fair broke him up having to go to the police station and apply for sustenance. He'd've done anything rather than admit things'd got so bad with him.'

'Single men have been worse off,' Bill said. 'The Unemployment Relief Committee has pushed the council into providing jobs for most of the married men, and got the government to inaugurate a prospecting scheme which is offering single men fifteen bob a week. But that's not a living wage; and we've got to keep on bringing pressure to bear on the government to raise it.'

'The workers on this field are gettin' a rougher spin than they've ever had, I reckon,' Dinny muttered.

'That American bloke here a while ago,' Sam remembered, 'said we'd ought "to make the standard of living follow profits and maintain it as they fall".'

'Easier said than done.' Tassy's fat, jolly laugh rumbled. 'We've got the worst houses and pay the highest rent for 'em, in Australia. But profits from the mines aren't going into any housing scheme.'

'The mines of the west've produced gold valued at over £200,000,000 up to date,' Bill said. 'To say nothing of the millions paid in dividends. And the bulk of all that wealth came from the Golden Mile. But what do the mine owners care how the people live here?'

'Six times yesterday the ambulance from the mines passed along the road,' Sally murmured.

'There's been more accidents than ever, lately.' Dally was no

221

longer working underground, but he took a melancholy interest in every fatal accident. 'Sixty deaths in twenty months, since the penalty clause has been introduced. The boys say it's the rotten gear they've been usin' and bad fracteur.'

'No blame attachable,' Tassy chuckled, quoting the usual verdict when there was in inquiry into the causes of an accident underground.

'And the mine owners makin' a handsome profit on the fracteur they sell the miners,' Blunt Pick pitched in. 'But the unions hailed 'em into court over it. Costin' us a pretty penny, takin' the case from the Supreme Court to the High Court; but Bronc Finley reckons we'll get a verdict. 'T any rate, on some of the mines the price of fracteur's dropped already.'

The talk swung to national and international affairs as it usually did these days.

'See Count Felix von Luckner, Hitler's emissary to the youth of the world, is visiting Australia,' Sam Mullet said.

'The government didn't prohibit him landing like it did Egon Kisch, when he was a delegate from the World Peace Congress,' Sally remarked.

'Been received by the Prime Minister, and made a great fuss of in Sydney,' Blunt Pick jeered.

'But not by the workers,' Dinny countered. 'They're organizin' demonstrations against him, pointin' out he's an enemy of democratic peoples, a fascist and a spy. He has to be given police protection when he shows his face in public.'

'If he comes here he'll get the works,' Bill told them. 'The union has passed a resolution objecting to the use of the Kalgoorlie Town Hall for any meeting to be addressed by von Luckner, and threatened a lively demonstration if he's given the right of way.'

Warned of the hostility of the miners, von Luckner dropped Kalgoorlie from his itinerary.

'Well, that's one bit of fascist intrigue workers on the goldfields have helped to frustrate, Bill,' Eily commented happily. 'Makes you feel our work hasn't been all in vain, trying to make people understand what fascism is, and what it has been doing in Europe.'

Bill was loath to deny Eily the satisfaction which this small triumph gave her; but at the back of his mind lay a consciousness of the ominous darkness of the international situation, making all their efforts to improve the lot of workers in Kalgoorlie and Boulder seem puny and futile. It was there as he worked over the plans and specifications for development work on the mine: when he was giving instructions for and supervising the sinking of a winz, or opening up new ground; and at night as he read ravenously all the papers and books he could get on the military strength of the powers, the economic and political factors dominating national policy. He did not neglect any of his ordinary organizational activities. This was no time to sit back and relax, he warned himself. Every effort must be intensified to expose fascist tendencies and maintain the rights of the people.

A mood of utter depression overwhelmed him with defeat of the Republican Government in Spain. People on the goldfields had responded generously to appeals for money to send an ambulance and medical aid to Spain. A committee of working men and women had adopted Spanish children and dispatched funds to provide them with food and clothing. Now all the energy and hope which had been poured into that campaign were lost. The forces of reaction had triumphed and in the months which followed fascism appeared to be in the ascendant.

Soon it was trampling rough-shod over the peoples of Europe. Newspapers bemoaned the collapse of Austria and Hitler's designs on Czechoslovakia. But governments in Great Britain and France continued to wring their hands like helpless old women afraid to interfere in the rampage of a punch-drunk bully. Notwithstanding, or because of, Hitler's abuse of democratic institutions, they vaunted a policy of appeasement as the only safeguard of peace, although a full military, political and economic alliance between Great Britain, France and the U.S.S.R. had been mooted as a formidable alignment of powers likely to curb German preparations for war.

'Better fascism than communism,' huckstering industrial magnates and conservative statesmen were saying; and their political roundsmen and hangers-on echoed that cry, despite national interests and the national peril. Bill had heard them on the goldfields; but not among the miners.

Most of the miners refused to listen to him when he talked about communism; but they 'wouldn't have a bar of fascism' as they said. They prided themselves on being 'staunch labourites'; voting solidly for the Australian Labour Party and knew where any tenderness for fascism was coming from. 'Better fascism than communism' was a rich man's slogan, intended to split the workers, the miners recognized; but religious prejudices beaten up to discredit communism and the Soviet Union had affected them a good deal. There was as much ignorance and confusion on both subjects here on the goldfields as everywhere else, Bill feared. But what could you expect, he asked himself. Most workers got their news from the daily press. Few of them wanted to read *World Peace*, or any of the working-class papers he and Eily tried to sell them on pay day, or by calling from door to door along the mile-long streets of Boulder and Kalgoorlie.

CHAPTER XXIII

'Dinny's had a letter from Pat,' Sally said, when Bill sat down on the veranda steps. 'Pam wrote to me soon after they left, but we haven't heard from them since.'

She knew, of course, that Bill had been receiving the same sort of blue envelope, with the address in a bold, vivid scrawl, every week. But he had been curiously reticent about it, and she told him of Dinny's letter teasingly, as if he might be ignorant of Pat's news. Bill understood her impulse was to draw his fire. The lines round his mouth creased, and a shy, tender smile hung in his eyes with a lover's secret satisfaction.

It was a hot night. Dinny and his cronies puffed away at their old pipes, dumb and broody, having exhausted their usual topics of conversation.

'How are they gettin' on?' Tassy asked lazily.

'Been havin' a show-down with Paddy, and no end of fun,' Dinny said.

'Pat and Pam are twenty-one now,' Sally murmured.

'Paddy give 'em a big party, I suppose?'

'He wanted to.' Dinny enjoyed the importance of knowing just what had happened. 'Before the girls' lawyer interviewed him, that was. Seems the lawyer bloke demanded an account of trust funds Paddy's supposed to have invested on the girls' behalf, and due to them when they came of age under the terms of their mother's will. So Pat and Pam had a rumpus with Paddy instead of the party.'

'Tare'n ages, it'd be a nasty jar for Paddy, that!' Tassy's big belly shook with the convulsions of his laughter.

'Paddy's been livin' with the girls at their old home,' Dinny went on. 'It's a mansion of a place, Pat says, with beautiful gardens, and Paddy's regarded it as his since the girls' mother died. But it belongs to Pat and Pam, now; and Sir Patrick hit the roof when their lawyer informed him that the Misses Gaggin requested him to vacate the rooms he was occupying before the end of the month!'

'Holy smoke!' Tassy spluttered. 'Paddy evicted. That's a good one.'

'Best joke I've heard for many a long day,' Dally gasped when the laughter subsided.

Blunt Pick added, coughing and wheezing, the tears running down his lean cheeks:

'Who'd've thought it? A couple of girls like that, game to stand up to Paddy Cavan!'

'He didn't take it easy, I'll bet?' Sam Mullet observed.

'Too right he didn't,' Dinny grinned. 'Pat says he was like a volcano in eruption for days. All the way over in the train, and for the first months they were in Melbourne, Paddy was soft-soapin' them — tryin' to make up for a bad time he'd given them here, in Kal, before they left. Wanted them to believe he was a good sort and they were a happy family and would always get on well together. There was no need to alter any of their arrangements because the girls would soon be twenty-one. Of course they'd be free to do as they pleased. If he'd laid down the law a bit in the past it was no more than any other father would have done. Not wantin' them to get into mischief with red-raggers, or be imposed on by fortune-huntin' scoundrels. But all the time, he was quakin' in his shoes, because they might want to take their money out of his hands as soon as they could.'

'That'd hurt Paddy. That'd hurt him more than anything else,' Dally muttered.

'You bet it would,' Blunt Pick agreed.

'He raved and blustered, almost blubbered, beggin' the girls not to dump him,' Dinny rattled on, throwing himself into his story and unconsciously dramatizing it for the benefit of his audience. 'That was when he knew they didn't want him livin' in the house with them any more. Couldn't believe the girls'd treat him so badly. Such ingratitude! Such a crazy idea, thinkin' they could take their investments out of his hands! What did they know about handlin' large sums of money? Who could give them better advice than he? Who could make bigger profits for them? Who could they trust more? Wasn't he willin' to make them his heirs? Leave them every penny he'd got. And he'd see they had handsome allowances during his lifetime. All the money they wanted to play with. Thousands, if it came to that. What more could any young women ask for?'

' "We don't like your business methods," Pat told him. "And are quite capable of employing a competent stock broker to deal with our investments."

' "God A'mighty, y' don't know what y'r talkin' about," Paddy roared. "It takes the shrewdest brains in the country to do what I've done, more than double the value of every asset y'r mother put in me hands: show four hundred per cent on some of 'em. Where are ye goin' to get a stock broker could do that for ye? They're all thieves and rogues, will fleece ye in no time."

' "We're not interested in making money," Pam told him. "We want to do something useful with what we've got."

' "Y're mad," Paddy raged, "y're not fit to have money to throw away on y'r hare-brained schemes. Y'd ought to be locked up! It's a crime and a cryin' black shame on the country, ye can rob me of capital I've built up and need to stabilize me financial position."

' "You can't have it both ways," Pat told him. "You support a system which gives us the right to squander money we haven't earned. And you haven't either, if it comes to that. You've swindled everybody you could when you got a chance. Pam and I don't intend to let you swindle us, if we can help it."

' "What we do with our money is our concern, not yours," Pam said.

' "It is me concern," Paddy bawled. "Isn't y'r money tied up with mine? D'y' think I'm fool enough to let ye withdraw any asset that'll jeopardize me position? Y'r damned lawyer can threaten legal action, but that won't do ye any good. Y'll squander a fortune on legal proceedings, I tell ye. But nobody's ever beaten Patrick Cavan. Nobody ever will. And who the hell put ye up to stabbin' me in the back like this? That scoundrel

Lucius Gaggin, or that lousy paintin' feller? Maybe some of me old enemies on the goldfields, Dinny Quin and Mrs. Gough, or that blasted red-ragger! God-damned bloody liars and crooks, every one of 'em. What have they ever done for ye? Why are they makin' up to ye, now? Want to get hold of y'r money, that's all, and wipe off a few old scores against me." '

Everybody was gurgling and gasping over Dinny's version of Paddy Cavan's row with his step-daughters.

'Paddy's up against something he didn't bargain for, all right,' Sam Mullet commented, smoke clouding up round him.

'That's about the strong of it,' Dinny stoked his pipe.

'Paddy'll kick harder'n a bull camel when he's crossed.' Blunt Pick had to have his say.

'My oath he will,' Dally drooled.

'What does it matter how he kicks, if the girls get away from him?' Sally demanded.

'That's right, gran,' Bill said.

'Who's this Lucius Gaggin, 't any rate?' Tassy asked.

'Their father's younger brother,' Dinny replied. 'Seems he put the lawyers up to takin' action on the girls' account. Got his knife into Paddy because he did him out of a wad of brewery shares. "A bit of a drunken old reprobate, Uncle Lucius, but rather a dear," Pat says. And he's got a lot of evidence that'll make things awkward for Paddy when the case comes into court.'

'Be the Great Livin' Tinker, looks as if Paddy'll be gettin' something of what's been comin' to him for a long time,' Tassy chuckled.

'Uncle Lucius got the police to prevent Paddy removing some of the furniture when he took his departure,' Dinny murmured contentedly. 'And Uncle Lucius gave the bride away when Pam was married, a few weeks ago.'

'Did she marry "the lousy paintin' feller?" ' Tassy wanted to know.

'She did,' Dinny said.

'Shawn Desmond was with the International Brigade in Spain.' Bill spoke up to defend Shawn. 'He's a fine man, from all accounts: was wounded and came out to join Pam. They were married as soon as he arrived.'

"Struth,' Blunt Pick chortled, 'there's a sheila I wouldn't've minded marryin' meself. Though to tell y' the truth, it's her sister I've got more of a hankerin' after. Blow me, Charles, if I don't feel like buyin' meself a new suit and goin' over to Melbourne to try me luck.'

He winked at Dinny, and slid a sly glance in Bill's direction.

'Y' might save y'self the trouble, Blunt,' Dinny said. 'Pat's got somebody in her mind's eye.'

'Who is he, the dirty dog?' Blunt Pick cried wrathfully. 'Doin' me out of me prospects, and the love of me life into the bargain!'

'Go on, Blunt Pick, you old bag of bones,' Sally laughed. 'You don't imagine any girl would look at you, do you?'

'Me heart's broke! Me heart's broke!' Blunt Pick lamented, though he was grinning at Bill, and everybody understood why.

Bill took the chiacking with a faint smile. He knew that Dinny and all these old friends would have liked him to do as Blunt Pick suggested, buy himself a new suit, and go off to Melbourne and marry Pat. But he could not allow them to enter the hallowed area of his consciousness where he wrestled with his love for Pat. These old people were all on Pat's side, he guessed. Romantic and sentimental, they liked to think happiness was just round the corner for him to grab. Marry the girl and damn the consequences, would have been their advice, had he asked for it. Except Sally. She felt as he did about Pat, Bill was afraid. She thought this wild-fire amour between himself and Pat would fizzle out. Although he was possessed by its insurgence, he still could not bring himself to abjure the hard and strenuous way of life he had chosen, or explain all that to Dinny and his mates.

There was nothing for it but to laugh off the inquisition of their kindly gaze with a casual:

'Well, wish Pat the best of luck from me, Dinny!' and fling a jaunty: 'So long!' at them, as he walked away.

229

CHAPTER XXIV

DAPHNE had got a job as waitress in a pub at Boulder. She was pleased to be earning again and hurried off eagerly every morning, in order to start work at seven o'clock. She was supposed to be free after seven in the evening, with a break during the morning, and two hours off in the afternoon. But she worked right through the first day and came home exhausted.

'I must be collar-proud,' she exclaimed ruefully. 'There's only one other waitress; and the manageress, Miss Sheepshanks, is a fair cow. Puts everything on to you she can, Ivy — that's the other girl — says, and there's no time off if she can help it.'

'Oh, dear, I know how it is with a woman like that,' Eily said. 'She likes to let you know who's boss, and run you off your legs.'

'That's right,' Daphne smiled. 'Ivy says she sleeps with old Doherty, and is scared stiff if a girl looks at him. Plasters the rouge on, gets her hair dyed, and dresses smartly to look young; but is one of those thin wizened-up women who looks worse than if she didn't. And she's got a voice like a saw. It just screeches at you.'

'You don't have to take this job, Daph,' Eily protested. 'You know I've got enough to provide for both of us.'

'I'll stick it,' Daphne said firmly. 'I'm not going to have you going short of things you need on my account, mum. Besides, it's up to me to provide for myself and the Tomlet.'

Stick to that job she did, doggedly, valiantly, going off in the morning, a brisk, energetic little figure, and coming home at night, too tired to eat, too tired to do anything but kick off her shoes and flop on her bed, scarcely able to speak.

'It's not good enough, darling,' Eily said, distressed to see Daphne so knocked out, one Saturday night, 'you can't go on like this.'

'We had an awful rush today,' Daphne explained wearily. 'Fifty men for lunch and more for dinner, and everything in the kitchen at sixes and sevens. Sheepshanks was in a fiendish temper. She always is after one of her "sick headaches" — gets on the brandy, Ivy says — and we suffer for it.'

'Sling the rotten job, Daph,' Bill urged. 'You don't need to let anybody work you to death. I'm earning good wages, and can help you and the little chap.'

'Thanks, Bill.' Tears of weakness swam into Daphne's grey eyes. 'But I just can't bear not to pay my own way, and jobs are scarce. As many girls as men unemployed in Boulder and Kal just now. Ivy's father and brother have been out of work for months, or she'd have walked out of Doherty's before this, she says. She's older than I am, with one of those hard, shrewd faces, but she's a good sort. Between us we ought to be able to stand up to Sheepshanks, before long.'

'The sooner the better if you ask me,' Bill said.

'Week-ends are the worst,' Daphne told him. 'There's always a crowd of men for midday and evening meals. They're very decent, of course, chivvy us a bit; but that female rouses and grouses until we don't know whether we're standing on our head or our heels. She pushes all sorts of jobs on to us and then reckons we're behind with everything. We've got to make the salads now! This morning she came bustling into the kitchen to say: "Put plenty of salt in the salads, girls. Don't forget it's pay week-end!"'

'Wants the men to get up a thirst and take it out in the bar,' Bill growled.

'Ivy was feeling sore about having to do the salads, so she told Sheepshanks straight, she ought to put on another girl: had no right expecting us to make salads. It was all we could manage to get through our morning's work, Ivy told her, and we did a darn side more than waitresses were expected to do: washed up after breakfast, scrubbed out the dining-room, cleaned the silver and fixed up the tables for lunch. "If you don't like the job, you know what to do with it," Sheepshanks said, and stalked off.'

'You're the ones who ought to have stalked off,' Bill said.

'Ivy thinks we ought to put the union on to her,' Daphne went on. 'She works us any old hours, and we never get a break in the morning, and only half an hour in the afternoon, sometimes, if we're lucky.'

'Of course, that's what you ought to do,' Eily declared. 'Nell McIntyre's a fine girl. She's done a lot to make hotel and restaurant keepers in Boulder and Kal respect award rates of pay and working conditions.'

After a night's sleep, Daphne's youth and spirit rallied. She hurried off in the morning, ready for her day's work, determined to get through it as efficiently as possible, and not to be rattled by that shrill voice saying: 'Get a move on, girls, get a move on!' when she was moving as fast as she could. She was a good waitress; she could serve half a dozen men at a time, expertly, and return their chaffing gallantries, without losing a moment, during the rush periods of the midday or evening meal. But there was always flurry and disorder in the kitchen to contend with. She had to hang round, waiting to get her orders supplied, or, if the cook was drunk, pile food on to plates herself, and dash out with them. There was no method or attempt at regulating the service behind the swing doors into the dining-room on days like that. Ivy and Daphne had to tackle it as best they could, and come out of the scrimmage with loaded, back-breaking trays, and minds clear as to what each customer had ordered.

Daphne had been at Doherty's for three months when the union secretary called during the slack period in the afternoon, after lunch.

Ivy and Daphne were sitting over a cup of tea, at a table in the dining-room, when they heard Nell McIntyre inquire at the office:

'Is the proprietor in?'

'He is not!' Miss Sheepshanks replied, distrusting any good-looking young female who inquired for the boss. 'I'm the manageress. What do you want?'

'Miss Sheepshanks, I believe,' Nell McIntyre remarked sweetly.

'I'm the secretary of the Hotel and Restaurant Employees' union. I would like to see your time and wages book, please.'

'She looked so young and pretty, standing there,' Daphne explained afterwards. 'So innocent, with her big blue eyes, and a soft little smile on her face, that Sheepshanks could scarcely believe her ears. Then her face wrinkled and twisted up as though she were going to have a fit.'

'Get out,' she shrieked. 'Get out, you impudent hussy! You and your damned union can go to hell as far as I'm concerned. Time and wages book! Of all the bloody cheek. It's no business of yours how I run this place. You keep y'r nose out of my business, miss, or it'll be the worse for you!'

Nell stood her ground.

'You misunderstand me, Miss Sheepshanks,' she said firmly. 'It is my business, as a representative of the union, to be here. I have a legal right to ask to see your hours and wages book.'

Miss Sheepshanks arose screaming with fury. 'I'll show you whether you've got any business on these premises,' she raved. 'I'll show ye who's got any legal right here! And I'll wipe that smirk off y'r face if you don't clear off quick and lively!'

Then the boss came out of the bar, Daphne said. He'd heard the row and wondered what it was all about. Miss Sheepshanks was in such a rage that he could hardly make out what she said.

'Insulting little bitch,' she kept screaming. 'She's insulted me, Ted. She's one of these union agitators. Thinks she can walk into the place and tell me what to do with my staff. Give orders to me! Me that's run this place for twenty years.'

'I merely asked to see your hours and wages book, Mr. Doherty,' Nell said quietly, although she looked rather pale, and as if she were quaking inside. 'And I would be obliged if you would explain to this lady that as secretary of the union, I am entitled to do so.'

'Get out,' Ted Doherty roared. 'And keep out. We don't want no union interference in our business. And the girls workin' for us don't neether. If y' don't clear out I'll throw y' out.'

He looked like doing it, too: walked towards Nell menacingly, with his fist raised. Daphne and Ivy behind the doors to the dining-room were ready to rush out and defend Nell. But she looked Doherty in the eyes, and said calmly:

'I am sorry, Mr. Doherty, that you force me to take other action. I will return in an hour to see your hours and wages book.'

Nell walked away, looking as pretty as a picture in her pale blue linen suit, but quite undaunted.

'Doherty and old Sheepshanks were cock-a-hoop thinking they had driven her off the premises,' Daphne said. ' "Scared the liver and the lights out of her," he chuckled. And came to warn Ivy and me we'd get the sack if we had anything to do with the union. "We're sacking ourselves when it suits us," Ivy told him. "If you put on any scabs, we'll see how many unionists will drink in your scabby pub, Mr. Doherty"!'

'We'll wait and see what happens when Nell gets back,' Ivy had said to Daphne. 'If we're going to walk out, we'd better stay until dinner time, and let the boys know why we're going. They'll stand by us.'

Steve Miller had been finding it convenient to take his meals at that pub while Daphne was working there. She did not doubt he would induce other unionists to walk out with him when he heard her story. In about an hour Nell was back with a big policeman beside her. He appeared rather sorry for himself and as if he were not relishing his job.

'Thought of all the pots of free beer he'd be losing by going against Doherty, I'll bet,' Bill laughed.

'I regret having had to claim the protection of the police to do my duty, Mr. Doherty,' Nell said with mild dignity. 'I must ask you again to let me see your hours and wages book.'

'The young lady's within her rights, Doherty,' the policeman mumbled apologetically. 'You'd best show her the book.'

'And if I refuse?' Doherty blustered. 'I'm damned if I'm going to be dictated to by an impudent chit of a girl who's only out to make mischief, and — '

'Now, now,' the policeman warned good-naturedly, 'y'can't

do that, y'know. Not unless y' want an action in the courts — and all the unions in the town up agin yer.'

Doherty fumed and swore distractedly, but presently produced his book. The records were in a terrible mess. There had been little or no attempt made to keep them accurately. The policeman sat alongside while Nell went through them, making notes and taking her time to make them thoroughly.

Daphne and Ivy giggled and jigged delightedly watching her through a peep-hole in the frosted glass of the dining-room doors. They were thrilled by the way Miss McIntyre had handled the situation, refusing to be intimidated, and determined to defend the interests of working girls like themselves. They had to scatter and pretend to be setting the tables for dinner when Doherty came to speak to them.

He was quite anxious to placate them: said he had spoken 'a bit hasty' about sacking them, and begged them not to walk out on him for dinner that night. Miss Sheepshanks had collapsed with one of her sick headaches, he said; and they were good girls. He'd see about giving them a bit of overtime if they would stick to him, and not let the union secretary put anything over them about the shindy that afternoon.

'We're both unionists, Mr. Doherty,' Ivy said, 'and will stick by the union. If any overtime's due to us, Miss McIntyre will see we get it.'

As a result of Nell McIntyre's investigations that afternoon Ivy discovered that she could claim £50 for overtime and arrears of wages. She had never possessed so much money in her life, and it seemed a godsend. The amount owing to Daphne was much less because she had not been working at Doherty's as long as Ivy. When Doherty refused to pay either claim, Nell McIntyre took him to court and won her case. Ivy was jubilant and decided to take a holiday. Daphne could not bring herself to work at Doherty's without her, and started to look for another job. But although she applied for work at nearly every pub and restaurant in Boulder and Kalgoorlie, there was nothing available.

When Ivy went to Wiluna as waitress in the hotel, she promised to let Daphne know if there was any possibility of finding work for her. Before long she wrote to say that she had told the boss the work was too hard, and she wouldn't stay unless he put on another girl. The wages were good, and the work a treat after Doherty's, so Daphne could have the job if she came at once. Daphne wanted to take it; and Eily persuaded her to. She thought it would be good for Daphne to feel free and a girl again. Tommy was toddling about now, and she would love to look after him, Eily assured Daphne.

'I hate to leave him, mum,' Daphne said, 'but I must earn a living for us both. And it's better for him to be with you than with me.'

She went off to Wiluna, which was only three hundred and sixty miles away, as if she were going to the other end of the earth. It made Eily's heart ache to see her looking so young and sad, yet there was a love and fortitude in Daphne's eyes, of which she was proud.

'Don't worry, darling,' she pleaded, kissing Daphne goodbye. 'We'll take great care of Tommy. And don't forget, you needn't stay a day longer at Wiluna than you feel inclined. We've grown so close to each other, Daph, I'll miss you dreadfully.'

DUST storms hid the scattered townships on the flat below the Boulder Ridge in a red fog at the end of the summer: a fog making men and women in the streets look distraught puppets in an inferno. Blinding, suffocating with gritty, infinitesimal particles, it hung in the air when the wind dropped, a lurid veil between earth and sky. The sun burned like a lump of slag behind it. The earth seemed to be rising in those clouds of dust, drawn by some magnetic element into the molten mass of the sun.

Inside their houses women sweated and sweltered in an airless twilight. They had closed their doors and windows to keep out the dust, but it seeped through the cracks and crevices of flimsy walls, lying in a red film over everything. Floors, beds, furniture and food were all covered with it.

Sometimes a dust storm passed without rain, and no more than a remote rumbling of thunder. The days went on again with their dry insatiable heat, drawing the moisture from every living thing, draining men and beasts of their vital energy. Through the hot still nights people slept fitfully, breathing dust, eating dust, dreaming of rain. When thunder broke with crashes which shook the houses, or cyclonic gusts sent the sheet iron flying from roofs rotted by the sun, everybody, except the folk who lost their roofs, heaved a sigh of relief. Each crash of thunder and crackle of lightning in the turgid sky brought the rain nearer. When it fell, sweeping out from heavy masses of torn and dirty clouds, flashing and slashing at the hard-baked ground, men, women and children rejoiced. Soon the gutters and dry creek beds were running with swirling streams. The thirsty earth could not swallow the downpour quickly enough. It lay on the flat, shining silvery, as if by magic a great lake had been created there.

Dinny wished Pam could see it. Two years had passed since

Pat's and Pam's visit to Kalgoorlie. Dinny still heard from them occasionally and knew that their suit against Paddy Cavan was dragging a slow course through the law courts. But Bill's blue envelopes were arriving less frequently, Eily said. She thought his love affair with Pat was petering out.

Again, all night, after that devastating dust storm at the end of the summer, it rained. In the morning, La and Nadya reported gleefully that the creek had overflowed its banks and the streets round about were flooded. They splashed to school, bare-legged, through the muddy water: and Eily had to rescue her hens from a perch in the shed where they were marooned.

When Bill came in from work, he said the road was awash, and workers' trams held up on the track to the mines. Storm waters had entered the workings of some of them. Men on the day shift could not go underground on the Boulder Reef, or the Iron Duke. The North Kalgurli had suspended operations until further notice.

And gran's front fence was down! He had found Sally and Dinny on the roof, in the wind and rain, trying to nail down a sheet of iron which had blown off the roof. The rain had poured into the sitting-room, and ruined the wall-paper; but like the pair of sturdy battlers they were, they were making a joke of all the damage and discomfort the deluge had caused them. They remembered too well what they had been through in the early days, when men perished for lack of water, and a downpour was a godsend in drought-stricken country, to say anything disrespectful of the rain, they told Bill. Bill laughed at them, and called them a pair of superstitious old fogies as he chased Sally off the roof and gave Dinny a hand himself.

After the rain stopped and hot sunshine gleamed, youngsters swarmed everywhere, paddling in the muddy pools. They made themselves cockle-shell boats of pieces of old iron or empty boxes, and when they tipped over, splashed, screaming merrily, in the shallow water.

The mothers and wives of miners off work for a few days were not so pleased about the heavy rain. They would be on short pay, and were depressed because when their men started work, they would be working on levels which had been affected by the storm. There was always a greater number of accidents in a mine where the workings had been under water.

'And would you believe it, they haven't had a drop of rain on Warrinup for months?' Sally exclaimed to Eily.

Usually, plentiful rains kept the timbered ranges and fertile valleys green, the rivers brimming, but that summer had been hot and dry in the south-west.

Sally went on talking about a letter she had had from Den's wife. 'Charlie says that bush fires are raging all round them. The heat has been terrific, and she and Den have been fighting the fires for days. The whole countryside is shrouded in smoke and they've lost the feed in their home paddocks. Seems she and Den were away fighting a fire on her father's place, when the wind fish-tailed and swept the flames down on the big belt of timber behind Warrinup. Before they could get back, the barns and milking sheds were ablaze. Nearly all the milking machines and a new separator have been destroyed. Den's very broken up about it, Charlie says. It will cost them well over £1000 to repair the damage that's been done.'

'Poor old Den, he's had a lot of bad luck lately, hasn't he?' Eily said, with her ready sympathy.

Sally was worried as to how Den was going to meet the losses and heavy expenditure that this disastrous bush fire would entail. She wanted to go and help him through his difficulties in any way she could. He was the only one of her sons still living, and she had promised to spend Christmas with him that year. But Marie was ill, bed-ridden now by the arthritis which had been crippling her for years. Her heart was in a bad way, the doctor had warned Sally, and Marie might slip away at any moment. She had been so impatient of being helpless that she had strained her strength to the utmost before she would give in and realize that she could no longer even dress or wash herself.

Steve Miller had taken a job at Wiluna, and Sally arranged for his mother to live in the house with Marie, and look after her;

but every day, she spent an hour or two with Marie, gossiping and yarning as they had always done. Marie read a great deal and was as interested in everything and as quick-witted as ever, but those hours with Sally were the only pleasure she had. It was difficult to believe their long and intimate friendship was nearly over. They both needed the gay and loving tenderness they had always given each other to stifle the pain of these last days together. Sally felt that she could not leave Marie, even to visit Den, while Marie's eyes watched the door, and her voice trembled as she said: '*Chèrie*, but it is so good to see you!'

Sally was haunted, too, by her dread of another war. Den would be safe at Warrinup, she thought. He would have to stick to his cows and producing butter fat. But she could not endure the prospect of Bill being drawn into the madness of another orgy of destruction. The last war had taken two of her sons. Lal had been killed and Dick's life wrecked. How could people reconcile themselves to such a disaster: be prepared to face so much horror and misery again? Yet Bill was arguing that an end had to be put to fascist aggression. Fascism threatened the world with a system of brutal tyranny and endless wars. Its power could be broken only by the combination of democratic peoples against it. The air was thick with rumours of war, fears and prognostications of what the next few months might bring.

It was as if the dust storms which had raged on the goldfields were blowing about the world. Gritty particles of news flung about by frenzied speculators and corrupt politicians cut into the mind. A dense fog overhung diplomatic manœuvres. The people everywhere were struggling against a blinding dust being thrown in their eyes. They were suffocating in an atmosphere of vicious intrigues designed to dupe and betray. That was all Sally could see in the chaos of international affairs.

Bill might know what he was talking about, she admitted to herself. He could give disturbing facts and figures from all those books and papers he read; but she doubted whether Dinny and his mates knew as much as they thought they did. How could they know the truth, or judge the significance of what was happening overseas? They liked to chew over the news in the morning newspaper, and draw their own conclusions.

There were some conclusions anybody who had the interests of plain, ordinary working people, and their country, at heart, could draw from certain events, Sally admitted. When million-aires and mine managers were urging any line of action, it was time for the workers to draw in their horns and ask why; and whose interests were being served by an appeal for popular support. For a long time, men who had been advocating con-cessions to the fascist powers, making flattering references to the order prevailing in Germany and under Mussolini's regime in Italy, had been conniving also at the growing military and economic strength of Japan.

For years Japanese designs on Australia had been no secret. Since the last war there had been innumerable incidents to justify apprehension. A Japanese statesman announced 'the burning desire of Japan for hegemony in the Pacific'. Japanese sampans had been caught prowling along the north coasts. Japanese goods, produced by cheap labour and ruthless exploita-tion, had been dumped on the Australian market, hampering the development of Australian industries and depriving Australian workers of jobs. Yet, while it was believed that the dark and stormy conditions prevailing in Europe would inevitably lead to war, and the part Japan would play in the war became a matter for gloomy foreboding, the export of iron ore and scrap iron from Australia to Japan continued.

For a long time workers on the goldfields had been aware that scrap iron from the mines was being sold to Japan. They had seen it being loaded into trucks in the railway yards, and lying on the wharves at Fremantle, awaiting shipment. But it was the old Kalgoorlie steam-roller which drew attention to the traffic. When it was rumoured that the Kalgoorlie Municipal Council was going to sell a broken-down steam-roller, as old as the city itself, to a buyer of scrap for a fiver, there was a public outcry.

241

'Be the Great Livin' Tinker, it'll be comin' back to us in bombs and bullets,' Tassy exclaimed.

But protests about the steam-roller were nothing to the upsurge of wrath and indignation when it was known the government of Western Australia had been negotiating with the agents of a Japanese combine for the working of immense iron ore deposits at Yampi Sound. To this news was added the information that an agreement had been drawn up between a Japanese combine and one of the largest industrial companies in Australia for the export of half a million tons of iron ore to Japan.

The Prime Minister, Mr. Lyons, stated that the development of Yampi iron ore was a matter for the Western Australian Government to deal with, and that the Commonwealth Government felt no more justified in prohibiting the export of iron ore to Japan than in prohibiting the export of wool. But the people of Australia would have none of this proposition to lease Australian mineral resources to the Japanese. The will of the people spoke like the voice of God, and the proposition had to dropped. Private enterprise, however, maintained the export of iron ore and scrap iron to Japan.

Bill had told Dinny and his cronies about a great meeting held in London to launch a boycott of Japanese goods and appeal for aid to China.

'The International Federation of Trade Unions with a membership of sixty millions,' he said, 'supports the principle of the boycott. Dockers in Marseilles have refused to unload Japanese goods, Norwegian dockers, as well, and waterside workers in British ports. There have been bonfires of silk stockings, and other Japanese goods, on an American square, demonstrations by university students, and in New York, many large stores have stopped selling Japanese goods.'

Eily and Bill addressed meetings to arouse enthusiasm for the boycott. They described the massacres and terrorism of Japanese aggression in China: what invasion had meant to millions of defenceless people in that country.

Bill had a copy of the Tanaka memorandum which outlines

the Japanese policy of expansion in Asia and the plucking of Australia as a ripe plum for the Japanese Empire. From statistical reports he quoted facts and figures to show how Japan was obtaining essential war materials from other countries, particularly Great Britain and America. If Japanese markets were restricted by the boycott, he argued, the Japanese Government would have difficulty in obtaining foreign loans and war materials to pursue its marauding career in China, or to attack and invade other countries.

Sally was so enraged and alarmed by the record of Japanese crimes in China, and the threat which Japanese imperialism held over Australia, that she worked eagerly with Bill and Eily to make the boycott effective on the goldfields.

Sometimes she distributed leaflets with Eily, and helped her to paste up posters which said: 'Don't buy Japanese goods, they're bloodstained.'

The shops were full of cheap, shoddy wares: china, stockings, garments, toys, gadgets and tools, not always marked 'made in Japan'. Sally and Dinny had gone shopping to sniff and snort when they turned over these articles.

'Selling Jap stuff?' they asked the shop assistants. 'The workers won't stand for it. Didn't you know there was a boycott on? Better tell the boss.'

It was a temptation for the wife of a working man to buy as cheaply as she could. But Sally had persuaded several of her neighbours to go about with her, urging miners and their wives not to deal with shopkeepers ignoring the boycott. Shopkeepers depended on the goodwill and wages of the miners and their wives, and before long only one store continued to show Japanese goods. Its windows were cleared after the premises had been empty of customers for a day or two.

Fremantle lumpers refused to service Japanese whaling ships, although pressure was finally brought on them to do so. But it was the Port Kembla waterside workers who were remembered with most pride when people on the goldfields talked about their effort to halt the rising power of Japan.

'When the Port Kembla workers refused to load the *Delfram* with seven thousand tons of pig-iron for Japan, I reckon they put up a good fight for the defence of Australia,' Dinny liked to say. 'They weren't bound by law or contract to load pig-iron and refused to do the job.'

As often as not he would go off to hunt up a pamphlet which was one of his treasures, and put on his spectacles to read from it.

'This was written by the Right Honourable Sir Isaac Isaacs, G.C.B., G.C.M.G.,' he announced proudly. 'He was Chief Justice at one time and then Governor-General of Australia. And here's a bit of what he says about the Port Kembla dispute:

' "For myself, I honour the men who stood out as long as they could, and those who supported them. They went far, and with sincerity of heart and purity of motive, sacrificed much to vindicate, for the whole Australian community, a general humanitarian sentiment and the right to insist on personal freedom of conscience where unrestrained by law." '

There was much more of Sir Isaac Isaacs's analysis of the coercion exercised by the Commonwealth Government against the Port Kembla workers, and its significance with regard to the government's obligations as a signatory to the League of Nations covenant. But Dinny usually wound up with a paragraph which said:

'In taking an active part by compelling the loading of pig-iron, the Commonwealth Government in the circumstances was thus clearly guilty of a breach of neutrality, and committed what is known as an "international delinquency".'

'Peace was hanging by a thread, accordin' to British statesmen, when the *Delfram* incident occurred in January 1939,' Dinny always pointed out. 'And Mr. Anthony Eden had declared: "There can be no more one-way traffic down Appeasement Avenue"; but new trade treaties were entered into with Japan, and the Japs got pig-iron and scrap for the making of high grade steel, from Australia, with the protection of the government.'

CHAPTER XXVI

T HE clouds lowering over Europe threw their dark
shadow over the goldfields. Gloomy forebodings filled
the daily press. The atmosphere was as oppressive as
before a storm burst.

Everybody was talking about war. Would there be war?
Would nazi-fascism rule the world or would the democratic
powers take up its challenge to their existence?

Arguments raged this way and that. Friendships were broken:
men came to blows in the pubs. Even Dinny and his old cronies
had their differences of opinion which almost destroyed the
mateship of years, that bond of hardships and experiences shared
in the early days of prospecting on the goldfields which was so
dear to them. Sally could hear them going hammer and tongs
as they reviewed the phantasmagoria of the past year, thrashing
over the defeat of the Spanish Government, 'the rape of Austria',
'Eden sacrificed to Mussolini', Hitler's invasion of Czechoslovakia. Fascist domination of Greece, the Balkans and the
Baltic States. Germany's demand for colonies. The Berlin-
Rome-Tokio Axis, the Japanese offensive in China, Lloyd
George's demand for an alliance with the U.S.S.R.

' "Without the help of Russia we are walking into a trap,"
he said,' Dinny observed. 'That was when Chamberlain
announced that Britain would support Poland.'

'And Mr. Montague Norman, Governor of the Bank of
England said, early this year,' Sam Mullet reminded him: ' "We
will have to give Germany a loan of £50,000,000. We may
never be paid back, but it will be a less loss than the fall of
nazism." '

'What's a plain, ordinary bloke to think,' Tassy grumbled.
'One of 'em saying we've got to line up with the Bolshies, if
we get into this war. And t'other all out to see the blasted
Germans don't get the worst of it.'

Tassy's disapproval of Bolshevism was well known. Ever since the struggle in Spain, he had constituted himself an opposition in Dinny's parliament.

Tassy said he was a Holy Roman, though a bad one. He believed the Reds had got control of the government in Spain, and from what he had heard were chiefly occupied burning churches and raping nuns. He disapproved, also, of the abdication of Edward VIII to marry a woman who had been divorced, because the church did not 'hold with' divorce. Eli Nancarrow, for different reasons, had sided with Tassy in opposition to Dinny, Blunt Pick and Sam Mullet, over the questions of Spain and the right of a king to marry the woman he loved.

Eli was 'a narrow-minded sanctimonious old bastard' about the royal love affair, Blunt Pick said, and 'too much of a skinflint and too afraid of his wife, to subscribe to Spanish relief funds'.

'What a plain, ordinary bloke's got to decide now,' Blunt Pick spluttered, 'is whether he stands for fascism or whether he doesn't.'

'You know as well as I do, Tassy,' Dinny protested, 'it was French and British armament firms helped Germany to re-arm, defyin' the terms of the Treaty of Versailles. It was British and American loans put the wind in Hitler's sails. What the hell do y' mean now, pretendin' y' don't know which side y' ought to back? There's men in Great Britain and France — and Australia — would rather back Hitler to smash trade unionism and working-class organizations, than give their own people a chance to get a better deal.'

'Be the Great Livin' Tinker, did I ever say I didn't know it?' Tassy bawled. 'It's havin' anything to do with bolshies and this damned communism, I'm objectin' to.'

'Fascism and communism, there's nowt of a difference between two of 'em, far as I can see,' Eli piped up.

'Then y'r blind as a bat,' Blunt Pick shouted.

'Only the difference between night and day,' Dinny said dryly. 'Fascism spits on the workers, turns them into machines

246

for makin' profits and wars. Communism says the world and everything in it belongs to the workers, and organizes for peace.'

'Ses you,' Tassy muttered stubbornly.

'Godless and immoral, her be,' Eli persisted. 'Same as this here fascism.'

'Y' lousy old wowser,' Blunt Pick blazed. 'God and morality don't mean any more to you than hangin' on to what you've got and lettin' everybody else go to blazes.'

'There's this about it, Eli,' Sam Mullet butted in with the intention of placating everybody, 'you've got one idea of God and morality. Tassy's got another: and there's a lot more ideas of what's good and moral than either of you think is right. It's deeds not words we must judge men and isms by. Well, take what fascists've done in the world today; and what the communists've done.'

'Don't know as the workers are much better off in Roosia than anywhere else,' Eli muttered.

'Y' don't know and y' don't want to know,' Blunt Pick flung at him, 'Y're a bloody fascist at heart, that's what y' are.'

Eli rose with the quick, brittle wrath of his seventy-odd years.

'Y' can call me a lousy wowser, and a sanctimonious old bastard, if you like, Blunt,' he said, 'but, by goom, if y' call me a bloody fascist agin, I'll crack y'r jaw.

There was an outburst of gusty laughter, and something like good humour was restored as Blunt Pick crowed:

'Y're comin' on, Eli!'

Dinny and Sam Mullet were going up to the mines on pay day to sell copies of the monthly journal of the League of Peace and Democracy. It was called *World Peace*, but did not advocate peace at any price. It urged co-operation of the democratic powers to defend the principle of collective security and resist fascist aggression, exposed the political intrigues of powerful groups of financiers and munition makers which lay behind the policy of appeasement, and explained the complications of the present situation which had forced men and women who hated war to realize there could be no organization for permanent peace between nations, while the power of fascism to dominate international affairs remained undefeated.

Eily sold *World Peace* and other working-class papers on the street corners, and Sally was astounded to discover she too believed that this war had to be fought to defeat fascism.

It was a crazy world she was living in, Sally thought despairingly. Everything was topsy-turvy. The friends of peace were demanding war, while the war-makers wore sheep's clothing to spar for peace. Not a peace which would end war; but 'a peace which would guarantee their power to make endless wars', Eily said.

During the sultry atmosphere of those days when war was brewing in Europe, Sally relived the sorrow and suffering the last war had brought her. She was horrified to hear Bill and Dinny, who had been talking against war for years, saying, now, that the issue was clearly fascism or democracy; and that they would have to support the war if it came.

It would be a war to defeat fascism, the most arrogant form of militant capitalism, they reasoned. This war must be fought to safeguard the rights of democratic peoples and keep the road open for social progress.

Sally was deaf to their arguments: dazed by her horror of another wholesale destruction of human life. This war would be more terrible and devastating than the last, there was no doubt. New weapons, poison gases, the bombing of cities and civilian populations which had taken place in Spain, indicated how appalling the havoc would be.

'Oh, Marie,' she cried, 'you can't believe we should support this war — if it comes.'

'What else is there to do?' A flush rose in Marie's withered cheeks and her eyes flashed. 'We cannot permit Hitler and Mussolini to triumph. "Mad dogs" they are being called. Must they be allowed to torture and kill when they will? Would you not 'ave them chained, or destroyed?'

'Of course.' Sally regretted that her question had stirred

248

Marie so much. The slightest exertion set her heart fluttering painfully, she knew. 'But you must not upset yourself, dear. Let's talk of something else.'

'But no,' Marie insisted, 'I must say what is in my mind. There is no other way, *chèrie*,' she went on after a moment. 'One must destroy or be destroyed. It is the tragic impasse of our times.'

'But it's the innocent who suffer most in a war,' Sally said bitterly. 'Thousands and thousands of young men, and the guilty get off scot free.'

'You speak as a mother whose sons have been torn from her,' Marie said. 'I, too, feel like a mother; but a mother for the sons and daughters of other women. How can žis misery be borne? How can we ever hope there will be any peace in the world for them? Only if we face the facts, and are stronger, braver, more resolute than our enemies . . . to remove evils which prevent organization for peace.'

'But the last war was supposed to be a war to end war,' Sally wailed.

'There is only one way to end war,' Marie said. 'And you know it, *chèrie*. "Take the profit out of war, and there will be no war," as Dinny says.'

'That means socialism,' Sally replied. 'But the mine owners and big business men are saying, even now, that the defeat of Hitler fascism would only mean they will have to fight Russia and the spread of socialism, later on.'

Marie's smile glimmered and faded.

'Maybe, it will be so,' she sighed. 'But the father of my Jacques used to say the tide of social evolution cannot be turned back. It moves, slowly, surely.'

'I wish it weren't so slowly,' Sally interrupted, her impatience and smile intended to reassure Marie.

'It is good to think we may have done a little to help flowing in of the tide,' Marie said wearily. 'I will not be here to see it. Perhaps you will not, either, chérie, but —'

'Oh, Marie,' Sally cried, giving way to the grief which had

not been expressed between them, 'I can't bear to think of you — not here.'

Marie's eyes met hers with their deep, serene gaze. 'You must not let it hurt you when I go, darrling,' she said. 'Between us there 'as been so much love and 'appiness. We will think only of that, yes?'

Sally's eyes brimmed as she kissed her.

Mrs. Miller had come into the room then with Marie's evening meal, and Sally left her. But she returned the same evening, afraid Marie had overtired herself by talking so much that afternoon. She had had a nasty heart attack, Mrs. Miller said, but was easier now. Sally went into Marie's room, and sat beside her. Marie was sleeping; but by the dim light of the lamp near her bed, Sally saw that a change had come over her wan features. It was as if the life were drifting out of them. Marie opened her eyes, and tried to smile as she saw Sally.

'I thought I was dreaming you were with me, *chèrie*,' she whispered.

Sally sat in the darkness beside her all night. It was morning, and Marie was still sleeping when she had gone home to bath and get the men's breakfasts, telling Mrs. Miller that she would come back as soon as she could. Mrs. Miller came running over to her about an hour later.

'She's gone,' Steve's mother said in great distress. 'I was lifting her to give her a cup of tea, and she gave a queer cry and fell back. I did all I could, Mrs. Gough, but it was no use.'

'My dear Marie,' Sally cried brokenly. 'My dear, dear Marie.'

CHAPTER XXVII

'AUSTRALIA also is at war. . . .'

The words fell heavily, booming and droning as they came over the air. Sally was stunned, unable for a few seconds to think or move.

Then pain and misery filtered through all her senses. She felt as if she had been struck a powerful invisible blow. She knew that millions of other women would be feeling as she did, appalled and helpless. She realized that the mania which makes a business of wholesale slaughter was beginning again with its tragic waste and insane brutality. Another generation was to be sacrificed to the enemies of mankind: to their rapacity and lust for power. That was all she could realize: all most of the women who lived near and came running to see her could realize.

Those of them who had lost a son or husband in the last war, or whose menfolk were still suffering from its aftermath of injuries, shattered nerves and unemployment, exclaimed and wept angrily. Others who dreaded the same fate for their men were distraught by fear and anxiety.

There was none of the excitement and exaltation about women of the neighbourhood which the last war had aroused. No war fever or patriotic emotion could blind them to understanding of what this war was going to mean. Memories of the last were too clear in their minds. It was a calamity about which they had no illusions: a calamity which could not be endured except by believing it had been forced on them in order that a worse might not befall. Only the younger men and women, who had not suffered during the last war, discussed the Prime Minister's announcement without leaden hearts and sombre resentment.

'But this war will be different,' Dinny said, trying to cheer Sally. 'This time we'll be fightin' for the rights of the people. The show-down'd got to come. We've been askin' for it.'

'That's all very well,' Sally replied bitterly. 'But the people who'll fight and die, aren't the ones who've been boosting fascism, giving Hitler the money and arms to make war. He couldn't've carried on the way he has done, if they hadn't. They've run us like sheep along the same old track to the slaughter yards. How do you know they won't do it again?'

'I don't,' Dinny admitted. 'They've been buildin' up fascism as a bulwark against bolshevism. But Hitler's got a bit too bumptious. National interests are threatened in France and Great Britain. And there's enough democratic feelin' in both countries to see where things are leadin'. The people won't stand for it. So they've got to fight.'

'Why don't they start by shooting the criminals responsible for helping Germany to make another war?' Sally demanded.

'They'll be the great patriots now,' Dinny pointed out. 'It will pay 'em to be. And where'd we get the arms and munitions to beat Hitler, if the governments clamped down on their profits?'

'God,' Sally groaned, 'will it ever end; this killing off of young men, for the benefit of a few old money-grubbers and their rotten schemes? If the Soviet Union hadn't changed their tune about Germany maybe there'd've been no war.'

'Now, now, missus,' Dinny expostulated, 'you don't want to do your block. All along the Soviet's been askin' for an agreement with the Allies, and they've been shilly-shallyin' over the proposition. The Soviet Government's got its own people and country to think of, and if a non-aggression pact with Germany'll keep them out of the war, they've got a right to make it. 'Specially as they know the governments of Great Britain and France've been tryin' to save themselves by soolin' Hitler on to fight bolshevism.'

He was by no means happy about the Soviet-German Pact. It had been a shock even to Bill, although he defended it, and understood the underlying purposes for which it had been framed. Sally, in her frantic resentment of every move which precipitated the war, was prepared to blame anybody and everybody responsible for its outbreak.

'Oh, well,' she said querulously, 'if you've got no confidence in the governments running the war, what's the good of it?'

'We've got confidence in the peoples behind the governments,' Dinny said. 'We reckon they'll see the war is fought to smash Hitlerism and all it stands for.'

'Wish I could believe it,' Sally grumbled.

Dinny could not persuade her that the war would be fought for the purposes being blazoned in the daily press: to defend democratic peoples from the aggressive designs of Hitler Germany. Mussolini was not yet a belligerent, or fascism referred to disrespectfully. But the most conservative newspapers and politicians were talking of democracy as though they loved it: talking about our 'democratic traditions', 'democratic institutions', 'democratic ideals', and 'the democratic way of life', as though they had always been associated with these praiseworthy manifestations of national vigour. Sally was not impressed. She did not believe that men who had been lauding Hitler and Mussolini, and approving of their regimes only a few weeks before war was declared, could change their spots over night. She was as uneasy as a cat in a new house, unhappy, suspicious, her fur on end. Bill and Dinny both teased and reasoned with her; but Sally continued to miaow apprehensively, and nurse her grouch against them and the war.

During the following weeks, she seized on every pretext to air her grievances about the war, this war, and wars in general. She argued stubbornly with Dinny and Bill and Eily, grouchy and unreasonable.

'We've just been pitch-forked into it,' she said, voicing one of the objections to the Prime Minister's announcement, which was being freely expressed. 'Why wasn't the Federal parliament consulted before Australia was committed to the war? The governments of Canada and South Africa haven't been in such a hurry to drag their people into support of the blundering policy of the British Government. They, at least, have given the people's representatives a chance to make a decision.'

Dinny and Bill and Eily agreed she had something there;

but the result would have been the same, they contended. They had to approve of the principles which underlay Australia's participation in the war. It was with reluctant acceptance of a disaster that they, and most men and women, moved into preparations for putting Australia in a position to meet the military demands which would be made on her.

Sally saw the drab, familiar scene about her change as it had done twenty-five years ago. She heard the tramp of marching feet in the streets, the blare of military bands: watched men crowded round the recruiting offices, with despairing grief. It seemed to her that the same sensational rumours were spreading. Well-known citizens became 'enemy aliens', overnight, and were interned. Spies had been arrested. Mysterious signalling stations and wireless transmitting sets were being discovered in strategic positions along the coast.

People talked of nothing but military needs, air-raid precautions, citizen forces being organized for home defence, women's committees forming to knit and sew, or provide amenities for the troops. But with it all grew a more intense realization of the national peril than there had been before. There was nothing like the hysteria and war fever which had possessed people in the early days of the last war, Sally began to perceive. Isolated and remote from the battlefields in Europe though Australia was, the probability of Japanese co-operation with the Axis partners created a sober recognition of the dangers facing the country.

Goldfields folk swung automatically into the war effort. Miners were in a reserved occupation, but many of them enlisted: some for the militia which was to be retained for the defence of Australia: others for active service overseas wherever they might be needed.

When Bill came to tell her he had volunteered for active service, Sally wailed:

'That's the last straw! It's what I've been afraid of.'

'I've got to go, gran,' Bill said. 'I've been telling people for the last three years we must stop Hitler's bid for world power.

We've got to prevent the spread of fascism. I can't expect other men to fight if I don't.'

'I suppose not.'

Sally felt as if all the vitality were being drained out of her. This was what she had been dreading for months. Just this, that Bill's young body, his gay, sensitive spirit would be hurled into the brutal chaos. She had hoped that never again would she have to endure the pain which gnawed at her brain. But there it was, the gripping anguish she had gone through for Lal and Dick. And there it would remain, she knew, until — she could not, for the moment, imagine the day when this war would be over, and Bill would stand before her, sound in body and mind, as he was now. Lal had been killed in Palestine, and Dick shattered by the last war. How could she dream this dearly loved grandson would survive the horrors of this war?

And yet, she must not let Bill suspect her pessimism, Sally told herself. She had a superstitious idea that any sense of fatality would impair his will to live.

'Don't worrit, darl,' Bill said, putting his arms round her. 'I know it's hard for you to let me go. But I've got to fight for the things we believe in, this way, as well as any other.'

His voice was so like his father's that Sally's tears welled. She drove them back.

'I know, Bill,' she said. 'And I've got to back you up. Not make it any harder.'

'That's the stuff,' Bill exulted. 'Tom used to say you'd stand up to anything, gran. It started him thinking, you know, when he was a youngster: made him want to get a fair deal for all the men and women who were battling along like you.'

'Did he? Did he say that?' Sally queried. 'I didn't always stand by Tom when I should have, Bill. And now — I seem to be getting such an old crock, just doddering along, with no courage left.'

'Not you!' Bill hugged her. 'You're game as they make them, Sal-o-my.'

'Oh, Bill!' His father's name for her, which Bill only used in

255

moments of rare intimacy like this, shook Sally. She clung to him, her tears brimming, a smile breaking through. 'I'll try to be,' she promised.

During those first weeks of the war, grim appraisement of what it was going to mean oppressed everybody. The danger lurking for Australia from the Japanese alliance with Germany loomed above all else. But Sally had come to understand with Bill and Dinny that the vital issues would be decided in Europe; that the challenge of Hitler's armies devastating Poland would have to be met by the British and French forces, united to throw back any attack on their frontiers. Guns had opened fire along the Maginot Line. The *Athenia* had been sunk by a German submarine. There was a British bombing raid on Kiel. Italy's strategic position on the Mediterranean, and her collusion with Germany, allowed for no doubts as to how they would presently affect the situation.

Before long emergency regulations issued by the Menzies government were distracting attention from the war news. They gave the government dictatorial powers which would strangle the democratic rights of the Australian people. There was an outcry against them. How could men fight for democracy abroad when their rights were being filched from them at home, workers on the goldfields demanded. Eily was aghast at this attempt to penalize trade unionists determined to maintain their standards of organization, communists, and people like Sally herself, who had overcome a loathing of war in order to support this war by democratic people against fascism.

'Why, gran,' Eily exclaimed, 'these regulations are attacking the most active anti-fascists in the country. What does it mean?'

'Don't ask me,' Sally replied crossly. 'The war's caused troubles enough, as far as I can see, without adding to them.'

'There's never been such repressive legislation against the rights of the Australian people,' Dinny said. 'It's aroused indignation, not only among the workers. All sorts of intelligent men and women who value their rights as citizens are protestin' agenst it. There was a letter in the *West*, a few days ago, signed by the Anglican Primate of Australia, Dr. Le Fanu, and a professor of the University of Western Australia, Mr. Walter Murdoch, sayin' that the regulations which prevents "any reference to the war, to Russia or its government, to strikes within the Empire, or any allied country, or to industrial unrest, in any publication the government may care to classify as 'communist' is a dangerous restriction of civil liberties in this country".'

After Hitler's victory had been arrested by the Red Army's march into Poland, and Soviet pacts with Lithuania, Estonia and Latvia, the daily press began to reflect sentiments favourable to the U.S.S.R. Dinny liked to cut them out and chuckle over them.

He read them to Sally. 'Hitler has been outwitted and discomfited by the Soviet-German Pact. Russia has enormously advanced her strategic position and Baltic influence. Hitler in short has paid a disastrous price for the neutrality of the Soviet Union.'

'Stalin has used Hitler as a catspaw and compelled him to disgorge half his booty.'

'There are angry heart-burnings in Germany over the Russian occupation of the Western Ukraine and White Ruthenia. Hitler is now champing to settle the score.'

The Soviet-German Pact, denounced as a 'stab in the back' of Allied diplomacy, was now regarded as having strengthened the position of the Allies, smashed Hitler's plans for an all quiet on his eastern front, and inspired the peace feelers which were waving tentatively in a murky atmosphere.

There had been little fighting on the western front. The belligerents were jockeying for position before opening an offensive, the newspapers said. This was a positional war. 'A phoney war', people began to growl, wondering what was going on behind the scenes of the Allied commands. Dinny declared that the anti-Soviet diehards were trying desperately to come to terms with Hitler and switch the war against Russia. Through the mud and fogs of a northern winter, the armies of

France and Germany remained facing each other, stalled down and impotent.

When the French Cabinet had arrested a hundred communist deputies and thrown them into prison, and Thorez, secretary of the Communist Party of France, left the trenches, accusing the government of being more concerned to suppress the movement of the people towards socialism than to fight Hitler, Dinny's and Eily's attitude towards the war changed.

Dinny was not a communist, but he was satisfied, he said, that the war was being used not only in France and Great Britain, but in Australia also, to serve the interests of reactionaries and destroy the organizations of the workers. The will of the people for service and victory had been broken by attacks on their rights and liberties, and outrageous prosecutions.

'It's a damned capitalist war like any other,' Dinny growled. And Eily was chalking up slogans like: 'Fight Fascism at Home and Abroad.' Sally had seen them in big crooked letters on the pavement and on dingy bare walls.

She was demented by the shifts of opinion about the war. No sooner had she been won to regard it as a war for democracy against nazism and fascism, than Dinny and Eily were saying it was a capitalist war being used to destroy the democratic organizations of the British and French people, and making only a pretence of fighting Hitler fascism. The workers were being betrayed at home and in the trenches, they said. The talk about freedom and democracy was all a bluff to get men into the army.

What was she to do, Sally asked herself. How was she to glean the truth from the specious propaganda going on all round her? She heard public speakers applauding the government, and people in the street abusing the government and the war leaders. Slogans and lies dinned in her ears. She knew all about 'the convenient euphemisms with which statesmen hide the real objects of their policy'. Bill had often used that phrase when he was addressing a meeting, and explained what it meant. But now she seemed unable to distinguish between 'convenient euphemisms' and honest statements about the war.

She remembered what Tom used to say: 'Judge people not by what they say, but by what they do.' But Bill was a soldier now, and part of the war. As an engineer, he had been sent to the Eastern States for special training. Could he get out of the army if he tried? Bill had wanted to fight fascism. He wanted to fight until fascism was defeated. But from his letters recently, it was evident he was as disturbed as Dinny and Eily about those drastic regulations and the prosecutions which had occurred. He accused the government of causing disunity among the workers and of sabotaging the war effort. Sally was sure that if Bill was as convinced as Eily and Dinny were that the war was being used to defeat the very purpose for which it was supposed to be fought, he would not go through with it. But he had not yet come to that conclusion and while he was in the fighting forces, Sally felt she must be helping and working with them.

It was well known that the defences of Australia were totally indequate. Neither equipment nor man-power at their present strength could effectively resist Japanese attack and invasion, the military authorities had admitted. There had been a good deal of opposition, therefore, to the government's proposal to send an expeditionary force overseas. A Labour senator's amendment to the bill empowering the government to do so, stated that 'Australian man-power is required for the defence and safety of Australia', and that 'the Senate is opposed to the dispatch of expeditionary forces'. It failed by five votes.

The first troops for service overseas embarked soon afterwards. Bill sailed with them. Sally and Dinny went down to see him when the troops passed through Perth.

Secrecy had to be maintained about the movement of troops, but Bill had written to say he would be in the gardens opposite the old post office on a certain date, and Sally knew what that meant. No information could be obtained as to when a troopship was due. Friends and relatives of the men on board were advised to meet them in the city, and some of them had heard when the first expeditionary force would arrive.

It was a breathlessly hot day and a restless, disgruntled crowd milled about the streets, waiting for a glimpse of the first Australian soldiers going 'to fight Hitler and the bloomin' nazis', as a man said to Dinny. He had a son among them, and wanted to go down to Fremantle to meet him. But the wharves were under guard he was told. Crowds would not be allowed to welcome or farewell the troopships. The troops were marching up from Fremantle, and would be here presently.

Footsore, sweating and dispirited, they dragged their way through the city. They had marched twelve miles under a blazing sun, in their shoddy khaki uniforms and heavy army boots. A striking contrast to men of the first A.I.F. who had gone abroad during the last war! Sally remembered the Light Horsemen riding through the streets, perfect specimens of manhood in the pride and vigour of their youth, well-disciplined, well-equipped, gay and confident. These men looked, for the most part, of poor physique, weedy, unkempt and ill-trained. There was no waving of flags, no cheering as they passed. Only a sombre, heavy-hearted realization of what lay before these citizen soldiers, leaving their own country to take part in a war which threatened to be more violent and disastrous than any the world had ever known.

When the lines of weary, straggling figures broke up, the men dropped exhausted in the shade of trees along the city streets. They took off their boots and coats, stretched out along footpaths near the gardens and went to sleep, or swarmed into the pubs.

Bill found Sally and Dinny waiting for him in the gardens, under the jacaranda trees which spread a fleece of lilac blossom against the blue sky. He was looking well and wiry, though fagged after the gruelling march from Fremantle.

'The worst of it is, the troops've been getting round barefoot on board ship for over a week' he said with a wry grin. 'And they were issued with new boots for this stunt. I stuck to my old ones, but some of the lads, what with the heat and these blasted boots, went out to it on the way. Had to be picked up by the ambulance and dumped in hospital.'

'Why can't the army take decent care of men when it gets them?' Sally exclaimed wrathfully. 'It's a crying shame to have made those poor boys walk all that way on a day like this, Bill.'

'Many of them have been recruited from the unemployed,' Bill told her. 'At least the army feeds them. Some of them hadn't had a decent feed for months till they joined up. I suppose that's got something to do with the way they konked out today. But I dare say we'll have tougher stunts to face before we're through.'

'Oh, darling,' Sally wailed. 'I can't bear to think of it.'

She had a present for him which she thought would amuse Bill.

'Who do you think came to see me, the other day?' she queried. 'Kalgoorla! She had heard "that feller Young Bill goin' away fight'm, big war". And she brought me this for you, darling.'

Sally handed Bill a small package wrapped in brown paper.

'Kalgoorla was very mysterious and solemn about it,' she went on. 'Said it's a movin she made for you, with blackfeller magics to keep you safe and bring you home again.'

'Strike!' Bill laughed, unwrapping the brown paper Sally had put round the package Kalgoorla gave her. 'What am I supposed to do with it?'

'I could have cried when she brought it to me,' Sally said. 'She's ill and feeble, nearly blind these days, and walked in all the way from Rill Station.'

Kalgoorla's movin consisted of a bundle of twigs and feathers, wrapped in bark and tied with a piece of hair string. The laughter died out of Bill's eyes and moisture welled as he looked at them.

'It was all she could do for you, I suppose,' he said. 'Poor old Kalgoorla! Tell her I'll keep her movin here.'

He slipped it into the wallet he took from the breast pocket of his tunic. 'It will be a little bit of the goldfields to take away with me, at any rate.'

Sprawled on the grass beside them, Bill yarned about his experiences and impressions of life in the army.

He was interested in it, and liked the contact with all sorts of men who had joined up, but had felt like chucking the whole show, he confessed, when the French deputies were arrested and the Menzies government started its campaign of repressive legislation. The feeling in the Eastern States was that the government had so antagonized the workers it could not carry on. If there was to be unity for victory, Labour would have to take office. And Bill was gambling on pressure from the peoples of Great Britain and France to ensure more energetic prosecution of the war.

'I reckon there's a job for me to do in the army as much as anywhere else,' he said, frowning thoughtfully. 'Tell Eily that, Dinny.'

'That's how I thought you'd feel,' Sally said. 'But do be careful. Don't take any unnecessary risks, will you, Bill?'

Bill's smile flashed at her.

'You bet I won't,' he said cheerily. 'Promised Pat, too. We've been seeing quite a lot of each other when I was on leave in Sydney. She's in the W.A.A.F. And Pam's got a baby daughter — the funniest little doll with a mop of black hair and brown eyes like Shawn.'

That was news Sally could glow over because Bill himself seemed so pleased to give it to her. There was more he would like to say, she felt sure, though he was shy of putting it into words.

'Well,' she said teasingly, 'are you engaged — or what?'

'What, mostly,' Bill replied with his provoking reserve. 'If we feel the same way about each other — after the war, I dare say we'll be married.'

'Oh, dear,' Sally beamed at him, 'I'm so glad. If only the wretched business were all over!'

'I reckon you hadn't a chance when Pat took a fancy to you, Bill,' Dinny crowed happily.

Dinny took them to lunch in a café near the Town Hall. Men

in khaki were swarming through the streets now: some of them drunk already, and singing lugubriously as they hung on to each other, or strode unsteadily along. Others swaggered by with girls they had captured; and small boys clung like flies to any solitary soldier. There were brawls outside the pubs and here and there a two-up ring collected a crowd, but the police made no attempt to interfere.

'The boys've taken charge of the town all right,' Bill grinned.

'It's their last day of freedom, I suppose they reckon,' Dinny said. 'Their last day in Australia — for a long time. You can't blame 'em if they're making the most of it.'

After lunch Bill decided he would like a swim. They went to Cottesloe and Sally hired a bathing-suit to go for a dip with him. Dinny sat on the beach watching them, scared that Missus Sally would be carried out by the surf. It was still hot, but a breeze had sprung up, lifting great green combers and sending them sprawling towards him.

Bill wanted to know all the news of the fields and the family. As he lay on the sand beside her, the scene seemed the same to Sally as it had been that day years ago, before Lal went to the war, and Lal and Den had run into the surf or tumbled sky-larking here on the sand. The same hordes of children made a fringe to the edge of the sea: the same figures in brightly coloured bathers under big gaudy umbrellas were scattered about the beach: the same lovely, sun-browned bodies of men and girls posed negligently in the brilliant sunshine. And far out across the blue sea, in a light mist screening the islands, the grey shapes of transports and their convoy lay waiting to take men into the hideous carnage of war.

Sally was distraught as she thought of it and that Lal had never come back. Perhaps she had only a few more hours to spend with Bill —

They had dinner at the hotel and went down to the port with Bill when it was time for him to return to his ship. He had no idea when it would sail. In the early hours of the morning, he imagined. Sally would have liked to sit on the beach all night and watch those dim grey shapes glide away beyond the horizon. She persuaded Dinny to go back to the rooms they had taken in Perth, and let her stay at an hotel overlooking the sea at Cottesloe.

But when she looked out over the sea at dawn it was empty. The transports and destroyers had gone from the roadstead.

CHAPTER XXVIII

A MOOD of utter despondency overwhelmed Sally during the next few months. Dinny wanted her to go down to Warrinup to see Den, but she could not bring herself to leave home. Lonely and miserable, she moped about the house and in the garden. She missed Marie and was depressed about Bill having been hurled away from her so soon.

'Why should men be sent overseas when they're needed so badly to defend Australia?' she asked grumpily.

Most people seemed apathetic. They were talking as if they had been deluded by a war scare, saying this was 'a phoney war', vaguely expecting it to end soon. The mines were still working: the every-day life of the town going on much as usual, the picture theatres and dance halls crowded: the pubs full of men drinking and roistering.

It was difficult to believe that the war, stalled down in the mists and snows of a European winter, could very much affect their lives, any more than that weather. Goldfields folk were sweltering in the heat and dust storms of summer. But when the Russian campaign against Finland began people quarrelled as violently as if they had been in the midst of it. Sally and Dinny had never had a serious quarrel except when she and Frisco were lovers; but they quarrelled bitterly over Finland.

'Poor little Finland!' Sally exclaimed indignantly, as so many of her neighbours were doing.

She was pleased to agree with them for once in a way. Dinny argued frantically that Finland was a fascist-controlled state, that Hitler could use it as a jumping-off ground for attack whenever he chose, and that the Soviet Government had made generous offers of territory and compensation for strategic positions to safe-guard Leningrad. But Sally maintained a stubborn disapproval of Russia's attitude, until it was announced that British and French troops, planes and arms were being dispatched to aid the Finns.

'Can't y' see now, missus, what the wire-pullers are up to?' Dinny demanded hotly. 'They want to switch the war. All the time there's been a chance of conflict between the German and Russian armies in Poland, they've been sittin' back, waitin' for them to fly at each other's throats. But now, they think they've got an opportunity to queer the Soviet pitch.'

Sally saw; and lost her bearings about the war again. She felt hopelessly and utterly confused by the complications, undercurrents, political chicanery and national intrigues racking the Allied forces. It seemed futile to knit and sew. Every time she picked up her work, she could see Marie's hands flying with delicate swiftness over the materials; and then how crippled and ugly Marie's hands had become. She brooded over the cruelty of life for so many people she had known: the waste and destruction, by war, of all decent men and women valued most. The abuses of authority, double-dealing, profiteering, frenzy of prosecutions going on under the cover of patriotism, appalled her.

At Geraldton, there had been an outrageous case. A returned soldier of the last war and his wife were convicted and sentenced, each to six months' imprisonment, for having 'unlawful documents' in their possession. These were newspapers and pamphlets issued long before there was any ban on them. Mrs. Owen had a baby of eighteen months and a boy nine years old, but that did not prevent the authorities from removing her from her children and keeping her and her husband in jail for six months.

Most of the prosecutions had been levelled at communists, or persons found in possession of some pamphlet like 'No War on Soviet Russia'. But there were ludicrous instances, like that of a sailor, one of the few survivors of a ship sunk by a German raider. Two or three months later he was fined £60 — 'in default imprisonment for one month' — for having in his possession a pamphlet entitled, 'The Coming War in the Pacific', and several other pamphlets which it had become unlawful to own.

To escape her obsessing misery, Sally grubbed about, disinterestedly, in the garden. But soon, trying to keep a few plants alive while men were being slaughtered, irked her unbearably.

Why should she bother whether her roses bloomed when the lives of men and women were being blasted, she asked herself. What did it matter that her wild hibiscus was a bouquet of diaphanous mauve petals, or the bird of paradise bushes gay with yellow wings and vermilion tails? How could she have any joy in their beauty when death and destruction were ravaging helpless peoples?

She had given up going to Red Cross or Comforts Fund meetings. If Dinny had not watered the garden, nobody would have. He found time to do that and any chores round the house Sally neglected.

'You'd ought to take a pull at y'self, missus,' he said reproachfully. 'There's no sense in not giving the flowers a drop of water, even if things are in a bad way. I know how you feel about the war and these damned reg'lations. But there'll be a change. You see. The people can't be fooled by what's happenin' much longer.'

'I hope you're right, Dinny,' Sally said, unable to shake off her depression. 'It's thinking about Bill: his life being wasted, that's got me down.'

Eily had been very hurt because Dick passed her in the street now with a casual: 'Hullo, mother.' He had not been to see her since he was married. He was in uniform now, and speaking at a patriotic meeting recently had urged that drastic action be taken against any reds on the goldfields, disrupting the war effort by circulating illegal literature.

'He knows all we want is a real fight against fascism,' Eily wailed. 'How can Dick talk like that?'

'Never mind,' Sally comforted her. 'Everybody sees through his game. Bill's been fighting in Libya for months, and Dick's just joined up. He's out to ingratiate himself with the authorities and get a commission.'

Suddenly Hitler moved again, with a lightning blow at Norway: Denmark, Holland and Belgium were invaded. France fell. British forces were withdrawn from Dunkirk. Disaster confronted the Allied forces.

Aroused and disgusted with herself Sally started to knit and go to Comforts Fund meetings again. She fretted to be doing something more effective to relieve the suffering of peoples in the occupied countries: something which would turn the fury of the war against those armies of triumphant fascism: something which would strengthen the defences of Great Britain and Australia.

Dinny and Eily maintained that the only hope for victory lay in an alliance with the Soviet Union which would force Hitler to fight on two fronts. They were talking about it everywhere: distributing leaflets which put the facts of the situation before the people and urged them to bring pressure to bear on the government for the adoption of a policy to ensure a full military, political and economic alliance with the Soviet Union for winning the war.

Sally was surprised to see Frisco push back the garden gate, late one afternoon, and stumble along the path to the veranda.

She had seen him only once or twice since he had closed his office and gone to live with Mrs. Rooney in a house at Boulder. Nora said they were married and had a child. Frisco had been very shaky and unkempt when Sally had seen him before, but today he was wearing his old uniform: looked alert and well-groomed.

Dinny went to meet him, and Sally heard them talking as they sat in those, big sagging chairs on the veranda.

'I'm in harness again, Dinny,' Frisco said, his voice jerked out of him under some nervous strain. 'There's not much use an old crock like me can be. But they've put me on secret service. I'm supposed to keep track of subversive activities. Breaking my oath, and all that, to come here and tell you. But there's a new regulation coming out. It's going to hit the coms pretty hard. Wanted to warn you, and get you to tell Eily to clear out every scrap of paper or book she's got connected with the Communist Party, or any organizations affiliated with it. If she doesn't, the chances are she'll go to jail.'

'Cripes,' Dinny growled, 'what are they comin' at? All the

coms want is to make the government play the game, and get on with the war — if it is a war to smash fascism.'

'I know that,' Frisco said. 'If I didn't, I wouldn't be here.'

'Hell!' Dinny hooted. 'If they'd round up the fascists and pro-fascists in this town, it'd be more to the point.'

'That's what I say,' Frisco declared, his sardonic humour crackling. 'But we've put a guard on the post office and the broadcasting station, in case the coms try to start something.'

He got up to go, straightened his belt, and turned his head towards the open door. Sally thought he had heard her moving about in the sitting-room, and was hoping she might come out to speak to him. She could not yet forgive him for what he had done to her: for the pain and humiliation of their broken romance, and for depriving her of her illusions about him.

Frisco seemed to realize she had been listening, but had no intention of coming to speak to him.

'Oh, well,' he exclaimed with the jaunty derision Sally knew so well, 'tell Missus Sally I've done this for her. I'd always perjure my soul for her sake.'

Sally had gone with Dinny to warn Eily after Frisco's visit. They helped her to burn a pile of newspapers and pamphlets. Some of her books she would not destroy. She packed them carefully, and Dinny promised to take them to a safe place he knew in the bush. Sally, herself, took charge of Bill's papers and books.

'Over my dead body they'll get them,' she said.

But Dinny persuaded her to let him take Bill's books, also, to his safe place.

The Communist Party, the League for Peace and Democracy, and several other organizations, were declared illegal. It became an offence to have in one's possession papers or pamphlets published by them even months before the ban. Several men and women were arrested and imprisoned after security police had raided their homes and discovered a copy of one of these forbidden pamphlets or papers.

But nothing was found in Eily's home on which to base a prosecution, thanks to Nadya. When detectives called early in the morning after that regulation had become law, Eily remembered suddenly there were two old newspapers under the cushion of her kitchen chair which she should have destroyed. While detectives ransacked her sitting-room and bedroom, going painstakingly through every cupboard and drawer, turning over her underclothes and reading her letters, they would not allow her out of their sight. She could only call to Nadya to look after Tommy and give him his breakfast. How could she have been so careless, Eily asked herself. There was no doubt in her mind those papers would be found and that she would go to jail for having them in the house.

Nadya was sitting on the floor playing with Tommy when the detectives searched the kitchen. There were no incriminating newspapers under the cushion on Eily's chair.

'You often put things under that cushion, mum,' Nadya said calmly, when the detectives had gone. 'I thought I'd better see if there was anything you'd forgotten.'

'Oh, darling,' Eily cried, hugging her, 'did you burn those papers?'

'Of course,' Nadya replied, in her staid matter-of-fact way, though her eyes behind their round glasses held a naive satisfaction.

La, who had been kept in his own room, came rushing out, indignant that the detectives had taken away some of his history notes: notes on the Peasants' War, and Wat Tyler's rebellion which he had been given at school for his scholarship work.

'Never mind,' Eily laughed, 'they've taken dad's copy of the Koran, and Carlyle's *French Revolution*, too, so perhaps those detectives will be learning there were other times when the people had to defend their rights.'

Dinny was enraged by the new regulations. They made no difference to Eily's conviction that it was her duty to bring before the people leaflets and pamphlets which protested against this attack on civil liberties, and pointed out that it was aiding fascism, as well as undermining the war effort. She explained to the children why she was doing this, and arranged with Sally to look after them if she were arrested. Dinny tramped about half the night helping her to distribute the illegal leaflets and pamphlets.

Yarning with Sam Mullet, Tassy Regan, Blunt Pick, Eli Nancarrow and Dally on the veranda, Sally heard him denouncing the regulations and the government. But he had been doing it in the pubs, and talking to men on the street corners in the same way, she knew. Men and women had been sentenced to six months' imprisonment for saying much less than Dinny was saying, or having in their possession one of those 'illegal publications' Dinny was passing round among miners and their families.

He often quoted Maurice Blackburn, a Labour member of the Commonwealth parliament, who had declared: 'These regulations are intended to stifle criticism of the policy of the government and its war effort . . . There's nothing you can say in criticism of them that may not be held likely to cause public alarm, or discourage recruiting, or to lower civilian morale.'

' "If these reg'lations stand," Blackburn says,' Dinny explained wrathfully, ' "anyone who dares to criticize the government, does so at his peril." '

'Look out, Dinny, y'll be run in,' Dally chiacked.

'I'd rather be run in than keep me mouth shut about the rotten things that are happenin',' Dinny replied. 'Didn't we go into this war to fight fascism? Didn't Bill Gough and Perth Molloy, two of the best-known coms on the goldfields, go off with the first A.I.F.? Then what the hell do these reg'lations mean? Government by reg'lation, that's what we're gettin'. That was Hitler's game.'

'It was over the fence jailing an old man like John Coleman for having a communist paper in his house — published months ago,' Sam said slowly.

'Particularly when he was arrested and sentenced to four months' imprisonment on a warrant made out for his son,' Sally interjected. 'I've known the Colemans for years. They've reared a big family, and a decenter, finer old couple you couldn't meet. One of the boys is a communist; but things have come to a pretty pass when an old man's got to go to jail for what his son thinks.'

'It's become a crime to say or publish a word favourable to the Soviet Union,' Blunt Pick growled.

'Or to be "suspected of being about to commit", an offence against the reg'lations,' Dinny barked.

'Churchill says,' Sam Mullet observed, 'the British Government's dropped regulations "at variance with the English temper, sense of justice and fair play".'

'That's right,' Dinny agreed. 'In England the regulations have been amended, so that only "false statements intended to assist the enemy or hinder national defence", are punished. But here, there's a real campaign of terrorism goin' on. If anybody's holdin' up the war effort, the government is. Chamberlain couldn't shunt the English people about the way he wanted, and I reckon Menzies and Co. can't shunt the people of Australia about much longer, the way they've been doin'.'

Angry and disturbed though she was, Sally wished that Dinny and Eily, and the two or three men and women working with them, would desist from their attempts to distribute forbidden leaflets and papers.

'You're just knocking your heads against a stone wall,' she said testily. 'No good will come of it.'

'But we've got to do it, gran,' Eily objected. 'Bill would expect us to protest, wouldn't he? A rage against wrong and injustice isn't enough, if you do nothing to change them. And it's only by struggle against oppressive legislation that there's ever been any progress.'

Sally was not convinced. She nursed a grouch against everything and everybody: the governments responsible for the incompetence and blunders defeating the Allied forces, as well as Dinny and Eily whose changes of opinion about the war had thrown her mind into such confusion.

Bill was still in North Africa. There had been fighting in the western desert. A hospital ship brought hundreds of wounded men back to Australia. Sally wished she could have been a nurse. She was too old to start training even; but she went up to the big shabby hospital of wood and corrugated iron that had stood in

272

Kalgoorlie for years, and offered to scrub the floors or do any work for which help might be needed.

She spent two mornings a week on her knees from then on, and frequently helped to provide meals for troops passing through Kalgoorlie to training camps in the east, or near the coast. But she could not stifle her unrest and dissatisfaction. She felt as if she were shirking something she ought to be doing. What it was she did not know until Dinny said irritably:

'Me leg's gone crook on me. I can't go out with Eily tonight, and I don't like lettin' her go round pastin' up leaflets alone. You'd ought to go with her, missus.'

'Me? I'm not a communist,' Sally demurred.

'No more am I,' Dinny retorted. 'Only an old labourite. But that doesn't mean I'm goin' to let the people be done out of their rights without raisin' a finger to stop it.'

'All right,' Sally said slowly. 'I'll go with Eily.'

Eily had tried to dissuade her.

'It's not fair for you to take the risk, gran dear,' she said. 'I can manage quite well by myself.'

'If Tom were here, or Bill, they'd go with you,' Sally said stubbornly. 'So I will.'

She had trudged round the deserted streets, hiding a pot of paste and a big brush in her shopping bag, while Eily carried the leaflets which accused the government of attempting to destroy vital and democratic rights of the Australian people. Sally kept watch while Eily slapped leaflets on fences, telegraph poles, seats in the street and buildings near the mines. When any late prowler hove in sight they would pick up their papers and paste pot and stroll away.

'If we're stopped and questioned as to why we're out at this hour, we've been looking after a sick friend, don't forget,' Eily said.

'Who?'

'Mrs. Miller, Steve's mother. She'll understand.'

It was all very unpleasant and terrifying to Sally. She was afraid they might be arrested at any moment; but it was absurd to be scared, she told herself. Her natural instinct to defy any threat to her freedom of conscience, and to go through with anything difficult and dangerous to do, asserted itself. She trotted along gamely beside Eily, joking and making even Eily feel there was something rather amusing in their escapade.

When a man on a bicycle slipped past, just when they had decorated a telegraph pole, Eily thought he might be a spy and going to give information to the police; but Sally laughed at the idea. After two old drunks had followed them for some distance, she wanted to use her paste brush on their faces to get rid of them.

But when it was all over, and they were having a cup of tea in the kitchen at home, she was angry and distressed that Eily should have to do things like this and be treated as a criminal.

'We had to do it in the anti-conscription campaign,' Eily reminded her. 'A few men and women have always had to fight for the rights of the people. Soon, it will be understood this state of things can't go on. There'll have to be a change of government, and a different attitude to the war.'

'I hope you're right,' Sally said wearily. 'I didn't do much to help before. But I want you to know I'll do all I can to stand by you, now, Eily.'

'Dear gran,' Eily said lovingly as she got up to go, 'you've always been a tower of strength to me, anyhow. Thank you for coming tonight. Bill used to say: "She's such a sturdy old battler, gran!" That's what you've shown me, tonight. How a sturdy old battler just battles on.'

With the German attack on Russia and the conclusion of an alliance between Great Britain, France and the Soviet Union, the war took another turn which altered the course of events in Australia. It put red-baiters on the fields, and everywhere, in an awkward position, although they maintained a surly opposition to local communists, and the suggestion that communist organizations had anything to do with the stiff resistance the Red Army was putting up to the German armies which had careered victoriously across Europe.

But before long Eily was being treated as something of a

heroine. She was spoken of as 'a brave little woman' who had defended the rights of the people, and against all opposition put forward a policy for winning the war which was now being accepted. Folk who had looked the other way when she smiled and said: 'Good morning', to them, now nodded and remarked shamefacedly: 'You were right after all, Mrs. Gough!'

'All the reactionaries in the town are chewin' the rag,' Dinny chortled. 'But they've got to admit the Red Army's "saved Britain in her hour of gravest peril".'

He enjoyed himself mightily pointing out to Tassy and Eli, and anybody who had talked about the Russians not being able 'to fight their way out of a paper bag', just what the Red Army was, and why it had been able to stand up to the Germans' military machine. It gave him no end of satisfaction to bail up Dick and remark chirpily: 'So you backed the wrong horse, after all, Dick!'

Daphne wrote to say she was coming home. Steve had decided to join up and persuaded her to leave her job at Wiluna.

Eily smiled when she told Sally this news. They both hoped there was more in it than Daphne had said. Sally was sure there would be when Steve came to see her, a week before Daphne returned.

'Wiluna's the most God-forsaken spot on the fields,' Steve said, 'and Daph's got too thin working there. A big town's grown up near the mine; but the country round about is a blasted desert. White dust from the arsenic plant, falling everywhere, has destroyed the scrub and herbage. People can't keep a cat or a dog. Before long the arsenic kills it, and the heat this summer's been terrific. The sun, up there, blazes like a huge oxy-acetylene welding lamp, shrivelling your skin and blinding you.'

It was no wonder men on Wiluna drank heavily, Steve thought. There was nothing else for them to do during the long hot nights, and in that sultry atmosphere a man had to drink to keep going. Particularly men working in the arsenic plant. They wore masks and silk underclothes to minimize the effects of the poisonous dust on their skin. But few of them worked there for long, knowing that the arsenic dust seeping through their skin would destroy the cartilage in their noses and genital organs if they did so. Most of them took the risk for high wages, but pulled out after a few months.

Steve made no secret of the fact that he had gone to Wiluna to be near Daphne. No jobs underground were available so he had worked on the arsenic plant. It was just as well he had gone along to look after her, he said. There were few women in the town: most of them the wives of miners or shopkeepers, and when hundreds of men were on the booze, a good-looking, un-attached girl drove them crazy. Steve had been able to stand by Daphne, and take care that it should be generally understood she was his girl. That was true as far as he was concerned, he told Sally; but Daphne could not make up her mind to marry him. She had begged him to leave the arsenic plant, though, and promised to sling her job and come home if he did.

'So here I am,' Steve wound up. 'And I want Daphne to marry me before I go into the army. Even if she doesn't care for me — like I do for her — it would make things easier for her and the little bloke. And, cripes, I do love her, Mrs. Gough. You know how it's always been with me.'

'I know, Steve,' Sally said. 'There's no one I'd rather see Daphne married to, than you. Daphne got so hurt, before, I think she's been afraid to care for anybody since.'

'I'm such an ordinary sort of chap,' Steve said apologetically. 'I don't see how Daph could care much for me.'

'You're one of the best,' Sally declared. 'Just make love to Daphne for all you're worth when she comes, and see if she doesn't change her mind.'

'You bet I will,' Steve promised, his eyes lighting, his broad, pleasant face all smiles.

'Oh, yes,' Eily said happily, when she saw Sally next day. 'Steve came to see me, too. And I had a letter from Daph, last night. She says Steve's been awfully good to her, and she's very fond of him, really. Maybe we'll be having a wedding on our hands soon, gran.'

WHEN Daphne returned, she was so happy to be at home, so busy with her little son, Steve thought she no longer needed him. He feared it was only because she had been lonely and miserable at Wiluna that she had turned to him for love and companionship. He hung round the house for a while, every day; chopped wood for Eily, played good-naturedly with Tommy and gazed fondly at Daphne. She took his devotion for granted; but eluded all his attempts at love-making with gay, friendly banter.

'I'm joining up, tomorrow, and will be going into camp in a few days, I suppose,' Steve remarked casually one evening.

'Oh no, Steve!' Daphne glanced at him with startled eyes.

'Why not?' Steve asked.

'You're in a reserved occupation. You don't have to,' Daphne protested.

'I reckon it's up to me, all the same,' Steve said gravely. 'Since the bombing of Britain, and invasion of Russia, I've felt I couldn't stand out any longer.'

'But I can't bear it! I can't bear the thought of you going into all that terrible fighting,' Daphne cried. 'It was bad enough when Bill went; but, oh Steve, if you go, too — '

Her voice broke: she could not put her panic into words.

'I didn't think you'd mind, Daph.' Steve could not altogether repress the joy her troubled face gave him.

'I do mind,' Daphne said stormily. 'I mind much more than I thought I would. I'd do anything to stop you, Steve.'

'Even marry me?'

'Yes.'

'Oh, Daph!' Steve's arms enfolded her.

'But I'd have to join up all the same,' he said, feeling she might not have understood that. 'It's not only what's happening overseas we've got to think of, now. But the position here. It's mighty serious, Daph. I was talking to a chap from the Eastern States, yesterday. He said his brother-in-law, who's a big shot at Military Headquarters, told him our defences are in a bad way. If the Japs come into the war, as the Germans reckon they will before long, there's practically nothing to stop them invading Australia. There are plans to evacuate North Queensland, and the west will not be defended.'

'Do you think it's true?' Daphne was too astounded to believe what he had said. 'It can't be, surely, Steve?'

'Looks to me as if we can't afford to take any chances about whether it's true or not,' Steve replied. 'The Japs've been carrying things with a high hand lately and they know the nor-'west coast like the palm of their hands. Divers on the pearling grounds've seen to that. There's nothing to stop a raid on Fremantle except an old fort and a few guns on Rottnest Island. The boys training down at the coast tell me they haven't enough rifles to go round, and as for our air force, it wouldn't stand a chance against modern bombers and fighting planes.'

'And thousands of our men have gone overseas,' Daphne cried, overcome by sober realization of a situation many people were aware of, but she had only just grasped.

'That's why every man left has got to learn this soldiering business as fast as he can,' Steve said. 'I could kick myself for not having got into it sooner.'

'Oh, Steve,' Daphne's hand stole into his, 'let's get married before you go into camp.'

Steve's arms tightened round her and he kissed her again and again. Then he eyed her steadily: 'Are you sure you want to, Daph? It's not only because —'

'You're going to wear a smelly khaki uniform,' Daphne laughed. 'No, you idiot. I made up my mind, months ago, I'd marry you, some day, Steve. But there's Tommy, you know. I've been scared to love you. Not wanting to; and now I feel I can't lose you.'

Steve held her close.

'If only I could save you from every sorrow and hurt and

278

danger, Daph,' he groaned, knowing that as a soldier he was going to bring more sorrow and pain into her life, perhaps. 'As for Tommy, he's your kid — and mine, now.'

Daphne's love bloomed to the wholesome strength of his body beside her, the passion and tenderness with which he enveloped her.

'I could really say for better or for worse, Steve,' she told him.

Telling Eily afterwards that she and Steve were going to be married soon, Daphne said: 'Oh, mum, it's almost too good to be true! I'm so happy, and so much in love with Steve, that what happened before seems just a bad dream!'

'That's just what it was,' Eily said firmly. 'We mustn't think of it any more.'

Steve was in uniform before he and Daphne were married, a month later. He had leave only for a week-end, and Daphne went to the coast to be near him while he was in camp. The shadow of the war lay over their wedding. There was heavy fighting in North Africa, bombs were raining on London, the Russians retreating before the offensive of the German armies. But at the little party Eily gave for the bride and bridegroom, Sally and Eily, Steve's mother and Dinny glowed with satisfaction in the happiness which had come to the young people they loved. Such a fine couple they looked as they stood together, united by their joy and faith in each other.

'A wedding in war-time!' Sally said sadly, when she and Dinny were going home. 'It always seems to me like defying the forces of death: carrying life and hope into the future.'

'That's what it does,' Dinny agreed.

'If only Bill and Pat could have been married,' Sally reflected sadly, 'I wouldn't feel so bad about what the war's doing to him.'

'I dare say they had a preliminary canter,' Dinny chuckled.

'Why, Dinny — ' Sally stared at him.

'Y' can't blame the young people if they grab a little of what the war's deprivin' them of,' Dinny said defensively.

'I'm not blaming them,' Sally replied. 'I'm hoping you're right about Pat and Bill. That's all.'

Bill's letters had been few and far between lately. They were short and scrappy when they did arrive. Sally and Eily read and re-read them, but could get little comfort out of them except the knowledge that Bill was still alive. The censorship was strict, of course: much stricter than it had been during the last war. There was almost nothing Bill could say about his whereabouts or what was happening round him, they knew. He joked about hardships, assured them he was well and fit, thanked them for food parcels, begged them not to worry about him, asked for news of the family and friends. That was about all there was in his letters. Now and then there were passages into which Eily thought she could read a second meaning.

'When the boys receive newspapers giving them bad news from home, they're ropable,' Bill wrote. 'It takes all a man's got to say we'll smash the blasted fascists on this front, first, and deal with the rotten dogs playing their game at home afterwards.'

Eily and Sally had to be careful in writing to him, too. Women had been prosecuted for mentioning matters in a letter to a son, husband or lover, which might give 'information useful to the enemy' if a ship or plane carrying mail for the troops were captured. The censorship, too, inhibited the expression of intimate thoughts and feelings. Everybody knew letters were being opened and read, not merely to prevent any leakage of information with regard to the movement of ships and troops; but to keep track of the political affiliations of soldiers and their families.

When the Labour Government took office, workers on the goldfields were jubilant. John Curtin, the new Prime Minister, was a West Australian member of the House of Representatives. Even business men with no Labour sympathies agreed that the National Party, national in name only and representative of the most conservative interests in the country, had created so much distrust and antagonism, it could not carry on. John Curtin was recognized as the man of the moment to unite the people and bring new energy into the war effort.

This was what his government set out to do. It opposed the

sending of more troops overseas, discarded repressive legislation against the trade unions, opened friendly negotiations with the Soviet Government for the exchange of ministers, restored the legality of the Communist Party, and other organizations prepared to throw their weight into winning the war.

With the Japanese attack on Singapore and Pearl Harbour bringing the war to the very threshold of Australia, two months after it had taken office, the Labour Government faced stupendous tasks and responsibilities. It was a period of greater danger than the people of Australia had ever encountered, and they knew it. There was no limit to what men and women, young and old, were willing to do to meet the threat of invasion. The government demanded service, and the sacrifice of personal interests from everyone, and rallied support even from its political opponents.

Volunteers poured into the recruiting centres. The mines were almost deserted. Only skeleton staffs remained to keep them in working order. Few able-bodied men walked the streets of Kalgoorlie and Boulder, although the aged and unfit hung round the pubs and starting-price betting shops, gambling on the races, and gossiping aimlessly, as usual. The number of race meetings had been curtailed and races were tolerated, it was said, only to indicate there was no panic in reorganization of the war effort.

Day and night, troop trains passed through Kalgoorlie, moving east or west with recruits, artillery and air force units. Men in khaki or dark blue uniforms surged through the town for an hour or two: were shouted in the pubs, fed and fêted by the women's committees. Women and girls in the smart blue uniform of the W.A.A.F., or the neat tan of the W.R.A.N., strode along with a brisk marching step.

Sally envied them. She would have liked to be wearing a uniform herself to show she was taking an active part in the defence of her country. She and Eily went to ambulance classes and hoped soon to have their first-aid certificates. Eily was working several hours a day at the hospital, which was understaffed, so many nurses having gone into the army. Sally still did her chores there, and knitted frantically whenever she had a minute to spare between whiles of doing her own housework, packing parcels for the troops, or serving meals at a canteen on the railway station.

The fall of Singapore, and the loss of Australian regiments and men, struck a shattering blow at national security early in the new year. Men from the goldfields had taken part in the disastrous jungle fighting. Now they were dead, missing, or prisoners of the Japanese. For a long time many mothers and wives did not know what had been the fate of their men. To their frantic anxiety was added the mourning of those who were informed that a son, husband, or brother had been 'killed in action'. Fear and consternation rose while desperate fighting continued over the islands which formed a barricade along the north of Australia.

Then Java, too, collapsed before the Japanese typhoon. Refugees from Malaya, Java, Sumatra and all the lovely tropical islands of the Timor Sea, poured into Australia. With them were several soldiers who had escaped from Singapore. Two of them made their way to the goldfields, and Dinny and his mates listened horror-stricken to their tale of the unpreparedness, lack of competent leadership and aerial defence, which led to the surrender of what had been regarded as an impregnable position. Their criticism was stifled when military police removed and imprisoned them. It was staggering to ordinary citizens that these men should be treated as deserters, and that General Gordon Bennett, over whose escape there had been general rejoicing, should be censured for not having remained in Singapore to share the lot of his troops. Public opinion was with Gordon Bennett who maintained he had considered it his duty to preserve his effectiveness for the defence of Australia.

He took over command of forces in the west, and there were quick and vital changes to strengthen strategic positions. When the Japs raided Darwin, wiping out the town in their first attack, leaving hundreds of dead and wounded lying on the beaches, and in the ruins of its flimsy tropical buildings, no one could doubt what was going to happen if other towns on the northern and north-western coasts were bombed, and the enemy planes flew further south.

There was a grim realization that invasion by the Japanese had to be regarded as something which might occur any day; but at the same time, the will of the people stiffened and hardened to resist any enemy landing by every means in their power. Everybody knew that military equipment and man-power, never adequate, had been dangerously depleted by the sending of men and munitions with the expeditionary forces to fight overseas. Some divisions were being recalled; but meanwhile the situation was critical, and renewed raids on Darwin, Broome and the north-eastern coast intensified the nightmare in which people were living.

A few pessimists contended that it would be futile for unarmed citizens to offer any resistance to the Japanese, if they landed. But most working men and women declared: 'We'll fight with what we've got. Like the Spanish workers did, and the Chinese.' They were making hand-grenades from bottles and jam tins in their back-yards and empty garages.

Someone at a Comforts Fund meeting told Sally the story of a lady in South Perth who had said: 'Perhaps it wouldn't be such a bad thing if the Japanese did take Australia. At least we'd have good servants then!' But there were not many people like that. It wasn't until later a pro-fascist organization, prepared to capitulate to the Japanese, was unearthed. Its few members would have got short shrift, had they shown their faces on the goldfields, Dinny declared.

Hundreds of miles from the sea, Kalgoorlie and Boulder were regarded as safe places to which children could be sent from the coastal towns. The enemy would not penetrate so far, it was thought, unless the coastal defences had been overpowered. Bombing raids might destroy the railway and pipe line, however, goldfields people foresaw: isolate them from supplies of food and water. That was their most serious danger for the time being. They drew comfort from the idea that distance from supply bases might deter the Japanese from attempting the conquest of Australia at this stage of their campaign; and that the vast dry spaces of the inland constituted a natural defence against the movement of enemy troops from the north.

Most people attributed miraculous qualities to the aircraft they saw making reconnaisance flights at dawn and in the evening. Nobody doubted the valour and skill of Australian pilots. Few knew the weakness of the air force in fighting planes and trained personnel.

With the launching of the Japanese offensive in the Pacific, the government had made strong representations to the High Command for recognition of the importance of Australia as the strategic base for Allied operations in the Pacific. It had embarked on an independent policy of wooing United States support for their point of view.

The arrival of an American convoy and troops nevertheless came as a surprise to the Australian people. The Yanks were greeted with cheers and the wildest enthusiasm. Coming as they did at the darkest period of the war, for Australia, their magnificent equipment, guns, planes and motorized services sent everybody's spirits skyrocketing with the assurance that now there would at least be modern armaments and a tremendous increase in the forces available to meet any attempted invasion.

When the first lads from the United States Navy came sightseeing to the goldfields, Sally was so excited that she stopped to shake hands with some of them.

'I'm glad to see you, boys,' she said. 'Thanks for coming.'

'For cryin' out loud!' a round-faced, rather abashed dough-boy exclaimed.

'To tell ya the truth, ma'am, we didn't know where we were comin', and are mighty glad to be here,' another explained.

'I'm tellin' the cock-eyed world Australia's a grand place,' still another declared laughingly. 'You got nothing to worry about now, ma'am. The Japs won't get you while the United States Army, Navy and Air Force are on the job.'

'We wouldn't have been in such danger if so many of our own boys hadn't been sent overseas.' Sally bristled to the defence of Australian men and boys. 'They've been fighting in North Africa and over Germany for the last two years.'

'Huh, that's tough,' the Yanks agreed cordially.

They wanted to know where they could pick up a bit of gold.

Sally took them home and introduced them to Dinny. He gave them each a small slug as a souvenir from a bottle of specimens he was hoarding, and set off to tramp with them round the mines. The Yanks hailed the first passing taxi, and they all piled into it with Dinny talking sixteen to the dozen about the early days and the fabulous wealth which had come out of the Golden Mile.

It was a great day for him, though he came home rather under the weather. The Yanks had been mobbed wherever they went: hauled off into the pubs and shouted enthusiastically. In the end they had gone off with some girls they picked up in the lounge at the Reward, yelling to Dinny that they'd come right back when the war was over, and get him to stake out a claim for them where they could make their fortunes.

'They're fine lads,' Dinny said. 'Reckon they're rarin' to blast hell out of the Japs!.'

'All the same,' Sally grumbled, 'I wish our own boys were coming home.'

It was a long time since she had heard from Bill. The last letter had been from Greece. Since then Greece had been evacuated. Some of the Australian regiments were· in Crete. But now Crete, too, had been captured by the Germans. Every day Sally was hoping for news and dreading what she might hear.

CHAPTER XXX

'MISSUS SALLY — what luck! I was hoping there'd be time to dash out to see you. But the Trans is late, and we've got to go straight through to Perth.'

Sally looked up from the trestle table she was swabbing down at a canteen on the railway station. A girl in the uniform of the W.A.A.F., with an officer of the United States Air Force beside her, had stopped suddenly as she was passing.

For the fraction of a second Sally did not recognize Pat in the smart dark blue uniform and peaked cap. Her mind was still busy with men from the troop train which had pulled out an hour before, hundreds of them swarming over the platform, in their shoddy khaki, unwashed and hungry. They were travelling in open cattle trucks to the coast; lads, most of them, with big guns loaded into their trucks, about which they were as proud and protective as young mothers,. So like Bill they were with their sun-brown faces, cheery grins and rowdy chiacking, as they shoved and wrestled for a place at the table near her. She felt as if she had been handing out cups of tea and bulky corned-beef sandwiches to innumerable Bills — although a gunner's shabby beret was pushed back on their heads, not the felt hat with its turned-up flap Lal had worn so jauntily, then Dick, and Bill. That hat was more the distinguishing mark of an Australian soldier than the badge he wore on his sleeve. Sally was thinking of Bill as she cleaned up after the gunners had gone. Where was he? What had happened to him? It was so long since she had had a letter, or any news. She was worrying about that when the transcontinental train pulled in, and civilian passengers, officers of the army and air force, sailors going to rejoin their ships at Fremantle, streamed past to board the western express at the far end of the station.

Pat dropped her suitcase, and turned to the man beside her. 'This is Mrs. Gough,' she explained blithely. 'Meet Mrs.

Gough, Major Anthony Jefferson Dekker of the United States Air Force. I've been posted to Geraldton, Missus Sally, and he's going further north. We met on the train. What's the news of Bill? I haven't heard from him for months.'

'Neither have we,' Sally said, acknowledging the major's salute mechanically with a nod and smile.

'I won't believe anything could happen to him,' Pat cried. 'I just won't. These days,' she added, her face crumpling in vague distress, 'you've got to do your job and not think of anything else. I've just been given a responsible position. Look at my pips — ' she turned to show the stripes on her sleeve and its air force wings. 'Three hundred girls under me, and our training's stiff. At first I thought I could never stand it. But, now, I'm as hard as nails: can walk miles, eat like a horse and be as shrewd and stern as a sergeant-major, maintaining discipline in the W.A.A.F.'

'If you want that drink, lootenant,' Major Dekker remarked, glancing at his wrist-watch, 'we'll have to hustle.'

Pat saluted briskly and picked up her suitcase.

'Marching orders,' she laughed back at Sally. 'We've got about ten minutes to catch the express and I'm dying for a glass of Hannan's. Give my love to Dinny. And Daph! How is she?' Already she was moving away with the Major's arm under hers. 'Let me know if — when you hear from Bill,' she called. 'I'll write from Geraldton. Hop over to see you when I get leave.'

Sally lost sight of her in the crowd surging towards the bar and restaurant further along the platform. Most of the men were frantic for a drink after two days of crossing the sun-blasted desert of the Nullarbor plains, and with the prospect of a hot night before them, sitting up in the rackety western express. As Sally stood watching Pat and the American, pain and uneasiness stirred her bemused weariness.

So that's what Bill's love affair had come to: something to be mentioned casually and thrust aside. There was no place for it evidently in Pat's mind at present. She was very pleased with herself, and her importance as an officer of the W.A.A.F., Sally thought. She had cut her bright hair and tucked it away under that smart cap with the gold embroidered badge in front; she looked robust and handsome in her trim uniform. Military training had improved her physique, and Pat was more concerned, it was evident, to be correctly military in her bearing, than to exercise any feminine charm on either Major Jefferson Dekker or Bill's grandmother. But she had not abjured feminine charm altogether, Sally perceived. She still reddened her lips, and the siren lurked in her grey-green eyes as she smiled at the American. Major Jefferson Dekker had caught a glimpse of the siren, Sally guessed, and wondered whether Pat had become 'Yank happy' like so many other girls who were fluttering gaily with American soldiers.

It was a shame the way the girls were 'carrying on', Sally considered. Of course, Australian soldiers in their ill-fitting, shoddy, khaki uniforms were not so well turned-out as the Americans. They did not have as much money to spend. They did not address a girl friend as 'Beautiful!' and make her feel she was as alluring as Dorothy Lamour. But it was galling for Australian soldiers to see how girls fell for the Americans. At the picture theatres, every Yank had a girl beside him, and men on leave from distant training camps glared at them, sore and disgruntled. The perfidy of the girls and the swanky superior airs the Yanks gave themselves had caused many a brawl.

It was to be expected, people were saying, that thousands of young and vigorous men, separated from their own women folk, on the eve of battle, as it were, should make the most of any time left to them for gay living. Drink and women gave most of them all they required: the pub lounges were full: queues lined up outside the brothels. But so many Australian women and girls, deprived of their husbands, lovers and sweethearts for over two years, were forgetting them for the newcomers that ill-will between men of the A.I.F. on active service and the United States forces was smouldering.

The Yanks had charming manners, plenty of money and were generous and amusing, the women said. The young girls, particularly, thrilled to the happy-go-lucky Yanks who looked like film stars, picked them up in shops and milk bars, presented them with orchids, took them about in taxis, and made whoopee every night of the week when they were on leave. There were letters in the newspapers about drunken girls in their teens going round with soldiers, being sick in the streets of the big cities, and lying about with them in the parks. Public outcry had demanded the passing of regulations to make it an offence to serve girls in their teens with alcohol in an hotel, or to take them to an apartment for immoral purposes.

The spate of sordid sexuality, scandals, brawls, domestic tragedies, divorces, crimes of passion and perversion, continued. It was recognized that all this was part of the cost of war. And, of course, there were romantic love affairs, engagements and weddings, as well. But the reaction of Australian men to the Yanks who were ousting them from the favour of their women had become bitter and resentful. Men on active service, or men coming home on leave from training camps, who found themselves jilted lovers or deserted husbands with broken homes, neglected children and gossiping neighbours to contend with, nursed a sombre grouch against the Americans.

Now the battered 6th and 7th Divisions who had been fighting in Libya and Greece were returning, it was rumoured. They had threatened to settle scores with the Yanks.

It was a bad business, Sally knew, this hostility which had cropped up between men of the A.I.F. and the United States forces.

'What the flibbertigibbets do doesn't matter,' Dinny said. 'Or the women who make a living by the game. But I feel as mad as the boys when a man coming home from Libya and Greece finds his wife's cleared out with a Yank.'

'You can't help being sorry for the Americans, too,' Sally demurred. 'Their wives and sweethearts. Some quite decent lads've been caught by real trollops.'

'More fools they,' Dinny had growled.

Sally hoped Bill would be coming home with the 6th Division.

Thinking of Pat and Major Jefferson Dekker, she wondered whether Bill, too, might have a score to settle with the Yanks.

Late one afternoon when she had been collecting for the Red Cross, Sally turned down the end of Brookman Street, where most of the houses were brothels, barricaded round with barbed wire. Troops had been swarming through the town that day, and a racket of gramophones, radios, raucous voices laughing and singing uproariously, came from the drab, weather-beaten houses. Brazen sunshine beat down on the wide, dusty street, and Sally was hurrying along, shamed and hurt by the sight of those high fences and barbed-wire barricades, as she always had been, when the eerie wail of a familiar air caught her ear — 'ma chandelle est morte . . . je n'ai pas de feu. . . .'

Sprawled on the door step of a house more dilapidated than the rest, she saw a drunken old woman in a pink chemise. Her shrunken limbs were exposed: her withered face had been carelessly rouged, her lank, disordered grey hair hung about her, yellowed by peroxide. She was a tragic and pitiful spectacle. Sally fled from it.

'Poor Lili,' Dinny said when Sally asked him what had happened to Lili that she should have sunk so low, 'she's been havin' a rough spin, lately. She and Belle were livin' in comfort, like ladies; but when Belle died a man, name of Guarez, took over the house Belle was running and put Lili to work for him. He had to hold her down, screamin', at first, the local boys say. Now she's rotten with disease. None of them would go near her. But women are scarce. The bludger who owns the place picks up drunken soldiers and sailors and tells them Lili's a high-class French piece. He's made a lot of money out of her, Tassy says.'

'God!' Sally exclaimed, outraged and furious. 'It's unbelievable. We must do something to stop it, Dinny. For the soldiers' sake — as well as Lili's.'

'That's right,' Dinny agreed. But he did not want Missus Sally to take Lili under her wing. 'The military can stop a diseased prostitute bein' used like that. I'll have a word with

Tassy and some of the old-timers. P'raps we can pass round the hat and have Lili moved into a room of her own, somewhere.'

Dinny got busy. When action was threatened against the brothel keeper if Lili remained on his premises, Dinny and his mates took charge of her. They arranged for her to live with two old friends of hers, Mrs. Rosy Ann Plush and Mrs. Amelia Green. Rosy Ann and Mrs. Amelia prided themselves on being respectable, although when they had had a glass too many they were often in trouble with the police. They were good sorts, and not so respectable that they would look down their noses at Lili, Dinny pointed out. As a matter of fact she had wept and kissed Dinny and all the old men, when they left her with Rosy Ann and Mrs. Amelia.

''E was a wicked, bad man, *ce cochon de Guarez*,' she said tearfully, 'and verry cruel to poor Lili. It will be so good to be togezzer with friends, now.'

Sally had been to see her soon afterwards and found Lili very frail but with something of her old sprightliness, living contentedly with Mrs. Plush and Mrs. Green. Rosy Ann had had a win on the races that day, so they went off to the Reward to celebrate. Sally had never been there except with Marie, and the 'Ladies' Room' in which they used to take their pot of beer with other old-timers, after a shopping excursion, looked dingier and shabbier than ever. God-Save-Us-Sarah had disappeared from her dark corner. Lili would be missing Belle, too, Sally thought.

As Rosy Ann and Mrs. Green gabbled hilariously to the barmaid, who had served their drinks, about their luck on an outsider, Lili raised her heavy schooner and whispered: '*Aux amies parties.*' Sally did not understand those words; but she drank with Lili, knowing they were both thinking of Belle and Marie.

CHAPTER XXXI

'MAKING tracks and quick ones.'

Bill's telegram threw Sally into a frenzy of excitement. It was months since anybody had heard from him. Not since his battalion had been moved from North Africa, as a matter of fact. He did not say then where he was going. The Australian forces had been evacuated from Greece before Sally guessed he might have been there. Demented by anxiety she and Eily had searched the casualty lists.

They found the names of other goldfields lads in those lists and knew Bill's battalion had suffered heavily, but that was all. The thought that Bill was no longer alive haunted them, though they told each other he might have been wounded or taken prisoner. And now there was this glorious wire dissipating their fears. Sally's spirits flew to the seventh heaven of crazy rejoicing. The telegram had been dispatched from Perth, too, which meant that Bill might be arriving at any moment.

Dinny chuckled over the telegram. It was typical of Bill to remind them of an old goldfields joke.

When Carr Boyd, a prospector and explorer of the early days, with a reputation for telling tall stories, was describing some of his hair-raising adventures to a city audience, a lady had inquired sweetly: 'But, Mr. Carr Boyd, if an infuriated native were facing you with a nulla-nulla in one hand and an uplifted spear in the other, what would you do?'

'I'd make tracks, and — quick ones,' Carr Boyd had replied, swallowing the usual adjective, considered unfit for a lady's ears.

Sally started up Dinny's old rattletrap and drove off to give Eily the good news. Then she and Dinny went to the railway station to find out something about trains. They had no idea whether Billy would be arriving by the daily express from the coast, or by one of the troop trains which passed through Kalgoorlie nearly every day on their way to the Eastern States.

Railway officials would give no information about the movement of troop trains; but yarning with a porter he knew, Dinny discovered that two troop trains were due. At what time, the porter could not say, though he warned Dinny not to wait for them there. Troop trains, now, pulled up at a siding some distance beyond Kalgoorlie, he pointed out: well out of the range of pubs and wine shops.

When the express rattled in, Sally and Dinny stood beside the wicket gate on to the platform, scanning the face of every man in uniform, so agitated they could scarcely see. The passengers surged past and drifted away. Bill was not among them.

'Maybe y'll have better luck with the troop trains. I'm expectin' a son back with the 6th Divvy, meself,' Dinny's porter said.

Dinny made Sally stop at a restaurant and have a cup of tea before they trundled out to Parkeston. But she was on pins and needles all the time, scared Jiggledy Jane might play up or break down, and make them late for the arrival of the troop train.

She and Dinny sat for hours in the blaze of the sun. They felt suffocating in the car; but there were no slender, thin-leafed trees to scatter tattered fragments of shade on the stretch of bare red earth near the siding. Army huts which had been built to accommodate passing troops struck through the heat and glare, their roofs dazzling. Men in khaki, some of them half-naked, dived in and out of huts, preparing for the arrival of the troop train, too busy to notice the old couple and their ramshackle car drawn up near the siding; and Dinny and Sally were too afraid of being ordered off what was perhaps military ground to draw attention to themselves by asking questions.

When at last the troop train clattered to a standstill before them, hundreds of lads in worn and shabby khaki, with battered slouch hats dragged down on their heads, and loaded down with gear, tumbled on to the platform. That they were overseas troops, Sally did not have to be told. Dazed and blinded by her emotion, she could not distinguish one man from another. Almost any man might have been Bill. So alike they were, these gaunt, leather-skinned, tight-lipped men, with eyes sunk deep in their sockets, though there was a lot of chiacking, laughter and cursing, as they swarmed across the hard red earth, and gazed at the barren goldfields landscape without a redeeming pub in sight.

How on earth was she going to find Bill among all these war-worn men, Sally asked herself frantically. He might have changed so that she would scarcely know him. She and Dinny stood at a little distance from the platform, waiting and watching. They hoped Bill would recognize them. They hoped they might be able to distinguish his figure, or features: that slight swagger and grin which they thought they could recognize anywhere. The railway platform was nearly bare when Dinny had a word with a soldier straggling behind his mates.

Yes, these were men of the 6th Divvy — what was left of it. Been fighting in Libya and Greece? Too bloody right they had. Know a bloke name of Bill Gough? No. Couldn't say he did. But he called to another soldier: 'Hi, Ted, know a bloke name of Bill Gough?'

'Smiler?' The other replied. 'Cripes, 'course I do. Copped it in the retreat, but was with us in Crete. Ought to be some-where around. Saw him yesterday. Maybe he's on the second section.'

It was evening before the second section of the troop train arrived and Bill with it. Dinny first saw the young soldier mooching along with rifle and heavy pack slung over his bowed shoulders. There was something about that figure which was familiar. He shouted: 'Hi, Bill!'

The soldier looked up, and it was Bill's grin which met Dinny's. Sally was flinging her arms round Bill and nearly throttling him the next instant: Dinny prancing up and down and yelling: 'It's good to see y', lad! It's good to see y'!'

'Good to be home, Dinny,' Bill said in a queer, strained voice. 'Sort of thing I've been dreaming about,' he added with a shaky laugh, 'and a man's mind plays him tricks sometimes!'

'You're home, all right, darling,' Sally blithered, hugging

him to her. 'It's a decent meal you need right away, and to sleep for a week.'

Dinny picked up Bill's rifle and pack and marched off, as proud of them as if he were the returned soldier.

'I could do with a bit of shut-eye,' Bill admitted.

He stretched his legs beside Sally in the car and Dinny hopped in behind them. There was a gash of coppery gold in the western sky when they turned away from the siding. As it faded the red earth was steeped in the garish glow of a goldfields sunset and the distant scrub turned to a purple darkness. The sky became a dome of translucent amber, with wisps of wind clouds, pink and filmy, drifting across Kalgoorlie. Sally thought the city had never look so dilapidated and dust-raddled. Heat haze and dust seemed to be lurking still among the rusty roofs and white-washed buildings although a luminous mist overhung them. Even the kurrajongs and pepper trees, which usually kept their bouquets of fresh green all through the summer, were dull and drooping as the last light touched them along the wide streets.

But Bill glanced about him with a faint smile.

'Most beautiful town I've ever seen,' he muttered.

Sally laughed happily, guessing what he did not say: that the sight of this familiar place was as miraculous to him as it was to her to have him beside her. For a while, she had almost lost hope, and yet here he was, talking and looking at her with eyes so like Dick's that she could feel Dick was still alive in his son. She kept looking at him to assure herself that it was really Bill: that the body and soul of him were intact, still Bill's, though seared and changed by the experiences they had undergone. She did not want to talk of those experiences now; or of the silence which had kept news of him from them for so long. There would be time enough to hear about everything later. She sensed Bill's reluctance to think or talk about the war, too. All that mattered was that he was alive and here.

When they reached home, it was a shower and clean clothes Bill wanted most. He stayed under the shower so long, that Sally called laughingly to know whether he had been washed away. Her grilled steak and eggs were ready for him when he reappeared wearing a pair of Dinny's pyjamas, his hair still wet.

Dinny went off to tell Eily that Bill had arrived, and presently they all came running in: Eily and La and Nadya, Daphne and Tommy. There were hugs and kisses all round. Everybody was so happy and excited to see Bill they hardly knew what to say or do. Sally made Bill finish his meal and then he sat and gossiped with them about what had been happening at home as if he had only been away for the week-end, though he broke off in what he was saying to stride about restlessly, now and then: seemed not to hear what they told him, and smoked incessantly. Dinny rolled fags for him from a tin of makings. Often, these days, you couldn't buy decent tobacco in Kal for love or money, he explained; but he promised to ransack the town in search of cigarettes for Bill next day.

'In Crete we'd treasure a butt — and share it with a mate,' Bill said.

The youngsters were a little in awe of him. Such a grim, gangling stranger Bill seemed to have become. There were tight lines in his thin, leathery face, and his hair lay like a bleached weed on his head. Though his eyes smiled, Sally knew they were straining through the shock and horror of what lay at the back of his mind.

He was not to be with them for long, Bill told them quite soon. At the end of a fortnight he would be reporting for duty again. This time, the remnants of the Division would be going to New Guinea or the islands, he suspected.

Sally made a great outcry about it, blackguarding the military authorities for not giving Bill more time to rest and recuperate. She realized Australian troops were needed in New Guinea, and that holding of this strategic position off the north-east coast was essential to the defence of Australia. But it was hard to let Bill go into the fighting again.

'I'm enough of a soldier to know where I ought to be,' he said gravely. 'And the battle for Australia is going to take all we've got. The 6th and 7th Divisions wouldn't've been recalled unless the situation's pretty serious. I want to fight until the Nips can't threaten this country.'

'That's all very well,' Sally wailed, love and grief tearing her. 'But you can't fight until you're fitter, my lamb!'

'I'm tough,' Bill assured her. 'As tough as old boots — only a bit tired.'

During the next days, it was his utter weariness and remoteness from them all that troubled Sally most. Bill would sit silent and brooding for hours. Nothing of his old exuberance remained. Only that wry smile, and an occasional glint in his eyes, reminded her of the gay, urchinish lad who was her most beloved grandson.

'It's a fact, we've all had the wind up since the fall of Singapore, Bill,' Dinny told him. 'When the Japs got Java we knew we were for it. The raids on Darwin and Broome were much worse than the newspapers let on at the time. But men from the north've been talkin'. We know now the Jap bombers just sailed in and smashed up Darwin . . . There's been raids on Cairns, Townsville, Newcastle and Sydney, too, as well as on our west coast. Rumours are goin' round that a Jap plane's been as far inland as Wiluna — though it didn't do any damage.'

'I know.' Bill's forehead ruckled. 'The troops've had it all by mulga. They've heard too, that in the event of Jap landings on the west coast, this state was to be evacuated — and the north-east coast as far as Brisbane.'

'That's all been changed,' Dinny said eagerly. 'There's been a big difference in plans for the defence of this country since the Labour Government took office. Even men who are opposed to him politically are sayin' John Curtin's done a good job reorganizin' defences and uniting the people for an all-out war effort. A couple of months ago, it looked as if the Japs would be on our doorstep any day. Old men were doing Home Guard duty along the coast without enough rifles to go round. There was even a pro-fascist gang sayin' it would be hopeless to put up any resistance: best thing we could do was surrender and save useless bloodshed. But Curtin said: "We will fight in every town and city. Every township will become a fortress in a last

297

ditch fight." People started makin' jam-tin grenades in their back-yards and garages. Missus Sally and me among 'em. That's how it was, Bill. The workers in this town were ready to put up a fight with anything they'd got. And that's how it was all over Australia. But were we mad — knowin' the bulk of our navy and fighting men'd been sent overseas, leavin' us in the lurch — just a walk-over for the Japs?'

'We reckoned we'd got to take a hand smashing Hitler, don't forget,' Bill objected.

'I'm not forgettin',' Dinny said heatedly. 'Or that Britain was in a bad way herself until the damned fascists invaded the Soviet Union. But after all we're part of the Empire, aren't we? And everybody knew what the Anti-Comintern Pact meant. Frisco says there wasn't a combat plane in the country worth a damn when the Japs swooped on Pearl Harbour and Singapore. Our airmen went up against the Japs in old Lockheed Hudsons and Wirraways over the islands. They hadn't a dog's chance against the up-to-date bombers and fighters the Japs were usin'. It was the most reckless gallantry y' ever heard of, the way those boys went up in their rotten Wirraways to meet the Japs, and were shot down every time. Later we got a few British Spitfires and Beauforts. But Curtin had acted before we knew: put the hard word on America for troops and equipment: got the High Command to consent to the recall of some of our troops overseas. Then McArthur arrived and everybody's cock-a-hoop now. New roads and airfields are bein' built: new factories turnin' out war material: every able-bodied man and woman's been called up. The prosecution of coms has been stopped. They're in all the services — and were never so popular. Everybody reckons the stiff resistance the Red Army's put up has saved Britain from invasion.'

'No doubt about it,' Bill grinned. 'Or that Curtin and Evatt've done a good job. Cripes, it put new life into the troops in North Africa and Syria to know the Labour Government was taking a stand on the rights of Australia in this war. Evatt's announcement that Australia had made an alliance with the Soviet Union was great news, and that he'd urged "a firm and unbroken alliance between the Empire, U.S.S.R. and the U.S.A." Before Pearl Harbour, wasn't it, he notified the British Government that the Commonwealth Government would not agree to any further appeasement of Japan that would be detrimental either to China or the U.S.S.R.? And claimed the right for Australia of absolute equality with Great Britain in any mission or councils dealing with military and political affairs in the Pacific.'

'That's a fact,' Dinny chortled. 'But there was a great rumpus after Curtin's speech pointin' out Australia must look to America rather than Great Britain for any substantial aid "if war swept the Pacific". Gents of the opposition reckoned it was downright subversive and disloyal. But John Curtin was fightin' the battle of Australia when he made it, Bill — before the fall of Singapore. Wait a jiff! I'll get me scrapbook and read that speech to you.'

Dinny trotted off and came back with the old exercise book into which he had pasted newspaper cuttings for years. He put on his spectacles and Bill let him burble over the sentences which he himself had read to a group of anxious and disgruntled soldiers in a desert camp.

The words came ringing back:

'No nation can afford to submerge the right of speaking for itself because of another nation's assumed omniscience. . . .

'I will make it clear . . . that Australia looks to America free from any pangs about our traditional links of friendship with Britain . . . We know that Australia could go under and Britain could still hold on . . . We are determined that Australia shall not go. We shall exert our energy towards shaping a plan with the United States as the keystone, giving our country confidence and ability to hold out until the tide of battle swings against the enemy.'

'And later on — ' Dinny skimmed the pages of his scrapbook — 'Curtin told the Americans "the battle for America may very well be won or lost by the way the battle for Australia goes".'

'It was real statesmanship, making that move — and bringing us home,' Bill said.

He liked to yarn with Dinny about what had been happening while he was away: about the mines and the mining industry, air-raid precautions, spy scares, black marketing, and how the people were taking Curtin's slogan: 'Work, fight or perish.' And Dinny rattled away eagerly, giving him the facts and the gossip, between whiles of trotting off to a meeting of air wardens, or to do odd jobs he had undertaken at the hospital.

For two or three days Bill lounged about the house, reluctant to go out, meet people, or to talk about his own experiences. They were never out of his mind, Sally guessed. She had heard him calling out in his sleep: shouting hoarsely, incoherently muttering.

When a plane passed, one morning, flying low and roaring over the house tops, Bill glanced at it with a quick, involuntary movement, his face blenching.

'Cripes,' he exclaimed shamefacedly, 'I was just going to hug the ground and hope for the best.'

Tassy and Sam Mullet came along every evening, bursting with eagerness to hear what Young Bill had to say about the war. But Sally had warned them Bill was not to be asked to talk, so they sat with clamped jaws while Dally drooled about the shortage of beer and tobacco, or Dinny babbled aimlessly over his day's work, in order that Bill should not feel constrained to say a word unless he wanted to.

Bill knew, all the same, what Dinny and his mates were waiting for. Slowly, at last, he began to tell them of desert marches, fighting patrols, the capture of Bardia. Sally could not imagine how he had survived the desperate fighting with fixed bayonets, and the furious air raids. Arab villages and the ruins of white Italian towns; treacherous desert sand dunes; the dry beds of wadis and the wreckage of ships strewing the blue waters of the Mediterranean; she could see them as Bill talked, or hear the zoom and drone of enemy planes, the cracking rattle of anti-aircraft guns, the whistle and crash of bombs falling, terrific explosions.

The old men were shaken to the marrow of their bones by

Bill's story, and Sally wept in the darkness. Then he told them about the retreat of the Australian forces in Greece and his escape from Crete.

'They called us "the fighting 6th" after we took Bardia and knocked the stuffing out of the Italians in Libya,' Bill said bitterly. 'I saw the report of an English war correspondent when I was in hospital in Alex. He said: "The key to the British victory was the Australians' epic smash-through." Reckoned, at Bardia, we'd kept up the tradition of the Anzacs when they landed on Gallipoli. But in Greece we got it in the neck. Were rushed across and up to the mountains. White with snow, they were, with Olympus towering into the clouds. The country on the way looked green and beautiful after the desert. There were fruit trees in blossom, vineyards and olive groves with villages tucked among them. But it was tough work hauling the guns up those mountain passes. Our job was to hold them. But the Germans'd massed terrific forces for the campaign. A Panzer Division broke through on the Greek sector to the south-east and another to the north at Monastir. We were being hemmed in when orders came for delaying actions to cover a retreat to the coast.

'The British armoured brigade at Monastir got smashed to pulp, and the Maoris at Pinios Gorge flung back infantry attacks six times, charging with blood-curdling yells right up to the enemy guns. At one stage, seven hundred Aussies were up against twenty-five thousand Germans for two days and two nights. An Australian battalion held back two German Divisions but the Jerries had the tanks and guns that carried them through.

'When my unit made a break, through the pitch darkness and blinding rain, I got a crack, and thought I was all in: must've stumbled off the track a bit — not wanting to be a burden to the boys. It was a long trek to the coast.

'In the morning I could just see the road, blocked with bodies and tanks that had been blown up: crawled away a bit and lay under a clump of bushes. All day the Jerries were sweeping the sky and blasting the whole countryside. Their infantry, tanks and armoured cars poured along the road. A Greek peasant found me that night and dragged me to his hut. The women fixed up my wound. It wasn't too bad, not much more than a scalp wound — though it had knocked me out and bled a lot. They were stone poor: fed me on bread and wine until I was able to walk. Then the old man went with me down to the coast: got a relation of his who had a fishing boat to pick me up and drop me off Crete. Cripes they were good to us, those Greek peasants up country: and it was as much as their lives were worth to be caught hiding an Aussie soldier.'

Nobody spoke. As if feeling he ought to relieve the heaviness of the emotion he had caused, Bill wound up with forced gaiety:

'The boys reckoned I ought to take a ticket in Tatts, when I struck them. I'd swum ashore with no more on me than a life-belt: wangled a pair of pants from a fisherman when I crawled ashore, and found out from him the nazis had taken the village. We were holding a position at the back of it. Was making my way towards it, taking advantage of any cover along the track, when, blow me Charles, if the bullets didn't start flying round me! I'd run into one of our outposts that wasn't taking any chances. Thought I was a spy.'

He laughed, but not even Tassy could laugh with him. Dinny and Blunt Pick tried: and a queer choked gurgle came from their throats.

It was Sam Mullet who muttered:

'We're just flabbergasted, Bill. You read about things like you've been telling us; but don't realize 'em. And to think the blasted war's goin' on like that, everywhere, with all the blunderin', sufferin' and heroism not half-known or understood by most people.'

'It's going on,' Bill said grimly, 'until the fascists are beaten. What happened in Greece and in all the countries of Europe where the nazis got away with their blitz, could happen here — although the Japs are our proposition. Their tactics are the same. But we've got the men who'll clean them up or die in the attempt. It's the guns, planes and tanks, we've always been short of. Now the Yanks are bringing those along. And in Europe, the Russians are going to crush Hitler's armies out of existence.'

'You're pretty sure of that, Bill?'

'What do you think?' Bill grinned, rising and stretching as if he were facing the future with renewed confidence. 'It makes all the hard knocks we've taken worth while.'

SALLY had told Bill about seeing Pat on the railway station. Bill listened as though he were interested, but in a curiously detached way.

'Does she know you're here, darling?' Sally asked.

'Don't suppose so,' Bill said slowly. 'We seem to have lost track of each other. Pat wrote often, at first — and then not for a long time. A crack I got in Crete went septic and put me in hospital when we got back to Alex. Then we went into camp for reorganization and training: had another bout of desert fighting. I managed to collect some shrapnel before we struck Syria, and was carted back. But all that time, I seem to have had a sort of blackout: couldn't remember anything but the job on hand. Nothing seemed worth remembering.'

'But you remember now?' Sally asked anxiously. 'You want to see Pat, don't you?'

Bill's shy smiled slewed to her. 'If she wants to see me,' he said dubiously.

'Send her a wire, today,' Sally begged. 'Geraldton's not so far away, after all. Perhaps we could drive over — or she could come here.'

Bill sent his wire, and the next day — it was a Sunday morning — Sally was delighted to see Pat pushing back the garden gate. She was not so pleased to see that the American officer who had been so possesive on the railway station was with her. There was no time to warn Bill. He had taken it into his head to overhaul Jiggledy Jane, and was giving her a thorough greasing and clean up when Pat descended on him, with the American in tow.

In his working clothes, grimy and dishevelled, Bill did not look the sort of man for a spick and span young officer of the W.A.A.F. to get excited about. But Pat flung her arms round him, exclaiming rapturously: 'Oh, Bill! Bill, darling, how marvellous! I couldn't wait to let you know I was coming. Tony just happened to be there when your wire came. I got him to fly me over. Tony — my fiancé, Bill Gough! And Dinny — Mr. Dinny Quin, Major Anthony Jefferson Dekker. Mrs. Sally you have met. Oh, dear, I'm so excited I don't know what I'm saying! When did you arrive, Bill? How long have you got?'

Bill disentagled himself from Pat's embrace to salute the visitor. Dinny grabbed Major Dekker's hand and wrung it while Pat rattled on:

'Tony's on maintenance and supply: been up at Marble Bar. Came down last night on a spot of leave. I wangled the day off and persuaded him to take me for a joy ride. Sporting of him, wasn't it? We'll both get into hot water if we're found out. But I couldn't resist making a break to see Bill. So here we are!'.

'You must have a cup of tea.' Sally turned towards the house and everybody followed her.

'Make it cawfee for Tony,' Pat laughed. 'These Yanks are always saying we don't know how to make cawfee, Missus Sally. But that's because they haven't tasted yours.'

Bill darted away to have a wash and brush-up. He looked more presentable afterwards; but was still wearing the dust and grease-grimed giggle suit in which he had gone about delousing enemy minefields, or crawled out into no-man's-land at night to blow up gun emplacements.

'He looks very thin and grim,' Pat whispered to Sally. 'Not a bit like Bill used to be.'

'No,' Sally said. 'He's not a bit like Bill used to be.'

She wished Bill had been wearing his new uniform. The one which had just arrived from the coast. He had been through an officers' training camp and got word of his commission before he left Egypt: been instructed to apply for his equipment in Perth and report for duty in the Eastern States. The new uniform was as smart and well-made as Major Dekker's. When Bill tried it on, Sally thought he looked slim and handsome: almost too slim, but broad shouldered, with good leg muscles, the nerve and strength of a well-bred stallion. If only Pat could have seen him in his new uniform instead of those dirty overalls! Sally had tried to wash them, but the dust and grease would never come out, she was sure.

Major Dekker was a good looking, if not so young man, Sally considered, although he had the fat bottom and smooth dough-coloured face of so many Americans she had seen. As he lolled in his chair, eating the sandwiches and drinking the coffee she had made, Major Dekker was taking stock of Bill out of the corner of his eye, and making comparisons between himself and Bill. No doubt he was wondering what Pat saw in so ordinary and insignificant a young man as Bill looked just now. That he hoped to cure her of any foolish attachment was evident. His eyes followed Pat with amused tolerance. He lit her cigarette as if it were a sacred rite, and was all attention to whatever she said. Pat was playing him for Bill's benefit, and her devotion to Bill for his, in order to pique Major Dekker and flatter Bill by her preference, Sally imagined.

Bill seemed aware of that. He became silent and withdrawn, listening to the patter Pat and the Yank exchanged: felt outside the familiarity which had been established between them, no doubt. They kept up a wise-cracking about jobs and people Bill knew nothing about. Their air force jargon was difficult to follow, and the war appeared to be still something of a 'show' to them: a show in which they were playing an important but not too hazardous part. Like so much of the civilian talk he heard, Bill found it hard to stomach. To take the war as a sort of bad joke was beyond him.

Major Dekker noted Bill's abstraction and the tightened lines of his face. This young soldier was nervy and not finding it easy to adjust himself to social amenities of the home front, he suspected. More particularly to finding his girl consorting with a Yank, as were so many Australian women and girls whose men were away fighting. All was fair in love and war, Dekker considered; but, himself an amiable, easy-going, middle-aged Lothario, he was loath to add fuel to the ill-will growing between

306

the United States' forces and Australian soldiers on the woman question.

'You guys put up a swell show in Libya,' he remarked with the intention of being tactful and placating Pat's boy friend.

'The whole position was lost when they flung us into Greece,' Bill replied, indisposed to be patronized.

'Cock-eyed, that campaign — without adequate air support.' The American ran a hand over his sleek head and examined his polished finger nails.

Bill's face ruckled. 'It doesn't bear thinking of. There was none. I saw only one British plane all the time I was there. It tackled a mob of German bombers and was shot down. They bombed every goat track and scrap of low-growing scrub on the hillsides. The wonder was any of our men got away.'

'Sure,' Major Dekker agreed. 'And yet, round about 46,000 troops, British and Australian, were evacuated.'

'The navy, and Greek fishermen, did a good job,' Bill brooded. 'But it was the Australian and New Zealand battalions who held up the German advance — rearguard actions fought at terrific cost that made the retreat possible. A British armoured brigade at Monastir, too, held on until it was cut to pieces.'

'Why they dumped you in Crete's got me guessing,' the major went on with good-humoured condescension. 'That was no goddam rest camp from all accounts.'

'It was hell,' Bill said. 'Enemy planes came over like a cloud of grasshoppers, dropped troops and stores by parachute. We shot them down and grabbed their ammunition at first, but hadn't a dog's chance. The Jerries ferried thousands of men and guns over by glider and air transport. They swarmed everywhere. There was nothing for it then but guerrilla tactics, raids and skirmishes. All sorts of odds and sods, cooks, mechanics, clerks and orderlies, tackling a group of Jerries in the olive groves, grabbing rifle and bayonet from a dead man's hands and fighting till they dropped. Orders came through we were to make for Sphakia on the far side of the island. The 2nd/7th of the A.I.F. — what was left of it — took on holding a ridge until the rest of the men got away. Some made the town in two days: others took three or four, without food, and short of water, climbing the pass over a rugged range of mountains. Many got lost, or died on the track.

'I stayed to mine the position when the battery retreated, and got a slug in the left shoulder. A couple of gunners lugged me away. We hid among the rocks until we could make our way down to the coast, crawling along at night, mostly. Some blokes we struck in a cave there said the cruisers had taken off hundreds of men, but a good many were still hiding along the beach.

'They saw the last stand of the 2nd/7th when they lined up on the beach with their backs to the sea. They'd flung back every attack on the ridge until their shells were exhausted. The Jerries came charging down on them — but the cruisers were just about out of sight along the horizon. A war correspondent I was talking to in Alex reckoned holding that ridge above Sphakia was one of the most gallant actions in British military history. But those of us who were on Crete can only curse when we think of it . . . The rest of us were picked up by a navy cutter a week later.'

Pat got up and went to sit beside Bill. She slipped her hand into his.

'I had no idea it was as bad as that,' she said.

'It was worse than anything you can imagine,' Bill said harshly. 'And worst of all the bungling and blasted waste of it all.'

This was not the sort of talk Major Dekker had expected from one of the tough, hard-bitten lads who, according to the newspapers, were returning from their baptism of fire in Libya and the campaigns in Greece, Crete and Syria, full of gusto and grim humour, burning to show what they could do to the Japanese.

Dekker was discomfited by Bill's grouch. The way Pat had sidled up to Bill, caressing him with warm soft eyes, was disconcerting also.

'I'm not belly-aching about the job that's got to be done,'

308

Bill said, with a wry smile. 'I reckon we can do it. We've got to do it. But if you'd seen men taking off their boots to creep quietly on an enemy position, rush their guns and fall back, wounded and done for, you'd know how I feel. The spirit of men who did things like that, thousands of them, whose daring and courage have been forgotten already, shouldn't go for nothing. There's got to be a more realistic understanding of what we're up against in this war, and less guff about smiling through, and playing the game as if it were a football match. The men are saying we'll win this blasted war in spite of the brass hats. And we will too.'

'I don't doubt it,' Major Dekker replied soothingly.

' " 'Cause the Aussies and the Yanks are here," ' Pat sang.

> We're all together now, as we've never been before,
> The Aussies and the Yanks, sure we're gonna win the war,
> And now throughout the ranks everyone can give their thanks,
> 'Cause the Aussies and the Yanks are here.

'With fighting planes, guns, equipment — and Yankee efficiency,' the Major's air of benign superiority was restored, 'the tide's going to change in this war.'

'Dinny's got a yarn about e-fficiency,' Pat said. 'Tell it to him, Dinny.'

Nothing loath, Dinny sailed into the yarn which everybody else knew. The major laughed heartily, although he sensed something of a laugh at himself in the yarn. He rose, straightening his belt and reaching for his cap.

'Maybe you could spare time to show me over the Golden Mile, sir,' he said, addressing Dinny. 'Our young friends no doubt have got a lot to say to each other; and Pat and I'll have to take off for Geraldton at four o'clock.'

' 'Course I could,' Dinny declared.

'You know I'd go to hell and back for you, lootenant,' the American added with the casual gallantry to which he had found

Pat was susceptible. 'But we've got to be back on the station before your goddam C.O. starts making inquiries.'

'I'll be ready when you say the word, sir,' Pat assured him.

Major Dekker rather stiffly saluted Sally and thanked her with formal courtesy for her hospitality. He and Dinny went off in the air force car which had brought Pat and himself from the drome.

'He's rather a dear, isn't he?' Pat exclaimed, subsiding beside Bill. 'It was awfully sweet of him to bring me over to see you, wasn't it, darling?'

'Awfully,' Bill agreed, a glint of his quizzical grin making her feel for the the first time there was really the Bill she had known in this glum and rather indifferent stranger.

'What's the matter, darling,' Pat asked, taking his hand in both of hers and holding it to her. 'Aren't you glad to see me? Don't you want to talk to me?'

'Of course I'm glad to see you,' Bill said. 'I want to talk to you. But it doesn't seem you and me who are here any more, Pat. I'm different. I know I am. So are you. It's no use trying to pretend we're not.'

'Yes, but —' Pat demurred.

'I feel outside the ordinary civvy way of life,' Bill explained with a weary exasperation. 'Not fit for it. Hate it. Hate everything that's not bringing the war nearer an end.'

'You don't love me any more?' Pat queried.

'Love?' Bill scoffed. 'I can't feel anything but a savage misery about the men who were blasted to bits out there. And people at home carrying on much as usual, not caring a damn really, having a good time and making money out of the war. There's nothing left in me but enough life to go on fighting and try to clean up the bloody mess.'

'Oh, Bill —' Pat pleaded. She knew Bill resented her having brought the American to Missus Sally's: that Bill was sore about the way they had talked. It was hard to explain to him how lonely and distraught she had been while he was away, and that she had filled in her time with Tony and others in order to stop fretting. It didn't make sense, of course, her love for Bill and her willingness to let other men make love to her. But that's how it was.

'Don't worry about me,' Bill said bitterly. 'I'm not blaming you for taking any fun you could get.'

'That's not fair,' Pat cried angrily. 'I've been working hard — damned hard — all the time you've been away. Thought at first I couldn't stand the drills and physical training we went through. But I stuck them out — felt I was being of some use. I've been proud of these darned pips because they meant I had done a good job. And now — now, they don't mean anything to you. You don't want me, or my love.'

'It's not that,' Bill spoke more gently. 'But I reckon life could still be good for you, Pat, without me. Better than with me.'

'You don't believe in me, Bill. You never have,' Pat cried, still hurt and angry. 'You think because I've played about with other men — Dekker among them — that I don't care for you. But Tony and the rest don't matter a damn — though if I had any sense I'd try to forget you and marry him.'

'Why don't you?'

'Bill!'

'Oh, well,' Bill's grin quivered, 'I quite expected you to break the news to me. So many of our chaps came home to find their wives have gone off with a Yank, or their girls are Yank happy.'

'I'm not,' Pat protested. 'Tony's a good sort and I like him. But I love you, Bill. I always will.'

'Pat!'

In each others' arms, their kisses obliterating the anger and sadness which had arisen between them, Bill recaptured some of the magic Pat held for him; and she was content to have won him again. They murmured foolish endearments, leaning against each other, exclaiming happily, childishly, each permeated by the satisfaction of being close to the other. Pat drank from Bill's eyes all she desired in him; and he filled himself with her. For this brief, miraculous meeting so little was enough: to have found each other in the midst of the war, to have this respite from the fears and horror which had engulfed them. The sensuous sweetness of their nearness held them in a trance. Passion and pain were in it, but repressed by an instinct to preserve a joyous consciousness of this time together.

Those deeper emotions were surging unbearably when Sally came to tell them Major Dekker and Dinny had returned. Dekker was waiting for Pat in his car at the gate.

Pat wrenched herself from Bill's arms.

'Oh, blast him' she wailed. 'How can I go? How on earth can I leave you, Bill?'

Bill pulled her to him, murmuring incoherently, tenderly. 'Some day,' he said at last, 'when the blasted war's over, we'll be together for keeps.'

'If I didn't believe that I couldn't go now,' Pat said. 'I'll be longing and waiting for the day, Bill.'

A horn tooted imperiously.

Pat jumped up, tidied her hair, whisked a lipstick over her mouth and jammed her air force cap down over her head.

'It'll be hell for us without him, won't it,' she cried, turning to Sally. 'But Bill's got to do his job, I suppose — and I've got to do mine.'

'There's nothing else for it,' Bill agreed.

They clung for a moment, then Pat ran out to the car. Bill followed her.

When he thanked Major Dekker for having brought Pat over from Geraldton, the American could scarcely believe it was the same young man he had met a couple of hours earlier. He attributed Bill's exhilaration and assurance to his love-making with Pat; but there was a winning grace in Bill's manner, and he wore those grimy overalls with a dignity which reduced Major Dekker's estimate of his own attractions for the girl beside him. Still, he consoled himself, he was just as well pleased to know where he stood with Pat.

She played game, chattering gaily with Dinny and Sally until the car started.

'Keep your fingers crossed, darling,' she called to Bill.

'Don't worry,' Bill said lightly. 'I'll be all right. I've still got Kalgoorla's movin.'

The car threw a cloud of dust as it rushed off to the airfield. Pat wept tempestuously when she was no longer able to see Bill as he stood with Dinny and Sally beside the garden gate.

'Garsh, honey,' the American protested, steering adroitly with one hand and putting an arm round her, 'he's a swell guy! But you don't have to break your heart over him.'

SCRAPPY notes came from Bill to say he had reached Sydney. Sally guessed that for a while he was in camp in Northern Queensland. Then he wrote about big forests all round him, a steamy jungle mist rising, blue sea sparkling away to the horizon, and she realized he was probably in New Guinea or one of the islands nearby. There were no details in Bill's letters. He was very guarded in whatever he wrote.

Sally knew why. Planes carrying mails might be shot down, or ships torpedoed. Bill was not giving any 'information likely to be of use to the enemy'. He told Sally all she wanted to know: that he was alive and well: in his own words 'jumping out of his skin', and 'keeping his fingers crossed'. Although she doubted these assurances, and lived in a state of suspended anxiety from one letter to the next, she went about her daily work, as well as her Red Cross and Comforts Funds jobs, as indefatigably as ever, contriving to impress everybody by an air of staunch optimism.

Her mind, however, had become obsessed by thoughts of the jungle Bill described. She felt as if her psychic essence, whatever that might be, were drifting among the great trees packed so closely together, interwoven with leaves, creepers and dense undergrowth, that it was almost dark among them at midday.

The jungle, which awed and impressed Bill, its silence, mystery and vast depths, shrouding tracks to the interior of the island and providing ambush for the enemy, terrified her. Sometimes she could see brilliant butterflies hovering in green twilight over the jungle trails as Bill described them. He wrote too about yarns with the natives: handsome copper-coloured boys with fuzzy upstanding hair, in which they sometimes stuck frangipane or a flower of the scarlet hibiscus. He told her about their courage and friendliness: the care with which they carried wounded soldiers down the steep mountain passes, through crocodile-infested rivers and the shifting slime of treacherous swamps.

Occasionally Bill mentioned having met some goldfields boys and foregathered with them for a 'wongie' about home. Daphne said that in one of Steve's letters he spoke of having run across Bill. She was elated when Bill wrote to her, telling her about this meeting with Steve: how he was looking, and how popular Steve had become with the men of his unit.

Daphne read her letter to Sally and Dinny. 'I always knew Steve was one of the best,' Bill wrote. 'And he's proved himself here, all right, Daph. We talked a lot about you and the kid. Steve showed me the snap of you both he carries in his wallet. Gee, isn't he proud of it. And reckons he's the luckiest man on earth to have got you for his missus. A bit of the luck's on your side, too, to have got Steve, darl. You know that though, don't you? When this blasted war's over you and Steve are going to have a good life. . . .'

'When the war's over!' Daphne exclaimed, assailed by a horde of creeping fears. 'Meanwhile I've got to go through every day wondering whether Steve has been killed or wounded.'

'You mustn't think like that,' Sally said sharply.

'I know.' Daphne's voice shook as she thrust away her despondency. 'But the Japs are within thirty-two miles of Port Moresby, and there's been fighting at Milne Bay. I suppose Bill and Steve were both in it. I can't help feeling anxious.'

'I know, dear,' Sally replied. 'You must keep busy and try not to fret. If we believe Steve and Bill will come back to us, safe and sound, it must help. Not only ourselves, but them.'

Everybody had been downcast during those days. Six hundred men of an Australian militia battalion who had trekked for the first time through the dark steaming jungle and across flooded rivers to the summit of the Owen Stanley Range were being driven back by the Japanese. Those Australian lads had defended Kakoda, a collection of native huts on the strategic pass, against three thousand Japanese for a month. In desperate fighting, Kakoda changed hands three times. But when the Japs brought

315

up reinforcements the Australians, reduced to half their number, were forced to abandon the position and make their way back to Moresby. It was a disastrous situation everybody at home knew. The Japs, swarming over the southern slopes of the range, were threatening the garrison of what was recognized to be a vital outpost for the defence of Australia.

Sally could not tear her thoughts from what was happening in New Guinea. Every morning she absorbed the meagre news in the paper; and all day wrestled with the fears and anxieties which kept surging up and had to be thrust into the background of her consciousness. She was so preoccupied with Bill and the war, raging now over those beautiful islands lying beyond the horizon away to the north-east, that she had almost forgotten trouble could come to her from any other direction.

She had thought Den and his family were living in peaceful security. There had been no need to worry about them. Den was too old for active service, and besides, dairy farmers were not permitted to leave their land. They were required to maintain and increase food production. And Den's only son was too young to be touched by the war.

Charlie's telegram fell like a bomb out of clear blue of the sky. 'Come at once. Den seriously ill. Relapse after pneumonia.'

Dazed and distraught, Sally threw a few clothes into a suitcase and caught the afternoon train. She was in Perth next morning: had to wait until evening for a train to the south-west, and it was mid-morning next day before she reached Warrinup Siding where Marion, Den's eldest daughter, was waiting for her, red-eyed and grief-stricken.

'Oh, gran, it's awful for you, I know,' she sobbed. 'Dad was only ill a few days, then suddenly — last night — it was all over.'

Sally was too stunned to speak. Marion took her arm and led her to a seat. They sat there until Sally felt she could walk to the truck Marion had brought to meet her. Marion told her something of what had happened as they drove over the familiar bush tracks, through the fragrant tangled scrub, across a bridge which spanned the silver, slowly moving river; but Sally comprehended little of what she said. In a stupor of misery, she could understand only that Den was dead, and that this tall, swarthy girl, wearing riding pants like a boy, was Den's daughter.

'I didn't have time to change,' Marion had explained. 'There's so much work to do. Cows've got to be brought in and milked, cream delivered at the factory — no matter what happens.'

Charlie and Marion helped Sally into the house. She was ashamed of her weakness, and to be an extra burden to Den's wife. But, helpless under the shock and anguish which had struck her, she could only lie in the room to which Charlie took her, and try to overcome the pain racking her body and mind.

'Oh, Den, Den,' she cried distractedly. 'I thought you would be so safe here. Why did you have to die? Why have all my sons been taken from me?'

'He was happy here, mother,' Charlie said, weeping beside her. 'We were good mates . . . I don't think Den would have been so happy anywhere else. Warrinup meant a great deal to him.'

'I know,' Sally said wearily. 'It was the dream of my life that he should come here. When he did, and loved the place, it seemed too good to be true. Then you gave him love and happiness, Charlotte. I hoped Den would have so much my other boys missed in their hard life on the fields.'

'Life on a dairy farm is never easy,' Charlie reminded her. 'In the old days, when Warrinup was a cattle station and there were more men to run it, things weren't so difficult, perhaps. Den was worried about the mortgage as well: that we might lose the place. He worked too hard. Particularly since the war. Our two men joined up, and Den said, if he couldn't fight, he'd got to feed the troops.'

'He would,' Sally said bitterly. 'Remembering what Lal said to him during the last war: "Food supplies have got to be kept up. You'll be doing as good a job on Warrinup, lad, as in the army." '

'It's been a terrible winter,' Charlie went on. 'Rained for

317

months. Den's been out in all weathers, working from four in the morning until after dark. When he caught a chill he wouldn't lay up. He was driving himself too hard, I knew; but nothing I could say would make him sell some of the cows and take things easier. It wasn't until he had a frightful pain in his chest and could hardly breathe, he would stay in bed and let me send for the doctor. Our nearest doctor now is sixty miles away. When he came, Den was delirious. Doctor Thompson said it would be no use trying to take him into the district hospital. I sent you the wire then.'

That was the whole story as far as Sally could make out. Charlie had nursed Den, day and night, for three days: the two elder girls looking after the cows and milking. Even the funeral had to be arranged so as not to interfere with the milking. It was to be next afternoon. Sally would not go, and she didn't wish to see Den in his coffin. She wanted to think of him as her own vital, warm-hearted boy and not the cold stranger he would have become. But he was the last of her sons, and all the passion of her grief for them went into her mourning for Den.

During the next few days, she realized it was not fair to Den's wife and children to sit idle and brooding when they all had so much to do. The everyday work on Warrinup had to go on: cows and pigs could not be neglected. Sally tried to help; but found herself strangely stupid and ineffectual: unable to concentrate on what she was doing.

'Things have to be kept going,' Charlie had said desperately, heart-broken though she was. 'I'll have to provide for the children and keep the place in good order. We can manage, I'm sure. Marion's been Den's right-hand man for a long time, and, of course, I know what ought to be done and how to do it.'

Sally marvelled at the way Den's family adjusted itself to doing without him. Soon the work of the farm was being attended to, much as usual. Cows trailed towards the milking sheds in the early morning and late afternoon. The separator whirred: poddies blared from the yard beside the barn: pigs were fed, eggs gathered. Marion was busy out of doors all day, bringing the cows in, fixing the milking machines, taking butter fat to the factory. Charlie looked after the milk and the separator, all the washing and cleaning of gear. Every child had its job. Gwenda cooked and did the house work. Susie, Una and Peggy, the three little girls who rode to school bare-back on an old white horse when he was not needed for ploughing or carting hay, helped with the milking, fed the poddies and fowls. Even John, who was five years old now, brought in fire-wood, and trotted about, in his mother's way most of the time, but pretending to assist in whatever she was doing.

It was time she was going back to the goldfields, Sally felt. She had swept and cooked with Gwenda: given a hand with the washing and ironing, mended small garments, but could not be of much use; was even something of an embarrassment to Den's wife and children.

Sally looked at this home of her childhood through tears, as if she were seeing it for the last time.

Warrinup, the grey stone homestead with apple blossom foaming in the orchard beside it, cleared paddocks lush green, with the river glinting beyond, forests darkening to purple on the hillsides all round — it had never looked more beautiful. Her father, one of the earliest pioneers in the south-west, had hacked it out of the wilderness. And how Den had loved it, and tended it, proud of the improvements he had made in herds and pastures, orchards and milking sheds. It was hard to believe he was no longer part of Warrinup. The sun shone, birds were singing, trees blossoming, and the work of the place was going on much as if he were still there, full of pride and joy in it all.

What would happen to Warrinup now, Sally wondered. She did not doubt that Charlie, who had known as much about cows as Den did when they were married, could manage the place as well, or almost as well, as Den had done. Charlie had said something, too, about Marion wanting to marry a local lad who was with the forces in New Guinea. Perhaps, after the war, Charlie thought, Marion and her husband would take over the management of Warrinup.

Dinny came down from Kalgoorlie for a few days and Sally made up her mind to return with him. He had arranged to help Charlie to meet some outstanding financial obligations.

'We'll be all right, now, Dinny,' Charlie said, thanking him in her sober unemotional way, 'though it will be hard to manage without Den for a while.'

Sally was reluctant to say goodbye to her, and to Den's children, Marion, Gwenda, Susie, Una, Peggy and John with the gingery hair and freckled eyes Den used to have as a small boy. She would always love them, Charlotte and Den's children, Sally told herself. Charlie was such a sterling person, and they were like wild flowers, Den's children, with their impish, shrewd, innocent and shy faces. Something of herself and Den would survive in them.

But there was nothing for her now in this fertile land of green valleys and blossoming orchards, Sally realized. She belonged to the vast arid country of the goldfields. Her existence depended on the interests which had grown up round her there.

Den's death had obliterated them and the war from her mind for a while. Now she was frantic for news of Bill.

Dinny said there had been no letters. But the newspapers were full of accounts of the fighting at Milne Bay which had resulted in the first defeat on land of the Japanese.

CHAPTER XXXIV

FOR a month after she returned to Kalgoorlie no letter came from Bill. Sally fretted dementedly. She tried to fill in her days by scrubbing and polishing floors there was no need to scrub or polish: cleaning out the fowl house and digging the garden, quarrelling with Dinny and working more strenuously on the Comforts Fund Committee.

Daphne, too, had not heard from Steve. Sally's only relief came from talking to her: going over with Daphne all the reasons there might be for their letters not having arrived. Instinctively, she exerted herself to cheer Daphne, and felt better herself for clinging to the hope they could both have that all sorts of transport difficulties might have interfered with the delivery of their letters.

It comforted Daphne to make cakes as usual to send Steve. Sally and she often did their cooking together, packed their cakes into tins, sewed wrappings of unbleached calico round the tins, and posted them prayerfully. They discussed eagerly the cigarettes and tobacco they were hoarding to stow away in other tins, with raisins, beef extract, packets of salt, and any small luxuries they could think of to supplement the boys' army rations. It was foolish to attach so much importance to these little things they were able to do, Sally knew; but it kept up their spirits when they could not deceive each other and their eyes held an unspoken fear.

Then six letters arrived by the same post: three for Daphne and three for Sally. Dinny laughed as if it were a good joke to see them reading those precious almost illegibly pencilled scraps of paper, and chattering excitedly over them.

'Anybody'd think y' were a pair of sweethearts,' he said teasingly, glad that Missus Sally could have that momentary excitement and happiness; but afraid too. Afraid that since Den's death, she was concentrating too much on Bill All her love and hope were centred in him.

'Exigencies of the military situation demanding the utmost secrecy!' were responsible for delay in the mails, it was understood.

In the battle of the Coral Sea, the United States Navy had shattered an invasion fleet intended for the capture of New Guinea. But after their defeat at Milne Bay, the Japs in their southerly drive across the Owen Stanleys had threatened Port Moresby. Now, the United States Air Force was bombing their supply bases, and Australian troops pushing the enemy back across the ranges. Men who had fought in North Africa, Greece and Syria were tramping the Kakoda trail, and commando units, trained in guerrilla tactics, harried the retreat of the Japanese.

When they read reports in the newspapers of desperate encounters with the enemy, Sally and Daphne could see Bill and Steve in every one: attacked from machine-gun nests in rank depths of the jungle: dodging the bullets of Japanese snipers hidden in tall trees. But Sally resolved to seal her mind against the fears which had beset her when her letters were overdue.

She said to Daphne: 'We must believe Bill and Steve will come home — and not worry unnecessarily.'

Optimism was in the air, despite the casualty lists dribbling through the daily press, and accounts of how the men had been suffering from malaria, dysentery, tropical ulcers and the festering sores caused by poisonous insects and jungle vines. Wounded soldiers were being carried back along the dangerous winding trails by native bearers in a slow and continuous procession. 'Fuzz-wuzzy angels' these native bearers had been called, so gently and patiently they tended their helpless burdens.

It was natural, Dinny recognized, for Missus Sally and many other goldfields people to be preoccupied with what was happening in New Guinea. They did not forget that the fighting in New Guinea was only part of the war in Europe, Sally protested, but after all how could she and others help being chiefly concerned about the defence of Australia, and their own men-folk battling against terrific odds in one of the 'toughest campaigns of the war', according to some of the newspaper men? There was no answer to that, Dinny admitted, though he reminded her that the war had to be won in Europe for victories in the Pacific to have any value.

Stalingrad had become the strategic centre round which the maelstrom swirled most violently. It was generally understood that the defeat or triumph of Hitlerism would depend on the fate of Stalingrad. Military strategists had agreed, according to Mr. Winston Churchill, that the opening of a second front in Europe was essential to victory. Delay in the opening of this front provoked a controversy which raged fitfully on the goldfields. Dinny was for opening of the second front immediately; and Sally fearful of what any diversion of planes and munitions might mean to Australian troops in New Guinea.

She accused Dinny of being willing 'to let down our own boys in order to help the Russians'.

'That's not the point,' Dinny argued heatedly, 'but winning the war. The same bunch of reactionaries who used the non-intervention policy to defeat the Spanish Government, and who tried to prevent our alliance with the Soviet Union, are busy again. They're talkin' of lettin' the Red Army and the Germans exhaust themselves in Russia, and comin' in on the last round, so as they can make peace terms to suit themselves.'

Sally was not convinced until a letter came from Bill in which he said:

'It seems madness not to open the western offensive which would shatter Hitler's rear and relieve Stalingrad. The boys here are all for it. People opposed to the second front want to prolong the war. We've got the Nips on the run, now, and can hold our own. Keep your tongue wagging for the second front, gran, and see that Dinny does, too.'

'Oh, dear,' Sally sighed, 'seems I was wrong again!'

She told Dinny she had a curious feeling that if she kept her mind on Bill, putting an aura of protective magic about him, nothing could hurt him. It was almost as bad as believing Kalgoorla's movin could safeguard Bill, she confessed. Had she been unconsciously influenced by native superstition, she wondered.

Or was she merely relieving her anxiety by this subterfuge: taking refuge in a mysticism which her common sense derided?

There was so little she could do for Bill that she had fallen back on a psychological trick to comfort herself, she suspected. And it did comfort her to think her spirit was always hovering near him, in communication with his, trying to shield and sustain him. Bill knew that, Sally was sure. Some day, when he came back, she might tell him how foolish she had been. If only he came back — whole and sane! That was all she asked. There were such terrible stories of the way the Japs tortured prisoners. Sally was haunted by them. She tried not to let her mind dwell on what had happened at Toll and Waitavalo.

Tol was a tiny native village with a coconut plantation surrounding it, some distance from Rabaul. When the Japanese made their first landings there, at the beginning of the campaign, a small party of Australian soldiers had surrendered, their way of escape cut off and 25,000 of the enemy surrounding them. Leaflets, promising decent treatment as prisoners of war to those who surrendered, had been dropped by planes a few days previously; and at first the captured men, deprived of their arms and any personal possessions, were treated reasonably well. Then, tied together in parties of ten or twelve, with their hands bound behind their backs, they had been bayoneted and shot with the most barbarous cruelty. Two or three of the men, left for dead, survived. Two, badly bayoneted in the stomach, managed to crawl to a native hut, but were found by the Japs who set fire to the hut and burned them alive. Another man, stabbed in the back, over the kidneys, was lying in agony when a Japanese stood over him and stabbed him six times. Finding himself lying under a heap of brushwood, this man had later dragged himself to the beach thirty yards away, bathed his wounds and been picked up by a party of Australians hiding in the jungle. He told this story when they were rescued and reached Port Moresby.

At Waitavalo plantation, eleven soldiers, bayoneted and shot from behind with the same vicious brutality, had been left for dead. Six of them survived and escaped. It was estimated that one hundred and fifty men had been massacred at Tol and Waitavalo.

Prisoners had been spread-eagled naked for two days and nights on barbed wire, left without food or water in the blazing sun, tormented by ants and mosquitoes, or any passing Jap who cared to bash their faces or prod them with his jungle knife.

And who could forget the nurses who had swum ashore when their ship was wrecked near Muntok, on Banka Island? They had been driven back into the water by the Japanese, and tommy-gunned with their backs to the shore. Only the last girl in the row had escaped with a wound in her shoulder. She lay, as if dead, in the water until the Japs ran off to wipe out a group of ship-wrecked soldiers and sailors who had landed further along the beach. She had crawled into the jungle then and been found by another survivor of the wreck. Together, with the aid of friendly natives, they had hidden and finally found their way to safety.

Many stories were being told of the heroism of Australian soldiers, and Sally treasured them in her heart, because these lads fighting so desperately through the jungles, swamps and across the terrible mountains of New Guinea, were like her own boys.

When his unit was held up near Milne Bay by heavy fire from a machine-gun post hidden in three weapon pits, John French, a young Queensland corporal, ordered his men to remain under cover while he reconnoitred the position. Dragging himself over the ground to within a few yards of the first pit, he had flung grenades into it: made his way back for more grenades and silenced the second pit. One of his men reported: 'Corporal French came back again for grenades and went to put the third pit out of action, firing a tommy gun from his hip. He was hit, and staggered, but went on with his gun still firing, flung his grenades and silenced the third pit.' When the unit went out to clean up the post, they found Corporal John French dead in front of the third pit: but every Japanese in the three pits had been killed.

There was the young pilot who had been shot down over Lae. His wrecked plane crashed into the sea. Wounded and followed by sharks he had been swimming for eight or nine hours when he reached the shore. Dazed and exhausted he had dragged himself on to a rocky beach. When he walked into the village, women fled screaming, and the men looked sulky and hostile. But two mission boys took him back to the beach. They gave him an army biscuit to eat, and guided him through thick dark jungle, across rivers, and up and down steep mountain-sides. Walking by day, climbing, sliding and wading through swamps up to their waists in foul black mud, devoured by leeches and mosquitoes, spending the nights now and then in a friendly village, or lying on banana leaves on the soggy ground, living on coconuts, paw-paw and the sweet native potato, they had come after thirty-three days to a settlement where the ragged, barefoot airman, whose bandages were caked with mud and blood, could be put in hospital, and his hungry native saviours be fed and rewarded.

It was only then they explained that they did not belong to the village near the beach, where the natives had intended handing over the white 'tabauda' to the Japanese. Villages had been burnt and their inhabitants murdered for sheltering Australian soldiers. The tribe, afraid of vengeance, hoped to ingratiate itself with the new masters. It was to the quick and courageous action of those two natives the young airman owed his life.

Others had not been so fortunate. Sally could not get out of her mind the picture of a young airman who had walked up the long hill track to the place where the Japanese executed their prisoners. A lonely, dauntless figure, he strode along, with Japanese guards behind him. On the hilltop he had faced them, just a flicker of his eyelids and a faint smile betraying that he knew his head would be lying on the ground, severed from his body, next moment.

A description of what happened was found in the note-book of a Japanese officer, months afterwards.

For some time, again, there had been little news and no letters.

Sally had read so much about the fighting in New Guinea that she thought she could visualize the scenes through which Bill was passing: identify herself with what was happening to him.

She felt sometimes as if she were watching the weary, un-shaven men, half-naked, or in their jungle green, trudging through tropical downpours as they climbed steep slopes of the ranges, slipping and sliding: dropping to rest by the track and going on, their leg muscles knotted with cramp, and their backs aching under the heavy kit they carried. They would be blotted out by mists: and when the clouds lifted, she could see them crawling like some queer tenacious larvae against a background of blue, jagged peaks, tier on tier of them in dazzling sunshine, with steamy mists rising from deep ravines and gorges on their lower slopes.

Her mind retained vivid images of everything she had read about the retreat from Kakoda, and the grim fighting which was driving the Japs back over the ranges. She could see machine-gun nests on the mountain-sides, and in dense thickets of the jungle, from which isolated Jap gunners flung deadly fire: attacks by patrols to silence them.

She remembered how one of these patrols had crawled several miles beyond the Japanese lines to find a gun which was landing shells on the Imita Ridge, where Australians were reforming for their advance along the Kakoda trail. When the Jap gun was discovered, two or three lads wormed their way forward until they were within a few yards of the gun, shot down the officer and gun crew, and with grenades and fixed bayonets charged the position and put the gun out of action. One returned to report that their captain had been killed, and two of their cobbers, badly wounded, were being dragged back through the jungle by two others.

These images and incidents wove through Sally's thoughts no matter what she was doing.

After the Japs had been driven back across the Kakoda Pass, after American bombers had swept enemy aircraft from the sky, correspondents sent glowing accounts of how Australian troops had outwitted and out-fought the Japanese in the jungles and mountains of central New Guinea. They had also borne the brunt of the fighting at Gona, on the far side of the island. Airborne American forces, landed further along, were driving the enemy from Buna; but although the Japanese floundered in a trap, their retreat cut off, heavy fighting was still going on in the thick jungles and over the white sands of those northern beaches.

Daphne received two mildewed, damp-sodden and almost illegible letters from Steve, and letters had come to other women Sally knew, from sons or husbands who had fought over the Kakoda trail to Gona. The men said they were 'O.K. and going strong', 'on the road to Tokio', in hospital with malaria, or had been wounded. But no letters came from Bill.

Rejoicing over the taking of Kakoda and the forward movement of our troops which had driven the Japanese back to the sea was overcast by the knowledge that so many men had been killed and that hundreds were coming home wounded.

Official information that their men had been killed in action, or were missing, had reached several goldfields folk Sally knew; and casualty lists were appearing in the newspapers every day. But little information could be obtained as to how a soldier had died, except from a brief letter written by some mate, or an officer, paying tribute to the gallantry of one of his men. There were many sad-eyed women in Kalgoorlie and Boulder: women who were mourning the death of a son, husband, or lover; men who went about heavy hearted because they had lost a mate, brother or dear lad of their own.

Sally fretted because she had not heard from Bill; but she would not allow herself to harbour any fear on his account. While her will was protecting him nothing could harm him, she tried to assure herself. The effort not to worry and the sense of waiting for news benumbed her faculties. One afternoon she was sitting on the back veranda knitting automatically, when she startled Dinny by a sharp cry.

'What is it?' he asked anxiously, dropping the newspaper he was reading, and peering at her over his spectacles.

Sally looked as if she had wakened from a horrible dream.

'I saw Bill crawling through the jungle,' she said, dazed and aghast. 'Slowly, carefully, as though he were hurt. And there was a Jap behind a tree watching him. I could see the Jap as plainly as I see you, Dinny. His clothes were dark green like the undergrowth, his face, too, and his eyes like a snake's. He had a short sword and lifted it to strike Bill. I screamed before I knew what I was doing.'

'Y're just worried because we've had no letters for a while,' Dinny said.

'That's it, I suppose,' Sally agreed. 'And there was that story of a wounded man who had a Jap with a dagger prancing round him all night. It's been on my mind.'

'I remember,' Dinny said. 'The lad had used all his ammunition. Kept himself propped against a tree, and held the Jap off with an empty rifle and fixed bayonet. But his mates went out to look for him at dawn and brought him in.'

'Yes,' Sally heaved a sigh of relief. 'He was a sapper too, like Bill.'

CHAPTER XXXV

'T HEY say Paddy Cavan's goin' to kick the bucket,' Dinny
told Sally. 'He's taken rooms at the Reward. Says the big
pubs are too noisy. Got a nurse and secretary with him:
wants to die in peace. Won't go to hospital: won't do a thing
the doctor tells him.'

'You don't expect me to shed a tear, do you?' Sally queried.

'No.' Dinny brooded. 'Funny thing, Bill Fethers says all
Paddy can talk of is the early days, and wantin' to yarn to some
of his old mates.'

'Mates?' Sally scoffed. 'He had none. If Paddy worked with a
man he'd do him down, sooner or later. Everybody knew that.'

'Well, Bill says, Paddy's asked him to send up any old-timers
who come into the bar, to have a yarn with him. He's got his
bed alongside the window and lies there lookin' out on the old
Reward claims. Reckons the happiest days of his life were spent
when he was a kid scroungin' for a livin', and bein' hail fellow
well met with every prospector on the rush.'

'God knows he's got enough on his conscience — if he's got
one — to make him uneasy about going to glory, if that's what
he's after,' Sally declared.

'You've said it, missus.' Dinny poked at the ashes in his pipe,
looking uncomfortable, as if he had more to say and did not
know how to say it. 'Tassy and me went into the Reward for a
pot, yesterday,' he continued, 'and Bill says:

' "Sir Patrick wants to see you, Dinny."

' "Tell him to go to hell. I don't want to see him," I ses.

' "He ses it's important. He's got something he wants to tell
you," Bill ses.

' "There's nothing I want to hear from Paddy Cavan," I ses.

' "Maybe it'll be to your advantage," Bill ses.

' "Won't do any harm to hear what the old bastard's got to
say," Tassy ses.

'Well, we went up. And strike, y'd've thought we were long lost brothers the fuss Paddy made over us. Y'd never know him. There he was lyin' in bed — an old bag of bones: just his eyes squizzin' about as sly and lively as ever.

'The young nurse who showed us into the room said: "Please don't say anything to agitate Sir Patrick. His heart is in a critical condition, and any excitement is bad for him." But it got my goat to let Paddy think I was willin' to let bygones be bygones, so I said straight: "Bill Fethers ses you've got something you want to tell me."

' "That's right," Paddy ses. "Sit down. Sit down, boys. God, but ye wear well. The both of ye could give me a good many years — yet there ye are lookin' as spry as a pair of two-years, and me a crock can't move off of this bloody bed. What'll ye drink? Nurse, ring for the barman."

' "That's all right, Paddy," Tassy ses, "we've had all the drinks we want in the bar. Y'd better say what ye've got to, and we'll get goin'."

'Sir Patrick sort of tipped we weren't standing for any of his baloney. His face fell in: went all flat and doughy.

' "Right," he ses, "what I want to say to you, Dinny, is I've got to see Missus Sally. I'd go to her if I could. But I can't. And there's something I must tell her before I die." '

'Why should I go to see him?' Sally said, angrily. 'If he thinks I'm going to let him get away with any death-bed repentance for what he's done to me and mine, he's greatly mistaken.'

'Please y'rself,' Dinny murmured, relieved she did not blame him for having anything to do with Paddy.

'If you make up your mind to go, though,' he added, pausing to smoke over what he was saying, 'it'd better be soon. That nurse — queer little thing, she was — reminded me of someone. Don't know who. Got big eyes . . . pretty brown hands . . . slinky way with her . . . she said Paddy can't last much longer. He's got cancer of the bowel and the doctors can't operate 'cause his heart's too weak.'

'Why should I go?' Sally demanded, arguing with herself

more than with him, Dinny realized. 'What has Paddy got to say that would make any difference to me now?'

'Search me.' Dinny guessed all the same Sally's curiosity was aroused. She might resent as bitterly as ever the wrongs done to her and her family by Paddy Cavan; but she wondered what he would say about them to her, if that was what was on his mind, as she suspected. There seemed no other reason for Paddy to want to talk to her.

'I'll go,' she said, presently. 'But you'll have to come with me, Dinny.'

The next afternoon Sally put on her best dress and hat, and a pair of black kid gloves she had not worn for a long time.

'Come on,' she said brusquely. 'We may as well get it over.'

The nurse Dinny had met before took them upstairs to Paddy's room. She smiled at Sally as though she knew her.

'Good afternoon, Mrs. Gough,' she said. 'You don't remember me; but I remember you.'

'Your face is familiar,' Sally replied, 'but — '

'I'll tell you why, later,' the girl said.

Her slight, graceful figure, in white linen, with the wings of her cap floating about her, moved away before them.

'Mrs. Gough and Mr. Quin have come to see you, Sir Patrick,' she said, arousing her patient from a doze.

'Oh, Missus Sally,' Paddy exclaimed, the ghost of a grin flickering across his emaciated features. 'So you did come! I thought you would — to settle accounts.'

'They were settled long ago, as far as I'm concerned,' Sally said. 'Dinny said you had something you want to tell me. I came to hear it. That's all.'

'Sit down,' Paddy replied querulously. 'It won't hurt you to sit down . . . while I talk.'

His breath came gustily. The nurse brought him a dose of medicine. Paddy gasped, drawing a malicious satisfaction from having induced Sally to come to him.

'Must please ye to see me like this. Ill and miserable — though

332

I've got plenty of money, still. That's what I wanted . . . money. And I got it. How . . . you two've got a pretty good idea. But confession's good for the soul, Father Flynn says, and I've got to make restitution for some of me misdeeds.'

'You can make no restitution for what you did to me and mine.' Sally spoke flatly, determined to show Paddy he could not expect any quarter where she was concerned.

'Thought y'd say that.'

Despite his weakness and the pain he was in, Paddy seemed to be enjoying himself: getting a sardonic amusement out of Sally's hostility: the unsmiling set of her worn face, and the rigid outlines of her figure as she sat in the chair confronting him. 'And ye don't know how true it is. I lost a lot of money when Pat and Pam took their affairs out of me hands — ungrateful little bitches. But I'm still a rich man . . . and ye might say, the basis of all the money I made was those shares I stole from Morrey, years ago. . . .'

It was out, and he grinned feebly as he gazed at Sally, his sunken eyes glittering above pallid, flabby cheeks, the outline of his face still square and pugnacious.

Sally's hands in their shabby black gloves moved spasmodically as she stared at him.

'Can't say I regret what I did,' Paddy cackled mirthlessly. 'Morrey was always a fool: wouldn't't've made as good use of 'em, as I did. He'd've gambled 'em away, or lost everything in some wild-cat speculation. But I hung on till Great Boulder scrip was worth something. Ye may say it gave me my first leg-up, and all the rest followed.'

'Helped you to send Morris and Tom to jail, and take Amy away from Dick.' Dry and hard as the breaking of sticks, Sally's voice sounded.

For a moment, it appeared as if Paddy was overwhelmed by her accusation and the weight of his guilt. Then his bony hand was raised in a feeble gesture of protest. His eyes caught the sparkle of a diamond on his little finger.

'Ye can't blame me for what happened about Amy,' he cried,

almost gleefully. 'I loved Amy . . . as much as Dick. And, be God, I'd do it all again to get her.'

Sally stood up. She had taken all she could from Paddy Cavan, Dinny knew.

'Y're not going,' Paddy cried in alarm. 'I haven't told ye yet what I asked ye to come for. I'm goin' to leave ye £5000 in me will, Missus Sally. Ye may not regard it as restitution. Ye may consider it makes no difference to the trouble there's been between us . . . But I'm a dying man and it'd ease me mind, if — '

'You can't buy me off, Paddy,' Sally said, her voice trembling to anger and the grief he had aroused. 'I don't want your blasted money. If there's a hell I hope you'll burn in it. I hope you'll suffer the way you made Morris suffer, and Tom and Dick. You stole another man's luck from him. You've lied and thieved all your life — never thinking about anybody but yourself. I'm not forgiving you, or caring if you've got any remorse now. I don't believe you have got any remorse. You've just said you'd do it all again to get Amy. You've escaped punishment here for all the wicked things you've done. May God damn and blast your rotten soul — if you've got one — for ever and ever, amen.'

'Don't say it,' Paddy turned away from her, covering his face with his hands.

'I do say it,' Sally declared, 'though I'd rather see you punished here and now for all the crimes you've committed; and are trying to crawl out of by talking about confession and restitution. They won't make any difference to the sorrows you've caused, or the men who are dead.'

As she stood by the window the nurse was swinging a tassel of the blind cord and singing to herself, as if indifferent to the conversation going on behind her.

'Stop it,' Paddy shouted at her. 'God damn and blast ye, haven't I told ye not to sing that thing! She's always singing it,' he whimpered, falling back on his pillows, limp and exhausted. 'I can't stand any more of it — this throwing things up against me.'

Sally thought the girl's absent-minded humming had disturbed him. But the nurse turned, and her eyes, big, beautiful brown eyes, met Sally's.

'That song reminds Sir Patrick of something unpleasant,' she said calmly. 'I sing it because my mother's name was Maritana.'

Sally remembered the air she had been singing then. It was: 'Oh, Maritana, wild-wood flower —'

'I didn't do it, I tell ye,' Paddy cried. 'I didn't murder Maritana — if that's what y're gettin' at. The boys said Fred and Maritana had a quarrel. He killed her . . . didn't mean to. It was an accident. Then he had to get rid of the body.'

'But you told him to shut her mouth, didn't you?'

'Maritana wanted her cut of the gold she collected,' Paddy blubbered, his bony yellow hands plucking at the sheet. 'She threatened to squeal if I didn't pay her. And she knew too much . . . about the plant and me dealings with Fred . . . what could I do? I'd've been ruined if it got about I was in the gold, those days.'

'So Maritana had to be put away,' the nurse said. 'And my father, and the children.'

'I never meant him to kill her. So help me God, I didn't,' Paddy wailed.

'But you never bothered to do anything for him — or us,' the nurse went on in her quiet, inexorable voice. 'We were sent to orphanages and institutions. They separated us and changed our names, so that we'd forget what had happened. I've never been able to find my brothers and sisters. Only you — and I waited a long time to get this job, and remind you of Maritana.'

'Get out of me sight,' Paddy howled. 'Ye're like a pack of crows squawkin' round me. But I'm not dead yet. I'll live long enough to get even with the lot of ye.'

The nurse went to the door and opened it. Dinny and Sally followed her into the passage.

As she closed the door behind her, the girl said quickly: 'Don't worry. I'll give him a needle, presently. Sir Patrick knows he can't do without me. He's had too many nurses who won't stand his bad temper and demands. I am a good nurse — I will do my professional duty conscientiously. Worked too hard to get my training to spoil everything now by neglecting or ill-using a patient. But Sir Patrick will hear that little song when he's dying.'

Paddy was already calling her.

'Nurse! Nurse!' His voice rose frantically as if he were afraid she had taken him at his word and left him.

Sally and Dinny could hear him screeching and wailing: 'Nurse! Nurse!' as they walked away.

Merita, Maritana's daughter had said her name was, although she called herself Rita West. There was nothing about the tall pale girl to suggest she had aboriginal blood except perhaps her eyes, Sally thought, and thin dark hands. They were like Maritana's, and Kalgoorla's.

Sally wished she could have talked more to Merita. She remembered the passionate devotion of the scraggy little girl to her younger brothers and sisters when the police had found her in the scrub near Fred Cairn's camp. Sally thought she might be able to help Merita to trace the children; but her mind was confused by the memories Paddy Cavan had aroused and her anger with him. She could scarcely control the nausea which had overwhelmed her in the heavy atmosphere of the sick room with its smells of disinfectant and physical decay.

It was good to be in the street again, feel the fresh air and sunshine wafting away that dizzy nausea, and soothing the tumult of her thoughts.

'Oh, well,' Dinny said, 'at least we know now what happened to those shares Morrey set such store by.'

'Much good that does us,' Sally said bitterly.

She was remembering the night when she had arrived on Hannans, so tired, and dismayed because Morris expected her to live in a brushwood shed behind the store. Then in the morning, when Morris found he had lost his wallet, there had been the terrible scene with Ma Buggins. Morris had always blamed her, Sally, for not taking proper care of his wallet — and the wretched shares tucked away in it. Those lost shares had been the cause of a secret grouch Morris held against her. He had always maintained that the chance to buy those original Great Boulder shares was the only decent luck he had ever had on the goldfields. Maybe Paddy was right, Morris might not have held on to them, as Paddy had done, and made a fortune out of them. But Morris believed he would have, and that Sally would never have had to endure such hardships when the children were young, if he had not lost those shares.

For years, Paddy had used and abused her confidence and Morris's: pursued them with the malignity of a guilty conscience, framing Morris and Tom on the charge of gold stealing, though she had been sure he intended to discredit Dick. Paddy made his love for Amy the excuse. He had got Amy in the long run: humiliated Dick and destroyed his happiness.

Sally reminded herself of the vague suspicion which had come to her after Morris's death that Paddy had stolen the wallet. And now he himself had admitted it. But that made no difference to the crimes Paddy had committed against her family, Maritana and people of the goldfields. She could not forget or forgive them, Sally told herself. She did not regret having let him know it.

'Maybe Paddy's what the system made him,' Dinny reflected. 'He was pitchforked into the struggle for existence when he was young: had to fend for himself, and did it ruthlessly, unscrupulously. Like many another man. Queer how all the wrong things he's done in his life are plaguing him now.'

'Don't you believe it,' Sally said impatiently. 'All that's worrying him is that he may have to pay for them in the hereafter. He's as ignorant and superstitious as he was when he was a kid.'

Her shoulders moved as if she were throwing off a burden.

'It's no use brooding over what's past and done with. I'm only sorry I let Paddy rake it all up again. While the war's on, Dinny, we've got enough to think of without worrying about saving Paddy Cavan's soul for him.'

337

'That's right,' Dinny agreed.

'Paddy's changed his mind about wanting to die on the gold-fields,' Dinny remarked a few days later, after glancing at his newspaper. 'Sir Patrick, accompanied by his nurse and secretary, left by plane for Melbourne, this morning.'

The death of Sir Patrick Cavan was announced the following week. There were eulogies of the deceased in the press. Dinny read Sally a glowing account, taken from an Eastern State's paper, of how Sir Patrick had risen from a bare-foot boy on the goldfields to be one of the wealthiest and most influential men in the mining world. He had left the greater part of his fortune to charities, it was stated. Requiem mass had been celebrated at St. Patrick's Cathedral and an imposing cortège had left the sacred precincts for the cemetery at Ivanhoe where the remains of Sir Patrick were interred.

EILY's sensitive face, never a mask for her feelings, told Sally there was bad news. So bad, that at first Eily could not speak when she came into the kitchen that morning.

'What is it?' Sally asked, although she knew, and was instinctively defending herself from the blow. 'Bill?'

'Oh, gran, he's missing,' Eily cried. 'Believed to have been killed.'

'Believed to have been killed,' Sally said slowly. 'What does that mean? If they don't know, how can they believe anything of the sort? Maybe he's lost in those jungles like other men have been. Maybe — they just haven't found him. Where's the telegram?'

Eily handed it to her. Sally put on her spectacles, her hands shaking. She held the flimsy piece of paper, staring at it uncomprehendingly. Eily saw that she could not read it: that her eyes would not focus on the swimming typescript.

Eily took the telegram from Sally's hands. The tears were streaming down her face as she read:

' "We regret to inform you that WX 28866 Captain Wilbur Gough was reported missing on November 10th, and is now believed to have been killed." '

'I don't believe it,' Sally said dully. 'I'd feel it — if Bill were dead. They've got no proof. He might have been wounded: crawled away and escaped. Others have. I was reading, only the other day, how an airman had been missing for six months, and been picked up, ragged, half-starved and nearly insane so that he couldn't make his way back.'

'I know,' Eily said despairingly. She could not deprive Sally of any hope to which she might cling. She thought herself that the military authorities would not have sent that message had there been any chance of Bill's survival.

Instances from the last war flitted through her mind, of men

339

reported missing and believed to be dead, who had returned home after a long time. On any other battle-front there might have been some consolation in the thought that a missing man had been taken prisoner. But everybody knew the Japanese were not taking prisoners in New Guinea. It was kill or be killed in the dark and steamy jungles and in the stinking swamps when Australian and Japanese soldiers got to grips. The massacre on Tol had warned Australians what surrender to the Japanese meant.

In the retreat from Kakoda, gaunt and fever-stricken men who had held the pass for a month against overwhelming forces of the enemy, remembered that. Again and again they had stood, dauntless and determined to pay for their death with as many Japanese dead as their ammunition allowed. Eily shuddered as she thought of it. Death was better for a loved one than to be taken alive by the Japanese, she knew. And she knew that Sally understood this too.

But rigid and dry-eyed, Sally stared before her, unable to believe Bill was dead. Was she deceiving herself in order to bear the shock of this news, Eily wondered? Or could there be anything in her faith that Bill was still alive?

'Perhaps you're right, dear,' she said, ashamed to be weeping while Sally's face wore that strange, stony expression. 'We mustn't give up hope.'

'No,' Sally said.

'Should I write to Pat?' Eily asked.

'Yes.'

Eily stayed all the morning, doing odd jobs round the house while Sally sat in her chair, gazing before her, dumb and motionless. Dinny had been out when Eily arrived. She waited until he returned from doing some shopping in the town to tell him what had happened. No one could help Sally more than Dinny, Eily was sure.

'I was afraid something was wrong,' Dinny groaned. 'We haven't heard from him for so long . . . My poor Missus Sally. How can she stand up to it?'

'I don't know,' Eily said.

'She's had too much to bear,' Dinny muttered.

'Go to her, Dinny,' Eily begged. 'I'm on duty at the hospital in half an hour; but I'll come in on my way home to see how gran is.'

Before she left, Eily saw that Dinny had drawn up a chair beside Sally, and that they were both weeping, holding each other's hands and talking brokenly together.

Next day, a letter came from an officer of Bill's unit. Eily read the letter to Sally and Dinny.

It said:

'Captain Gough had undertaken duties with a commando unit penetrating behind the enemy lines. It has been ascertained that he went forward with two sappers on the night of November 10th to blow up an ammunition dump in a native village held by the Japanese. After accomplishing their task, the party ran into an ambush. Patrols have combed the area and our troops are now in possession of the village; but no trace has been found of the missing men. The villagers say they assisted any of our wounded they found in the surrounding jungle to escape and that an officer answering to Captain Gough's description was shot by a Japanese sniper not far from where the ammunition dump exploded.

'Captain Gough was very popular with his men. His courage and ability to laugh off difficulties kept us all in good spirits under the most trying circumstances. Every man in his unit joins with me in regret for the loss of this gallant soldier, and in expressing our condolences to his bereaved family.'

Yet Sally would not relinquish her belief that Bill was still alive. She seemed to be living in a trance: seeing the forests of tall dark trees, their 'green twilight', as Bill had described it: feeling the steamy, fetid atmosphere in which life was generated and decayed so rapidly. She spoke sometimes as if she were wandering along the dim trails, searching for Bill, and again and again reminded Dinny of the stories they had read about airmen and soldiers who had been hidden by friendly natives, and returned to their own people after many weeks, even months, of wandering in remote parts of the island.

341

P AT came from Geraldton in a dusty rattletrap of a car. She had been driving all the day before, and it was a tired and distraught girl who flung herself into Sally's arms.

'Oh, it can't be true!' she cried. 'Tell me it isn't true, Missus Sally. My brain's bursting. I can't be brave. How can we bear it?'

Sally held her, exclaiming tenderly, brokenly. She took Pat into the house. They sat down on the old sofa in the sitting-room and Pat wept passionately, leaning against Sally. The tempest of Pat's grief swept Sally away from her own bitter sorrow. Her pain was merged with Pat's as the girl clung to her, shaken by an uncontrollable anguish. When Pat was exhausted and lay whimpering and moaning over and over again: 'Oh, my love, my love . . . my beloved . . .' Sally said gently:

'I'm glad you came to me, Pat.'

'I don't know how I got here,' Pat cried fretfully. 'I managed to hire a car and have been driving and driving. There's a black-out in my brain. I'm all torn and bleeding inside . . . All I can think of is Bill. Bill dead . . . Bill dead.' Her voice rose shrill and screaming. 'I feel as if I were going out of my mind. What am I to do, Missus Sally? What am I to do?'

'We've got to live through it, somehow,' Sally said. 'That's what Bill would say.'

'I know,' Pat wailed. 'But why? It doesn't seem worth while.'

'Bill would say there are hundreds and thousands of other women in the same position as we are,' Sally ventured, though to be reminded of that had brought her no consolation. It had only intensified her own sense of bereavement, to know that so many other women were suffering as she was, and to realize the colossal loss of life. She felt it was unforgivable to have said this to Pat. But what else was there to say?

'They haven't lost Bill,' Pat cried, unable to think of anything but her own grief.

'I have.' Sally's face ruckled and her hands wrung each other as she strove not to break down and weep as passionately as Pat had done.

'How selfish I am.' Pat put out her hand: its delicate intimation of their feeling for each other helped Sally to overcome the tumult of her own emotion. 'I know it's god-awful for you, too, Missus Sally.'

'You see,' Sally explained, to hold Pat's attention. 'Lal was killed in the last war. Then Dick died — Bill's father. I thought I could never love anybody again as I'd loved Dick. He was my first-born. But Bill came to mean as much to me as his father did.'

'He was like that, wasn't he, Bill?' Pat said wearily. 'You just had to love him. I didn't want to, at first. But then, I couldn't help it — and I had to make him love me, too, Missus Sally. I did my damndest. He didn't want to love me. But he did. Oh, he did! And now — to think I'll never lie in his arms — never see him again.'

It was a relief to Pat to have someone to talk to, Sally understood: someone to whom she could pour out the torrent of her love and grief. That was why Pat had come to her, Sally told herself. Pat knew her sympathy and understanding could be relied on, although at one time there had been a vague hostility between them. Sally afraid that Pat might be no more than a glamour girl beguiling herself with Bill during a few dull months on the goldfields; and Pat fearful Missus Sally would convince Bill there was no more to their love affair than that.

'I wish we had been married,' Pat went on tremulously, and a little uncertain whether Missus Sally would approve of what she was saying. 'I wanted us to be, before Bill went away the first time. But he thought I wasn't sure of myself. Just randy, and it would wear off. But it wasn't that way at all, Missus Sally. I wanted Bill for himself — all of him. I thought if I could show him nobody else mattered, I'd win in the end.'

'You did ' Sally said.

'Yes.' Pat's tear-drenched eyes held a flash of defiance. 'And we had a honeymoon in Sydney before he went to Egypt. I couldn't risk letting Bill go away without making him feel we belonged to each other whatever happened.'

'I'm glad,' Sally said. 'There weren't many bright spots in Bill's life. You gave him the best of them, Pat. He was always so taken up with the working-class movement, meetings and organizations, he hadn't much time to think about himself.'

'That's why I had to do most of the love-making.' A faint smile quivered about Pat's mouth, as if a vagrant memory could still defy the desolation of her mind. 'But I loved Bill for all that, as much as anything — though I was jealous, too, of whatever kept him away from me . . . It was just crazy to bring Dekker here, when Bill was on leave; but I didn't know I wouldn't see him again . . . we wouldn't have any more time together.'

'Bill was ill when he arrived,' Sally said. 'Mentally and physically exhausted. He didn't seem able to think of anything but the war: what had happened in Greece and Crete.'

'I knew as soon as I saw him,' Pat said sadly. 'We always understood what was going on inside each other as soon as we were together. I just glowed and dissolved into him if Bill was near me, Missus Sally. All the time, during this blasted war, when he wasn't here, I've had to pretend to be gay and cheerful. I had to go on living: doing my job as well as I could: make friends and let other men take me about, so as not to be moody and always worrying about Bill. Now — I can't go on. I'm just all-in — and there's nothing to do about it.'

She sat huddled-up: her face drained of its youthful vitality: her eyes empty. Dinny came in with a tray on which he had put cups and saucers, a tea-pot and some thickly cut bread and butter. Sally poured cups of tea for Pat and herself. Pat drank the tea thirstily, but choked as she tried to swallow.

'It makes me sick to eat,' she said apologetically. 'My works seem to be on strike.'

344

Sally wondered whether she should tell Pat that she, herself, thought those words 'missing' and 'believed to have been killed', left a faint hope Bill might still be alive. But the truth was she did not feel as sure of that now as at first she had done.

Steve had written to Daphne and told her all he knew about Bill's death. He seemed to have no doubt about it. Men of Bill's patrol, who knew he had been wounded, had scoured the area, Steve said. They had found a dead Jap wearing Bill's boots and wrist-watch. Still, Sally could not rid herself of a lingering hope that Bill might have wandered a long way from the military outposts, or have been taken to some isolated village by friendly natives escaping from the Japanese.

When she spoke of it, Pat listened intently. 'I've thought of that,' she said. 'If only you're right, Missus Sally! Mistakes have happened, I know. My C.O. is having inquiries made. But my heart's dead somehow. I don't seem able to hope.'

Pat was physically exhausted by her long drive over the rough inland tracks, as well as by sleepless nights, lack of food, and the emotional stress she had been under. She had got a week's leave. Sally put her to bed and gave her a mild sleeping-draught.

To have the girl to care for diverted Sally's attention from her own grief. She fussed over Pat with the motherliness of a broody hen, cooking dainty meals for her, coaxing her to eat, talking to her about Bill, sitting up with her when she could not sleep. And Pat, who had never been fussed over and cared for in such a way, found it comforting to know she mattered to someone, for Bill's sake.

Eily and Daphne, too, came to see her and made her feel that they regarded her as one of the family. Sally gave her Bill's letters to read, and even Dinny's old men had a protective concern for her as they sat on the veranda, in the evening, discussing the war news. But it was La and Nadya, by their gesture of childish sympathy, who broke the silent sorrow in which Pat had wrapped herself.

They had run into the sitting-room, on their way home from school, laughing and chattering noisily, one afternoon soon after

Pat arrived. Awed by her sad eyes and the dark blue uniform of the W.A.A.F. she was still wearing, they stood staring at her.

Eily took them outside and explained to them that Pat had been Bill's girl and she was heart-broken about him. Subdued and conscience-stricken because they had forgotten Bill's death so soon, the two went away.

Nadya had a little bunch of flowers in her hand when they returned an hour or so later: paper daisies, the dark blue dampiera which grew beside the tracks near the salt lake, and sprays of the wild cassia Sally loved. They had ridden out into the bush on their bicycles and picked the flowers for Pat.

'We're so sorry, Pat,' Nadya whispered.

'Mum says you're Bill's girl and heart-broken about him,' La explained in his blundering school-boyish way. 'We wanted to do something for you.'

Nadya cast a scathing glance at him. 'Of course, he would say the wrong thing!' she exclaimed afterwards to her mother.

But Pat had looked at the flowers and then at Nadya and La, her eyes brimming.

'Oh, darlings, how can I thank you,' she said, scarcely able to speak. 'Yes, that's what I am. Bill's girl and heart-broken about him.'

By the end of the week, she looked better. She was calm and clear-eyed, although shadows like bruises lay beneath her eyes. Sally knew she was not sleeping well: the violence of her grief had abated but its weight and pain remained. When Pat decided to go back to Geraldton and carry on with her work in the camp there, she said:

'That's what Bill would expect me to do.'

'My dear,' Sally folded Pat's hands between her own, 'won't it be too much for you?'

'No. I'm all right now.' The faint smile which flitted about Pat's mouth was so like Bill's when he was facing a tough proposition that Sally thought some of his spirit was surviving in the girl who had loved him. 'You've made it possible for me to go on. I was so alone and demented, before.'

346

'You need never feel like that again,' Sally assured her.

'At one time, Pam and I used to share all our troubles,' Pat explained, frowning slightly, as if apologizing for the need which had driven her to Sally. 'But now she's got Shawn and the baby, I don't like to worry her. Besides, she didn't know about Bill, and I couldn't think of anything but to come to you.'

'Come to me whenever you want to,' Sally said. 'But don't be too hard on yourself, Pat. You're young . . . and drinking tears will be bad for you.'

Pat went back to Geraldton, and after a brief letter to say she had arrived safely, Sally did not hear from her for months. Then she wrote that she had been transferred to the Eastern States, and was sorry there had not been time to come to say goodbye. No further news about Bill came from New Guinea.

The year ended: another passed, with the war still dragging on, although the tide had turned with the triumph of the Soviet forces at Stalingrad: rout of the German armies in the snows and slush of the country they had ravaged. The Red Army was driving the shattered remnants of Hitler's once invincible armies to defeat and capitulation on their own frontiers. British and American troops had occupied North Africa and Sicily. The collapse of Italy and bombing raids on Berlin foreshadowed the doom of the fascist forces. The Allied landings in France, which would hasten the end of the war, had not yet been accomplished, but were hourly expected.

Victory was in sight, people were saying, and waiting with eyes and ears strained for the first news which would end the years of dread and horror.

CHAPTER XXXVIII

THE streets of Kalgoorlie looked bare and empty during those last days of the war. Business was dead, the shopkeepers said: the mines still working skeleton staffs, and people buying only rationed goods, the necessities of food and clothing. Shortages of these had occurred, but nobody went hungry.

Everybody realized how close to invasion by the Japanese Australia had been, and any hardships the war brought were taken by working men and women on the goldfields with the matter-of-fact stoicism of people accustomed to hardships and discomfort as their normal lot. Besides, compared with the people of Great Britain and of the devastated countries of Europe, they knew how little they had suffered. As soon as arrangements could be made for the dispatch of parcels, they were busy sending food and clothing to friends and relatives in England. Eily and Dinny collected funds for organizations distributing relief to victims of the war in Europe.

But there was still fighting in the Pacific when the armistice was signed at Rheims, and the first peace celebrations were half-hearted and fizzled out with a few drunken brawls. It was not until the atom bomb had blasted Hiroshima, and the unconditional surrender of the Japanese concluded hostilities in which Australian troops were engaged, that people on the goldfields could throw themselves into a spontaneous orgy of rejoicing. Then mine whistles shrilled madly; men flocked to the pubs; crowds milled through the streets singing and dancing.

As she watched the flags flying from every building, heard the clashing of church bells and crazy racketing of crowds in the streets, Sally remembered she had seen and heard it all after the first World War. It had been difficult then to join in the frenzied revelry and was much more so now. Only people whose men-folk were returning could laugh and enjoy the wildest demonstrations, she thought. Men from the prison camps, emaciated wrecks, would soon be restored to their homes and families; soldiers, sailors and airmen be safe from the innumerable and hourly perils they had lived through for years; but many men and women were taking the peace celebrations soberly. Sally imagined they were feeling as she did: glad the horrible carnage was over, but mourning for the thousands of young men drowned at sea, lost in naval battles or air crashes over the North Sea and Mediterranean: sons, husbands, brothers, lovers and sweethearts whose graves were strewn over the desert sands of North Africa, under the snows of Greece, through the jungles of Malaya, New Guinea and islands of the Pacific. Sad-eyed, with pain in their hearts, those who had suffered deeply by the war turned away from the clowning and tumult in the streets. For them, a tawdry farce was being played on a theme of immeasurable tragedy.

And yet, fascism, which glorified war, had been defeated. 'It's the biggest victory for peace there's ever been,' Dinny said. Gaunt and yellow, Steve returned six months after the racket of the peace celebrations had died away.

Daphne knew that during the campaign he had been in hospital with dengue and malaria, and that he had been wounded several times, but Steve made light of those 'scratches' when he wrote: said he had been 'patched-up', and would keep going until the Nips were routed out of every dug-out they had made for them-selves within cooee of the Australian coast.

Daphne flew to meet him when he arrived in Sydney. But Steve had to undergo a serious operation before he could make the long journey to the west. Pieces of shrapnel had to be 'dug out of him', he explained lightly. There were six operations before Daphne could bring him home. But now he had been discharged and was hobbling about in his slop suit of new civvies, so pleased to be back again, so happy to be with Daphne and the sturdy youngster he regarded as his own son, that he hated to talk about the war and the horrors of jungle warfare.

'But it's got to be done, Daph,' he said. 'It's got to be done! People mustn't be allowed to forget what our men went through out there. The hell of it — fighting through that dank, dripping undergrowth, those rotten swamps — the stench, hunger, misery and exhaustion a man had to take as part of the game. I never reckoned I'd come out of it alive. Most of us didn't. That's why our chaps fought as if there were nothing to live for but killing Japs. And when our mates were picked off by snipers, or hidden guns, nobody cared about anything but wiping out the swine who'd done them in. Men like Johnny French and a score of others showed what could be done. After Bill died, I was made a sergeant, and got this.'

There was a ribbon which went with the M.M. on Steve's shabby discarded tunic.

'But it doesn't mean a damn thing,' he protested. 'I'm almost ashamed to be seen wearing it. Darned near every man who was in the fighting along the Kakoda trail, at Templeton's crossing, Eora Creek, Oivi and Gorari, to say nothing of our big push at Gona, earned that ribbon.'

'Don't you believe it, Mrs. Miller,' Shorty Leigh exclaimed.

Shorty was a goldfields lad who had gone away with Steve and come home on crutches a year before. He dropped in sometimes in the late afternoon when Steve was shivering with malaria, and liable to bouts of sickness and high fever. Shorty's 'Hi-yah, Sport! How's things?' was always cheery, and his gossip diverting. Talking to Shorty, Daphne learned more of why Steve had been awarded the medal than she had done from Steve.

'Steve's patrol was reckoned the most daring and reliable we'd got,' Shorty said. 'Steve went out on every stunt himself: sometimes single-handed, with a pocketful of grenades, a sniping rifle, a couple of bandoliers and a sharp knife stuck in his belt. Got nine lives, if y' ask me, to come through like he done. I've known him crawl a couple of miles through slushy jungle, get within a few yards of an enemy gun-post, lob his grenades and yell to the boys to come on and clean up the outfit. The Japs'd be yelling and squealing, their machine guns blazin', and a few buck-teethed rats layin' about them with big knives. Beats me how Steve got away from some of those scraps.'

'You didn't do so badly yourself, Shorty,' Steve remarked. 'Remember spotting that foxhole near Efogi and putting five Nips out of action on your own?'

'Aw, that was easy,' Shorty grinned. 'They were squattin' round a bit of a fire havin' their scran. A couple of grenades did the job. My luck was out, though, next day when I was snoopin' behind their lines. A green-faced bastard jumped on me, and I had to strangle him with me hands for fear he'd let out a yell and bring a swarm of 'em buzzin' round. Thought I'd cooked his goose, but he let me have a blast from his tommy gun as I was gettin' away. Near blew me guts out. I finished him off and reckoned me last moment had come. A cobber was trailin' me, though: picked me up and carried me in. Jeeze, it wasn't dyin' I minded, Steve, but bein' butchered by the swine like some of our boys were. Remember that mountain village where they found eight West Australians cut to pieces, in a hospital hut?'

'Shut up,' Steve muttered, glancing at Daphne's drawn and colourless face.

'Oh, well, afterwards I was a good spud-barber, and that's about all,' Shorty concluded.

Sally, of course, wanted to know all Steve could tell her about Bill. Very gently and carefully, he went over again what he had written. There was little to add to it. He had talked to two survivors of the operation in which Bill had been killed; and to men of the patrol who had searched the area. They had been able to tell him nothing that gave Steve any hope Bill was still alive. Native villages had been burnt as the Japanese retreated, and even if the fleeing villagers could have taken a wounded man with them into the mountains, he would have made his way to the coast by now. Something would have been heard of him.

Sally put her hands over her face. Against what Steve told her she could no longer maintain her stubborn resistance to believing Bill was dead. Realization broke over her in a dark wave of desolation. Dumb and bowed beneath it, she did not for a while notice Daphne kneeling beside her.

'Oh, gran,' Daphne whispered, 'Steve and I will try to make up to you.'

Sally's hands moved in a caress over Daphne's bright head, but she did not speak.

For weeks she remained wrapped in the darkness of her sorrow. It was as if she were mourning not only for Bill, but for all the sons of whom she had been bereaved. Her eyes became dull and strange, glancing at you and away with a disinterested moodiness. She could no longer be bothered about her appearance. Her hair was pulled back and carelessly knotted: loose, untidy strands hung, round her face. There was no powder to soften its grim, sorrowful expression: no colour on her faded lips. She rarely changed from the dress she worked about the house in during the morning to a fresh one in the afternoon, as she had done for years. Every movement was an effort: to get up from her chair even, or walk to the door. Although she cooked for Dinny, as often as not, she would not eat herself: sat gazing listlessly at a meal, and scarcely heard Dinny when he scolded her for half-starving herself. Dinny was worried. Nothing he could do or say, and nothing Eily or Daphne could do or say, had any effect in arousing Sally from the melancholy brooding into which she had fallen.

Mrs. Ike Potter was shocked when she went to see Sally one afternoon during that winter. It was difficult to recognize the Missus Sally she had admired since she was a girl, in the sombre, silent woman Sally had become.

Steve and Daphne were there, too, that day, and La and Nadya had run in after school to see their grandmother, as usual. She took no notice of them, or Steve and Daphne, and hardly spoke to Mrs. Potter.

After everybody had gone, Dinny made up his mind Missus Sally must be shaken out of that obsession with her grief. It was becoming dangerous, he thought, and he feared for Missus Sally's sanity.

'It's downright disgraceful, the way y' behaved this afternoon, ma'am,' he said, with all the wrath he could muster. 'I never thought I'd live to see the day when I had to apologize for y'r manners and looks. What if y' have lost heart — and are broken-up about Bill? Is that any reason to make others suffer? Is that any reason to treat Steve as if he's got no right to be here, because Bill isn't?'

'Oh, no, Dinny,' Sally cried distressfully. 'I don't want Steve to feel like that. I didn't mean to make him. God knows I'm glad he and Daphne can be happy together. It's just that such a misery's come over me.'

'Y've been lyin' down to it, and not carin' a damn about anybody else,' Dinny said, hitting hard to keep up his advantage.

'Why was I born?' Sally cried distractedly. 'Why did I ever bear children — if they were all to die like this?'

'You're not the only woman who's lost her sons,' Dinny replied.

'But I've got nothing to hope for,' Sally protested. 'Nothing to look forward to. Everything and everybody I cared most for has been taken from me.'

'You've stood up to too much to let things get y' down now, missus.' Dinny spoke scornfully. 'Don't you remember what Tom used to say: "Better to die fighting for a great idea than to drag out an aimless existence"?'

'But I don't want to fight any more,' Sally objected. 'Why should I? Tom and Bill are gone. Nothing seems worth fighting for.'

'You ought to be ashamed of y'rself to say so,' Dinny spoke so roughly and impatiently, with such repressed anger, Sally stared at him in amazement. She was accustomed to his feeling with her and for her: could not understand his roughness and impatience now. It disturbed her for days and gave a new direction to her dreary thoughts. Had she lost Dinny's sympathy? Was he hurt by her disregard of their friendship? But it was not of himself Dinny was thinking when he accused her of being so absorbed by her own troubles that she was not concerned about anything or anybody else, she knew.

It was true enough, and shameful, Sally admitted. She had

allowed her grouch against life and what it had done to her, to make her indifferent to what others might be feeling. She had been drunk with her own sorrows: become a besotted creature unfit for contact with friends and relations, she told herself. But what was she going to do about it? Could she continue to live with this anguish and despair? 'Drag out an aimless existence', as Dinny said. It was unbearable to think of. Her days would dribble away, flat and empty, as they had been doing recently. Might it be that to 'die fighting for a great idea' would give one something to live for?

When Mrs. Ike Potter went to see her, a month or so later, Missus Sally was more like the woman she had always known. Sally's brown eyes smiled with a warm friendliness though sadness still lurked in their shadowy depths. She had sewn a neat little embroidered collar Marie had made for her into her black dress, and plaited her grey hair into a heavy braid over the loose natural wave on her forehead. The grit and indomitable spirit which had enabled her to throw off the weight of her sorrow was in her face, renewing its vitality and indefinable charm. If the darkness of tragedy still hovered about her, Missus Sally was moving away from it, Vi Potter thought.

'I've got Dinny to thank for bringing me to my senses, Violet,' Sally said apologetically. 'And a poem in a book Tom gave me for my birthday years ago.'

She went on to explain how she had asked herself whether it was possible for her still to do something useful with her life. She knew well enough there was a great idea worth fighting for, she said; and she remembered that poem. It had always stuck in her mind.

> Then for a purpose of eternal worth
>   Human deliverance more vast than earth
> Hath known, give gladly of your body's breath. . . .

When first she read those words, a vision had come to her of deliverance from all that degrades and oppresses mankind, Missus Sally remembered. It had dazzled her; but absorbed with her family and housework, she had done nothing to help bring about that deliverance. It seemed a vague and idealistic illusion when Tom and Bill were working for it. But now, she felt as if to serve such 'a purpose of eternal worth' would give her something to live for. Life could not defeat her if she were working for something bigger than herself and her personal sorrows. That was what Dinny had been trying to tell her. And she understood, at last, how the help of insignificant people like herself, millions of them, in the end, could win the deliverance of which they dreamed.

Mrs. Potter was impressed by the strength, simplicity and grandeur of the idea which had enabled Missus Sally to rise above her misfortunes.

'It's the way I felt about singing, once,' she confessed. 'As if nothing else mattered. But now I'm just a big fat slug — too fond of my creature comforts to bother much about anything.'

She was glad, all the same, she told Dinny, to see Missus Sally's health had improved, and that she was regaining the energy she usually put into managing everything and everybody about her.

The mines had reopened, and gradually Kalgoorlie and Boulder resumed the normal spate of interests and business dependent on the mining industry. Men on leave from occupational forces in the Pacific, wearing faded jungle-green and khaki were seen in the streets: sick and disabled soldiers in slop suits looking for light jobs. On cold mornings miners went to work in their heavy service overcoats. Dilapidated felts that had weathered the Libyan dust storms, and tropical downpours, sat ignominiously on the head of an old native, or one of the town drunks who had never left his beat between pubs. Hundreds of young men like Steve had married and brought a wife and children to live with his or her parents. There was a great outcry for homes and a shortage of material for building them. Soldiers had money to spend. Pensions, deferred pay, war bonuses, were keeping shops busy that had been almost empty during the war years; but stocks were low, luxurious trifles and shoddy rubbish from overseas much easier to buy than the ordinary household goods, and clothing for men and boys, women were seeking.

Despite price control of necessities, the cost of living soared, and with the relaxation of regulations, every week more had to be paid for food and clothing. Rumours of a depression when post-war spending exhausted itself created uneasiness. With the cost of living rising, folk who could, bought what they needed before their money lost further value.

Many mines on the Golden Mile had almost ceased production during the war. Gold was not considered essential to effective prosecution of the war. Man-power had been drafted into the army, navy, air force, and into industries producing materials and munitions necessary to equip, feed, clothe and arm the fighting forces, as well as to provide for the basic needs of the civilian population.

But gold regained its significance in international relations; and the need for increased gold production had immediate repercussions in Kalgoorlie and Boulder. The mining industry of the west bestirred itself to increase production: applied for lifting of the tax on gold and for concessions affecting costs and regulations. Low grade mines which had threatened to close down if the miners were granted shorter hours or a rise in wages, continued to work at a profit, although at Wiluna and Youanmi the big mines around which prosperous townships had grown up ceased operations. They were worked out, it was said. New mines, however, like the Porphyry, a hundred miles north of Kalgoorlie, flourished; and prospecting for deep leads in the no-man's-land between old fields was given fresh impetus.

Overseas financiers were again casting speculative eyes over the five hundred thousand square miles of auriferous country round about Coolgardie and Kalgoorlie. A mushroom crop of new companies and development schemes sprang up. New finds on old mines and fields created a ferment of excitement.

Kalgoorlie and Boulder soon moved out of the doldrums of the war years into the new boom for gold production.

' "The Government and the Commonwealth Bank would have liked to continue the policy of gradually rebuilding Australia's gold reserve," ' Dinny read from his morning paper, ' "but the current dollar situation is so serious that it has been decided, for the time being, to sell current gold production to the United Kingdom as a special measure of assistance in her present difficulties. In view of its decision to sell current gold production to Britain, the Government might consider stimulating gold production in Australia." '

'What on earth does that mean?' Sally asked.

'It means,' Dinny said slowly, 'that Australia's backin' the Old Dart with $31,500,000 worth of gold a year. The British Treasury will credit the Commonwealth Bank in London with sterling balances. Of course, we might've gone on sellin' our gold to the U.S.A., like we did before the war: but if sterling — that's the standard value of British money — depreciates any further, Australian producers will be in the soup, with all the goods they sell to Britain. So it's not altogether what y'd call a patriotic gesture. Wool's a bigger dollar earner than gold, at present: brought £35,748,000 last year, accordin' to figures, here. Seems we sold £18,000,000 worth of gold in 1940-41 and another swag in 'forty-six — and most of that came from the West Australian goldfields. So we might blow our bags about doin' our bit in Kal and Boulder, to hold the British Commonwealth of Nations together, Missus Sally.'

'Gold won't do that,' Sally said.

' "Since it was discovered, ninety-eight years ago, gold has been one of our main exports," ' Dinny went on reading. ' "Australia had produced gold worth £795,000,000 and practically the lot of it has gone abroad to back currencies of other countries.

' "Before the last depression, the Commonwealth Bank was required to hold not less than a quarter of the value of the note issue in gold. This was reduced to fifteen per cent, and during the depression Australia had to part with practically the whole of her gold reserve to meet overseas obligations." '

'So that's what we've lived and worked for.'

Sally gazed at the bare, red, sun-blasted country she could see from her back door: at the rusty-roofed houses, their white-wash grimed with the dust of years. Rows and rows of them, they huddled across the flat, with stinking pans along the narrow back lanes. All the wealth of the mines had not changed the way workers on the goldfields were living in those dilapidated houses without adequate provision against the dust and heat, or proper sanitary conveniences. Her anger surged as she thought of it. The promises of a better life 'after the war' were being for-gotten, as they had been after the first World War.

Sally listened attentively now when Dinny and his mates discussed the chaos in international affairs, or the chicanery of economic policies undermining the peace. They had been talk-ing a lot lately about the dollar crisis, dollar imperialism and gold as a standard of value. It was not difficult to understand the struggle for power which was going on everywhere; but more difficult to believe, as Steve and Eily did, that capitalism was in its death throes and striving desperately to frustrate the movement of peoples all over the world towards socialism.

Steve and Daphne often came along in the evening to see Sally, and sat yarning with Dinny on the veranda. Sometimes they brought Shorty Leigh, and sometimes he dropped in on his own account, always ready for an argument with the old men.

Eily was too busy with her study classes and meetings to come often, although she liked to spend an evening occasionally listening to the yarns and opinions Dinny and his mates ex-changed. She brought her knitting or darning when she did come, and sat under the light, silent and unobtrusive.

Her hair was silvery where the light shone on it and her eyes cob-webbed with wrinkles, but she had kept the enthusiasms of her youth: continued to steer her life by them. There was a vitality and serenity about her Sally envied. Eily continued to work as she and Tom had worked together. Nothing had ever disturbed or shaken her devotion to her principles.

Dick was back in Kalgoorlie and swanking about as a returned soldier. He had not been out of Australia or seen any fighting. 'Got himself a soft job with the D.O.M.F. — the Darwin Overland Maintenance Force,' Daphne said. 'Trust Dick!' He had not been to see his mother and ignored the family.

As far as Sally was concerned Dick was a Judas, and unworthy to bear the name of her most dearly loved son. Despite her motherly grief and selflessness, there was a steel in Eily, too, which would never forgive Dick for using his knowledge of the men who shared her convictions to have them sacked from their jobs.

So strange, these shifts and complexities of human behaviour, Sally was reflecting, the evening they were all there together: Steve, Daphne, Shorty, and Eily with a bag of mending beside her.

The talk turned on gold, as it so often did these days: gold as a standard of value, the rising price of gold, the significance of gold in international affairs. Among workers on the goldfields there was always a fear that if gold lost its value, Kalgoorlie and Boulder would collapse; thousands of men and women be thrown out of employment, lose their homes, businesses and means of earning a living.

'Seen a pamphlet just got out by the Chamber of Mines?' Dinny asked Sam Mullet.

'Can't say I have,' Sam admitted.

'It says we're "sufferin' from too much money",' Dinny explained, his voice twanging. ' "Unless some remedy is applied immediately, the world is headed for the greatest financial explosion in history: an explosion which will cause as much devastation as the atomic bomb." '

'Well, what d'y know about that?' Shorty gasped.

'They're scared of another depression, bankruptcy of the capitalist system and what the workers will do about it,' Steve said.

'Beats me,' Dinny went on, 'why we have been exportin' gold to America for so many years. There's more than sixty-five per cent of the world's gold buried at Fort Knox, they say. And the U.S.A. is usin' it and her economic power to squeeze all the gold she can get out of every country in Europe.'

'There's no denying,' Sam Mullet weighed his words carefully as usual, 'that during the war, the production and use of gold declined in importance. The Allied nations exchanged goods on the basis of needs and values: set up a system of international barter.'

'That's right,' Dinny agreed. 'But don't forget the Bretton Woods Agreement was supposed to be a knock-out for the gold standard. "It is perfectly clear", one of the spokesmen said, "that most of the world will not accept return to the gold standard." But gold's come into its own again. Under capitalism, gold's the most convenient standard of value. Paper money's all right for use inside a country, but most countries won't accept any other country's paper money for settling international debts because they reckon it's based on the political set-up of a state, not its economic stability. Looks as if the Yanks want to corner gold. They're buyin' up gold mines, here and anywhere else they can get hold of 'em to maintain a stranglehold on gold production.'

'The U.S.S.R. is willing to trade on gold as a standard of value,' Eily reminded them.

'That's a pain in the neck for the big boys on Wall Street,' Dinny chuckled. 'When the Soviet Union jumped from fifteenth to second place among the gold-producing countries, they got windy.'

'A few years ago there was talk of the U.S.S.R. being able to dump gold on the market and bring down its value, "causing great difficulties for the capitalist world",' Sam remembered. ' "A flood of gold from Russia may be regarded as more dangerous than a flood of propaganda," one of the economists said. But the war blew up, and had to be won on the I.O.U.s we're up against now.'

'Gold increases in value and potency as currencies decline,' Dinny remarked as if he had memorized the sentence. 'An article I was readin' the other day said that. It pointed out the dollar's lost forty per cent of its purchasin' power before the war. The question is can it continue to boss the world. Dr. Charles Price was quoted as sayin' in the *United Nations World* that a rouble pegged to gold could "effectively compete with the dollar". It could "interfere with the monopoly of the dollar in international exchange".'

'And there's platinum,' Sam muttered. 'Russia's the largest producer of platinum and building up platinum stocks to compete with gold held by the U.S.A. and Britain. American speculators are keeping an eye on platinum as a medium of international exchange. Platinum's worth £18 15s. od. to £21 11s. 3d. an ounce and gold £10 15s. 3d., according to current Australian prices.'

'That's what's behind all the talk of another war,' Eily declared. 'The fear of an economy which doesn't need "to crucify mankind on a cross of gold".'

'Remember Bill Dyson's cartoon?' Blunt Pick's cackle cut across the silence which followed what Eily had said. 'Moneybags praying: "Oh, Lord, give us this day a little war?"'

'The Moneybags are praying for that now,' Steve said bitterly. 'And they think they've got the game sewn up with the atom bomb to do the job for them. But the workers won't fight again to make the world safe for them and their cobbers.'

The discussion had become too serious and weighty for Tassy's liking. He bucked it with a rumble of his fat, jolly laughter.

'The official price of gold may be £10 15s. 3d. an ounce,' he said, 'and the Yanks buyin' for 35 dollars. But everybody knows y' can get £30 in Singapore or India, and £44 in France. The gold stealin' detective staff's workin' overtime to catch the boys smugglin' stuff out of the country.'

'Knew one of those blokes had a treatment plant out in the bush near Binduli,' Blunt Pick grinned. 'They've been handlin' hundreds of ounces a week, and gettin' away with it. Had jest cleaned up four hundred when the dees bailed 'em up.'

'Dan Miles, a young wood-cutter, was tellin' me he had a

narrow squeak the other day,' Dinny let himself be drawn into the drift away from a topic Tassy had had enough of. 'He was bringin' in a load of green timber and not wantin' to run into the forestry inspector. There was an old Slav with him, and they missed the turn-off in a bit of thick bush. Followed the track of a truck that seemed to know where it was goin', and came on a treatment plant, with smelted gold jest poured into the mould. The blokes who'd been workin' on it must've lit out when they heard Danny's truck comin'. But the old Slav couldn't bear to see a lump of gold like that goin' beggin': wanted to get away with it.

' "Don't touch it," Dan said. "Either the blokes who run this plant or the dees'll nab you if you do."

'Dan got goin', quick and lively. For the good of his health, he reckoned, it'd be better for him not to know anything about that gold. Took him some time goin' back on his tracks and findin' the turn-off. But he pulled into town about midnight, dropped the old Slav and went home.

'The blokes who owned the plant, though, had been watchin' in the bush, when Dan drove up, and they reckoned the old Slav might turn informer. They got to him and squared up with him: persuaded him to go out and move the plant for them. Dan hit the roof a couple of days later when he came home and found the dees had been along half a dozen times that day, and scared the wits out of his wife with their questions. Dan waited for the dees next morning. Blinds were up all along the street and the neighbours watchin' when they arrived, and Dan let 'em have it for comin' round worrying his wife.'

'They'd got the boys who were running the plant, the dees said, and the old Slav when he went out to move it. They'd been in the bush with glasses on the plant when Dan struck it: wanted him to give evidence for them.

' "When I give evidence for the goldfields detection staff in a goldfields town, I'll be out of me mind," Dan said.

' "If you'd touched the plant we'd've got you, too," the dees said.

'So Dan's thanking his stars he knew enough not to touch anything lyin' around that plant though it looked safe enough, standing out there in the bush, miles from anywhere.'

'What's the strong of the yarn about old Spindlebury?' Steve asked.

'Spindlebury, the bank manager?' Dinny crowed. 'He got what's been comin' to him for a long time. You know young Percy Dutt, nice lad with a withered leg. He was workin' on a show out near the Yellow Feather, had been havin' a bad time and got into debt. He applied for a permit to treat sands. And Spindlebury got hold of him, put a proposition up to him for treatin' ore: offered him thirty bob a ton and arranged for Percy to bank a couple of thousand ounces for him and promised to protect Percy if there was any inquiry.

'When the dees went out to have a look at Percy's show, they found he'd been treatin' ore not sands. Investigated his banking account and Spindlebury gave Percy away. He was arrested and jailed for that couple of thousand ounces. His wife was going to have a baby and wild with Spindlebury for lettin' Percy take the rap. She accused the dees of prosecuting the little men and lettin' the big men off. They started investigatin' Spindlebury's deals, and he got a tough sentence.'

'There's some decent blokes among the dees, and some in "the take", still, the boys tell me,' Tassy chortled.

'Some mighty tough customers in the gold, too, these days,' Blunt Pick grumbled. 'A man never knows where he is with them. That bloke strung up for murdering a woman down in Perth was one of 'em. He cracked a young chap tryin' to sell him a bar of gold in a back lane, and got away with the gold.'

'There's been more arrests for gold stealin', lately, than for a long time,' Dinny remarked, meditatively.

'And more fatal accidents on the mines,' Sally said.

'They're opening up old mines. New chums are taking all sorts of risks in abandoned shafts.'

Everybody knew that: but although he was no longer working on the mines, Steve spoke as a miner who was still troubled

363

for his mates toiling underground. 'During the war, workings got out of repair, even on the big mines, and pushing up production has meant letting repairs slide to get out the gold.'

'You've said it, Steve,' Shorty said eager to support Steve.

'There's shows we thought were dead as a door-nail comin' to life again.' Tassy's optimism of an old-timer refused to be damped. 'Look at Daydawn, and Coolgardie! Be the Great Livin' Tinker, haven't we been calling Coolgardie a ghost town for the last twenty years — and now she's flourishin'. Company promoters sayin' the mines on the Golden Mile've only been scratched.'

Blunt Pick's spirits rose with Tassy's.

'The Mountain View at Daydawn's right alongside the old Fingall, and they broke six tons for something like £80,000, a couple of months ago. The new bore on Maritana's showin' values at depth. The Old Reward's been worked agen. Mt. Charlotte and the North End comin' to light as payable propositions. At Lawlers and Kookynie, there's been new finds and good crushings.' Blunt Pick rattled off the score as if he were personally responsible for it.

'And how about Camillo Reghenzani's blow-out at Parker's Range?' Tassy queried jocosely. 'Cam'd been loomin' round for weeks without seein' her. Reckoned his luck was out: threw every stick of fracteur he'd got into a pot-hole, and was goin' to pull out. But when he had a look round after firin', there she was — winkin' and glitterin' at him all over the auction. He'd broken the cap of a rich reef, and has been doin' pretty well out of her ever since.'

'Sounds like old times,' Dinny replied, humouring Tassy.

'But it's not old times,' Sally cried, always irritated when Dinny and his mates began to sentimentalize over old times. 'And it's the new times we've got to think of. What the miners and people of the goldfields are going to get out of any resurrection of the mining industry — and the depression that's looming.'

EARLY next year Missus Sally received a letter from Pat to say she was going to marry Major Anthony Jefferson Dekker.

'Don't think I've forgotten Bill,' Pat wrote. 'I'll never love anyone as I loved Bill. Tony knows that, and he knows how lonely and miserable I've been. He's been very persistent for a long time, about wanting to marry me, so I've given in at last.

'Why, I don't exactly know — except that it seems the easiest thing to do.

'I'll be going to New York as soon as I can get a passage, so I won't be seeing you again; and maybe you won't want to see me. Pam is furious with me for marrying Tony and going to America. She says I'm just "a slim gilt soul" after all and tired of the working-class movement: doing all sorts of humdrum odd jobs and making a mess of them. It's true probably. I feel as if I were letting Bill down by clearing out like this. But at least he won't know and can't be hurt any more.'

'You can't blame her,' Dinny muttered when Sally gave him the letter. 'She's young: needs a bit of happiness.'

'I don't begrudge Pat any happiness she can get,' Sally said. 'But is she going to get it this way?'

'A lot of people've forgotten what they said during the war,' Dinny reminded her. 'And a lot more've given up the struggle for the things they were supposed to be fighting for.'

'My God,' Sally flared, 'has Bill given his life for nothing? Have the lives of all the young men who thought they were fighting to give people a better life been sacrificed in vain? It makes me mad to think of the horror and heroism of the war being forgotten — the rotten betrayal behind it all.'

She did not doubt Pat had loved Bill: that Pat had been honest when she said she would be happy to live and work with him. Without him it had been too hard for her to live and work as

Bill would have done, apparently. Sally said she had hoped Pat would marry: that she had told Pat she must not let her love for Bill prevent her from finding happiness with some other man for whom she could care. She understood the loneliness and desolation of spirit which had driven Pat to appreciate Major Dekker's love for her. But was that sufficient reason for Pat to abandon the ideas and ideals which, she had persuaded Bill, meant a great deal to her? Pam was still loyal to them; but Pat had separated herself from Pam and her friends, still plodding along the hard road to realization of their dreams. She was taking the coward's way, the easy, irresponsible way, to satisfy a forlorn egoism. Sally's disappointment in Pat was tinged with an underlying bitterness. It irritated her to hear Eily say: 'Poor Pat!'

'Why do you say that?' she asked. 'Pat's given up the struggle: left others to do her fighting for her.'

Eily's smile went to her, tranquil and reassuring. 'Pat's lost faith in herself, and what we're working for. I'm sorry for anyone who has.'

'Goodness knows I ought to be the last one to throw a stone at Pat,' Sally admitted. 'I dropped my bundle, badly enough, a while ago. I know it's not easy to keep going like you've done all these years, Eily: taking the knocks and abuse, and not letting them make any difference.'

'I'm lucky to have seen the light when I was young,' Eily said simply. 'And to have been able to help the movement towards socialism even a little.' She was sewing and her needle flashed steadily as she spoke. 'Pat's desertion is symbolical of so much that's happening today. But you mustn't let it worry you, gran.'

'During the war we believed victory for the Allied democracies would mean a strengthening of the rights of the people,' Sally sighed. 'Now, it's as you were with all the old animosities, prejudices, intrigues and class struggles. We don't seem to get any forader.'

'But we do.' Eily smiled, her confidence unimpaired by recognition of the 'as you were'. 'You remember what Galileo told the priests who wanted everybody to believe the world stands still? They had forced him to recant and deny the result of his observations. "And yet, it moves!" Galileo said. Systems of society don't stand still, either. They move and change, as ours is changing now. Some people don't like that. They're trying to make it stand still, or force it back into an old rut.'

'There's Czechoslavakia, Poland, Romania, Hungary — and China — winning through,' Dinny butted in. 'No need to be downhearted, missus.'

'It doesn't alter the fact,' Sally persisted irritably, 'that in America and Australia, the workers are getting a raw deal — what with attacks on the trade unions, jailing people for being communists and using troops to break strikes. It's as if Hitler were defeated in Germany and his spirit had escaped; is being victorious in other countries. It's doing what he did to destroy the rights of the people and stampede them into another war.'

'Looks like it,' Dinny agreed, puffing away at his old pipe. 'But I reckon it's jest part of the struggle that's got to be expected.'

'In every stage of history when the tides of social evolution are changing there have been conflicts,' Eily said quietly. 'Feudalism had its labour pains before capitalism was born.' She looked up from her sewing, a faint smile in her eyes. 'Capitalism today's like an old woman pregnant with a lusty infant she's afraid will be the end of her.'

'And trying all the methods of abortion she knows,' Sally added, her smile meeting Eily's, as if Eily had dispelled her pessimism and the pain of her disappointment with Pat.

'That's about the strong of it,' Dinny declared jubilantly. 'So there's no need for us to be depressed about the state of things we're up against at present. "The madness of this sorry day" will pass, as Bill used to say; and we can still do our bit for tomorrow.'

It was Blunt Pick who, a few nights later, made the evening on the veranda at Mrs. Gough's an unexpectedly gay one. He arrived some time after Tassy and Sam Mullet had settled down to a comfortable argument as to who discovered the first gold in the Koonyonobbing range.

'I've g-got a bit of news'll knock you,' Blunt Pick stuttered, looking a little abashed, but quite pleased with himself, as he shifted uneasily in his chair. 'I'm g-goin' to be married.'

'Wh-at?'

'For the love er Mike!'

Blunt Pick took the exclamations of his old mates with complacency.

'Be the Great Livin' Tinker, y've been in no hurry to make up y'r mind about it,' Tassy gasped, his full-blown, ruddy face convulsed as he spluttered and gurgled uproariously.

'Never was one to rush things — 'less there was gold about,' Blunt Pick admitted. 'But I've had tickets on Rosy Ann since she was a barmaid at the Reward in the early days. She married the wrong man, she says, and has had a crook spin ever since. Thinks now we're both gettin' the old age pension, we could make a better do of things together than on our lonesome.'

'Strike,' Dinny chuckled. 'That's one way of lookin' at it. But aren't y' scared y'll have three women on y'r hands if y' marry Mrs. Plush, Blunt? What's goin' to happen to Mrs. Amelia and Lili?'

'Rosy Ann reckons they'll be all right on their own,' Blunt Pick said, as if this was a matter to which he also had given consideration. 'Seems they've taken to each other and Rosy's been a bit out in the cold lately. That's how we come together.'

He paused to draw on his stubby old pipe and his eyes glinted as he continued:

'I was passin' their place, Sunday mornin', feelin' pretty crook. Dally and me'd been bendin' the elbow a bit willin' the night before, and it was a chilly mornin', wet and miserable. Rosy Ann seen me over the fence when she was out in the yard tryin' to chop a great hunk of wood.

' "Hullo, you old So-and-so," she ses, "come and split a bit er wood for me." So I went and chopped a bit of wood for her.

' "How's things, Blunt?" she ses. "You look like I feel. And I've got a pot of soup on the fire. Come in and have some."

' "Too right," I ses.

'We went into the kitchen and Rosy Ann stoked up the fire.

' "Where's y'r cobbers?" I ses.'

' "Fact of the matter is, they were run in, last night, Blunt," Rosy Ann ses. "We'd been havin' a few over the odds at the Reward, and was bringin' home a couple of bottles when a cop started hustlin' us along. Well y' know Melie goes stone crazy when she's had a few and a cop talks about her bein' 'drunk and disorderly'. She went for him with one of the bottles. And Lili tried to stop him arrestin' Melie. So the cop blew his whistle and they was both hauled off to the lock-up."

'Rosy Ann was real sore about it.

' "Melie and me used always to be in things together," she ses. "But now Lili butts in, and gets picked up instead of me. It's the same all the time, Blunt. Melie doesn't want me hangin' round any more."

'Well, I tried to cheer Rosy Ann up and when the soup was ready, she put out two big platefuls. Steamin' hot, it was, and what with the cold and bein' so miserable, Rosy Ann couldn't keep the dew-drops off the end of her nose. She was sniffin' and swallowin' the hot soup as fast as she could. I got sort of fascinated watchin' and wonderin' if the drips'd race her and fall into the soup.

' "Look out, they're gainin' on y', Rosy," I ses, when a big drop was jest about ready to splash.

'That settled it. Rosy Ann wipes her nose on a bit of rag she had handy, finishes her soup and ses to me:

' "Blunt," she ses, "y're the kindest man, ever I knew. If I'd had any sense I'd've married y' years ago. But I chose the wrong man, and've been kickin' meself ever since. How about it?" '

'Sort of took me breath away, her comin' round like that, so I hummed and hawed: said I'd got out of the way of thinkin' of meself as a marryin' man. But Rosy Ann was set on the idea:

369

reckoned our old age pensions'd go further if we started house-keepin' together and weren't so lonesome: could cut out the booze. So' — Blunt Pick drew a deep breath and grinned at his audience — 'we're gettin' spliced in a couple of weeks, and Rosy Ann's comin' to live with me in me shack be the racecourse.'

'Good on y'r, mate!' Dinny chuckled.

'I'll give you a party, Blunt,' Sally laughed. 'You must come here after the wedding. It'll be a real old-timers' party: just ourselves and Mrs. Green and Lili.'

' 'Struth, ma'am,' Blunt Pick beamed at her, 'that'd be grand. Rosy Ann'll be tickled pink. I'd clean forgot I was so keen on her once, till she reminded me. And, now, it's like gettin' a bit of luck y'd dreamed of, and given up hopin' for — strikin' a rich patch on a claim y' reckoned was a dud.'

The old mates' gusty laughter and chiacking drifted away through the darkness.

Blunt Pick's wedding was something they were going to gossip and crow about for a long time.

CHAPTER XL

D INNY did not recognize the native who had stolen along the veranda, barefoot, and rapped gently on the wall beside his open door.

It was a hot still night: moonlight wan through a haze which hid the stars. The stagnant air tasted of dust and fumes from the mines; and that gaunt, dark figure by his doorway looked menacing, unreal, like the figure of a nightmare or the wraith of some bygone fear. Dinny stirred restlessly as though he were dreaming: his eyes swung instinctively again to the door.

The voice that reached him was urgent and pleading. 'Kalgoorla bin finish'm,' it said huskily. 'Come quick, Dinny. Mus' take'm away and bury'm, before dogs and pol-eece find'm.'

'Eh — what's that?' Dinny was half-awake. His mind, dragging itself from the lethargy of sleep, grasped only that Bardoc was standing there by the door and telling him something about Kalgoorla.

'Kalgoorla bin finish'm,' Bardoc repeated. 'Bin walk about longa bush close-up Big Boulder. Mus' take'm away before dingoes and dogs — maybe pol-eece — find'm. Everybody in camp mighty sick feller. Close-up finish'm.'

Dinny knew an epidemic of a particularly virulent type of influenza was raging. He had heard that the native camp on Rill Station was badly affected, although only one or two old men and a few women and children of the scattered tribes which had once sought asylum there, remained in the camp. During the war the younger men had been away working on defence projects, and now they were in demand on northern stations where there was a shortage of labour. Dinny understood natives well enough to know that Bardoc would not have come to him unless driven by a desperate need for assistance. It was because he was one of the few white men who knew something

371

of native customs, and because he had been kindly disposed to Kalgoorla, that Bardoc had come to him, Dinny guessed.

'Right,' he called, yawning and hauling on his trousers. 'I'll be with you in a jiffy, and we'll see what we can do, Bardoc.'

Bardoc squatted on the veranda. He was breathing heavily and shivering as though he had ague. Must have the 'flu himself, Dinny thought, and be feeling knocked out after his long walk from the camp.

From Bardoc's muttered explanations, Dinny gathered that Kalgoorla had wandered away from the camp. He had been looking for her in the bush and found her body in a dry creek bed behind the Boulder ridge. Everybody else in the camp was too sick to help to bury her and the boss was away from the station. Bardoc wanted Dinny to go back with him and give a hand with the job.

Dinny was wondering what to do about it, whether he could manage to drive Jiggledy Jane or whether he would have to stump all the way after Bardoc, when Sally flicked on the light and came along the veranda in her dressing-gown.

'What on earth's the matter?' she asked, glancing from Dinny to Bardoc, and guessing something was wrong as Bardoc dragged himself to his feet and she saw his heavy sombre face. 'You sick feller, Bardoc?'

'Weeah,' Bardoc muttered. He would not admit he was ill, Dinny knew.

Dinny told Sally why Bardoc had come to him.

'Seems there's not another man or woman in the camp able to get about. All the others down with the 'flu. So I'd better go along with him.'

'I'll come with you,' Sally said quickly. 'Bardoc looks all in. Put on the kettle and make him a cup of tea while I'm getting dressed, Dinny.'

It would be useless to argue with her, Dinny knew. Missus Sally had always spoken like that when there was a difficult situation to handle. As a matter of fact, if she drove the car it would simplify the whole business. His eyes were not much good

372

at the best of times now, Dinny realized; and driving at night, in this misty moonlight, would have been risky for himself and Bardoc.

He made tea, gave Bardoc a big mugful and a slab of bread and butter and poured out for himself and Sally.

'We'll take Jane,' she said when she appeared, dressed for the road, a couple of old blankets over her arm.

She drank the tea and went out to the shed which held Dinny's old car: switched on Jane's lights, backed her out into the yard, filled her petrol tank and radiator, inspected her tyres.

'You'll need shovels and a mattock,' she reminded Dinny when he and Bardoc joined her. 'And just see the water-bag's full.'

Dinny threw the shovels and mattock into the back of the car, refilled the canvas water-bag without which old-timers never moved far from home, and took his place beside Sally. Bardoc crouched behind them on the back seat.

As they chuntered along the road which wound out of the township, towards the back of the ridge and the distant scrub, he muttered and exclaimed to himself, breaking every now and then into an eerie wailing. He was not only mourning for Kalgoorla, Dinny explained, but in the devil of a stew about burying her like this, at night, and without any of the ordinary tribal rites and lamentations.

'The natives round here used to make a shallow grave, no more than two or three feet deep.' — Dinny was talking so that she would not be upset by Bardoc's wailing, Sally realized. — 'They put the body in, lying east and west, and covered it with green branches and sticks laid close together. That was so that the spirit could escape easily, and find its way to ancestors of the tribe wandering about. There was always a lot of singin', wailin' and dancin' round to scare away evil spirits waitin' to grab any newcomer in their midst. Dingoes and dogs from the camp, or crows, might root out the body and the bones be scattered about. But after about a year, the tribe would come back, gather up the bones and finish'm their funeral service with more singin' and wailin' about the man or woman who'd passed on; and a corroboree to signify they believed the spirit of the deceased had reached the home of its ancestors. Then they'd either bury the bones deep, or cart them away to some safe place in a cave or gorge, far away. That's what's worryin' Bardoc. There's none of the tribe left now to give Kalgoorla a proper send off.'

'My poor Kalgoorla,' Sally sighed, 'she would know that.'

The road beyond the ridge was rough and shingly. Jiggledy Jane climbed a hill groaning and stuttering; she scrambled down the further slopes, bucketing from side to side with brakes refusing to grip or control her crazy gait. Sally was glad she knew the road fairly well and could keep Jane out of the worst ruts and breakaways torrential rains had torn in its surface. But they had bumped along precariously for only three or four miles when Bardoc called to her to stop. He got out of the car and pointed to a track which wound off through the scrub. It was just visible and Sally's heart quaked as she turned on to it.

She drove as if in a nightmare, following the vague thread of the track as it twisted and turned between ghostly trees, the dumps and pot-holes of an abandoned rush. She could no longer avoid the ruts and roots which bumped her out of her seat and jolted her hands off the wheel. When they passed the poppet-legs over a deserted shaft standing out against the moonlit sky Sally gasped desperately:

'God, Dinny, how much further does he want us to go?'

Bardoc exclaimed suddenly when they were about two miles from the rush. Sally brought the car to a standstill and scrambled down from the seat.

She and Dinny got out of the car and Bardoc led them to the dry creek bed on which Kalgoorla's body was lying. A group of snap and rattle stood against a tangle of thorn bushes, the slender graceful sticks of the young trees spattered with silver, their foliage throwing sooty shadows which stirred and shifted as a breath of wind came like a sigh from the depths of the bush.

'She wanted to be here, near the place where she was born,' Sally said softly.

'Eh-erm,' Bardoc muttered. 'Bin walk about long time, fall down, jump up, fall down, jump up. Make'm camp here.'

Sally could see where a little fire had burnt out near Kalgoorla. She was lying with open eyes: the man's hat she had worn for years still on her head, her old coat wrapped round her, bare feet sticking out from it stiff and straight.

Dinny put one of the blankets over Kalgoorla and spread the other on the ground for Sally to sit on.

Bardoc seized the mattock and began to sling it at gravelly earth on the hillside, a little distance from the creek bank.

'You want we bury'm black feller way, Bardoc?' Dinny asked hopefully. 'Make'm little feller hole. By 'n' by you feller come along finish'm?'

'Bury'm white feller way,' Bardoc said. 'Finish'm. No more black feller round about.'

It was going to be hard work hacking out a deep grave for Kalgoorla but Dinny understood that, as there were no natives in the district to give last honours to Kalgoorla's bones, Bardoc wanted to be sure they would not be scattered.

Sally hung the water-bag on a tree and sat watching the two old men. They worked steadily at first, grunting and gasping as they slogged and shovelled away the heavy gravelly soil. After a while, they changed tools, Dinny took the mattock and Bardoc the big prospector's shovel. Dust fumed round them as they toiled, backs bent and sprung, to the dull monotonous rhythm of gashed earth and falling rubble.

Sally gathered some sticks and made a fire to give them more light to work by. Its leaping flames showed Bardoc's gaunt, dark, almost naked body, gleaming with sweat; and Dinny, spare and scrawny in a dirty white shirt and faded blueys.

The hot darkness had cooled to a breath of wind which stirred the tree tops. A vague chill filtered through the air and Sally shivered in the cotton dress she was wearing. Smoke from the fire threw the incense of smouldering bush timber about her, and her thoughts wandered from this thing they were doing,

375

burying Kalgoorla, to the griefs and disasters which had befallen them both, since those early days on the goldfields when they had first met.

Her tragedy and Kalgoorla's, they had something in common, Sally told herself. She and Kalgoorla had both been bereft of their children and the people they loved. Were they the victims of those 'ageless fates' Chris Crowe used to talk about, or merely part of the ordinary wastage of life? She felt like that shaft over an old mine they had passed near the deserted rush. Derelict and stranded, it had stood in the moonlight as if forgotten by time.

The light breeze, which ruffled the tips of the snap and rattle and the scrub nearby, was driving away the haze. Sally could see the moon now, dingy yellow, slinking down the sky beyond the dark heave of the ridge where the lights of distant mine buildings still glittered. The drone of batteries that had been pounding all night came to her with their reminder of the insatiable lust for wealth and power which still held the goldfields in its grip.

It had exterminated the native people to whom this stretch of country originally belonged. Kalgoorla was probably the last of her tribe.

Sally remembered the proud, angry figure of the aboriginal woman standing between her and the men of her husband's tribe: daring to oppose their decision not to hamper themselves with a sick white woman on a long stretch of their search for game and water. Kalgoorla had reminded them of their bargain with Morris: the food he had given them, the promise of more if they carried his missus back to her own people, and the vengeance he had threatened if they failed to do so. It had been touch and go for her life then, Sally knew, as it was when Kalgoorla had sat crooning beside her, brushing the flies and mosquitoes away from her face, giving her sips of cold water from the bag Morris had left, when he went on to the rush at Lake Darlot.

It all came back to her: how Kalgoorla had helped her when she started her bush dining-room on Hannans, and when the children were little. Never as a menial, or servant who could be

376

abused and ordered about. In what Kalgoorla did for her, Sally realized, there had always been an understanding of some indefinable bond between them. She herself was conscious of it, and of an affection which had never changed, although she reproached herself for not having done more for Kalgoorla, latterly. To most people Kalgoorla had become merely a dirty, disreputable old gin, who had been charged with being drunk and disorderly about the town on one or two occasions. But who could condemn her on that account; Sally asked herself. Who could measure the grief and despair which had overwhelmed this primitive woman with the breakdown of her tribal way of life and the extinction of her people?

Bardoc belonged to a tribe which hunted further to the northeast; but like Kalgoorla, with other remnants of disintegrated and dispossessed family groups, he had drifted to the camp on Rill Station. They two, among all the detribalized natives collected there, had been least affected by the white man's ways. They clung to their aboriginal beliefs and customs: held aloof from the strangers who had robbed them of the soil upon which their physical and spiritual existence depended. Other natives might cadge and cringe for plonk or tobacco, could be cursed and brow-beaten, but not Kalgoorla or Bardoc. They held themselves with sullen stoicism in their misfortune, their dark faces inscrutable, their demeanour dignified and aloof. If you gave them something, they did not say thank you, they took it as their right, disdaining the false gratitude white people expected when sharing any surplus of food or goods. It was contrary to aboriginal custom to admit that what was necessary for existence did not belong to all.

Sally wondered whether Bardoc was infringing some tribal taboo by making himself responsible for the burial of Kalgoorla. She had been his mother-in-law. When Maritana was his wife he would have steered clear of any contact with the old woman. But Maritana had been dead many years, and Bardoc had taken another gin by whom he had the son they had seen the day she took Pat and Pam out to the native camp, Sally remembered.

377

Bardoc was as proud of him as of Ralf, the handsome young stockman who had been Maritana's son and Frisco's, though Bardoc claimed the lad.

Sally's thoughts flickered to Frisco. Their love affair remained with the glitter of a stormy sunset in her mind: something which had flamed and vanished, leaving her a shamed and uneasy feeling of guilt.

There had been so much which had slipped into the background of her consciousness when she and Frisco were lovers. Those days on Hannans when Maritana had been living with Frisco: the baby he disowned: the murder of Maritana, which Frisco knew something about, but swore he had nothing to do with. Paddy Cavan was responsible for that crime, Sally was convinced, though he would not admit it as he had admitted stealing Morris's shares.

Maritana had been Meerie to her own people, though Sally knew now the slender bright-eyed girl on whom 'white men had cast their shadow', as Kalgoorla said, was only half native. Kalgoorla had told Dinny about that; and about the first white men she had seen: how they caught her and another young gin and kept them tied up in their camp until with a sharp stone Kalgoorla cut through the leather thongs which bound her and Wallingara, and they escaped.

Sally had mourned with Kalgoorla over Maritana's death and Kalgoorla had mourned with her over the death of her sons. Kalgoorla's bleary eyes and weird keening were so full of pain and sorrow, that Sally believed no one knew better the anguish she had suffered when the news came of Lal's death, when Dick had been killed, and Tom died.

Except Marie perhaps. Marie with her sensitive understanding of the complicated tangle of one's emotions. Marie knew her better than anybody had ever done. Marie had often interpreted her to herself. She had been aware of the stubborn loyalty of her love for Morris, the wild fire of her passion for Frisco, the hurt pride and jealousy which had driven her demented when she broke with him. But now they were all gone, Marie,

378

Morris, Frisco — and Kalgoorla: loves and friendships so closely woven with the core of her life.

There was no bitterness in Sally's mind now as she thought of Pat. But her heart ached for Bill. The cutting off of his life, the failure of so much he had tried to do for the welfare of his own people and for humanity, still hurt and bewildered her.

'We must not be satisfied with the myth, we must work for the reality of a commonwealth,' Bill had said, she mused. His vision of human deliverance was bound up with the idea of a commonwealth of nations. And why shouldn't the resources of this country and the labour of the people be used to make it a commonwealth in more than name? A reality which would regard the health and well-being of the people as its greatest asset, stimulating every phase of their development, giving ordinary men and women like herself new pleasures with a knowledge and understanding of the arts and sciences. Wheat and cattle were bred to their utmost usefulness. Why not men and women?

The life force strives towards perfection. What other imperative is there in living? The struggle had gone on through the ages. The vital germ in a seed attained its fine flowering and full fruit. How then could the great ideas and ideals of human progress be denied and annihilated? They could not. That was what Bill had believed, and what he tried to make people understand.

Sally remembered her pride in him, and her fear, when like a young Prometheus he had defied 'Power which seems omnipotent' to champion the cause of the workers in their struggle to organize for socialism.

His voice came to her with the gay assurance which had rung through the Boulder Town Hall on that wild stormy night long ago:

> . . . I tell you a cause like ours
> Never can know defeat.
> It is the Power of Powers.
> As surely as the sun
> Follows the great moon wave
> Will our cause be won.

That was it, Sally told herself, her courage rising. The spirit of mankind struggling through the centuries against injustice and oppression was the Power of Powers. It was the Power that would vanquish Power which only seems omnipotent. A spiritual fire had sustained men and women striving to free humanity from the drudgery and heavy burdens which hampered its progress in the past. It would sustain all who fought for such a purpose. They could not be defeated, as Bill's poem said, because that fire and their purpose would go with them into the future. . . .

Only Dinny remained of the company of old friends who had battled along so optimistically on the early goldfields. And Dinny was getting old. Old, and liable to meet death any day with a cheery grin. As a matter of fact, he must be years older than any of the others. How had he managed to survive? How had he contrived to look so wiry and energetic, so tough and indefatigable, to keep his youthful spirit? Perhaps life had dealt more gently with him, had not harrowed his soul with griefs and passions which still surged tumultuously through her own. Dinny had never been flayed by personal disasters as she had been, Sally argued with herself, although he had been in all of hers, sharing her sorrows and misfortunes as if they were his own.

Her life, now, would be unbearably bleak without Dinny. Their companionship had become very dear to her: the peaceful, pleasant reliance of old friends on each other. To be sure Dinny had always insisted on paying his way as if he were still a boarder in the house. He had enough money in the bank to keep himself comfortably in his old age, he said. There was no need for him to go out prospecting any more, or to undertake any heavy manual work, although he was always busy, doing odd jobs round the place, mending a fence or leaking spout. And he tramped miles, as usual, delivering papers or collecting funds for Eily.

What other man of his age would do what he had been doing? Spend half the night digging a grave for an old gin? Suddenly Sally was angry and alarmed about it. The work was too hard for Dinny. He had been swinging a mattock and shovelling dirt for hours as though he were a young man. It was crazy of her to have let him. He would overtax his strength, strain his heart. Goodness knows what might happen if she did not make him stop at once.

'Dinny,' she called sharply, 'you must knock off. It's nearly morning.'

'We're jest – about through,' Dinny replied, his voice jerked from him on a gusty breath.

Dawn was breaking before the grave was wide and deep enough to hold Kalgoorla's old body, her dilly bag and the blanket folded over her. Dinny and Bardoc lowered it into the hole they had made. Sally threw some green branches from the nearby scrub over it, and Dinny and Bardoc shovelled the gravelly earth into its place again.

Sally went back to where she had been sitting on the hillside. Dinny picked up his mattock and shovel, and stumbled over to her. He lowered himself painfully to rest a few moments until Bardoc was ready to go.

Bardoc squatted by the grave moaning and wailing, as if reluctant to leave Kalgoorla without a word of farewell and apology for depriving her of the native rites to which she was entitled.

Bardoc had been through a terrible ordeal, Dinny and Sally both knew. First of all wandering through the bush to find Kalgoorla, himself ill and afraid of the night: afraid of the evil spirits which lurked in and threatened him from every wavering shadow cast by a clump of mallee, or the writhing bone-white skeletons of dead trees; and then, too, of having broken tribal laws by burying her like this.

Distracted and terrified, he seemed to be explaining to Kalgoorla that he had done his best for her. He glanced about him fearfully as if Kalgoorla's spirit might be hovering near and resenting a lack of respect for the shell she had discarded. There were no women to weep and wail, tear their clothes and cut their bodies with sharp stones in mourning for her: no men to brandish their spears and yell fierce imprecations, scaring off the demons who might waylay her spirit on its journey. Only himself to shout and wave his arms wildly, trying to defend the old woman from any gnarloo or wandoo lying in wait for her.

Bardoc must have thought the two white people who were with him would not understand what he was doing, Dinny said. He did not make as great a show of daring and ferocity as he might have done. Perhaps he did not want to appear foolish before strangers to his race and customs. He knew they did not see the restless ghoulish forms taking shape out of the air about him, hear the gibbering and jeering going on all round. Although he defied the malicious influences and drove them away in a frenzy of fear, his voice trailed into an appeal, reminding Kalgoorla that she had been a strong woman, brave and wise in the magics of her people: she could defend herself still, as she had always done.

'Oh, dear,' Sally sighed. 'I hope he won't go on much longer.'

The light had grown beyond the dark wall of the ridge. It was filtering through the scrub in a dim silvery radiance, outlining the grave and the thicket of thorn bushes behind it. The air was still again, the trees motionless: stored heat began to rise from the sun-baked earth.

There was a faint clicking sound. Bardoc stared before him aghast. Then with a startled yell, he plunged away through the scrub.

'Look, look, Dinny,' Sally cried. 'It's a kalgoorluh cracked open and shedding its seeds.'

Dinny squinted across at the tangle of thorn bushes near the grave. Wiry vines of the wild native pear were clinging to the thorn bushes and one heavy pod had split. The spun silk of its thistledown was drifting down.

'Bardoc must've been scared, and cleared out, because he thought Kalgoorla's spirit's wandering round and touched them,' Sally said.

Lances of golden light were flashing through the bush now,

striking the heavy, drooping, dark green pods among the dead-looking thorn bushes. One after another the wild pears clicked and split, shedding a shower of gossamery thistledown. Sally picked up a handful and found each fragile, glistening orb of fluff loaded with a brown seed.

'Seeds with wings,' she murmured. 'Winged seeds . . . they'll find a corner where they can grow, even in this hard ground.'

Dinny grunted as he moved. His face was contorted with pain. Sally looked at him anxiously.

'It's been too much for you,' she said fearfully.

'I'm all right,' Dinny muttered. 'The old pumper playin' up a bit. That's all.'

'For goodness' sake!' Sally's alarm quickened. 'What can I do?'

'Nothing,' Dinny smiled to reassure her. 'It'll pass off presently.'

'Don't you crock up — and leave me,' Sally wailed.

'Not likely,' Dinny muttered, although it was an effort for him to speak. 'I'll rest here a bit, and be as right as rain in no time.'

Sally sat beside him and after a while he turned to her with a sigh of relief.

'There,' he said, 'it's gone! Nothing to worry about. Jest a wang that gits me, now and then. But I'm tough. Always there when you want me, missus — like I've said before.'

'Oh, dear,' Sally exclaimed in her distress, 'don't you dare to die before I do, Dinny. So many of the people I've loved are gone. Poor Kalgoorla — even she leaves a gap.'

Dinny's little laugh gurgled. 'When the Warden of the Universe comes lookin' for me, you'll still have Eily, Daphne and the children,' he said.

'It's not the same thing,' Sally snapped, her temper flashing because Dinny had brushed aside an intimation of his importance to her. 'You've been with me through so much. I've depended on you. I don't know how I'd have pulled through without you, sometimes, Dinny.'

'We've come a long way together,' Dinny mused. 'I reckon we can go on like we've always done.'

'Oh, Dinny, my dear,' Sally's eyes welled to her emotion, 'what would I do without you?'

'There, there, ma'am!' Dinny took her hand. He spoke with the gentleness and deference he had always shown her. 'There's some things better left unsaid, perhaps. But it's been the joy of me life to see you and be near you.'

His eyes had a shy, quizzical gleam. Sally caught it and her smile gave him its old radiance.

'Well, I simply couldn't live if you weren't there to keep me company — and don't you forget it,' she said briskly. 'We'd better be going home now. Then it's a hot bath and bed for you, my lad.'

Dinny hauled himself up from the ground with a grimace at the stiffness and screws in his back. Sally picked up the shovels and mattock. It would be an effort for Dinny to stoop and lift them, she knew. He reached out to take them, but she refused to let him.

And so they turned to leave the quiet spot where the slight graceful sticks of the snap and rattle and their light-leafed crests were dripping sunshine, and the glistening thistledown of the wild pear drifted down from the thorn bushes over Kalgoorla's grave.

Climbing the shingly hillside to the car, Sally contrived to put her arm under Dinny's. They stood a moment half way, close together, to get their breath and let the rackety pace of their old hearts subside. No flicker of dying sensual fires disturbed them. They were aware only of their affinity, their affection and fealty towards each other.

Manœuvring the car into position for their jaunt back to town, Sally trembled to think what would have happened if she had driven again while it was dark. She had pulled up on the edge of a costeen. And along the track near the rush she marvelled that she had been able to steer among the pot-holes by the light of her damaged headlamps and the elusive glimmer of a hazy moon. Even by daylight she found the track scarcely visible, winding among the stumps of dead drought-stricken mulga, snap and rattle and thorn bushes. You had to use a good deal of imagination, she said, to see it, and then there was a stretch of black ironstone gravel on which Jiggledy Jane skidded and swayed drunkenly.

'You did a good job last night, missus,' Dinny observed.

'Wonder we didn't break our necks,' Sally gasped.

Passing the scattered dumps of the rush, and the shaft over the deserted mine with its poppet-legs scrawled against clear pale blue of the morning sky, she said:

'I was feeling very sorry for myself last night, and thought I was just like that shaft left standing over an old mine, Dinny.'

'Cripes,' Dinny grinned, 'there's a lot of good gold come out of an old mine.'

Sally's smile wavered, although she could not take her eyes off the track ahead.

'That means, I suppose, there's a lot of work I can still do.'

'You've said it,' Dinny chuckled. 'The boys used to say,' he added slyly, 'she had the loveliest legs on the fields — the old Cassia mine.'

'Dinny!' Sally laughed at his effrontery and the glint in his eyes.

They were both laughing when they swung on to the road which wound round the great bluff of the Boulder ridge, coming out through the barricade of high-piled slime dumps beside the mines. Purple and grey, dusty red, dirty yellow and pink, the dumps towered in mountain peaks, sterile sierras, with shabby whitewashed tin sheds and offices cluttered against their sides. Sky shafts, tall chimneys over the roasting plants, and a forest of poppet-legs, stood clear-cut against the sky, while away below them sprawled the widespread encampment of the goldfields cities.

It was here Jiggledy Jane snorted, bucked and staggered to a standstill. Sally suspected she had been driving on a flat tyre for some time; but she had done that often enough and was hoping it would carry her home on this occasion. This morning, however, she was determined not to let Dinny wrestle with putting on the spare they always carried. Besides, it was not only the tyre that was the matter with Jane, Sally was sure. Neither wheedling nor bullying had raised a kick from Jane's decrepit engine.

'She's a contrairy female, and no mistake,' Dinny gurgled. 'After behavin' so well last night why does she want to stick us up now?'

'We'd better leave her and walk home,' Sally decided at last. 'It's not far, thank goodness!'

They climbed the rough shingly road to its crest and stood a moment looking down on the flat below. Dilapidated workers' trams were scuttling and rattling along their narrow rails to the mines: bicycles and dingy, old-fashioned motor cars forging towards the Block and disgorging black streams of men who looked like ants, threading their way across the red earth to the mine buildings. The roar of the day's industry had not yet begun, but the shrilling of whistles, the buzz and hum of a gigantic hive awakening, could be heard beneath the rush and crackle of ore feeding the batteries; the howl and hungry, hurrying tramp of the stamps.

Dust was rising in a red mist from traffic on the roads. Heat haze lay over the rusty and whitewashed roofs of ramshackle houses on the outskirts of Kalgoorlie and Boulder. The sunshine already had a burning glare and steeped everything in its incandescent brilliance.

Tired and overcast by realization of how often she had gazed at that familiar scene and hoped, some day, it would show signs of a better way of life for workers on the Golden Mile, Sally said bitterly:

'After all, everything that's been done to change things here amounts to almost nothing. The same crowd's swarming into the mines. There have been more serious accidents than ever, lately. And silicosis is on the increase. That's why there's this talk of the aluminium therapy. The value of gold was never higher, yet mining magnates are demanding government subsidies and removal of the fixed price. Even if a few contract miners are getting good wages, the majority of workers are bearing the brunt of the rising cost of food and clothing. Living on the goldfields is as hard now as it ever was.'

'Y're not quite right there, missus,' Dinny demurred. 'There've been some improvements in the way the mines are run. The mine owners can't have things all their own way. We've got ventilation, workers' inspection and a shorter working day. There's the laboratory and a better deal for sick or injured miners. None of that's been a hand-out from the bosses. It's been won by the organization and struggle of the workers themselves.'

'But,' Sally protested, 'there's not much difference in the system which grabs the gold and plays fast and loose with the lives of the people, bashing them into depressions and wars, whenever its interests are at stake.

'Don't you believe it,' Dinny exclaimed. 'I reckon a lot more understand the position now who didn't a few years ago. There's a lot of men on the fields who realize what's wrong with the present set-up and that it can't go on for ever. You'd be surprised the number of blokes who say to me: "Tom Gough was right. He knew what he was talkin' about." And "Young Bill," they say, "he had his head screwed on the right way. He told us what the fascists were up to, and why a man'd got to stand up for his rights: never let 'em be taken away from him." '

'Do they say that?' Sally queried. 'Do they really say that, Dinny?'

'S'help me goodness, they do,' Dinny declared. 'I reckon we had something to do with sowin' the seed for a better system, too, when we put up a fight for our rights in the old alluvial struggle, and in the big strike for union principles.'

Sally had a fleeting vision of that glistening thistledown with its heavy brown seed, drifting down from the tangle of dark thorn bushes to the barren earth. A shy hope and happiness inundated her.

'I believe you're right, Dinny,' she cried. 'The seeds we've sown will grow like the wild pears', no matter how hard and stony the ground where they fall.'

' 'Course they will,' Dinny chuckled. 'And it's up to us not to let anybody forget it.'

They walked on down the hillside, and trudged away along the rough road they had known for so many years, sure that nothing now could intimidate or defeat the spirit which had carried them so far on their life's journey.

Also of interest

THE LOVE CHILD
by Edith Olivier
New Introduction by Hermione Lee

At thirty-two, her mother dead, Agatha Bodenham finds herself quite alone. She summons back to life the only friend she ever knew, Clarissa, the dream companion of her childhood. At first Clarissa comes by night, and then by day, gathering substance in the warmth of Agatha's obsessive love until it seems that others too can see her. See, but not touch, for Agatha has made her love child for herself. No man may approach this creature of perfect beauty, and if he does, she who summoned her can spirit her away...

Edith Olivier (1879?-1948) was one of the youngest of a clergyman's family of ten children. Despite early ambitions to become an actress, she led a conventional life within twenty miles of her childhood home, the Rectory at Wilton, Wiltshire. But she wrote five highly original novels as well as works of non-fiction, and her 'circle' included Rex Whistler (who illustrated her books), David Cecil, Siegfried Sassoon and Osbert Sitwell. *The Love Child* (1927) was her first novel, acknowledged as a minor masterpiece: a perfectly imagined fable and a moving and perceptive portrayal of unfulfilled maternal love.

"This is wonderful..." — *Cecil Beaton*

"The Love Child seems to me to stand in a category of its own creating...the image it leaves is that of a tranquil star" — *Anne Douglas Sedgwick*

"Flawless — the best 'first' book I have ever read...perfect" — *Sir Henry Newbolt*

"A masterpiece of its kind" — *Lord David Cecil*

THE SHUTTER OF SNOW

by Emily Holmes Coleman
New Introduction by Carmen Callil and Mary Siepmann

After the birth of her child Marthe Gail spends two months in an insane asylum with the fixed idea that she is God. Marthe, something between Ophelia, Emily Dickinson and Lucille Ball, transports us into that strange country of terror and ecstasy we call madness. In this twilit country the doctors, nurses, the other inmates and the mad vision of her insane mind are revealed with piercing insight and with immense verbal facility.

Emily Coleman (1899-1974) was born in California and, like Marthe, went mad after the birth of her son in 1924. Witty, eccentric and ebullient, she lived in Paris in the 1920s as one of the *transition* writers, close friend of Peggy Guggenheim and Djuna Barnes (who said Emily would be marvellous company slightly stunned). In the 1930s she lived in London (in the French, the Wheatsheaf, the Fitzroy), where her friends numbered Dylan Thomas, T.S. Eliot, Humphrey Jennings and George Barker. Emily Coleman wrote poetry throughout her life — and this one beautiful, poignant novel (first published in 1930), which though constantly misunderstood, has always had a passionate body of admirers — Edwin Muir, David Gascoyne and Antonia White to name a few.

"A very striking triumph of imagination and technique... The book is not only quite unique; it is also a work of genuine literary inspiration" — *Edwin Muir*

"A work which has stirred me deeply...compelling" — *Harold Nicolson*

"An extraordinary, visionary book, written out of those edges where madness and poetry meet" — *Fay Weldon*

PLAGUED BY THE NIGHTINGALE

by Kay Boyle
New preface by the author

When the American girl Bridget marries the Frenchman Nicolas, she goes to live with his wealthy family in their Breton village. This close-knit family love each other to the exclusion of the outside world. But it is a love that festers, for the family is tainted with an inherited bone disease and Bridget discovers, as she faces the Old World with the courage of the New, that plague can also infect the soul...

Kay Boyle was born in Minnesota in 1902. The first of her three marriages was to a Frenchman and she moved to Paris in the 1920s where, as one of that legendary group of American expatriates and contributor to *transition*, she knew Joyce, Pound, Hemingway, the Fitzgeralds, Djuna Barnes and Gertrude Stein: a world she recorded in *Being Geniuses Together*. After a spell living in the bizarre commune run by Isadora Duncan's brother, she returned to America in 1941 where she still lives. A distinguished novelist, poet and short-story writer, she was acclaimed by Katherine Anne Porter for her "fighting spirit, freshness of feeling." *Plagued by the Nightingale* was first published in 1931. In subtle, rich and varied prose Kay Boyle echoes Henry James in a novel at once lyrical, delicate and shocking.

"A series of brilliant, light-laden pictures, lucid, delightful; highly original" — *Observer*

"In delicate, satirical vignettes Miss Boyle has enshrined a French middle-class family...The lines of the picture have an incisiveness and a bloom which suggest silverpoint"— *Guardian*